Th

Susan Lewis is the b... ...els and is currently working on her new novel, *A French Affair*. She is also the author of *Just One More Day*, a moving memoir of her childhood in Bristol, and lives in France. Her website address is www.susanlewis.com

Acclaim for Susan Lewis

'A multi-faceted tear jerker' *heat*

'Spellbinding! . . . you just keep turning the pages, with the atmosphere growing more and more intense as the story leads to its dramatic climax' *Daily Mail*

'Exciting and erotic' *Sunday Times*

'Mystery and romance *par excellence*' *Sun*

'Susan Lewis strikes gold again . . . gripping' *Options*

'Will keep you guessing till the last page' *19*

'A tense heartbreak of a read' *Good Book Guide*

'It's a sizzler. The tale of conspiracy and steamy passion will keep you intrigued until the final page' *Bella*

'A masterpiece of love, jealousy, passion and danger' *Bristol Evening Post*

'One of the best around' *Independent on Sunday*

Also by Susan Lewis

A Class Apart
Dance While You Can
Stolen Beginnings
Darkest Longings
Obsession
Vengeance
Summer Madness
Last Resort
Wildfire
Chasing Dreams
Taking Chances
Cruel Venus
Strange Allure
Silent Truths
Wicked Beauty
Intimate Strangers
The Hornbeam Tree

Just One More Day, A Memoir

THE MILL HOUSE

Susan Lewis

arrow books

Published by Arrow Books in 2006

3 5 7 9 10 8 6 4 2

First published in the United Kingdom in 2005 by William Heinemann

Arrow Books
The Random House Group Limited
20 Vauxhall Bridge Road, London, SW1V 2SA

Random House Australia (Pty) Limited
20 Alfred Street, Milsons Point, Sydney, New South Wales 2061, Australia

Random House New Zealand Limited
18 Poland Road, Glenfield, Auckland 10, New Zealand

Random House South Africa (Pty) Limited
Isle of Houghton, Corner of Boundary Road & Carse O'Gowrie,
Houghton 2198, South Africa

The Random House Group Limited Reg. No. 954009

www.randomhouse.co.uk

A CIP catalogue record for this book is available from the British Library

The Random House Group Limited supports The Forest Stewardship
Council (FSC), the leading international forest certification organisation. All
our title that are printed on Greenpeace approved FSC certified paper carry
the FSC logo. Our paper procurement policy can be found at
www.rbooks.co.uk/environment

ISBN 9780 09 945328 2 (from January 2007)
ISBN 0 09 945328 2

Typeset in Palatino by Palimpsest Book Production Limited
Printed in the UK by CPI Bookmarque, Croydon, CR0 4TD

To Toby
with love and thanks

Acknowledgements

I would like to express a huge thank you to Judy Douglas-Boyd and Simon Skelding for allowing me to use their magnificent estate in Cornwall and most particularly the Mill House as a setting for this book. I hope they will forgive some of the poetic licence I have taken, but even so, it is as beautiful and inviting as I have attempted to make it sound. Should anyone wish to spend a holiday there I couldn't recommend it highly enough. You can call 01208 832300 or email judy@jd-b.wanadoo.co.uk

I would also like to say thank you to Sergeant Garret Gloyn of Stroud Police who gave so generously of his time and advice whilst I was researching this book. If there are any errors in police procedure they are all mine. Thank you too to the custody officers who were on duty at the station the day I was there.

Prologue

The door flew open, his arms went wide and as she ran into them they laughed and laughed and spun round and round.

'Ah haaa,' he cried, pleasure resonating in his voice as he held her tight.

'Ah haaa,' she echoed, loving him madly.

It happened this way sometimes – he'd be home early from the office, and would greet her coming in from school as though they hadn't seen each other in weeks. It was a daft little ritual that pleased them immensely, always had, for as long as Julia could remember. He was her best friend, though she never admitted that to anyone, or they'd probably think she was weird – who had their dad as a best friend, for God's sake? Strange! Creepy. Grow up and get a life. But no-one else had a dad like hers. He was different, special, someone she could tell anything to, even which boys she liked and who'd asked her out. He listened when she had something to say, helped with her homework, got involved in her hobbies

1

and never minded about keeping a distance if he had to. It made him proud to know she was growing up and starting to manage without him.

Everyone else Julia knew, all the girls, had much better relationships with their mothers – when they weren't fighting and hating each other, that was. They shopped and gossiped together, borrowed each other's clothes and even slept in the same bed when their dads weren't around. Her sister, Pam, was definitely close to their mother, but neither of them went in for fun, girlie things, nor did they ever sleep in the same bed. Sometimes, their dad would snuggle in under the duvet with Julia when it was freezing outside, but they didn't ever mention that to anyone, because other people would only get the wrong idea, and they both knew there was nothing wrong in it, nothing at all. Her mother would say there was, though, so would her sister, but they were a much more serious pair, level-headed, introverted and even, some might say – and Julia was one of them – cold. No, give her her father any day, because he was always warm and light-hearted, silly when he knew it would make her laugh and full of sympathy and understanding if anything upset her. He knew how to make things better, whether it was a kiss on a scratched knee when she was three, or a cheer-up train ride to London after her first boyfriend dumped her when she was fourteen.

'He was a bit peculiar anyway,' he'd commented as they rumbled and rolled through the countryside on their way to Paddington and Piccadilly and the best theatre seats he could buy. 'His ears were too big.'

Heartbroken she might be, but a bubble of laughter managed to find its way through, and by the time they took the last train back to Gloucestershire she was at pains to remember the boy's name, never mind how much she'd liked him.

It was a shame that Pam was so quiet and withdrawn, because Julia knew their father loved her too, but Pam didn't like to be touched, or to share her thoughts, or even to spend time in the garden where their father laid out flower beds specially for them, and built swings and ponds and a very grand gazebo. Their mother took a great deal of pleasure in the garden, and Julia loved to listen to her praising her father's efforts, or to watch the rare moments of affection between them, for her mother didn't usually care for public displays of any kind.

'Daddy, do you and Mummy love each other?' Julia used to ask when she was little.

'Of course we do,' he'd answer. 'We're just different in the ways we show it.'

'Tell me about how you met,' she'd urge, because she never tired of romantic stories, particularly where her parents were concerned.

So he'd tell her about the first time he saw Alice Hope, a tall, extremely elegant young lady whose beauty had dazzled him, and whose quiet gentleness had totally captivated him. Julia loved the way his grey-blue eyes twinkled with mischief and merriment, indicating perhaps that he might be inventing some of the things he told her. But it didn't matter, his stories were always wonderful and exciting and full of the kinds of adventures she longed for. She'd sit there entranced for hours, never wanting them to end. Sometimes Pam would be found listening at the door, but whenever their father tried to encourage her in, she'd slink away and go back to the books in her room.

'She's a dedicated reader, my girl Pam,' their father used to say, 'but Julia, with her love of the bizarre and fascination for everything new, will be a famous writer one of these days.'

This had become Julia's dream. She would prove him right, because it was what she wanted more than anything, to be a successful writer, and to make him proud. Her mother would be proud too, she was sure of it, she'd just have a different way of showing it.

Then suddenly, just before her sixteenth birthday, the terrible thing happened. Julia never knew what it was, she only heard her mother's screams in the sitting room one night, and her father shouting back. She'd never heard him raise his voice before, so it frightened her more than the loud crashes and bangs that told her they were smashing the house apart, and probably even each other. She tried to get out of her room to go and make them stop, but Pam had tied one end of a rope to her door handle and the other to her own.

'You're besotted with that child,' she heard her mother yell. 'It's not right . . .'

'Don't you dare . . .' her father roared.

'You're sick!' her mother screeched. 'I want you to get out of this house, and never come back.'

'No!' Julia screamed, banging on her door. 'Dad, let me out! Let me out!'

In the end he came up to her, his face cut and bleeding, his lovely, lively blue eyes dull with pain. 'It's all right,' he told her, taking her in his arms. 'It'll be all right.'

'What happened? Why is Mum so angry?'

'Ssh, we won't talk about it now,' he told her, stroking her silky dark hair. 'Later. We'll talk about it later.'

But they never did.

'What do you mean, he's gone?' Julia cried, coming home from school one day the following week. 'He lives here. He can't go.'

'Well he has,' her mother responded, tight-lipped and pale, 'and the quicker you get used to it . . .'

'Nooooo! Where is he? What have you done to him . . . ?'

'Julia, pull yourself together. I'm not discussing this. It's better that you don't know . . .'

'You have to tell me.'

'Go to your room, now!'

'I will not. I want to know where he is.'

Her mother advanced on her, eyes flashing with fury. 'You're a wicked girl,' she seethed, 'and if there's any justice in this world that man will be locked up and never allowed near you again.'

'What do you mean? He's my father. He'd never hurt me . . .'

'Don't be a fool, Julia. You saw what he did to me. How do you think I got these bruises?'

Julia looked at her with wide, frightened eyes. Her father couldn't have caused those livid dark shadows or the red cut on her mother's eyebrow, he was gentle and kind and would never hurt anyone – but she'd heard them fighting, had seen the marks on him too.

Three months later their house, near Cirencester, was put up for sale and they moved in with her mother's brother and his wife. Julia had never cared for her uncle, nor had her father. They used to make jokes behind his giant back, and have to smother their laughter. If George caught them he'd try to make them join him in a prayer asking God for forgiveness, which would make them laugh even more.

Without her father there to turn the sombreness and sobriety into fun and laughter, the ordeal of living with her aunt and uncle became almost intolerable. Julia tried to make a friend of Pam, to find out if she hated it too, but Pam was even colder and more distant than ever, and it wasn't long before she left for college. So Julia was alone with her uncle's interminable prayers and her mother's growing hostility. They fought almost all the time, as Julia kept demanding to know where her father was, and refused to believe he didn't care for her any more. She waited, week after week, month after month, for him to contact her, but he never did. No-one she asked seemed to know where he was or what had happened to him, none of his friends, nor his colleagues nor their old neighbours – or if they did, they weren't saying. He had no other family but them, so there were no relatives to turn to, only her mother and uncle and aunt, and as her resentment at their silence grew it became edged with hatred. Julia could hardly wait to go to university, and when the time came she left vowing never to visit her mother again.

Not until she met and fell in love with Joshua Thayne did the ice around her heart start to thaw. He was a man she knew her father would have adored as much as she did, and who adored her too. There were never any doubts about marrying him, or about supporting him at the start of his career with her own generous salary as a book editor, or about having his children.

They were happy, fulfilled, and over the years, as their children grew, Julia came to think of her father less and less. The pain was buried deep inside her now, as were the longing and the memories of all the happy times they had shared. The horrifying suspicion of why he had abandoned her was something she only ever confided to Josh, reluctantly, but even with him she found it difficult to put it into words. It was best to keep the lurking fear hidden, locked away, for no-one had ever actually told her the truth, so why should she be the one to voice it? As far as she was concerned he was the man who'd loved and protected her, who'd always been there for her until her mother had made him go away.

Chapter One

Julia's dark eyes rounded with shock. 'What the hell is that?' she demanded.

Josh was amused. 'Well, what does it look like?' he countered.

She blinked and wished it would go away. 'I'll tell you what it looks like,' she responded. 'It looks like something I really don't want to be seeing outside *my* front door.'

'Oh come on, darling. It's beautiful – and it's *our* front door.'

Before he could go any further she turned to face him, struggling to keep her temper in check. 'Please tell me this isn't what I think it is,' she challenged, her flawless ivory complexion flushing to a shade of red that, did she but know it, rather matched the offending object at the gate. 'Tell me you are not making an early morph into a cliché. Take a breath, think about your answer, then tell me this is a joke.'

'It's not a joke.'

'I'll laugh,' she assured him.

He laughed.

'You are *thirty-seven years old*,' she heard herself trying not to shout, as though some nasty little shrew had swooped in from the wings to appro priate her voice. 'You're not supposed to have a toy like that until you're at least fifty.'

He laughed again. 'I don't know what you're getting so worked up about. It's only a car.'

'With two seats, Joshua. *Two*. By my reckoning, that makes one for you and one for Barbie.'

'Barbie?'

'Don't be obtuse. We're a family of four, remember? That means the kids and I are right here, living in this house, on this street, where you also happen to live, when you find time to drop in that is, and where, until this morning, a much beloved and trusty old Peugeot estate, which we need to function, *as a family*, was the sentinel at our gate. So where is it now, Josh? Did you trade her in? Is that what you've done to the fifth member of our family? Is that the fate the rest of us can look forward to, now you've decided to become peri-menopausal and get a Porsche?'

Josh's humour wasn't holding up. The playful light in his normally irresistible blue eyes had been effectively snuffed by the dig about him dropping in, as though he were an estranged father with visiting rights, rather than a man whose family meant everything to him, which well she knew. In fact, virtually none of their friends could boast the kind of closeness they had always shared, a closeness he valued above anything else in his life, which was why he really didn't appreciate remarks like that, any more than he admired the woman his wife seemed to be turning into lately. 'The Peugeot's at my office,' he said tightly. 'I was hoping to take you for a spin and then we'd go to pick her up.'

Julia regarded him with her exquisite, slanted eyes, the natural flare of her nostrils widening with temper, the fullness of her usually red mouth seeming pale and drawn. She wasn't even close to being pacified, though she was relieved to hear that dear old Patsy, who'd been with them since Daniel, their adorable eleven-year-old, had come blinking into the world, hadn't been shoved aside for a younger, sleeker and altogether racier model. In her heart of hearts she was terrified of such a thing happening to her. Being three years older than her glamorous, high-flying husband hadn't seemed to matter when they were twenty-four and twenty-one, and her remarkable beauty had turned as many heads as he had. Now that she was fat and forty, it was mattering a lot. Well, OK, not fat, exactly, but she'd definitely started filling out over the summer, mostly around the waist, and her long, lithe legs and taut buttocks needed much more work at the gym than previously. As for her bust, which had always been far too big for her slender frame, the battle was really on now to stave off its descent into knickersville, which wasn't easy after breast-feeding two – and with a husband who, at least until recently, had insisted she go braless at every opportunity. 'I'm a brunette. I'm not impressed by Porsches,' she snapped, wondering where this nastiness was coming from. What had happened to the tolerant and supportive wife who'd always adored her dashing husband and his moments of rashness?

11

Joshua rolled his eyes. 'If I thought it was going to create this much fuss . . .'

'What do you mean, *thought*?' her monster snarled. 'You didn't *think*, Josh, at least not in a rational, ordered, let's-discuss-this-with-Julia-first sort of way. You just acted. You went out and spent a hundred thousand pounds of our money . . .'

'It was not a hundred thousand pounds. Not even close.'

'Then a hundred and *fifty* thousand pounds of our money . . .'

'What's with the "our", all of a sudden? Last night you were hell-bent on telling me that all our money was actually mine . . .'

'While you continually insisted on calling it ours. Now it suits you, it seems to be yours. Well, that's OK. Yours it is. So you do just as you like with it. Be happy with your Porsche. You make a suitably flashy twosome, and just think how much you're going to enjoy screaming around town showing everyone what a great big dick you don't have.'

At that he laughed, as only a man confident in that department could, and she might have laughed too, had the dread that he really did have a strumpet all lined up for the passenger seat not been so great. 'So what's her name?' she demanded.

He frowned.

'The blonde? The one you're presumably trying to impress. Is she someone I know? Do we have another cliché on our hands here, in the secretary?'

'Marina?' he said incredulously.

'It doesn't have to be *your* secretary. It could be anyone's.'

He was looking past her now, to the entrance

of their exclusive Holland Park mews. 'Actually,' he replied smoothly, 'she's right behind you. Why don't you say hello?'

With a thud of horror Julia swung round, and almost collapsed with relief to see their fifteen-year-old blonde bombshell of a daughter, Shannon, sauntering towards them with a disturbingly sassy look in her eyes and a cripplingly heavy school bag on her shoulder.

'Oh, Dad, this is like soooo coooool,' she purred, dumping the bag and sidling up to the Porsche like a cat checking out a new sofa. 'You didn't tell me it was going to be red. I mean, black's wicked, but this is like, really out there.' She looked along the short garden path to where her parents were standing at the front door. 'So what does she think?' she asked, as though Julia weren't there.

Julia's head immediately swivelled to Josh. 'You discussed it with Shannon and not me?' she demanded.

'It was supposed to be a surprise,' he told her. 'One you'd enjoy and appreciate. The kids are getting older now. We don't always have to take them with us when we go out. I thought it would make us *both* feel young again.'

'You still are,' Julia retorted, trying not to be mollified.

'Daniel is going to be like, so blown away by this,' Shannon was informing them as she opened the driver's door and inhaled the heady scent of leather upholstery. 'Can I go for a spin first, Dad? Before he gets home.'

'I'm still hoping Mum might go first,' Josh answered.

Shannon's hyacinth eyes moved to her mother. Apart from the mane of sleek blonde hair that swooped coquettishly over one eye and swung around her shoulders as though she were a perpetual shampoo ad, she could hardly resemble her father more. She always had, from the day she'd come screeching into his arms straight from the womb. It was instant love all bound up by shared DNA and mutual delight, and over the years, as she'd grown into his looks, his charm, his mischief, even his mannerisms, they could almost have existed in a world of their own, they were so besotted with each other. It was very much how Julia remembered being with her father, which was probably why Josh and Shannon's closeness pleased her so much. Their rows, though, were much fiercer and more frequent, particularly since Shannon's innocent young body had started its journey into womanhood, and her interest in boys had really taken off. She was far more alluring than she was mature enough to realise, which was why Josh was so afraid for her, since he knew only too well how men's minds worked when they laid eyes on a female body as ripe and ravishing as his daughter's. Nevertheless, even Julia was astonished by his intransigence over the issue of boyfriends – as far as he was concerned, Shannon would be allowed one at the age of sixteen, and not a day before. He wasn't even open for discussion on the matter, which often frustrated Shannon to the point of violence, though thankfully it was usually her pillow that caught it, while Julia sympathised and promised to try and talk him around.

Today, however, Josh was obviously firmly on his pedestal, as Shannon enquired of her mother, in a tone that said she already knew the answer, 'You're not in one of your strops, are you? Honestly, Dad, forget about her. Take me. I think it's really cool. I mean, like, no-one else's dad has got a Porsche.'

'I think that's Mum's point,' Josh told her. 'She doesn't want me to be different.'

'If that were true,' Julia responded, stealing a moment while the inner monster seemed to be focusing on Shannon, 'I'd never have fallen for you in the first place.'

'Ah, so you admit you did care once,' he quipped.

She returned his look and could see her reflection in the teasing, knowing depths that she'd always sunk into so willingly. She wished she could give herself as readily now, but it just wasn't possible. In spite of his insistence that he still found her as beautiful and desirable as the day they'd met, the growing insecurity that was wreaking havoc behind the scenes of their perfect marriage was right there, holding her back.

'The car's for you, not me,' he told her softly. 'Happy birthday.'

Her surprise showed.

'But her birthday was a month ago,' Shannon protested loudly. 'That is so not fair. It's my birthday next, so why don't I get a Porsche? And you didn't tell me it was for her. You said it was for you.'

'What on earth would I want with a Porsche?' Julia asked Josh, still basking in the magic of his gaze. How easy they'd always found it to be like young lovers, yet how fleeting those moments had become.

'I thought it might help you find yourself a younger man,' he murmured.

'But I've already got one.'

'Ah, so you remember.'

His mouth was coming closer to hers.

'Oh no!' Shannon cried. 'Puhleeze not out here. Someone might see.'

Laughing, Julia and Josh pulled apart, and feeling a wonderful spark of light-heartedness that enabled her to kick the monster into touch, at least for the moment, Julia started down the path towards the car. 'OK, so let's see how this beast handles,' she declared, holding out a hand for the keys. 'Shannon, there are four phone messages for you. Is something wrong with your mobile?'

'Out of power,' Shannon answered, standing aside to watch her mother lower herself clumsily into the driver's seat. 'You're going to have to practise that a bit,' she told her.

Julia poked out her tongue and jabbed around for a place to slot the key. 'Daniel might call in the next ten minutes,' she said. 'If he does, tell him to ring Dad's mobile.'

'Where is he?'

'Cricket practice.'

'Dad, I've got to have the next spin,' Shannon insisted, leaning in the driver's window and shouting across her mother as the engine roared into life. 'OK. Right? I'm next in this car. Don't you dare let Daniel go before me.'

'It's not mine,' Josh reminded her. 'You have to plead your case with your mother.'

'But she's bound to let him go first,' Shannon wailed.

Julia's eyes were inches from Shannon's as they stared at each other in mute understanding – for Julia, Daniel always came first. Leaning forward, Julia planted a kiss on her daughter's soft, peachy cheek. 'Don't wait up,' she murmured, and sliding the car into gear she touched the accelerator and roared off down the mews.

Josh was at the wheel now. They'd swapped places after Julia had flashed around Holland Park and Notting Hill for a hair-raising twenty minutes before zooming up the West Cross Route onto the A40. For once the traffic had actually been moving, but by the time they'd reached the motorway Josh had slammed on an imaginary brake so many times she decided she might just as well let him stamp on the real thing, or the tension was going to start snapping his joints.

So now there he was, all Armani shades and movie-star looks, in total, hey-dude-I'm-the-man, bliss. The engine's roar was like an orgasmic lion, he'd insisted, while the seats moulded their bodies like kinky lovers. For someone who'd made his fortune in the literary world it was just as well, she'd informed him, that he'd applied his talent to agenting, and not to the page, or they'd be zipping about in a Trotteresque three-wheeler right now, instead of a turbo-charged testosterone-packed playboy toy. His laughter had stolen warmly through her, and for a while she'd felt nothing but pleasure to be alone with him like this. There was no pressure involved in being in a car, unlike in the bedroom, or the increasing number of occasions when both children were out.

Of course there was no way the Porsche had been meant for her. However, she had to hand it to her smooth-talking, quick-thinking, sometimes-too-perfect-to-be-true husband, if she decided she wanted it, he'd hand the key back and light the candles on a second birthday cake. Yes, he'd give her a hundred-thousand-pound car, if that was how much it had cost, and if it was what she wanted, because Joshua Thayne always had been generous to a fault, even when he'd had no money. Since many riches had started coming his way, his bounteous nature knew no limits: a grand, white-washed villa on one of Holland Park's smartest private streets, a move to swanky new offices just off Gloucester Road, the best schools for Shannon and Daniel, and now this gleaming cherry-red bullet that was clearly transporting him to heaven.

What next, she was wondering as they sped along the M40 at over a hundred miles an hour, apart from a speeding fine. She was trying to think of something expensive that she'd always craved, but wasn't coming up with much, besides liposuction and a facelift – though she had to admit that neither was exactly an emergency. In the car world Patsy really did it for her; in the house world, well they already had that; and in the bling world she lacked for nothing, because he got as much pleasure out of surprising her with jewels as she did from receiving them. How idyllic their relationship must seem from the outside, she'd often thought, and it should, because it was, or always had been until around this time a year ago. Their friends had frequently remarked on it, and because they were such a good-looking family people often turned to stare, whether they were merely having coffee at the café in Holland Park, going in or out of the cinema, or boarding a plane to jet off somewhere exotic. As a couple they had never seemed to tire of each other, though their relationship was definitely tempestuous, and they'd had their share of difficult spells, but there had never been anything they couldn't resolve, nor had they ever wanted to be with anyone more than with each other. She often wondered if that was part of what was frightening her so much – it was all too perfect, so how could it last?

'Josh!' she suddenly yelped, clutching the sides of her seat as he swerved across three lanes to hare up an exit road. 'Where are we going?'

'Anywhere,' he declared recklessly. 'Where do you want to go?'

Realising home would be a bit of a dampener, she looked around, and recognising where they were felt an immediate surge of annoyance. 'Well, as we seem to be in the general vicinity, why don't we pop in on your mother?' she said with acid sweetness.

'Hey, what a great idea!' he cried, as though he'd never thought of it himself.

Wishing he wasn't so adept at sidestepping her sarcasm, she reached for his mobile as it signalled an incoming text. 'That'll be Daniel,' she said.

'Could be a client,' he said, and whisked it back again. 'Daniel,' he declared and handed it over.

OK if I go 2 Tim's 4 n our?

Julia pressed in an affirmative and added, love you.

Lv u2, he messaged back.

She had to smile. He probably thought it was Josh who'd sent the text, but either way, Mum or Dad, he'd never been shy of expressing his feelings. If anything he was a little too free with his kindness and far too trusting of his friends. He had inherited Josh's open-handedness, but there was a guilelessness to Daniel's generosity that was totally lacking in his father. She often wished Dan really was more like Josh – he'd be far less likely to be used and walked over if he were.

'He's just a child, give him a chance,' Josh would protest whenever she voiced her concern. 'He'll toughen up. He'll show them what's what when he's ready.'

She hoped Josh was right, but he seldom saw Daniel's wide-eyed confusion when his friends took what they wanted of his, then dumped him. Nor was Josh aware of how readily Dan forgave them, so keen to be accepted. Did Josh really understand the embarrassment his son felt at the way some older girls teased him? Josh treated it as though it were some rite of passage to manhood. Maybe for some it was, but not for Daniel who didn't want to be kissed and touched and made a fool of in front of all his so-called friends, any more than he wanted anyone to know about his occasional seizures.

'They made my thingy go hard,' he'd told his mother with tears in his eyes, the first time the girls got to him. He'd barely turned ten at the time, and even she had to suppress a smile on that occasion, but when it kept on happening she soon came to realise that his distress wasn't only genuine, it was increasing. She might have gone to speak to the headmaster, had Josh not stopped her.

'You'll just make it worse if you do that,' he'd insisted.

'So you want them to keep on abusing him?'

'It's not abuse. It's normal kid-teasing. They'll get bored and leave him alone soon enough.'

As it turned out Josh might have been right, because Daniel hadn't mentioned it for several months now, and he even had a best friend these days, Timothy Lamont, who was as mad about computers, cricket and *The Simpsons* as Dan. They'd become virtually inseparable, so now instead of worrying about his premature experiences with girls, she was worrying that he might be gay. She'd yet to confide this latest concern to Josh for fear of the explosion. Not that he had a problem with gays, he was simply on a very short fuse when it came to Julia's constant fussing over their son. The trouble was, he'd never really seemed to connect with how vulnerable Dan was, or impressionable, or, well, just different to other boys his age. Shannon realised it, though, for in spite of all the bullying, rivalry and usual sisterly contempt, she was as protective of Dan as Julia was.

'Enjoying it?' Josh grinned, as they sped across Chalfont Common in a blaze of early evening sunshine.

She dutifully nodded and smiled. If she hadn't had so much on her mind she might have been able to share his delight, but she could already feel the dreaded restlessness stirring, and with so much crowding in on her lately, she found it impossible to relax for long.

'You look worried,' he told her. 'What are you thinking about?'

'As a matter of fact, I was thinking about how little time we actually get to spend together, just the two of us,' she said, 'and what a shame it is we're about to include your mother.'

He glanced over at her. 'If you want us to spend more time together,' he said, 'you know it can always be arranged.'

Feeling a twist of guilt in her heart, she turned to look out of the window.

He allowed a few moments to pass, clearly hoping she might respond, but in the end he let the subject go and said, 'We won't stay long.'

She was still feeling too guilty to reply.

'She'll love the car,' he declared in an upbeat tone, 'and you know what a kick it gives her to see how well things are going for us.'

'For you,' Julia corrected, keeping her eyes on the passing countryside, and trying not to feel annoyed by how much his mother's approval had always meant to him. Then a wave of unease swept through her as her irritation reminded her of how distanced they were becoming. It wasn't what she wanted, nor did she really know why it was happening, but though they were both trying to fight it, there was no denying the cracks that were, even now, threatening the very foundations of their marriage. She was to blame, she accepted that, because she was the one who'd turned from a loving, passionate and highly sexual woman, to an anxious, almost paranoid and even frigid wife. She just wished she knew what had happened to shut her down like this, for their sex life had always been one of the very best parts of their marriage, madly erotic and so varied and frequent that even they were occasionally dazed by just how good it was. But it had been months and months now since they'd made love with anything like their usual passion, and lately they'd shared no real physical intimacy at all, because she simply couldn't handle the fear that seemed to engulf her when they did. She'd experienced it once before in her life, just after Dan was born, but thanks to Josh's patience and some intensive therapy, it hadn't lasted long. This time it had though, and not even her recent sessions with a therapist or Josh's attempts to understand seemed to be helping her. If anything, the fear was getting worse, and since she'd abandoned the therapy a few weeks ago, and Josh had given up trying to persuade her to make love, she'd become even more afraid of where it might all end.

Emma Thayne, Josh's adoring mother, was as gushingly admiring of the Boxster as Julia dreaded and Josh expected. 'Darling, it's simply the best car I've ever seen,' she exclaimed, bony hands clasped to her meagre bosom as she circled the Porsche, treating it to an inexpert eye and a mother's crowing delight. Julia didn't miss the sneaky little glances she was throwing about the street, in the hope the neighbours were looking. She guessed that any minute they'd take off on a lap of honour, making sure the entire newly built estate that clung to the edge of a quaint old village, like a wart on the face of a beautiful woman, would be unable to miss the sight of the returning hero and his latest trophy. 'Dad would be so proud if he could see you now,' Emma informed her pride and joy. 'His father would be so proud,' she informed Julia, her dismay and despair.

'We all are,' Julia assured her.

Emma Thayne's protective ear didn't miss the dryness in Julia's tone, and since it implied criticism of her precious and only offspring, she was instantly bristling. Not a pretty sight, but Josh's looks had come from his father, not his mother. 'I'm glad you are, my dear,' she responded tartly. 'A man needs to know he's appreciated, particularly when he works so hard for his family.'

Julia started to respond, then decided not to bother. Occasionally she enjoyed sparring with Emma, but today she didn't have it in her, probably because the late-dawning suspicion that Josh was holding back a vital piece of news had suddenly come over the horizon. It could be what the Porsche was all about, to mask the white elephant that had moved in with them a few weeks ago and they'd resolutely refused to discuss since. If she was right, it probably meant it was something she wouldn't want to hear, and this was his way of softening the blow.

Emma was burbling on about her grandchildren now, and the pleasure she derived from their texts and emails – a modern wizardry they'd greatly enjoyed teaching their grandma, whose mastery of the techniques afforded them much amusement.

Julia was jealous, of course, because her own mother didn't share such a closeness with the children. However, a visit to her own mother could make a sneak peek inside Pandora's box seem the safer option, so she generally kept visits to Gloucestershire to a minimum.

'So, my dear, how are you filling your days now?' Emma enquired, as they left Josh spouting agent advice down the phone to one of his American authors who had carte blanche to call any time of the day or night. 'You must be rattling about in that big house of yours, wondering what on earth to do with yourself, with the children at school all day and Joshua working so hard.'

'Oh, but I barely have a minute to think,' Julia protested, 'what with trying to squeeze my personal trainer in between the manicurist and nutritionist, who have to work around my spiritual guru and the woman with swatches. Then I have to find time for the hairdresser and epicurean facialist, both great artists in their field who really won't be rushed ... Honestly, I don't know how I cope.'

Emma's glassy expression was full of contempt. 'I was merely trying to make polite conversation,' she said coldly. 'But as usual, you mock me.'

'I have a job, Emma,' Julia reminded her. 'I write and edit books, remember? So why would you think I have a problem filling my days?'

Emma pushed open the door to her spotless kitchen and made for the kettle. 'I thought you'd given it up,' she commented tersely.

'Why would I do that when Josh has bought us a house with a dream study just for me?'

'And you never go in it.'

Julia flinched. Clearly Josh had discussed this with his mother, which irked her immensely. 'Not true,' she said, reaching for mugs and wishing she could ask for wine. No point though, Emma only stocked undrinkable sweet sherry. 'My masseuse has plenty of room to set up her portable couch in there, and it's a good space for yoga.'

Emma regarded her with even greater disdain. 'I hope you don't mind me saying,' she said, clearly not caring a hoot if Julia did, 'but looking at you now ... Well, frankly my dear, if you've really got all that beauty back-up you could be wasting your money. Or should I say, *Josh's* money.'

The insult almost took Julia's breath away. OK, she wasn't looking her best these days, but for her mother-in-law to be so brutal about it, when she clearly knew, thanks to Josh, that Julia was having some problems with depression – or whatever the hell was wrong with her – was just plain cruel. But that was so like Emma, who seized every opportunity to belittle her daughter-in-law, and right now, this minute, Julia wasn't going to take it. 'The trouble with you, Emma,' she said scathingly, 'is that you still can't stand the fact that I took your precious son away, can you? As far as you're concerned I've always been the enemy, even while Josh was struggling to get his agency off the ground, and I was picking up all your bills. Yes, I can see that being dependent on your daughter-in-law would have been galling for a woman like you, but it wasn't me who left you in dire straits, Emma, it was your husband. There wasn't even enough to pay for his funeral, and do you know, to this day, you've never thanked me for sorting it out. Instead you don't even bother to disguise your contempt for me and everything I stand for. In fact . . .'

The stricken look on Emma's face brought her to a crashing halt. Christ, what was she saying? Just how deeply did she want to hurt this woman? She was getting on in years now, and though her motherly possessiveness and snobbish illusions were irritating, they were her only sins. So to rub her misfortune in her face by reminding her of all the heartache she had suffered when her husband had left her virtually destitute, was unconscionable, unforgivable, and only went to prove just how far down the slippery slope she had descended that she should hit back like this.

'Emma, I'm sorry,' she said hurriedly. 'I didn't mean . . . I shouldn't have . . .'

'Hey you two, what are you gassing about in here?' Josh demanded cheerily as he joined them. 'Roses are looking good, Mum. Still taking care of them yourself, are you? We can always get a gardener to give you a hand. Just say the word.'

Her son's presence brought a smile back to Emma's papery-white face. 'You're so kind, darling,' she told him shakily, 'but I enjoy pottering about out there. There's not much else for me to do these days, though Julia was just telling me about her beauty routine. I'm thinking about giving it a go. Maybe they'll have more luck with me.'

'You're gorgeous enough as you are,' her dutiful son informed her, completely missing the barb, which Julia took heroically, even gratefully, and let pass.

Tea was drunk – a viscous brown brew that Emma knew Julia detested – in the air-conditioned conservatory that Josh had treated his mother to earlier in the year. It was her special place, she repeatedly told him. In here she could enjoy her plants and read the paper with plenty of light, and admire her garden without getting burnt by the sun or eaten alive by midges and mosquitoes. They – Josh and Emma – talked at length about Shannon and Daniel, both glowing with pride at the children's various sporting and scholarly accomplishments, until finally they landed themselves on the glistening beach of their absolute favourite topic, Joshua.

Emma listened raptly as her son regaled her with tales of his most recent battles with legendary publishing figures, all of which he'd won, of course – she wouldn't be able to handle the failures, so only Julia was made party to them. Next came his most recent trip to New York, followed by an unexpected dash to LA to finalise a movie deal, and crowding up his diary for the weeks to come were dozens of book fairs, literary festivals, keenly contended prizes and the endless round of breakfasts, lunches, dinners, launch parties, cocktails, author tours and glittering award galas that went with the territory of being one of London's hottest literary agents. 'So I might not be able to pop in quite as often as you'd like for a little while, Mum,' he told her.

All this demand and heady prosperity was thanks, in the main, to a chance meeting some seven years ago with a fluffy-haired nymphet from Leeds University by the name of Claudia Barnes, who'd written an hilarious and brilliantly crafted story about two aliens – Paul from Pluto and Suzie from Saturn – who met whilst attempting to blend in with the community of a North Yorkshire town. Almost immediately it had struck the right chords with Josh, who'd managed to whip up an impressive publisher's auction, both sides of the Atlantic. This had resulted in a staggeringly high figure for a first novel, that had since turned into a series of books, three movies and worldwide publication. And all due to Josh Thayne's eagle eye for a winner (or a blonde) and tenaciously adroit negotiating skills. Now, every author with breath in their body, and publisher with dollars on his mind, wanted to be in Josh's magic sphere, which Julia could hardly blame them for, as it was a wonderful place to be – except when he was chalking up his attributes with his appalling mother.

'The trouble with you,' he told her, as they finally roared out of the estate and down through the highly desirable village of Chalfont St Giles, with its quaint village green, designer shops and olde worlde pub, 'is you have a phobia about mothers.'

Julia rolled her eyes. 'Since I am one, that doesn't really add up,' she responded.

'Yes it does. You can't stand your own, you can't stand mine, and you can't stand yourself either.'

Her head came round.

He glanced at her, shifted down and came to a straining pause at a roundabout.

'Two out of three,' she told him.

He circled to the right, and sped along an empty Amersham Road. 'Is that you claiming to like yourself?' he asked.

'I'm not in the mood for this conversation,' she replied crisply.

Silence prevailed until, without warning, he swerved into a pub car park and turned off the engine. 'Come on, I'll buy you a drink,' he said, starting to get out of the car.

'Josh! For heaven's sake, look at me. It was bad enough having to face your mother like this, I don't want to go into a pub.'

'What's wrong with you, for God's sake?'

'How can you say that? My hair's not washed, I've got no make-up on, these trousers are practically as old as Shannon . . .'

'White wine or vodka tonic?' he cut in.

'Did you hear what I said?'

'I'll bring the drink out,' he urged.

'Good answer. That way you get your drink, and don't have to be seen with me.'

Sighing, he let his head fall back against the seat. 'I don't think I'm going to win this,' he muttered.

'Is it a contest?'

His eyes came round to hers. 'No. It's just me wanting to buy you a drink. Is that too much to handle?'

She pushed open the door. 'White wine,' she said. 'I'll go and sit at the table over there, by the cartwheels.'

As she waited she sent texts to the children, then tried very hard to keep her mind in neutral, because she didn't want to think, she only wanted the wine when it came, and then Josh to tell her what she most longed to hear – that the book she'd submitted six weeks ago was going to be published. It wasn't going to happen though, she knew that already, because if it was, he wouldn't be trying to distract her with a Porsche, he'd have been plying her with fizzing magnums of expensive champagne.

Her insides churned with so much disappointment that for a moment she felt almost panicked by the depth of it. It was as though a lifeline had been dangled and was now rapidly being drawn in, leaving her to flounder in a darkness impossible to escape. She took a gasp of air, then closed her eyes tightly. She knew this reaction was out of proportion, that if she'd let him Josh would provide all the safety she needed, so she must get herself under control. It wouldn't be the end of the world if the news was bad, they'd all survive, and her terror that she might not was due to her over-vivid imagination rather than anything real.

Feeling the sun on her skin she turned to look around, trying to distract herself by watching cattle grazing in the next field, tails flicking, muzzles chomping. A soft breeze moved through her hair. She listened to the birds, the traffic and music inside the pub. The air was scented by jasmine growing nearby, dung from the field, and fumes from the cars. Then she looked up as Josh approached and loved him so much it hurt.

After putting their drinks down he sat facing her across the wooden table, watching her sip the wine, while he drank a beer. When her eyes finally came to his, he covered her free hand with his own, and felt her fingers lacing into his.

'They've turned it down, haven't they?' she said softly.

As he nodded her heart contracted so painfully that childish tears filled her eyes.

She looked off into the distance, and felt him watching her, his regret and love trying to reach her.

'I'm sorry,' he said, his fingers tightening around hers.

She made no response. What was there to say? Her first book hadn't been a success, and now clearly her second wouldn't be either.

She used a large sip of wine to help swallow the lump in her throat. All those years as an editor, all that knowing what made a book work and what set it apart from the rest, yet she couldn't do it for herself. She was a failure, worthless, a woman who contributed nothing to her own life, was totally dependent on her husband who might, at any time, decide to leave her.

She guessed now that McKenzies had only published her first book as a favour to Josh. A seventy-thousand-pound advance had made it a very big favour, for she knew the business, and seventy grand was huge in comparison to most first-book deals. It had made no difference to the critics though, for they'd been vicious. As a result the public shunned it, so the bookshops ended up returning it by the truckload. She'd been devastated. Inconsolable. How could she have got it so wrong? Everyone in the business knew who she was, so how was she ever going to find the courage to face them all again? Her grief was so profound it was as though she'd lost a child to some hideous disease. Shannon and Daniel tried to comfort her, and in turn she tried to reassure them, but the rejection had all but annihilated her.

For once in his life Josh had been lost for words. In the end he'd taken them all to the tropics where they'd swum, dived, snorkelled, waterskied, sailed and relaxed with magazines, never books. Gradually, mainly thanks to him, she'd managed to pull herself together, and as they'd rebounded and rebonded as a family, she'd promised herself that when she got back she'd write to every author she'd ever treated to a harsh review and apologise for the hurt she'd caused.

Of course she hadn't. What good would it do them now to know she was suffering from a belated fit of guilt? And if they'd read what had been said about her book, they'd feel the sweet dessert of justice had been royally served. Which it had. And now here it was again, a bitter second helping, for having forced herself back to the computer, she'd written another, even better book than the first – at least in her and Josh's opinion – but clearly no-one else out there thought so.

'So what's wrong with our judgement?' she said bleakly. 'Why doesn't anyone agree with us?'

Josh shook his head sadly. 'I wish to God I knew,' he murmured.

Looking searchingly into his eyes she saw the pain of her rejection reflected in their depths, and realising how hard it must have been for him to break this news, she squeezed his hand and lifted it to her lips. 'It doesn't matter,' she said, making herself smile. 'I've got so much to be grateful for, you, Shannon, Dan, a beautiful home, plenty of money. What more could I ask for?'

He regarded her uncertainly.

She continued to smile. 'Anything else is icing,'

she insisted, 'and since I've never had a sweet tooth I'm happy with just plain cake.'

Irony arched his brows. 'You try to give your wife the world,' he said drolly, 'and she calls it plain cake. What I want to know is, when will she call it enough?'

Her eyes went down. 'You are enough,' she told him in a whisper.

'Are you sure about that?'

Knowing he was referring to their lack of intimacy, she felt the ghastliness of it starting to engulf her. It wasn't that she didn't want him, there had never been a time when she didn't, she simply needed to try and make him understand the terrible fear that overcame her at the very peak of their lovemaking, but how could she, when she barely understood it herself?

In the end she lifted her head to look at him. His eyes were steeped in concern, and as her heart filled with gratitude for these few precious moments with no bickering or biting, she leaned across the table to kiss him. 'Tell me everything'll be all right,' she said. 'Tell me there isn't anyone else.'

A fleeting look of exasperation crossed his face. 'Darling, you're the one who put a stop to our sex life,' he reminded her gently. 'You know it's not what I want.'

She nodded and lowered her eyes again, horribly aware that he hadn't denied it, and knowing that even if he had it wouldn't be enough to dispel the fear and make her feel safe. She wasn't sure what could do that. If she were to achieve success, maybe that would at least mean she'd never have to depend on anyone again, not even him.

Much later that night, after the usual round of snatched dinners, fights for the phone, homework, flute and violin practice, and the protracted journey to bed, Julia was standing in her and Josh's bathroom, staring at her reflection in the mirror. Her short dark hair was framing her face in curled feathery wisps, her almond-shaped eyes seemed almost feverish. Her mouth was naturally red and moist, her skin was smooth and barely lined – and still tanned from a long, hot summer in France. She recalled how she and Josh had strolled through the surf, arms around each other, her wearing nothing but a brief bikini bottom, because he loved other men to see her breasts while knowing they were exclusively his to touch. Usually it turned her on to exhibit herself like that, and to know what it was doing to him, but this year it hadn't worked at all. In the end, angry and frustrated, Josh had almost seemed to welcome a crisis call from an author in Scotland, for it had allowed him to fly off for a few days, leaving her with the children, and the horrible suspicions of why he'd really gone.

Now, as she looked at herself in the mirror, she was aware of the rise and fall of her breasts, and the way her heart was thudding beneath them as it filled with unease over what was to come. But she had to try, even though she already knew she couldn't do it.

Relinquishing her gaze she put her toothbrush back in the cabinet and closed the mirrored door, wishing she could shut away her dread so easily. She'd already let him know that she wouldn't push him away tonight, and had even allowed him to kiss her deeply before she'd come into the bathroom, but then kissing never had been a problem. They still kissed often and lovingly, even through these difficult times. It was only when it seemed likely to lead on to other things that the trouble began.

Not tonight though, she told herself firmly. Somehow she'd wrest back control of her body and let him do with it as he would, the way she always had. She thought of his hands moving over her, his mouth on hers, and the sounds he made as he loved her. She reminded herself of the heights he could transport her to – it was nothing for him to take her to three, four or five orgasms in quick succession. Now she was profoundly terrified of even going close to one. It made no sense and she knew it, for she'd always felt so safe in his arms, willing to let go and give herself completely – and there was no reason for her not to now, so somehow she must make herself do it.

Wishing there was a magical way to drop the extra weight she'd gained around her middle, while knowing it would make little difference to him just as long as they could go back to the way they were, she took one last look at herself in the mirror before turning out the light and going into the bedroom.

Only the lamps were on, casting a warm, mellow glow over the bed which was covered in crisp white linens and draped with copious folds of voile. The rest of the large room, with its plush oriental carpets and chic Italian furniture, was cast in shadow, and both sash windows were masked by raw silk blinds. Josh was standing in front of one of them, laying his watch on the surface of a black laminated chest, and as he heard her come in, he turned to look at her.

She looked back and attempted to smile. He was so tall and dark, seeming so powerfully male and confident, but even so, she could tell he was nervous. She guessed he was naked beneath his robe, possibly already semi-aroused. That he could still want her after all she'd put him through made her detest herself completely and love him even more.

His eyes were sweeping the near-transparency of her nightie, pausing at the hard swell of her nipples. Then he came towards her, and stood looking into her eyes, and as he lowered her straps to let the nightie slip to the floor, she struggled with the urge to cover her nudity and push him away. She wanted him, she reminded herself, she loved him, and as he took her in his arms, she lifted her mouth to his. His hands moved gently over her back and buttocks. He didn't pull her closer, but she could already feel his erection, and as she forced herself to press against him she heard him groan with desire.

'Are you OK?' he murmured, cupping her face in one hand.

She nodded and made herself untie his robe.

Feeling him naked against her, she slipped her arms round his neck and pressed her belly to his. He was hard and ready, and as his tongue moved deeply into her mouth she fought back the need

37

to break free. The reluctance was false, she was deceiving herself, because her body was responding, she could feel it in her nipples, between her legs and in the sheer pleasure of his skin on hers. She didn't want this to stop, so she wouldn't make it.

Taking her to the bed he lay down with her, and for a long time he merely toyed with her, using his fingers and mouth. The more exquisite the sensations became, the more tightly she could feel herself tensing. She knew he could sense it, but he didn't stop. His fingers were between her legs and though she was moist and inviting, she was already turning rigid inside. She wanted to cry and scream, run away and hold onto him. Why couldn't it be the way it always had? Why was she so afraid to let go?

Lifting his mouth from her breasts, he lowered it to hers and used his hand to part her legs. Her head was starting to spin, sweat was breaking out on her skin.

'Ssh, it's OK,' he soothed, as he lay over her.

She tried to relax. She put her arms and legs around him, and closed her eyes tightly. Her heart was thudding a powerful beat. She tried to think only of that, as he started to enter her. Somewhere, at a distance, she could feel the craving for him to go all the way in, but already her hands were pushing against him because the panic was coming. She tried distracting herself with thoughts of Shannon and Dan, the silly things they said, what they needed for school, what their schedules were for tomorrow. He was moving in and out of her now, not fast, but not gently either. She gripped the sheet either side of her and kept her eyes closed as he raised himself up to look down at their bodies. A horrible and devastating thought suddenly flashed in her mind. When was the last time he'd been inside a woman? Had it been her, or was it someone else? She started to choke, fighting for air.

He was moving faster now. Her hands flew to his shoulders. He didn't stop. She pushed, but still he didn't stop. And then the terrible blackness was there, swooping around her, trying to obliterate her, sucking her down and down. She couldn't breathe. She was so afraid she wanted to scream, but no sound came.

'No,' she finally gasped. 'Please, I can't.'

'Julia, for God's sake.'

'No!'

'I'm almost there ...'

'Josh stop!'

But he didn't, and as he continued to pound she started to fight, so desperate to make it stop that she didn't care if she hurt him.

'Julia, anyone would think I was raping you,' he protested.

'Just stop. Please,' she begged.

Biting down on his frustration he rolled off her and onto his back. 'Jesus Christ,' he growled, as she shot up from the bed. 'Just what kind of a marriage is this?'

'I'm sorry,' she gulped, scrabbling for her nightie. 'I'm so sorry. I wanted it to be ...'

'Don't say any more,' he seethed. 'I've heard it all before ...'

'But I tried, I swear ...'

'Well obviously not hard enough. Christ, I'm sick of it. *Damned well fucking sick* of it.'

'Well, it's no fun for me either,' she cried. 'You surely can't think I want it to be like this.'

'Frankly I don't know what you want, but I'm sure as hell not going to lie here discussing it. There's no point pretending we've got a marriage here, because it's just a farce, a total fucking charade. So why don't you just go off to the spare room, where you usually hide . . .'

'I go there to prevent this kind of scene,' she shouted, 'not because I'm hiding, or because I want to. And don't you dare try ordering me out of my own bedroom . . .'

'Then get into bed, for Christ's sake, and stop shouting or you'll wake the children.'

Still smouldering with anger and shame, she waited for him to move over to his own side, then slipped in under the sheet next to him. Neither of them spoke again, but she could sense his fury as though it were an actual presence in the bed with them. With a horrible burn of fear she recalled the last time they'd had a scene like this, and how he'd accused her then of wanting to push him into someone else's arms. But that was crazy, because she'd almost rather die than think of him with anyone but her. She'd wondered at the time if he'd been setting himself up with an excuse, blaming her for an affair he was either already having, or was about to have, and she was asking herself the same questions now. Had he found someone who welcomed his passion and even matched his skill as a lover? Was he starting to fall in love with her, whoever she was? The very idea of it tore at her so painfully that she couldn't bring herself to entertain it a moment longer.

She turned to look at him, listened to him breathing, then reached out to touch him.

'Don't,' he growled.

She took her hand away and swallowed hard on everything she wanted to say. He was right, it had all been said before, and repeating it wouldn't help. But they obviously couldn't go on like this, she had to find out what was wrong with her, why this was happening, even though she hardly knew what more to do. She'd been through hours and hours of therapy, she'd even had physical check-ups to make sure nothing had changed inside her. The results had shown her to be a perfectly normal woman with a healthy body and rational mind that, OK, bore the scars of her past, but whose didn't? And she'd faced up to everything now, talked it all through with Josh and the therapist, so there was no reason to think any of it was coming back to haunt her.

A terrible hollow seemed to open up in her heart, because she knew, she just didn't want to admit, that the past was somehow involved in this. She couldn't go there again, she simply couldn't. She'd almost rather blame Josh and his suspected affair for the way she was rejecting him, than have to do as the therapist advised and confront all the horrifying reasons why her father might have abandoned her. Besides, it made no sense for some-thing that had happened almost twenty-five years ago to be having such a profound effect on her now. And even if it was, there was no reason for it to be impacting on the way she responded to

Josh, so maybe his infidelity really was at the root of the problem. Maybe, subconsciously, she'd suspected him of an affair for much longer than she realised, and if anything would play havoc with her sex drive, that definitely would.

Chapter Two

The following morning Julia was up long before everyone else, so was able to shower, dress, load the washing machine and set up breakfast in the garden before the usual morning mayhem got under way. It was a bit of a treat to eat outside on a school and work day, but it was beautifully warm and sunny for September and she wanted to do something for Josh that she knew he enjoyed, even though she didn't for a minute think it was going to make up for last night.

Dan was next to emerge, all sleepy blue eyes and tousled dark hair, yawning loudly as he told Julia about some new gizmo they were talking up on GMTV. After promising to consider it, she steered him into the laundry room for a clean pair of socks, then watched him go motoring off around the garden, pretending to be a Porsche.

Josh was close behind him, wearing his black suit trousers and a crisp white shirt and reading the paper that had been delivered through the door. Julia watched him as he descended the last few steps into the basement kitchen, but he didn't look up. He merely glanced at the empty table, then registered the one in the gazebo, before picking up the coffee pot and carrying it outside.

Unsurprised, though dismayed by the cold shoulder, Julia said nothing, simply followed him out with the milk and sugar and was just filling Dan's bowl with cereal when Shannon came thundering down the stairs yelling, 'Mum! Mum!'

Julia turned as she came flying out through the French windows clutching a magazine. 'Oh Mum,' she cried, clearly highly distressed. 'Orlando Bloom's shaved off his beard and had his hair cut and now he looks just like *Dad*!'

Josh's head immediately came out of the paper. 'What's the matter with that?' he demanded hotly.

Unable to suppress a laugh, Julia took the magazine to look at the offending photo. Actually, Shannon was right, her heartthrob did rather resemble Josh with his fine-cut features and shorter hair.

'This is like, so horrible,' Shannon wailed. 'He can't look like Dad. He just can't.'

'Actually, I think Dad's quite good-looking,' Julia commented, handing the magazine back.

'Yes, but he's *old*. And he's not supposed to look like Orlando. Oh God,' she cried, looking at the picture again. 'All he needs is a bald spot.'

Julia and Dan burst out laughing at Josh's look of indignation. 'I don't have a bald spot,' he protested.

'No, but it's like thin at the back, and, oh Mum. What am I going to do? I can't put this on my wall.'

Suddenly grabbing her, Josh dragged her onto his lap and gave her a resounding kiss on the check. 'I could save us a lot of money on those rubbishy magazines and give you some pictures of me,' he told her.

'Yeah, right,' she responded, fighting him off. 'I'd really love that.'

'I'll have some pictures of you, Dad,' Dan piped up. 'I can use them as a dartboard.'

Julia had to laugh as Josh turned in outrage on his son, and only just managed to stop Dan crashing off his chair as he ducked clear of Josh's advance.

'Phone!' Shannon suddenly yelled. 'I'll get it,' and she shot back inside the house, shouting, 'Let it ring till I get upstairs.'

Josh looked at Julia. 'Is she expecting someone?' he asked.

'It would seem so,' she responded lightly.

His eyes stayed on her. 'If it's a conversation we're not supposed to hear, it must be a boy,' he decided.

'Not necessarily. Girls that age are usually secretive, especially where their parents are concerned.'

'But a boy rang here last night.'

'Yes, Freddy, from her drama class. You've met him.'

Josh grunted, and after throwing a look at Dan he returned to his paper. Since Freddy was at least two stone overweight and as camp as Butlins there was no cause for concern there. 'Just as long as she's not getting into any trouble,' he mumbled.

Julia pulled a face he couldn't see and poured milk over Dan's Frosties.

'What's this one called, Mum?' Dan asked, his attention now focused on a butterfly that had perched on the edge of the sugar bowl.

'I don't know. We'll look it up, if you like.'

The butterfly flitted off and Daniel turned to his father. 'What time will you be home today?' he asked, sticking his head in under the paper.

'Not sure. Why?' Josh answered, ruffling his unruly hair.

'There's a dads-and-lads game in the park at half past six. Remember?'

Josh frowned, showing that probably he didn't. 'Am I the only one around here who works?' he grumbled. 'Who on earth manages to get home by that time?'

'Dad!'

'All right, I'll be there if I can,' he said. 'What position do I have to play?'

Dan grinned. 'Goalie.'

Josh's eyes narrowed and Daniel laughed delightedly, for the last time Josh had played in goal their team had been trashed, four–nil. 'Only joking,' he cried, as Josh made to swat him.

Leaving them to a lively exchange about a sport she had no interest in, Julia picked up the mail and started to open it. It wouldn't be long now before they all shifted up a gear to begin the final dash from the house, but until then she was happy to sit here in the gazebo, soaking up the sun, listening to Dan's chatter, and holding all her negative thoughts at bay, because there would be time enough later to deal with the crushing disappointment over her book, and the slow deterioration of her marriage.

She glanced at Josh, detesting the silence between them, but there was nothing she could say with the children around, and since last night was probably best left unmentioned anyway, she handed him his post and went to check on the clematis. It appeared some kind of rust was afflicting the leaves, but that was a problem easily sorted, as was the luxuriant bed of hydrangeas that needed to be watered.

This garden was like a little haven, she'd always found, with its rich green lawn and the late-blooming flowers. A lily pond sparkled across one pebbled corner, where a small waterfall trickled over rocks and swirled around the feet of an ornamental stork. They could barely even hear the traffic out here, or smell the fumes, so the thrumming chaos of London could have been miles away. She sighed gently to herself. Mostly she loved it here. Anyone would, it felt so tranquil and safe, but there were times when she felt almost suffocated by it. She could never say why exactly, for she sensed no hostile presence, nor knew of any sordid history, but occasionally, usually when she was alone, a feeling of doom would come over her that was as bewildering as it was unsettling.

Feeling Josh's eyes on her, she turned to look at him. It was hard to tell what he was thinking, but under the harshness of his gaze she became uncomfortably aware of what she was wearing. What kind of perversity, she wondered, had made her put on the cream leather skirt he'd bought her over a year ago, that was slit high in the front to reveal her tanned thighs and that he'd always found irresistibly sexy? And despite the thin straps and low cut of her top, she could easily have put on a strapless bra, so why had she chosen to come downstairs in an outfit she'd normally use to seduce him, when they both knew she wouldn't?

'What are you doing today?' he demanded roughly.

Certain he was going to suggest she contact the therapist again, she quickly began listing off all she had to do, from taking Patsy for a service, to buying new shoes for Dan, to answering the dozens of messages on their joint email address. She was careful to leave out the lunch she was having with her closest friend, Sylvia, for he'd automatically assume she'd be discussing their problems, which she probably would. Besides, he rarely felt easy about the time she spent with Sylvia, in case her friend's exceptionally glamorous lifestyle and firm commitment to the single life started giving Julia ideas. He was much less reticent about Sylvia's talent as a writer, however, for he'd long wanted to take her on as a client, but Sylvia was fiercely loyal to the agent she had, and felt quite strongly that any kind of professional liaison could pose a problem to a friendship she valued very highly.

Julia was about to ask if he needed her to do anything for him, when Shannon shouted from her bedroom window, 'Mum! It's for you.'

Feeling as though it was an eternity rather than just a few moments since the phone had rung, Julia wandered into the kitchen and picked up the extension. 'Hello?' she said, helping herself from a bowl of blackberries.

No reply.

'Hello,' she said again.

Still no reply.

She listened, trying to hear some kind of background noise, but there was no breathing, no distant clatter, not even any interference. Looking round as Shannon came down the back stairs, she hung up, saying, 'There's no-one there. Who was it?'

To her surprise Shannon looked slightly uneasy. 'He said . . . Well, he said he was your father,' she answered.

Julia's eyes widened with shock.

'That's what he said,' Shannon assured her, as though afraid of being disbelieved.

A strange humming sound seemed to have started in Julia's ears. 'Well what else did he say?' she asked.

'Not much really.'

Julia looked up as Josh carried a tray of dishes in through the French doors. 'Apparently my father just called,' she told him. 'He rang off before I got there.'

Josh stared at her in amazement. 'Your father?' he said. 'But . . .' He turned to Shannon.

'Don't look at me,' she cried. 'I only took the call.'

'So what did he say?' Julia prompted.

'Nothing. He just asked if he could talk to you.'

'He must have said more than that,' Julia pressed. 'You were talking to him for a good few minutes.'

'Think, Shannon,' Josh urged. 'What exactly did he say?'

With a sigh of impatience she said, 'Well, first he asked if he had the right number . . .'

'How did he get this number?' Julia said to Josh.

He cast her a look then told Shannon to go on.

'Then he asked if I was you, Mum, so I told him no, I was your daughter. He asked if my name was Shannon, so I said yes, and then he said he wanted to talk to you. So I asked who was calling, and he said, "I'm your grandfather. Julia's father."'

Julia was feeling faintly dizzy. Her eyes were fixed on Josh, as his were on her. 'Has this happened before?' he suddenly demanded.

'Of course not,' she cried. 'I'd have told you if it had.'

'Did he ask if I was here?' he said to Shannon.

'No,' she replied.

'Josh, you can't seriously think I'd hide it from you,' Julia said.

'Did he give his name?' he asked Shannon.

'I just told you what he said.'

Dan was standing in the doorway listening. Seeing him, Julia felt a sudden, overpowering instinct to hold him, to hold them all, then turning to Shannon she said, 'Did he leave a number?'

'No, but we could try 1471.'

Josh was already dialling. 'Nothing,' he said, after listening to the recorded voice.

'What's the big deal?' Dan asked.

Julia stared at his look of confusion. 'No big deal,' she told him with a smile, 'just that no-one's heard from him in more than twenty years.'

Dan's eyes widened. 'Wow! That's a long time. Where's he been?'

She shook her head.

'Have you ever met him, Dad?' Shannon asked.

'No. He disappeared before Mum and I met.'

'Why?' Dan asked.

'Nobody knows,' Julia answered.

'What about Grandma Alice, she must know,' Dan insisted, referring to Julia's mother.

Julia shook her head again, and felt the cold fingers of dread starting to clamp around her heart. If her mother ever got wind of this . . . She shuddered and snapped the thought off before it began dabbling in all the horrible implications of that.

Seeming to read her mind, Josh said, 'We don't need to mention this to Grandma Alice. She hasn't been too well lately . . .'

'This might make her feel better,' Dan said helpfully.

'It won't,' Julia assured him, relieved that Josh now seemed to be believing her.

'But she must have been worried, if he's been gone all that time.'

'*Duh.* He walked out on her, stupid,' Shannon informed him. 'She probably hopes he's dead. I know I would, if I was her.'

'Why did he walk out on her?' Dan asked.

'I expect he found someone else. And who can blame him? Grandma Alice is soo . . .'

'That's enough,' Josh snapped.

'Well, she is.'

'What is she?' Dan demanded.

'You know what she's like,' Shannon responded sneeringly, reminding Julia of herself. 'She hates everyone, even us.'

'She does not hate you,' Julia said sharply.

'She hates you,' Shannon retorted.

'She doesn't hate Uncle George,' Dan piped up. 'He's her brother, so she can't hate him.'

'Wanna bet?' Shannon challenged. 'You're my brother and I hate you.'

Dan rushed at her and grabbed her in a headlock. 'No, you don't. You love, love, love me,' he shouted.

'Yeah, like, please hold the bucket someone while I puke.'

Josh and Julia looked at each other. 'I have to go,' he said, checking his watch and reaching for his briefcase.

Julia followed him upstairs to the hall, where he stopped to pick up his keys. 'What shall I do if he calls back?' she said.

'I guess that depends what he wants.'

'What do you think he wants?'

'Who knows.'

'Josh, I swear, he's never called before,' she cried. 'I wouldn't keep it from you if he had.'

'Are you sure about that?'

'Of course I am. Why would I?'

'You know perfectly well why,' he responded. 'You don't want to face who he was, what he is, so if he's trying to get in touch and you're trying to avoid him ...'

She was about to cut in when the phone rang again. They waited, listening as Shannon picked up down in the kitchen, then realising it was one of her friends, Josh started for the door.

'Will you be back in time for Dan?' Julia asked.

'I said I would if I could.'

'Josh!'

He turned round, his expression irritable, impatient.

'It's important to him that you make that match.'

'I know, and I'll try,' he replied.

Her eyes remained on his. 'Don't make him pay for crimes that are mine,' she said quietly.

Anger tightened his jaw, and taking a step towards her he said, 'That's the trouble with you, Julia, you think everything's about you. Well, since we're on the subject, don't you think it's time you got back in touch with the therapist, because frankly, I'm not prepared to put up with much more of this.'

'I'm not a machine, for God's sake. I can't just turn myself on and off . . .'

'You've never had a problem before. Not like this.'

'Well, maybe if you weren't always fresh from screwing someone else I might find it a bit easier to get in the mood,' she hissed.

'Oh for Christ's sake,' he seethed, and without bothering to kiss her he slammed out of the house.

Already regretting her last words she listened to his footsteps, the opening and closing of the car door and roar of the engine as he pulled away. No pretence over whose car it was this morning, she remarked grimly to herself.

'Mum!' Shannon shouted up the stairs. 'I can't find my blue top, the one with drop shoulders. It's not in the laundry room . . .'

'It's hanging up in your wardrobe,' Julia told her, collecting her thoughts as she started back down the stairs. 'Why do you need it now?'

'I'm going straight to Gilly's after school. She's having a kind of party, you know, for her birthday.'

'OK. Before you disappear, give me a hand loading the dishes. Where's Dan?'

'He went into the computer room.'

Julia opened the dishwasher. 'So who's going to be at the party?' she asked as Shannon passed her a stack of cereal bowls.

'Just a few of us hanging out, you know, while Gilly opens her presents and stuff. Her boyfriend's taking her out on Saturday. They've asked me if I want to go. I mean, like, there'll be a gang of us, not just me and Gilly and Guy.'

Julia gave her a look. 'Are the other boys Guy's age?'

Shannon shrugged. 'I don't know. I suppose so.'

'Then I don't think Dad will agree, darling. Guy's nineteen.'

'But Mum, I'm never going to have a boyfriend if he keeps me locked up all the time.'

'You'll be sixteen before you know it, sweetheart, he'll relax the rules then, he promised.'

'But everyone else has a boyfriend, except me,' Shannon protested. 'I hate being the only one who doesn't. I feel like a freak.' With pouting lips and tears in her eyes she squirted a dollop of liquid into the dishwasher and slammed the door shut. 'Anyway, even if Dad was cool about it, it wouldn't make a difference,' she said, turning her woeful face to Julia. 'No-one's ever interested in me.'

'Oh darling, it'll happen,' Julia assured her, drawing her into an embrace. 'You're so beautiful it can't not.'

'But even the mingers in school have got boys after them. It's so embarrassing, being the only one who never gets asked out or anything. It's just not fair, because when my friends talk about the things they've done I can't ever join in. I haven't even ever been kissed, and some of them have gone all the way already.'

Pressing her lips to the top of Shannon's head, Julia rocked her from side to side. 'I know it's hard,' she whispered, 'but you don't want anything to happen with someone unless he's the right one, do you?'

'No.' Shannon's head came up to look into Julia's face. 'Was Dad the first man you ever slept with?' she asked.

Julia thought fast. 'That's a question for another time,' she said, smoothing her hair.

'Which means he wasn't.'

Julia fixed her with a meaningful look. 'Come on, or you'll be late,' she said.

'But it's all about sex, really, isn't it?' Shannon persisted. 'Dad doesn't want me to go out with anyone because he's afraid I'll have sex with them.'

'Certainly it's a concern,' Julia admitted.

'But you wouldn't mind if I had sex, would you? You gave me the condoms . . .'

'I would mind a great deal,' Julia interrupted. 'I gave you the condoms so you'd know what they are, or in case you found yourself in a situation that . . . Well, let's just hope you don't find yourself in such a situation. And whatever happens, you mustn't let Dad know I gave them to you.'

Shannon squeezed her hard. 'I love you so much, Mum. You're the best mum in all the world.'

'Can I quote that next time you're yelling at me for not allowing you your own way over something?'

Shannon's lovely blue eyes seemed more earnest than amused as she said, 'I think Dad really loves you too, Mum. I don't think he's sleeping with anyone else.'

Julia's heart twisted. 'You've been eavesdropping,' she said, cupping Shannon's face in her hands.

'Only a bit. I wish you'd be nicer to him.'

Julia smiled and shook her head. 'What a mixed-up lot we are,' she sighed. 'Me trying to sort you out, you trying to sort me and Dad out ...'

'Oh yuk! Is this a girlie love-in?' Dan protested from the door.

'Not exclusively,' Julia responded, holding out an arm. 'Certain boys can join in.'

'No thanks,' he replied. Then abruptly changing his mind, he charged towards them like a bull, and caught them both round the waist.

'And you want a boyfriend?' Julia said to Shannon as they staggered against the sink.

'Not one like him,' Shannon retorted, and grabbing Dan by the ears she planted a resounding kiss on his cheek before flashing off up the stairs.

'OK, so what's on your agenda today, young man?' Julia said, starting to put the breakfast cereals away. 'Do you have any sports?'

Dan's face fell. 'I don't know. I lost my agenda,' he said bleakly.

Julia rolled her eyes in exasperation. 'Dan, term only started a week ago, you can't have lost it already.'

He hung his head. 'I didn't mean to,' he said.

With a sinking heart Julia realised that someone had probably stolen it as a prank, hidden it, and now he couldn't find it. 'We'll get you another,' she said gently. 'Then just make sure you hang onto it.'

'Can we look up that butterfly now?' he asked. 'Dad's computer's on. We can use his.'

As she followed him into Josh's hallowed territory that they all regularly invaded, she found her thoughts going back to the mysterious telephone call and wondered if it really had been her father – and if it had, why he would be in touch now, after all these years. It was bizarre, and such a shock she wasn't entirely sure she'd taken it in. Maybe she'd ring her sister, see if he'd tried to call her, though she knew she wouldn't, because if Pam hadn't heard anything the old rivalry would begin again. And if Pam had . . .

A memory of her father's face cut off the thought, his soft grey-blue eyes, long nose, square chin and high forehead. He'd always seemed to be laughing, never cross, unfailingly interested in what she was saying, or ready to take part in her new adventures. She tried to hear the sound of his voice, the playfulness and laughter; his pleasure when she did well and concern when she didn't. It was all there somewhere, along with the feelings of love and contentment, the excitement and eagerness to please. She just couldn't seem to reach past all the closed doors between now and then to find it.

'Sometimes it feels as though I'm not a real person any more,' Julia was confessing to Sylvia later. 'It's as though I've come adrift from myself and my family and I'm not sure how it happened, or how to find my way back.'

Sylvia's perfect eyebrows arched with irony. 'You're forty and a mother,' she responded lightly 'Crises go with the territory.'

Humour sparked in Julia's eyes as she said, 'You're always such a comfort to me, Sylvie. How would I manage without you?'

As Sylvia looked up from the bottle she was opening, she was smiling in the affectionate, teasing way Julia knew so well, for they'd been friends since their early twenties, and though they'd made very different life choices back then, they'd always remained as close as their conflicting commitments would allow. Surprisingly, they'd hardly ever considered each other as rivals, for in spite of both being beauties and sharing the ambition to write, they'd never had the same taste in men, and Julia knew very well that to begrudge Sylvia her success as an author would certainly do nothing to enhance her own. Besides, she was far too fond of Sylvia to wish her anything but good, and was even delighted by the added success she'd been enjoying lately with her highly unusual ceramics. It was why she'd taken this bijou mews house in Notting Hill, to be in a more bohemian environment, which Julia found both amusing and intriguing, for Sylvia, with her haute-couture wardrobe and aversion to even the slightest muddle, had always been the epitome of Chelsea chic and stylish living up till now.

'You'll get through this,' Sylvia assured her, 'you love each other too much not to.'

Liking the sound of that, Julia watched as she pulled the cork from the bottle, and thought how lovely she looked in the sunlight that was streaming through the open French windows. It was turning her long, silky blonde hair to a silvery mane, and shrouding her in the kind of light that made Julia understand why some referred to her as the ice maiden, for everything about her seemed impenetrably cool and collected, and aloof almost to the point of disdain. Julia knew, however, that passions ran very deeply beneath that perfect facade, for Sylvia's love affairs had been many and tempestuous, and if there was a lover who'd been willing to let her go when she'd decided to move on, Julia was at a loss to remember him now.

'Is Pauline still joining us?' Julia asked, reaching into a cupboard for glasses as Sylvia made ready to pour.

'As far as I'm aware,' Sylvia replied. 'She should be here any minute,' and after filling three glasses she handed one to Julia before picking up another for herself.

'I miss seeing you,' she said, gazing directly into Julia's eyes. 'You don't come often enough . . . OK, I know you have demands on you, but you really ought to take more time for yourself. You look in need.'

Julia sighed and grimaced. 'I feel it,' she confessed, 'and believe me, there's nothing I'd like more than to come here for at least two weeks to indulge myself in us, being a woman, pretending to be a writer . . .'

'Is there any news about your book?' Sylvia cut in gently.

Julia assumed a defeated smile, and clinked their glasses. 'Let's drink to you,' she said, 'and be thankful that at least one of us is living the dream.'

Sylvia was about to respond when the doorbell rang. 'It'll work out,' she said, giving Julia's hand a quick squeeze, 'I know it will,' and putting her glass down she crossed the open-plan living room to buzz Pauline in through the workshop downstairs.

As Julia watched her, she was admiring the shimmering turquoise wrap that seemed to float behind her like a cloud and the matching bikini underneath that sat so smoothly on her slender hips and over her neat, unpretentious breasts that it might almost have been a part of her. Then with no small dismay she found herself reflecting on how long it had been since she'd felt that willing to show off her figure, even though the dress she was wearing now complemented it and her legs quite beautifully – she was just lacking the confidence to exploit it, the way she used to.

On returning to the kitchenette Sylvia began unwrapping the tapas she'd picked up at the deli, while Julia carried plates and cutlery out to the small roof terrace where the table was already partly laid. 'Is Pauline seeing anyone at the moment?' she called back over her shoulder.

'Not that I'm aware of,' Sylvia answered. 'She didn't mention anything when we spoke last night, but you know Pauline, everything could have changed between then and now.'

Smiling, Julia stepped back into the room, and was about to return to the kitchenette when she spotted a large, harp-shaped porcelain vase she hadn't seen before. 'Sylvie, this is exquisite,' she declared, going to it. 'The shape is so unusual. So delicate. I take it it's one of yours?'

Sylvia's eyes shone with pleasure as she nodded.

'Can I pick it up?'

'Of course.'

Julia was about to do so, when she remembered how much Josh had paid for Sylvia's last piece, which they'd bought – at discount – at one of her exhibitions. Deciding not to risk it, she stood back to admire it where it was, while imagining how lovely it would look gracing a plinth in their drawing room, along with the several others they now owned.

'Going back to how you're feeling about yourself, and your family,' Sylvia said, licking oil from her fingers.

'No, let's talk about when your next book is being published,' Julia cut in. 'It must be quite soon now.'

'Actually, not until the beginning of November, but review copies will go out in advance, so let's hope they treat me gently.'

Julia smiled, for critics and public alike usually adored Sylvia's psychological thrillers, and she couldn't imagine this latest would be treated any differently. 'Have you started a new one yet?' she asked.

Sylvia shook her head. 'No, I'm taking a year off to focus on my ceramics,' she answered, looking across the room as a large bunch of flowers entered, followed by a striking, deeply tanned woman, with gleaming white teeth and a perfectly toned body.

'Julia!' Pauline cried, casting the bouquet aside. 'Sylvie told me you were coming. How lovely to see you. It's been too long.'

'At least a month,' Julia smiled, looking into Pauline's lively brown eyes and feeling happier than ever about being here. She embraced her warmly, then cupped her pixie-like face between her hands. 'How come you never age?' she demanded. 'You still look the right side of thirty, for God's sake, and you're older than me.'

'Hey, you're the beauty amongst us,' Pauline protested, in the cultured Bostonian accent that had served her well over two decades in London. 'Mine's all Botox, highlights and a sadistic personal trainer. You look fabulous, my love.'

Julia cast her a sceptical glance. 'I've put on at least half a stone, my hair needs some serious attention and . . .'

'At your height half a stone means nothing. And stop with the self-criticism. You look gorgeous, so accept the compliment and revel in it. I know this one will,' she added, holding her arms out to Sylvia. 'You look so scrumptiously unattainable, my darling, I'd tumble into bed with you right now if I was that way inclined.'

'How much easier life might be if we all were,' Sylvia responded, kissing her on both cheeks. 'Now, you've come at the right time, because Julia's having a midlife crisis and she needs our help.'

'Are you really?' Pauline cried, all fascination and concern. 'You know, my second husband was a psychiatrist . . . Where's the wine?'

Sylvia passed her a glass and left them discussing the woes of becoming forty while she finished preparing lunch and carried it out to the terrace. Then, once they were all settled in amongst a forest of succulent pot plants and the riotous colours of more flowers than there was room for, she said, 'I didn't catch everything you were saying just now, so has Julia told you her second book hasn't been accepted?'

Pauline's eyes filled with sympathy as she turned to Julia.

'Please don't let's go there,' Julia protested. 'Everything about my life is a mess at the moment so I'd rather forget it . . .'

'Hey, come on,' Pauline interrupted. 'It's a big deal. Don't just brush it away. It hurts like hell to go through something like that.'

Realising that nothing ever hurt quite so much when she was sharing it with her friends, Julia said, 'But I have to ask myself, is it crushing because I truly believe in myself as a writer, or because I'm trying to be somebody in my own right and it's not working out?'

'But you are somebody,' Sylvia declared, offering her a plate of plump jalapeño-stuffed olives. 'A very important somebody as far as Josh and the kids are concerned. And your friends too.'

'But I need to be somebody for *me*,' Julia responded forcefully, as she helped herself. 'I know it sounds corny and clichéd, but everything I am, everything I have, is down to Josh. I haven't achieved anything myself . . . OK, I know you're going to remind me of the kids again, and of what a support I've been to Josh, but that's all happened because of him, not in spite of him, and I'm just feeling the need to have something of my own – something that no-one can take away, because it's *all* mine.'

Pauline was looking at her quizzically. 'Now that's a scream for independence, if ever I heard one,' she commented. 'Which has to mean you're feeling insecure. Do you ever dream about losing your car?'

Julia looked surprised. 'Actually, yes I do from time to time,' she confessed.

Pauline shrugged. 'It's a symbol of independence, gets you from one place to another, you're in control . . . You lose it, you lose control. I'm sure you're getting the picture.'

'Does Josh know how you're feeling?' Sylvia asked.

Julia gave an incredulous laugh. 'Are you kidding? You know it's playing havoc with our sex life – at least I assume that's what's behind my reticence – and now I keep worrying about how, if he left me, I'd have nothing. I don't do anything to support myself . . .'

'You're a brilliant editor,' Pauline protested. 'Everyone knows you'd be running McKenzies by now if you hadn't gone freelance.'

'I haven't had a serious commission in over two years,' Julia reminded her. 'Anyway, let's stop this. I don't want to squander our precious time together talking about me, tell me what wildly hedonistic adventures you've been having.'

Sylvia frowned. 'If you've got a problem, what else are friends for?' she said gently.

Julia felt absurdly emotional for a moment, and lowered her eyes.

'Don't keep it bottled up,' Sylvia pressed.

Julia swallowed and reached for her wine.

'Actually, I have some other news,' she said. 'I think my father might have called this morning.'

At that, Sylvia's glass stopped in mid-air and Pauline put down her fork. After exchanging glances they both sat back in their chairs.

'What do you mean, *might* have called?' Pauline prompted, as Julia tore off a morsel of bread and dipped it in a dish of truffle-flavoured oil.

'Someone called, and told Shannon he was her grandfather, my father, but by the time I got to the phone he'd rung off.'

'You sound as though you're not convinced it was him,' Sylvia said curiously.

Julia shrugged. 'I've got no way of knowing.'

'But why would anyone pretend to be?'

'I've no idea,' Julia responded and continued to eat.

Sylvia was frowning thoughtfully as she leaned forward to help herself to a sliver of quiche. 'It must be over twenty years since he left,' she said, 'so why now?'

'Twenty-four and a half, actually,' Julia said. 'Not that I'm counting. I'm way over it.'

Sylvia looked at her askance.

Julia laughed. 'I've had the therapy, dealt with the abandonment, so I'm ... What am I?'

'Totally cool about the way he skipped out of your life without a word of warning or explanation, and never contacted any of you again?' Sylvia suggested.

'Something like that.'

'Remind me again when you last tried to contact him?' Pauline said.

'It was just after Shannon was born. I felt so

proud, and I wanted him to see her, so Josh got on the case, and I'm sure if we'd kept at it we'd have found him, but then I lost my nerve and made him stop.'

'Why?' Pauline asked.

'Probably because I'm afraid of finding out things I'd rather not know.'

'Such as?'

'Like I said, I'd rather not know.'

Sylvia turned to sit sideways and as she crossed her legs her wrap fell open to the waist, revealing her slim, tanned thighs and perfectly toned tummy. 'Have you told your mother about the call?' she asked, continuing to eat.

Julia shuddered, and for a moment the sun seemed to disappear as fearsome images of her mother shouting and slapping her, blaming her for her father's desertion, ripped out from the shadows. Quickly she pushed them away again, for it wasn't a time of her life she ever cared to revisit.

'Was he depressed before he left?' Pauline asked. 'Had something happened? Do you remember any rows, or anything like that?'

'There was one huge row, not long before he went,' Julia admitted. 'I'm not sure what it was about, I just remember my mother telling him he was sick and . . .' She broke off quickly. 'He ended up with cuts and bruises all over his face and a fractured rib, I think. I don't know if they spoke to each other again after that, they certainly slept in separate beds. Then one morning he left for work and never came back.'

'And never tried to contact you again?'

'Not that I know of. My mother might have kept

it from us, but he could always have tried another way, if he'd wanted to.'

Pauline was wrinkling her nose as she looked at Sylvia. 'Do you think there was another woman involved?' she asked, turning back to Julia.

'If there was, why would that stop him seeing me and Pam?'

'Your mother might have stood in his way, but again there would have been other routes he could have taken.'

Sylvia was refilling their glasses. 'So has this prompted you to try again to find him?' she asked.

Julia sighed. 'I don't know. Part of me feels as though I should, but it's been so long now . . . And if he wanted to be found, why not leave a number?'

'What does Josh think?'

'We haven't discussed it yet, but no-one would be happier than him if I went back into therapy and got myself sorted out once and for all, because he's convinced my father's desertion is at the root of it all. What he's not considering though, is that it might just end up making everything ten times worse.'

'Worse than no sex at all?' Sylvia said doubtfully. 'Hard to imagine.'

Julia smiled, then pulled a face as she realised Sylvia might have a point.

'You know what I think,' Sylvia suddenly decided, 'I think you need an affair.'

Julia blinked in astonishment. 'I'm off sex,' she reminded her. 'And if I weren't, Josh is who I'd want to do it with.'

'But are you sure it's sex you're off, and not him?'

Julia shifted uncomfortably. 'Quite sure,' she responded. Then after a moment's thought, 'Well, the fear that he's sleeping with someone else is definitely playing a part in putting me off sex, so I suppose, in a way, it could be him.'

'*Is* he sleeping with someone else?' Pauline asked, incredulously.

'No. I don't know. I don't think so.'

'Of course not,' Sylvia answered, going inside to fetch more wine. 'But that's not to say Julia shouldn't, so is there anyone you fancy? Someone you could try flirting with to see if it gets you going? If nothing else, it might kick-start the old libido, get things moving again.'

Julia was shaking her head. 'No-one I can think of. Anyway, I don't want to go that route. I love Josh, I'm totally fulfilled by our sex life – when we're having one – and I have no desire to be involved with anyone else, even on the most superficial level.'

Sylvia sighed and cast a mournful glance at Pauline as she came out again. 'I never did get monogamy, did you?'

'Only when I'm married,' Pauline confessed, 'but coming at it from this side, it seems positively quaint. Honestly, Julia, to think you're still crazy about the same man after how many years?'

'Almost eighteen,' Julia provided.

'Incredible. I don't know whether congratulations or commiserations are in order. However, we *are* talking about Josh, so maybe it's not so peculiar. Is he a generous lover?'

Julia nodded. 'The best,' she replied.

'What if I told you,' Sylvia said, 'that he *is* having an affair?'

Julia's smile fled, and as she turned to look at her, her entire body turned cold.

'I'm just posing the question,' Sylvia assured her. 'I'm not saying he is.'

Relief flooded in so fast that Julia felt instantly light-headed. 'You really scared me then,' she chided, glancing at Pauline.

'She sure did,' Pauline commented, appearing curious as to why Sylvia had taken this line.

'I think you're using it as an excuse,' Sylvia explained. 'You'd almost rather persuade yourself Josh is having an affair than face up to the problems that are clearly still hanging around from the time your father left. Something happened to you back then, the trauma was huge, it must have been to cause so much damage that your mind just can't heal it. Sure, it goes into retreat for a while, and lets you lead a normal, untroubled existence, but it keeps coming back, and it will continue to if you don't get it out there and address it.'

Julia was starting to feel overly hot.

'He walked out when you were about Shannon's age,' Sylvia went on a little more gently, 'so there could be a resonance there that, on some level, is bringing it all back, and it's not going away again this time, is it?'

'You know, I think we're all jumping to conclusions about this being connected to my father,' Julia began.

Ignoring her, Sylvia said, 'Have you spoken to your sister about the call?'

Julia shook her head. 'I was always his favourite,

so if he's called me and not her .. I just don't want to go there.'

'How old was she when he left?'

'Eighteen.'

'So does she know why he went?'

'If she does, she's never confided in me, and God knows I tried hard enough to get it out of her at the time. It never even gets mentioned now – well, it wouldn't when we almost never see her.'

'Did your mother ever blame her the way she did you?' Pauline asked.

'Once I heard her saying Pam should be thankful he'd gone after everything that had happened, but I don't know if you could call that blame.'

'So really, it was only you who got saddled with that?' Sylvia said.

Julia nodded and drank more wine.

'Did she ever say what you'd done to drive him away?'

Julia felt herself stiffen as the old and terrible misery threatened to engulf her. Then with a bitter laugh, she said, 'Would you believe she told me it was disgusting for a father to love his own daughter the way he loved me. She called him a pervert and accused me of leading him on.' Even as she said the words she could feel her insides heaving with the shame she'd felt back then, and still did, even though she knew very well she'd never done anything wrong. 'It's not true,' she added quickly. 'He never laid a finger on me that way, but the accusation stuck. I've never been able to forget it, or to forgive her.'

'Have you ever brought it up again? Asked her to explain?'

'Of course, but if you knew my mother you'd know what a waste of time that is. She has a very selective memory and has chosen to forget she ever said such a thing. And she never, but never discusses anything she doesn't want to.'

'Is she still living in Gloucestershire?'

'Of course. She'll never leave that place. Pam's back there now, with her husband and daughter, living in the same village, less than a minute's walk away. She sees my mother every day, and as far as my mother's capable of being close to anyone, she seems to have managed it with Pam. Neither of them ever call me, in fact Josh is the one who keeps the contact going, mainly for the kids, but I'm not at all sure she appreciates it.'

'The only female on the planet who hasn't fallen prey to the legendary Josh Thayne charm?' Sylvia quipped.

'Actually, I think she quite likes him. It's me she can't stand.'

'What about the kids?'

'She can take them or leave them, whereas Rachel, Pam's daughter, is the apple of her eye, which is quite something for a woman who can't bear anything less than perfection. And Down's would definitely qualify as an imperfection in my mother's book.'

Getting up to answer the phone, Sylvia said, 'I think you should confront her over your father once and for all. Force her to tell you the truth of what really happened back then.'

'I agree,' Pauline said.

Julia's eyes drifted, as the mere thought of such a showdown began stirring the horrible, suffocating feeling she so dreaded. 'The last time I broached the subject she told me my father was dead,' she said flatly. 'I knew she was lying, which was borne out when Josh asked her where the grave was so we could visit. She wouldn't discuss it again after that.'

Pauline was watching Sylvia as she spoke quietly into the phone. 'It seems pretty clear to me,' she said, turning back, 'that someone else was involved when he left. It would explain your mother's bitterness. Do you suppose it might have been a man, rather than a woman?'

'I've considered that and it's certainly possible, since homosexuality is something my mother would find utterly abhorrent and deviant, and totally impossible to mention by name, never mind discuss in detail.'

'Would it give you a problem if he were gay?'

'Of course not, as long as he was happy. It doesn't chime with my mother's delightful incest charge though, does it, or the hints she dropped a few times about him being in prison.'

Pauline's eyes widened. 'I don't think you've ever mentioned that before. What was he supposed to be in there for?'

Julia drew quote marks as she said, '"An unmentionable offence" – which could suggest some kind of lewd act if you want to go that route, but that would be playing her game, which is something I absolutely refuse to do.'

The sound of Sylvia laughing made them glance inside. 'I have guests,' Sylvia was saying reprovingly, 'so this isn't a good time.' She glanced up and gave them a wink. 'No, I'm not free later. I'll call you when I am.' She listened, smiled again and said, 'I should be at the River Café around nine, come and buy me a Martini.'

After putting the phone down, she fetched a bottle of Pellegrino from the fridge and came back to join them. 'So where were we?' she said, sinking gracefully back into her chair.

'Still talking far too much about me,' Julia replied. 'So tell us who that was on the phone, and who you're expecting later. A new love?'

Sylvia looked surprised. 'Did I say I was expecting someone?'

'You said you're not free, so I assumed . . .'

'Oh. No, I'm seeing my dealer – art, not drugs.' She kept her eyes on the sparkling water as she poured, then raised them to Julia and smiled. 'You know, I've been intrigued about your father for years,' she confessed, 'so I think it's high time we made it our business to find out exactly why he took off like that.'

'Think of it this way,' Pauline added, 'it could turn out to be the source for your first best-seller.'

Though Julia's expression remained light her insides sank in the darkness of the words, for it was starting to seem as though her whole life was about rejection – her father, her mother, her books, and, though she dreaded even to think it, Josh too. But it was going to happen, she could sense it as surely as the sun's burning rays on her skin. It was just a question of when, and how, and whether, when it happened, she could manage to survive it.

Chapter Three

Josh's expression was taut and pale as he got up from his desk and carried the phone over to the large bay window that overlooked Queen's Gate Gardens. Right now the view was blurred by a sudden downpour of rain, but his attention was far from the leafy enclave in the middle of the square, it was wholly focused on the appalling way he was handling the call he was on.

'Josh, I want to help,' Harry Greenstock, a good friend – and Julia's old boss at McKenzies – was telling him, 'but you know I can't overrule one of my editors like that.'

The truth was Harry could reverse an editorial decision, and they both knew it. However, he clearly wasn't going to, and Josh could hardly claim to be surprised. Nevertheless he wasn't ready to give up yet. 'But I think Fiona's the wrong editor for it,' he protested, deeply thankful that Julia couldn't hear any of this, for ballistic wouldn't even begin to describe her reaction. 'Let me send it to Lizzie Bloom, or Carson Maclure.'

'You chose Fiona because you know she's the best,' Greenstock replied patiently. 'And she's the most senior. The others won't oppose her decision.'

'But it's a wrong one.'

'Then you're free to take the book elsewhere.'

Josh checked to make sure his door was closed, for he didn't want Marina, his PA, to know about this conversation, particularly not what was coming next. 'Look,' he said, already wincing, for he'd never pulled a stroke like this before, and given a choice he sure as hell wouldn't do it now, 'we both know Moira Glaister's contract is coming up for renewal.'

The silence at the other end was deadly.

Hating himself, Josh continued to let the implication hang. Moira was an extremely successful crime-writer. Greenstock wouldn't want Josh taking her elsewhere, but though trading one author off the back of another did happen, when the author he was trying to promote was his wife, it smacked of the kind of nepotism anyone would find hard to stomach. In fact, as the silence drew on, he was becoming nauseous himself.

'Josh,' Greenstock said quietly. 'I understand how disappointed you and Julia must be with Fiona's decision, but we both know Julia wouldn't thank you for this. It's no way to get her published.'

Thankful at least that Greenstock realised Julia had nothing to do with this, Josh said, 'You could do it, though.'

'Of course, but the advance would be minimal, and the outcome could prove as painful as last time.'

All that really mattered to Josh was that Julia should start believing in herself again, so as excruciating, and undoubtedly misguided, as his line of attack was, he couldn't give up yet. 'I believe in this book, Harry,' he said.

There was only a brief pause before Greenstock said, 'Is that an objective view?'

Josh sighed and closed his eyes. It was well past the time to back off now. 'I'm sorry,' he mumbled.

'It's OK. You can count on my discretion. This conversation will go no further.'

After thanking him Josh rang off, pressed his hands to his face and tried to erase the humiliation from his mind. What the hell had he been thinking? Just what did he imagine he was going to prove by forcing Julia on her old publishing house? Everyone would know, and he shuddered even to think of how devastated she'd be if she ever found out.

Thankful to be distracted by another incoming call, he clicked the phone on again and returned to his desk. As he talked to the editor at the other end he glanced anxiously at his watch, aware that he was becoming edgier and more irritable by the minute, for time was marching him inexorably towards a meeting he should never have set up, but hadn't yet been able to bring himself to cancel.

The cab was booked for three thirty, so by the time the call ended he guessed it would be outside. Without bothering to check, he picked up his mobile and raincoat, strode past Marina who was busy on the phone, and ran downstairs taking another call as it came in.

'Sydney Street, I'll direct you from there,' he told

the driver, and continued into the phone, 'it's a good offer. Better than I hoped, but we can always shop it around some more, if that's what you want.'

The author at the other end was clearly torn between greed and a safe haven. Greed won. Josh told him he'd get back when he had more news, and clicked onto the next call. It was Marina, whose wry sense of humour was as great an asset as her unswerving loyalty, since he'd given her a job nine years ago at the age of fifty-one, when no-one else would.

'Just to let you know I've rescheduled your six o'clock this evening to five tomorrow evening,' she told him. 'I couldn't get hold of your four o'clock though, because I can't see who it's with.'

'Falcon Hotels,' he informed her. 'I'm on my way there now.'

'Oh? Why isn't it in the diary?'

'Over to you,' he responded. 'It was in mine.'

'OK. Well, if you manage to wrap that up by four thirty, quarter to five at the latest, you should be home in time to play cricket with Dan.'

'Football,' he corrected. 'Any news from Phyllis Long at Bowden's?'

'A fax is coming through now. Ed Granger just called from New York, he wants . . .'

'So that's who you were busy yabbering with as I left,' he teased. 'I'm jealous.'

'You'll get over it.'

He chuckled, and felt himself relax into her humour for a moment. How easy she always made life seem. Nothing ever managed to faze her – she was even mordantly witty about the husband who, ten years ago, had taken off to recapture his youth with a backpacking Scandinavian who boasted a bust size of double her age and an IQ around about half. Of all the dumb decisions the bloke had ever made, leaving a woman like Marina had to rate as one of the worst.

'Ed's coming over next week and wants to take you and Julia to dinner,' she was telling him. 'He's bringing a new author he wants you to meet, apparently the typescript's being couriered even as we speak. I said you might not have time to read it all before he gets here, but you'd probably manage the first three chapters. I'll precis them for you, and let you know if you think they're any good.'

Wondering how he'd ever cope without her, Josh said, 'I hope you'll be joining us for the dinner.'

'That's what I said about you, when he invited me,' she responded. 'I don't go anywhere without you while Ed Granger's loose in the town without a wife.'

'Did you tell him that?'

'Of course. He's keener than ever now. Hang on, another call coming in.'

As she went off the line, Josh checked where he was, and quickly instructed the driver to make a detour to Kensington Church Street.

'That was Shannon,' Marina informed him. 'She'll call on your mobile. So what's this about with Falcon Hotels?'

'A photographic history. Not sure how interested I am, but it's worth taking a look. That'll be Shannon trying to get through. Anything else?'

'If there is, I'll call you back.'

Clicking over the line, he said, 'Hi gorgeous, how are you?'

'What if it hadn't been me?' Shannon demanded.

'Sorry. Who's that?'

'Yeah, very funny, but only you would think so.'

'What can I do for you?'

'I've just spoken to Mum and she says I have to ask you if I can stay out late for Gilly's birthday on Saturday night. Mum's totally cool with it, but because you're like in the Dark Ages . . .'

'So how late is late?' he interrupted. 'And where are you going?'

'To this kind of club, but before you go off on one, it's specially for teenagers, which is what I am.'

'Does it serve alcohol?'

'*Duh.* Gilly's mum said I could stay over . . .'

'Out of the question. Home by ten.'

'Dad!'

'OK, ten thirty.'

'That is so not going to happen. There's no point me going if it is.'

'Let's have this conversation when I get home,' he said, as the driver pulled up outside the address he'd given him. 'I have to go now. Are you still at school?'

'Just finished.'

'Then straight home, no loitering about with boys.'

'You always say that, and it always winds me up.'

'I know. Love you.'

Silence.

'Love you,' he repeated, as he got out of the cab.

More silence.

'I'll let you have a ride in my Porsche.'

'I thought it was Mum's Porsche.'

He grinned. 'She gave it back. Right, I'm really going now. See you after Dan's football,' and ringing off, he pushed open the door of a lingerie shop where he and Julia had spent a small fortune over the years.

After selecting a transparent white negligee that would just cover the bottom, and a pair of hold-up stockings with lacy tops, he paid an unfamiliar assistant with cash, then gave a friendly wave to the shop's owner who was busy with someone else, before hurrying back out to the cab.

Minutes later he was talking to another client on his mobile, while mentally urging the traffic to do a Red Sea number to let him through to his four o'clock – or better still, just snarl up completely to stop him getting there at all.

When the cab finally arrived at Sydney Street it came to a stop outside one of the elegant town-houses that could easily have been mistaken for a private dwelling, but was actually a hotel.

'You must be Mr Thayne,' the receptionist said, finding his name on the computer screen as he came in through the door, 'you're not the first to arrive. Third floor, room 307.'

As the lift rose silently upwards, a dark mirror was showing him the reflection of a man who despised himself for being here, even though he could already feel the anticipation building. He thought back to the times when Julia had waited for him in hotel rooms, or restaurants, even taxi ranks, or cinemas, for they'd often pretended to be strangers meeting by chance as part of an erotic game that would end up driving them nuts with desire. In all their married life he'd never been unfaithful, had never even wanted to, though he'd never been short of offers. In spite of the rumours that he put it about all over town, no-one could ever point to someone he'd slept with, because until a few months ago there had never been anyone, except Julia.

The first time it had happened, it had been as much for the physical release as to punish her for the way she was rejecting him, though of course she knew nothing about it. And God forbid she ever would, because it hadn't stopped where it should have, and though he promised himself every time it happened that this would be the last, it still hadn't quite worked out that way.

Using the memory of last night's disaster to still his conscience, he tapped on the door of room 307, then pressed down on the handle and walked into the room. It was spacious, and bordering on the baroque with its ornately carved bedhead and old-fashioned furnishings – not the kind of place he'd normally associate with the woman he was meeting, for her style was much more minimalist and twenty-first century.

She was standing with her back to him looking out of the window, her blonde hair twisted into an elegant roll at the nape of her neck, her arms folded in front of her. She wore a cream silk suit, matching high-heeled sandals and a perfume he knew well. As he closed the door and put his parcel down he could already feel the erotic charge in the air, but knowing how she liked to play it her way, he said nothing, merely waited for her to turn round.

Several more seconds ticked by until she drawled softly, 'Punctuality has its rewards,' and as she turned to face him she slipped off her jacket, leaving herself naked to the waist.

Desire cut through him like a whip, but he only watched as Sylvia reached behind her to draw the clip from her silky blonde hair. As it tumbled around her shoulders she started towards him, her pale blue eyes moving over him like the burn of ice.

'Is this a business meeting?' she said as she reached him.

'If that's what you want,' he responded, and placed his hands over the small, perfect mounds of her breasts.

She looked down to watch his fingers as they began toying with her nipples, pulling and squeezing, and rubbing them with his thumbs.

'I could make you my agent,' she murmured, looking up at him, 'but it will depend on how you perform today.'

'You know I'll do whatever it takes,' he answered gruffly.

Her eyes narrowed with pleasure. 'That's what I like to hear.'

He slipped a hand around her throat and tilted her head back to look at her. 'I've brought something for you,' he told her.

She glanced at the parcel and recognising the name she said, 'I don't want to put anything on today. I just want to take everything off.'

'Then don't let me stop you,' he murmured.

As she unfastened her skirt she started to smile. 'I have a surprise for you,' she told him, and letting the silk slide down over her thighs she stepped out of it and back a few paces so he could see all of her.

'Oh Christ,' he groaned, when he saw that the lips of her sex were as naked as the day she'd been born.

She watched his eyes drinking it in, then lifting one foot onto a chair she said, 'Don't you want to touch it?'

Going to her, he pushed his fingers between her legs, to find her already wet and ready for him to do whatever pleased her the most.

For a while she just enjoyed the sensation of his fingers inside her, then moving away she walked over to the desk and dipped a strawberry into a pot of cream, before turning back to him and putting it in her mouth.

As he watched her eat he began removing his clothes. Her eyes never left him as he opened his shirt to reveal the muscles of his chest, and strength of his arms, then she murmured approval of how hard he was, as he lowered his trousers over legs that were firm and powerful and still tanned from the summer in France. By the time he was naked she'd smothered her breasts in cream and was waiting for him to lick it off. He wasted no time before drawing first one, then the other nipple deep into his mouth, and as he sucked he took the cream from her and began smearing it between her legs.

Her eyes were catlike and sensuous as she

watched him, then sitting back on the desk she opened her legs wide, ready for him to feast himself there too. Instead he put strawberries there, pushing them inside her, then feeding some to her before devouring the rest himself.

Her hand was reaching for him now, pulling his erection, guiding it towards her. As it touched her she moaned softly and let her head fall back. 'Give it to me,' she murmured. 'Give it to me harder than I can take.'

Her words inflamed him and as she circled his waist with her legs, she dug the heels of her shoes into his buttocks, and forced him into her so hard it made her cry out. 'Yes, oh yes,' she gasped, as he began slamming into her. 'Fuck me, Joshua. Make me scream.'

His hands were gripping her hips as he rode her savagely, jerking her body with all his might, making her back arch and her hair swing over the desk behind her. He met her coldly calculating gaze and wanted to hurt her more and more.

'You've wanted to do this for years, haven't you?' she taunted. 'You've been dreaming about it, tearing yourself apart over it. Well you're in me now, Josh. You're fucking me so hard . . .' She gasped as the first wave of an orgasm began to break. 'Do it harder,' she urged. 'Make me come like I've never come before.'

He could feel her shuddering and clamping him in a way that was bringing on his own climax. He threw himself at her in long, rapid strokes, then short brutal thrusts. She was sinking back on the desk, moaning with pleasure, and bucking her hips against his.

'Yes, oh yes,' she murmured, squeezing her own nipples and letting her head fall back. 'You're so big. I'm so full of you . . . *Oh God,*' she cried as he grabbed her knees and spread her so wide it hurt.

He was almost spent now, and knew that she was too, for the clasp of her inner muscles was growing weaker around him. His heart was thudding as though it might burst from his chest, while sweat poured down his back and his breath came in loud, grunting pants. Then the last of his climax was spurting from him, and as he held her fast, he ground her hard, waiting for the final ecstasy of release to subside.

When it ended he wanted to lie over her, to let his breath steady and his heart calm down, but he knew he didn't have the time and his mobile was ringing.

Without thinking he reached for it, and seeing who it was he instantly withdrew and turned away, tensing as Sylvia gave a murmur of protest.

'Hi,' he said, moving away from her and wondering what madness had made him answer this call. 'Everything OK?'

'Everything's fine,' Julia assured him. 'Are you in a meeting?'

'No. What's up?' he said, starting for the bathroom.

'I just had a call from Katya Young at Hodders. She wants me to edit Hamish Kincaid's new book.'

'Wow!' he responded, coming to a stop. 'That's great. Are you pleased?'

'Of course. I just wondered if it had anything to do with you.'

'Me?'

'I thought you might have had a chat with Katya, pulled a few strings.'

Swallowing his annoyance he said, 'Actually, the credit's all yours, so don't do yourself down.'

There was a smile in her voice as she said, 'Thank you.'

He wanted to get her off the line, but couldn't think how.

'Are you going to make it for Dan?' she asked.

'It's looking that way. I have to go now, I'll call when I'm on my way home.'

As he rang off he let his head fall against the bathroom door. 'Shit!' he muttered. 'Shit! Shit!'

Sylvia was regarding him from the desk, where she was sitting with her long legs demurely crossed and her hands spread out either side of her. 'I take it that was Julia,' she said mildly.

He turned to look at her. 'She's been asked to edit Hamish Kincaid's next book,' he told her, not quite knowing why.

Sylvia looked impressed. 'That's good news,' she responded. 'She must be pleased.'

His eyes closed as a terrible wave of guilt swept over him.

'Go and shower,' she advised, and leaned forward to take off her shoes.

A few minutes later he was standing in the bath under a fierce cascade of water when she sauntered in to watch, parts of her body still smeared with strawberry juice and cream. Her readiness for more was as easy to read in her eyes as it was in the response he could feel tightening in his groin. As they looked at each other he continued to wash, until finally he pulled her in to join him and they watched his hands soaping her, and the water washing it away.

'I don't have time,' he told her gruffly, as she circled his neck with her arms and hooked a leg around his waist.

'Just put it in,' she murmured.

He slid into her, then caught her before she lost her balance, and thrust into her again.

'I have to go,' he said. 'I promised Dan.'

She looked up at him, and reaching behind her turned off the water. 'For a bastard, you're a good man,' she told him.

'Don't you believe it,' he muttered, sliding gently in and out of her. Then forcing himself to pull sharply away, he stepped out of the bath and grabbed a towel. A moment later the shame of mentioning Dan's name while he was inside her, and the guilt of being where he was when Julia called, overwhelmed him to a point where he could barely wait to get out of there.

Hearing Sylvia climb out of the bath he kept his back turned, and continued to dry himself, until she came to stand so close behind him that he could feel her nipples against him.

'Josh,' she said, as he moved roughly away. 'It's only sex, remember?'

Lifting the towel he began rubbing his hair.

She put a hand on his shoulder and turned him to face her. 'We discussed this,' she reminded him. 'We agreed. It's best for Julia if you come to me for sex, because with anyone else you'd be running the risk of all kinds of complications. With me you know there'll only ever be this.'

'And that makes it right?' he said cuttingly.

'Josh, we're doing it because we care about her. When she's ready to sleep with you again, this will all be over. No-one will be hurt, and no-one, but us, will ever have to know.'

His eyes were still harsh as he looked at her. 'Don't you have a conscience at all?' he challenged.

Her face relaxed into a smile. 'Of course, when it's necessary,' she responded. 'But my motive isn't what another woman's might be, to split you up so I can have you to myself. It's to stop you looking elsewhere and keep you two together. And OK, to have some fun myself, because you're not the only one who's wanted this for a long time, I have too.' She continued to smile and regarded him with mounting amusement, seeing that his conscience was still punishing him. 'I wish she knew how much you love her,' she said. 'Correction, I wish she could make herself believe it.'

'She used to,' he answered, turning away. 'I don't know what made her stop.'

Sylvia reached for a fresh towel and began to pat herself dry. 'Actually, we kind of discussed that at lunch today,' she told him.

Hating the fact that she and Julia had so recently been together, he left the bathroom and began gathering up his clothes.

'We're all of the opinion,' Sylvia said, following him, 'that's me, Pauline and Julia, that it's tied to Shannon being almost the same age now as Julia was when her father left. On a subconscious level she could be reacting to the fear that you're going to do the same thing.'

'With no justification,' he said tightly. 'I mean,

what have I ever done to make her think I'm going to abandon her, for God's sake? And if she knows what she's doing, why the hell doesn't she stop?'

'I believe she's trying, but it's not easy, and being impatient with her doesn't help.'

'Nor do holidays, surprises, constant reassurance or seventeen years of total fucking fidelity.'

Letting that pass, Sylvia sauntered over to one of the sofas and sank luxuriously into it. 'It's interesting, this call from her father,' she said, picking up an abandoned pot of cream and spreading what was left on her breasts.

'It might be if he'd said anything,' he responded, keeping his back turned as he pulled on his trousers.

'Yes, but why now, after all these years of silence, when he might have been dead for all anyone knew?'

'I guess only he knows the answer to that.'

'I suppose it was him who called,' she said, casting him a look from beneath her lashes.

He barely caught the question as he combed his hair in the mirror and wondered if it would dry by the time he got home. If it didn't, and Julia was there, he'd say he'd snatched a quick fifteen minutes at the gym.

'Do you think it was him?' Sylvia prompted.

He shrugged. 'I don't see what anyone would gain from pretending to be,' he replied, grabbing up his jacket. 'Speaking personally, I hope it was, and I hope he calls again, because God knows I'm prepared to grasp at any straw that might bring back the woman I married.'

She looked up at him as he came to stand over

her. 'And what if she doesn't exist any more?' she asked.

Since that wasn't a prospect he was prepared even to consider he dismissed it, and let his eyes drop to the join of her legs. 'That was sensational,' he murmured.

Still watching him she rotated a finger around one of her nipples, then lifted it to her lips to lick away the cream.

Taking his cue he stooped to pull first one, then the other nipple into his mouth, while she let her head fall back against the sofa to enjoy the sensations.

When finally he drew away she looked up at him with maliciously teasing eyes. 'Is it as good as this with Julia?' she murmured.

Because she'd asked him that before, he was prepared for it, and knowing it would be less than gallant to tell her that what they had didn't even come close to what he'd shared with Julia, he simply said, 'You're different.'

She smiled at that, then laughed softly.

'This has to be the last time,' he told her, looking into her eyes.

'Of course,' she responded, and continued to smile as he checked he had his wallet and house keys before stooping to kiss her goodbye.

'I'm sorry to leave like this,' he said, glancing at his watch, 'but I have to get home for Dan. I'll settle up on my way out.'

She gave him a little wave, and watched him go, only remembering after the door had closed behind him that she'd forgotten to mention the harp-shaped vase Julia had admired earlier. But it didn't matter, she could always bring it up the next time she saw him, for as much as he might tell himself it wouldn't happen again, she knew as well as he did that it would – and because he'd seemed so delighted with her naked pussy, she decided she might not let it grow back again just yet, for she had to confess she rather liked it too.

It was early on Sunday morning. A languid sunlight was seeping through the curtains, while the street outside was quiet with just a few birds singing and an occasional car passing. Julia was lying beside Josh in their king-size bed listening to the steady rhythm of his breathing, and mulling over the chat they'd had last night about finding her father. She wasn't particularly convinced that her problems were connected to his disappearance, but she'd agreed to consider it, mainly for Josh, and because a part of her would delight in proving her mother wrong and revealing her father to be the gentle and loving man she remembered – not to mention alive.

In some ways, she could almost feel excited about the search, for she longed to show off Josh and her children, and have them know her father too. Strangely, she didn't even seem to be as afraid of seeing him again as she once had, but that was easy to say when the prospect was hardly imminent. Nor would it be for a while, because she'd soon have Hamish Kincaid's book to edit, which, considering the stature of the author, was going to require total absorption as well as every trick and nuance of her professional skills. Receiving that commission had boosted her morale no end, even if Josh had made it happen. She had to admit this was unlikely, for her reputation as an editor had long preceded his success, so she really must stop allowing all this self-doubt to keep dragging her down.

Hearing a floorboard creak outside their door, she waited for Dan to come in, but a moment later she heard him on the stairs, obviously going up to Shannon's room at the top of the house. She smiled to herself. He'd be off to check that his sister was all right after the unholy row she'd had with her father last night for coming home twenty minutes past his eleven-thirty curfew. She'd probably hoped Josh would be in bed by then and not notice, but he'd been right there in the hall as she'd come through the door, like an avenging Victorian father, and the scene that had followed wasn't one Julia cared to recall.

Deciding to go and check on Shannon herself, she pushed the covers back and carefully slipped out of bed.

As she climbed the stairs she could hear Dan and Shannon whispering to each other, and felt tempted to stand on the landing outside to listen, just for the sheer pleasure of hearing them. However, they were almost certainly having a good moan about Josh, and though she knew it would probably make her laugh, she decided to declare herself instead. When she pushed open the door it was to find them sitting cross-legged on the bed, both in pyjamas, and half-swamped by a sea of pink and lilac duvet.

One glimpse of her mother was enough for Shannon's temper to erupt in a storm of tears. 'It's not fair,' she sobbed into Julia's shoulder as Julia sat down beside her. 'I hate him and I'm *not* being grounded.'

'Ssh,' Julia said stroking her hair. 'He'll come round. You know what he's like.'

'But he treats me like a baby!' Shannon raged, drawing back to glare at her. 'I'm nearly sixteen, Mum, and you were cool about me staying out till midnight . . .'

'I didn't say that. I said whatever was OK with Dad . . .'

'And I said, even if it's midnight, and you said yes.'

Julia smiled and tucked her hair behind one ear.

'Do you want me to mend this for you?' Dan offered, reaching over to pick up the bracelet that had got broken in last night's tussle.

'Yes, please,' Shannon said, wiping her tears with the back of her hand.

For a moment or two she and Julia sat watching his clumsy fingers trying to work the beads, then turning an anxious gaze on her mother, Shannon said, 'I'm never going to have a boyfriend, Mum. He keeps me prisoner and everyone knows I'm like, not allowed to do anything that's even remotely out there.'

Wondering how many more times they were going to have this conversation before the big event finally happened, Julia said, 'Eleven thirty was late enough, darling.'

'But everyone else was allowed out till midnight, and even later.'

'He's only strict because he loves you and doesn't want anything bad to happen to you.'

Though seeming slightly pacified by this, a moment later Shannon was saying, 'Do you think there's something wrong with me, Mum? No-one ever fancies me. I think there's something wrong with me.'

'There's not, is there Mum?' Dan piped up. 'Ben James in my class thinks she's really fit. He wants me to get a photo of her.'

'Don't you dare!' Shannon snapped angrily. 'He's a right minger – and he's *only eleven*.'

Dan's hurt eyes moved to Julia.

Touching his cheek with her fingers, Julia kept an arm round Shannon as she said, 'Don't bite his head off, he was only trying to be kind.'

'Sorry,' Shannon said grudgingly.

'That's all right,' Dan said happily.

Julia tilted Shannon's chin up and looked down at her tear-ravaged face. 'It's not that no-one's interested in you,' she said gently, 'it's that you're not interested in them. Be honest now, there's no-one you really fancy, is there?'

In the end Shannon had to admit it.

'You wait till that happens,' Julia warned. 'You might be wishing you were back where you are now.'

'It won't happen, because I'm ugly, and fat and I've got spots . . .'

'You're beautiful,' Julia corrected, feeling for the teenage torment that managed to get everything out of proportion, or just plain wrong. 'Maybe too beautiful, which is why Dad worries. He doesn't want you to be hurt.'

'But why does being beautiful mean I have to be hurt?' Shannon cried in frustration.

'I'll be your boyfriend,' Dan offered.

'Don't be stupid.'

Dan grinned. 'I don't want to be anyway, because you're ugly and fat and you've got spots ...'

'That's enough now,' Julia interrupted, as Shannon jumped on him with a pillow, trying to stifle him.

As he came up for air Shannon caught him in a friendly headlock.

'I think she should be allowed to do whatever she likes,' Dan informed his mother.

'I'm sure you do,' Julia replied.

Letting him go, Shannon turned to sit comfortably facing her mother. 'How old were you when you had your first boyfriend?' she asked,

'Oh, let me see,' Julia said, thinking. 'I must have been about twenty-eight.'

Shannon bubbled with laughter and slapped her hand. 'Seriously,' she insisted.

'OK, probably about your age,' Julia confessed.

'And I bet your dad wasn't like *him*. I bet you could stay out late and go out with as many boys as you wanted.'

Julia's eyes moved to the middle distance. 'My dad left around that time,' she said, letting her thoughts drift – then finding herself tumbling towards some kind of abyss, she drew herself sharply up again.

'Why did he go?' Dan asked.

'I don't know,' she answered.

'If he had you and Aunt Pam, he shouldn't have left, should he?'

'No, but sometimes there are circumstances we

know nothing about that make it impossible for someone to stay.'

'Like what?'

'I don't know. Lots of people have secrets, and they don't always share them with their children.'

'You don't have secrets from us, do you?' Dan said, starting to look worried.

'No,' she smiled, touching his face.

'Does Dad?'

Though she didn't mean to, she hesitated.

'Dad's not going to leave us, like yours left you,' Shannon said defiantly, though her expression was full of concern.

'I hope not,' Julia responded.

Shannon's eyes widened.

Suddenly realising it hadn't been a firm enough answer, Julia said, 'No, of course he won't leave us. He loves you both far too much.'

'I don't want him to leave us,' Dan protested.

'He's not going to, silly,' Julia assured him.

'But you said you hoped not,' Shannon cried. 'That means you think he might.'

'No it doesn't.'

'Yes it does.'

'That's enough,' Josh barked from the door. 'I'm not going anywhere.'

They all swung round, and Julia's heart turned over to see the expression on his unshaven face.

'What the hell are you telling them?' he demanded.

'Nothing. They misunderstood . . .'

'Don't leave us, Dad,' Shannon wailed, springing up from the bed and running to him. 'I'm really, really sorry I was late last night and that I cheeked you back. I won't do it again. I promise.'

'I told you, I'm not going anywhere,' he responded, holding her tight and glaring at Julia.

Julia felt light-headed. From one thoughtless remark this was escalating way out of control.

'Are we friends now?' Shannon said, looking up at her father.

'Of course,' he replied, kissing her forehead.

Not quite knowing what to say, while sensing a dreadful row on the horizon, Julia turned back to Dan. In a split second everything else was forgotten. 'Oh my God!' she gasped, grabbing him. 'Dan! Dan!'

His eyes were rolling back in his head, and his teeth were clenched as his small body started to convulse.

Josh was there in an instant, taking him. 'It's OK, son,' he said firmly. 'I've got you. It's going to be all right.' Quickly they turned Dan on his side and held him as the seizure gripped his small frame. It was only a matter of seconds, but to Julia it was an eternity of terror, as she tormented herself with the fear of him not coming out of it at all; or emerging with brain damage. Could he stand to go through all those dreadful tests and hospital visits again? Could she?

At last he was still, and as he blinked and started to look around for her she gathered him up in her arms.

'Mum?' he said groggily.

'I'm here, darling,' she soothed, still trembling. 'Are you OK?'

His answer was to bury his face in her neck.

'There,' she said weakly, holding him close. 'It's all right now. Everything's all right.'

Josh turned to Shannon who was standing at the door, hands clasped over her mouth in horror.

'Is he all right, Dad?' she asked shakily.

'He's fine,' Josh assured her, going to comfort her.

'What happened? Why did he do that?'

'You know what happened,' Josh answered gently. 'We just haven't seen one in a while.'

'He's going to be all right though, isn't he?'

'Of course.'

Julia was rocking her son back and forth, her face pressed to his head as she fought back the tears. Almost two years with nothing, the longest spell they'd ever had, so why now? What had triggered it? In her heart she feared the worst, and the guilt she felt was only made worse by Dan's hand reaching up to her face.

'Shall we ask Dad to carry you back to bed, and I'll come and lie down with you?' she whispered to him.

He nodded.

As Josh took him from her their eyes met, and she saw instantly that he blamed her too. However, now wasn't the time to discuss it, Dan needed to rest, and after she'd called the doctor she wouldn't leave him until he woke up and she felt certain it wasn't going to happen again.

So it wasn't until the middle of the day, after the doctor had assured her it didn't sound serious, and Josh had taken Shannon to his health club for a swim, that she and Josh were alone in their bedroom and able to talk.

'You know very well,' Josh said through his teeth, 'that distress can bring on an attack, so what the hell were you thinking? Just what is going on with you, that you can let him think I'm leaving? You scared him half to death, Shannon too. Jesus Christ, Julia.' He clapped his hands to his head, his rage so profound that he barely knew how to contain it.

'I didn't tell him you were leaving,' she cried, trying to keep her voice down.

'I heard what you said! And you heard how they interpreted it. What's the matter with you, can't you see what's happening? Your paranoia is getting through to them on levels you don't even seem to be aware of.'

'It just came out that way. It wasn't meant . . .'

'You've got to get yourself sorted out,' he snapped. 'Something's going on with you, and using Shannon's age as an excuse just isn't good enough.'

Julia blinked. 'What do you mean?' she demanded, trying to remember when she'd mentioned that to him.

For a moment he seemed startled too, then recovering quickly, he said, 'You've got some kind of projection going on here, but whatever happened with your father has nothing to do with me. I'm not going to walk out on my children, I've never even thought about abandoning them, but I'll tell you this, if it weren't for them, then frankly there have been times lately . . .'

Her eyes flashed with fury. 'Go on,' she challenged. 'Finish what you were saying.'

He stared at her hard, clearly sorely tempted.

'You were about to say, if it weren't for them you wouldn't even hesitate,' she seethed. 'Well don't let me stop you. We can manage just fine without you.'

She saw the pain cut through his eyes, but was in no mood to back down now. He knew damned well she hadn't misled Dan on purpose, and though she blamed herself too, to lay into her like this was going too far.

In the end he was the first to turn away. 'I'm not going to let you screw up my children,' he snarled, and tore open the door.

'*Our* children!' she shouted.

Turning back, he slammed the door closed and took a step towards her. 'Then I suggest you start behaving like someone who gives a damn about anyone other than yourself,' he said coldly.

'How dare you? I've given everything to this family, and the problems I seem to be having now aren't going to go away just because *you* don't like them.'

'No, they won't go away until you start facing up to what your father was, and what happened back then.'

Her eyes were bright with fury and despair. 'That's easy for you to say, Mr Perfect Son from perfect parents,' she cried. 'You've never known a moment's doubt or insecurity in your life . . .'

'Try standing where I am right now.'

'It's not the same thing, and you know it.'

He was staring at her so hard she could almost feel herself backing away, then quite suddenly he seemed to let go, and looking at her with something close to contempt, he said, 'I don't know why

I bother,' and pulling open the door he walked out of the room.

A few minutes later she heard the front door close, and looking down into the street she saw him getting into the Porsche with Shannon. She guessed they'd go to his mother's, as they often did on a Sunday, usually with Dan, though not her if she could avoid it. She wondered how much of what had happened this morning he'd confide in his mother. With a horrible sinking feeling she realised how much easier he would find it to cope without her, thanks to Emma, than she would without him. There was probably nothing her mother-in-law would relish more than to step into Julia's shoes to take proper care of Josh and his children – which would happen over her dead body, Julia was thinking, as she went off to check again on Dan again.

She found him ransacking his bedroom, looking for a lost CD-Rom. How easily children forgot, she couldn't help thinking, and felt only relief for it. 'I can't find the wrestling one Dad gave me,' he exclaimed as she came in. 'It was in my computer, but it's gone.'

'Was it with the ones you took over to Tim's?' she asked, catching a flying trainer.

He stopped. 'Oh yes, I didn't think of that.'

She looked down at his handsome little face and smiled. 'How are you feeling?' she asked.

'OK. Can I go over to Tim's this afternoon?'

Not wanting to let him out of her sight, never mind the house, she said, 'Why don't you invite him round here?'

He shrugged. 'All right.'

'You need to get dressed and have something to eat first though,' she told him, going into his bathroom to turn on the shower. At the threshold she came to an abrupt stop. 'Daniel Thayne, how do you manage to make such a mess?' she demanded, taking in the upturned linen basket with clothes all over the floor, toilet rolls heaped in one corner, shoes half-tucked under rugs, a wet flannel hanging over the bath, a bar of soap on the floor, while the bath itself was littered with toys, shampoo bottles and the trainer that matched the one she'd caught.

'It's hard work,' he informed her chirpily as he came in behind her.

Laughing, she stooped to plant a resounding kiss on his cheek, and began the clearing up. Today he could get away with anything, which Shannon would probably proclaim was much like any other day, but then Shannon would.

'It scared me witless,' she confessed to Sylvia on the phone later. 'Fortunately it was only a mild attack, and he seems perfectly all right now ...'

'Where is he?' Sylvia asked.

'In his room with a friend, playing on the computer.'

'And Josh?'

'At his mother's, I think. We had the most awful row. He was absolutely furious. He even said if it weren't for the children he'd be gone.'

There was a pause before Sylvia said, 'That was just the heat of the moment. I'm sure he doesn't mean it.'

'But if there is someone else, and I carry on behaving like this ...'

'He just needs you to make love with him,' Sylvia said. 'Is that so much to ask when you love him?'

Julia's heart sank as she sat down at her desk and dropped her head into one hand. 'It might not seem so to you,' she said, 'it doesn't to me, when you're putting it into words, but if you knew what happened to me ... How it feels when he's ... The only way I can describe it is, it's like I'm being sucked into a vacuum of nothingness. Everything seems to go dark, like it's swallowing me up, or closing in on me, or smothering me ... I know it sounds crazy, but it's so ghastly that I just can't bear to go on, and quite frankly I'm starting to wonder if I'm more in need of an exorcist than a therapist.'

'Now that would be interesting,' Sylvia responded humorously.

Julia laughed, but a moment later unease was coming over her again. 'If he is having an affair I think I might kill him,' she declared.

'Julia, honestly ...'

'No, I'm serious. And the same goes for her, whoever she is. I actually fantasise about it – catching them together and blowing out their brains. So how's that for nuts?'

Sylvia took a moment before saying, 'Most women feel like that when they're afraid they're being cheated on. Have you mentioned it to Josh?'

'No. I think he really would leave me and take the children with him, if he knew I was having those kinds of thoughts.'

Sylvia sighed, and Julia heard the slap of clay going onto the wheel. 'If you ask me,' she said,

'Hamish Kincaid's book couldn't have come at a better time.'

Julia felt puzzled, and slightly unnerved by her loss of memory. 'I told you about that?' she said, trying to remember when. 'Anyway, yes, you're right, but it's not due for a few more weeks.'

'Then why don't you offer to do some reviews in the meantime? Or look into setting up some more writers' workshops. The last ones were a great success.'

'You're starting to sound like Josh,' Julia complained, 'and the trouble is, you're both right. I need to involve myself in something, or I really am going to drive myself nuts. And on that note, I'd better ring off, because I've promised to take the boys over to the park for a kick around.'

'OK. Before you go, I'm presuming there haven't been any more mystery calls from your father?'

'No. None, but I've promised Josh I'll do something about that once Kincaid's book is done. Any other developments I'll let you know.'

After saying goodbye, she went to round up the boys, took them for the promised treat, then returned to start preparing the Sunday roast, which they generally ate around six in the evening. And by the time Josh and Shannon came home the chicken was liberally seasoned, stuffed and roasting, the vegetables were prepared and she was enjoying a lavishly perfumed soak in the bath.

As she heard the front door bang closed behind them she began rehearsing her words of apology, even though she wasn't at all sure Josh would accept them, nor could she blame him if he didn't. But she'd try anyway, because the comment about not needing him had been hurtful, and not what he deserved at all, particularly when it could hardly be further from the truth.

After a while she heard his and Shannon's voices next door in Dan's room, though she couldn't make out what they were saying, except Josh was clearly making them laugh. Then she heard him come into their bedroom and start getting changed. Presumably Dan had told him where she was, but he didn't venture into the bathroom, nor did he call out to let her know he was back.

Submerging herself in the bubbles, she considered what it might be like to drown. She held her breath and listened to the muted thud of her heart. Long, other-worldly moments ticked by until she came up again, and took in air. She lay quietly. No sounds from the bedroom now. He must have gone downstairs.

Resting her head back on the towelling pillow behind her she let several more minutes pass, and was just thinking about getting out to dry herself when to her surprise the door opened and he came in.

The instant she saw him she felt her heart melting, for he'd mixed them both a drink and had brought them up here where they could be alone for a while.

'I'm sorry,' he said, coming to sit on the edge of the bath.

'Me too,' she responded, taking the glass. 'It was my fault.'

'No. I shouldn't have gone off like that.'

As their eyes met she reached for his hand.

'Dan seems OK,' he said, gazing down at their entwined fingers and the bubbles dripping onto his jeans.

'I think he's fine now.'

'What about school tomorrow?'

'The doctor thinks he should go.'

'Are you OK with that?'

'I think so. Are you?'

He nodded.

They both sipped their drinks, and continued to entwine their fingers.

'I've been thinking about this search for your father,' he said, after a while. 'I don't want to push you into anything ...'

'No, we agreed I should,' she interrupted.

'But only if it's what *you* want, not because it's what *I* want.'

Her eyes came up to his, and he dropped to his knees so her face was on a level with his.

'I want to,' she told him, the inner turmoil showing in her eyes, 'but what if he does turn out to be ...' She looked away, knowing she didn't have to put it into words, because he was the only person in the world she'd ever confessed her worst suspicions to, though she imagined Sylvia and Pauline had probably guessed them. She wouldn't discuss it with them though, for God knew she found it hard enough with Josh.

Taking the drink from her, he put both their glasses down and held onto her hand. 'All I want is what's best for you,' he told her softly.

Her eyes returned to his, and she lifted a hand to stroke his face.

'Want me to do your back?' he offered.

Yes, she did, but she said, 'I should probably get out now.'

His expression was impenetrable as he turned to reach for a towel, and held it out for her to step into.

She looked up at him hesitantly.

'You don't have anything I haven't seen before,' he reminded her. 'Or that I don't love.'

Feeling her heart expand, she drew herself up and stepped out into the towel.

'I'll go and check on the dinner,' he said, wrapping her up.

'Josh,' she said as he reached the door.

He turned back.

'I don't deserve you.'

His eyes held hers for a beat, then moved away. 'Dinner,' he said, and pulling open the door he left her to dry herself, and to wonder who, in their right mind, would reject a husband who loved them so much. The answer, of course, was the very same woman who simply couldn't bear to find out that the father she'd adored, and had mourned virtually every day since he'd left, was, in reality, the very worst kind of monster society could manage to produce.

Chapter Four

After six weeks of virtually non-stop rain the sun had finally re-emerged from the clouds, if not with a vengeance, then at least with enough warmth for Sylvia to open the door of her converted garage to let in some air while she worked the clay. Since she was in a mews it was unlikely anyone would pass and interrupt her, but once she was ready to start throwing, she'd close the door again and lose herself in the wonderfully sensuous and intensely private world of creation.

For the moment, though, her long, slim hands were kneading a new batch of clay on the marble workbench, taking out the air, and separating it into individual balls ready to throw, while she listened to a CD of Mirella Freni singing Tosca and enjoyed the feel of a fresh breeze on her skin. Under her bib-apron she wore only a thin white T-shirt and a pair of tracksuit bottoms, while her hair was clipped randomly on the top of her head.

These past few weeks had been an interesting time, she was reflecting as she worked, perhaps more for how often she'd seen Josh, than for anything else. For a while though, after their meeting at the hotel in Chelsea, she'd started to wonder if he would contact her again, because more than a week had gone by with no word, and during that time she'd learned, through Julia, that they'd become close again. Whether that meant physically, Sylvia had no way of knowing, since Julia hadn't said, however she doubted it. In the end Josh had called, and the fact that he was coming here, or asking her to meet him in other places, on a fairly regular basis now, was evidence enough that things hadn't improved at home.

Starting to wrap the clay balls in plastic, Sylvia found herself wondering what he might have told Julia about his overnight stay in Amsterdam a couple of weeks ago, or the two days he'd spent in Paris just after. Actually, she could easily guess, for he had clients and co-agents in both cities, so it wasn't rare for him to visit either place. They had been wonderful trips, full of fun and endless sex, when she'd put on the underwear he'd bought her, and had felt so unbelievably aroused by the sensation of wearing hold-up stockings with no panties, and a totally transparent negligee that only just covered her bottom, that even now she could feel the shudders of lust inside her to think of the effect it had had on them both.

Wiping her hands on her apron she went to change the CD, and eased her guilt with the reminder that she was only sleeping with Josh to stop him seeking his physical pleasures elsewhere, and with someone who might want to wreck his marriage. So this betrayal – if it had to be called that – was actually for Julia's sake, though heaven only knew how she could deprive herself of such a lover. In Sylvia's experience few men could compare to Josh, and God knew she'd had some excellent lovers in her time. If the truth were known, she was starting to find him a little addictive. She realised that was very possibly because she sensed he was holding something of himself back – however, she never questioned him about it, nor did she consider it a problem. His conscience was his own, and as long as she got the satisfaction she craved, she saw no point in making waves. On the other hand, she'd started to feel tempted these past few days, for it had been almost two weeks since she'd last seen him – one of which she knew he'd spent at the Frankfurt book fair, but that didn't change the fact that she was becoming highly desirous of his body.

Sighing gently to herself, she reclipped her hair and was about to carry on with her work when the phone started to ring. Experiencing a beat of hope that it might be him, she reached out to unhook it from the wall and tucked it under her chin.

'Hi, it's me,' Julia said. 'Am I interrupting?'

'No, not at all,' Sylvia responded smoothly. 'How are you?'

'OK. No, that's not true. Josh and I had a terrible row the night before last, and he's still barely speaking to me.'

'What was it about?' Sylvia asked, returning to the clay.

'I did a really stupid thing,' Julia confessed. 'I invited some friends round for dinner, when I should have known how tired he would be when he got back from Frankfurt. Anyway, we ended up saying some really dreadful things, both of us threatened to leave, I even thought he was going to hit me at one point . . .'

'I don't think he'd ever do that,' Sylvia assured her.

'I know, but he got so angry . . . Tell me, do you think I should have him followed?'

'What on earth for?' Sylvia asked, picking up a ball of clay and taking it to the wheel.

'To put my mind at rest about whether or not he is having an affair.'

Sylvia's eyebrows arched. 'No, I don't think you should do that,' she answered, pulling up a stool to sit down at the wheel.

Julia sighed heavily. 'You're right. He'd be furious if he found out . . .'

'How are the children?' Sylvia asked, feeling it was time for a change of subject.

'Oh, they're great. Dan hasn't had any more seizures since that last one, thank God, and Shannon's getting more depressed by the day about not having a boyfriend, though she's still managing to excel at school, which is definitely a blessing. Actually, in their own ways, they're a constant source of amusement and pride to us both, and I shudder to think where we might be without them, because they're definitely holding us together right now.'

'That's sweet,' Sylvia commented lightly, and pressed her foot on the pedal to start the wheel spinning. 'And what about Hamish Kincaid's book?'

'As a matter of fact, I'm on my way to have lunch with him now,' Julia answered. 'He wants to meet me and discuss the book before he hands it over. I'm the first new editor he's had in twenty-some years, so I have to be vetted.'

'You should enjoy that,' Sylvia said, not without irony, for they were both aware of the man's dreadful reputation. He had it in him to send Julia packing in the most brutal of ways, should he decide against her.

Julia laughed. 'It'll do me good to focus on something other than Josh for a while,' she said. 'Anyway, when are you off to New York?'

'Not until the weekend,' Sylvia replied, idly wondering if Josh might like to join her for a couple of days. 'I'm seeing my editor in Manhattan on Monday, then I've a couple more meetings lined up before I fly back.'

'I wish I was coming with you,' Julia said wistfully. 'I love my family to bits, but I could really do with a break and I've always so loved New York.'

Sylvia was about to respond when a shadow crossed the doorway and fell over her. Frowning, she looked up, then realising who it was she felt a tightening of her heart as a piercing lust cut through her below.

'Are you still in touch with Barry Spencer?' Julia was saying. 'Didn't he move over there a couple of years ago? He was always so crazy about you.'

'The last I heard he was married with kids,' Sylvia responded, keeping her eyes on Josh.

Julia laughed. 'Since when did that ever stop you?' she teased.

Sylvia's gaze didn't waver. 'I'm sorry, I have to go now,' she said. 'Someone's just turned up.'

'OK, no problem,' Julia replied. 'I'm almost at the restaurant anyway. Talk to you later.'

After clicking off the line, Sylvia put the phone to one side and kept the wheel spinning as she looked at Josh and randomly shaped the clay. With the sunlight behind him she couldn't see his expression, but there was no doubt in her mind why he'd come.

'So how are you?' she said, finally breaking the silence.

'I'm fine,' he answered. He cleared his throat and stepped into the shadows so she was more easily able to see him. 'Actually, I've come about the vase you mentioned a while ago. The one Julia liked.'

Sylvia nodded and continued to draw the clay into a tall, cone-like shape, squashing it down, then drawing it up again.

'We had a bit of a fight the other night,' he confessed. 'I went too far, said some pretty unforgivable things . . .'

'So you want to take the vase as a peace offering?'

He continued to look at her.

Her eyes lowered to her task. 'It's extremely expensive,' she reminded him.

'I know.'

She smiled, knowing that it helped ease his conscience to pay a lot, not just for betraying Julia, but to make himself feel better about using her for sex. How strangely moral he was. 'Just as well I hung onto it,' she told him, pushing her thumbs into the clay as it rose to a peak again.

He didn't answer, so she carried on with what she was doing, wondering if he was becoming aroused by the erotic movements of her hands as they cupped the phallic shape, because she certainly was.

'So how is Julia?' she asked after a while.

'OK.' He cleared his throat again.

'I take it she doesn't know anything about our trips to Amsterdam and Paris.'

His jaw tightened as he looked away.

'Sorry, I guess we're not supposed to mention them.'

His eyes came back to her. 'She's having lunch with Hamish Kincaid today,' he said. 'He wants to discuss his book before he hands it over.'

Her head tilted to one side as she said, 'That's nice.' Then after a beat, 'Tell me, how would you feel if she had an affair?'

He seemed surprised by the question, then sounded almost angry as he said, 'Considering the circumstances, I'd say murderous.'

Her eyebrows went up. So they weren't sleeping together again, but then, his presence here had already told her that. 'More or less how she feels,' she commented.

He said nothing.

After a while she said, 'Are you sure you didn't come here for sex?'

'It wasn't my intention,' he answered, the words ringing in a hollow of truth.

'I only ask, because I'm rather in the mood myself.'

It was a second or two before he moved, though they both knew he wasn't going to resist. Then walking round behind her, he took off his jacket, pulled up a stool and sat down.

'Mm, that feels good,' she murmured, as he reached under the bib of her apron, and lifted the front of her T-shirt. Since she never wore a bra, there was no barrier to his hands, and as his fingers closed around her nipples she rested her head back on his shoulder to bask in the sensation of what he was doing.

For a long time they sat like that, with the wheel spinning, the clay moving through her hands and his mouth on her neck as he toyed with her breasts and pressed his erection against her. Then he was lowering a hand over her belly, pushing it inside the waistband of her tracksuit and on down to discover that she was still baby-smooth below.

'Mm,' he murmured as his fingers slid into her, and as she turned her mouth to his he pushed his tongue deep inside.

'I think we need to go upstairs,' she said hoarsely, and leaving the wheel to spin to a stop she rose to her feet and let him remove her trousers before turning to lead the way.

Julia's lunch meeting with Hamish Kincaid turned out to be even briefer and more difficult than she'd expected, though happily, not even his rudely expressed doubts about her editorial skills, nor his insufferable criticism of her own book had managed to dent her confidence today – nor alter her admiration for his talent, come to that. On the contrary, she'd read enough of his past work to know that his would be a lasting literary legacy, so in spite of his loathsome character she couldn't help but feel pleased to be overseeing his next wayward masterpiece.

'The typescript will be hand-delivered on Friday, by my wife,' he'd informed her, his suspicious little eyes boring into hers. 'It'll be up to you to get it copied.'

Knowing his publisher would take care of that, Julia had merely smiled and assured him she was looking forward to receiving it, while flatly refusing to be intimidated by his manner, which she knew very well was his objective, for it was meant to make her reticent about giving notes. He'd find out soon enough how thorough she was, and unafraid to criticise, so no point going for a confrontation now, particularly when she hadn't read a single word – nor had he deigned to acquaint her with the subject matter, other than to hint that it would most likely be beyond her meagre intellectual capacity.

If he really believed that, the lunch would never have happened, she was thinking to herself as she drove back through Kensington, heading for home. She'd already tried calling Josh to let him know how the meeting had gone, but had been directed through to his voicemail, which probably meant he was in the middle of an important lunch of his own. She'd try again later, maybe after she'd spoken to Katya, Kincaid's publisher, who she knew would have a good chuckle with her over Kincaid's intractable dourness and outrageous insults.

As she pulled up at traffic lights she quickly checked the texts that had come in while she was driving, finding one from Shannon, and two from

Dan. It seemed neither of them would be home for dinner tonight, which meant she could make something special for Josh in the hope it might go some way towards helping them forget the horrible row they'd had the night he got back from Frankfurt. She might even, considering how buoyant she was feeling right now, manage to work herself up to ending the evening the way he'd appreciate most.

She grimaced at that. Making such a decision from the distance of several hours was extremely easy, so in an attempt to convince herself she really meant it, she made a sudden right turn at Kensington Church Street, and headed for her favourite lingerie shop. After that she'd drive over to the Portobello market to pick up all the special foods Josh liked – and already her insides were starting to knot, for she knew he'd understand the signals, and she could hardly bear to think of how awful it would be if she ended up pushing him away again.

Determined to ignore her misgivings, she searched for a meter close to the shop, and managed to shoot into a space directly opposite, much to the annoyance of a white-van man who gave her the finger as she ran across the street.

Plaisirs de Soie was an extremely expensive and discreet boutique that she and Josh had often visited together, for unlike most men he didn't have a problem helping his wife select her underwear, in fact he occasionally came alone to select it himself. The owner and her staff seemed to enjoy his lack of inhibition, and were often quite flirtatious with him, though they must have wondered where he'd been these past months. The thought made her hesitate before going inside, because maybe he had been in, and let them think he was shopping for her when it was actually for a mistress. Thrown by the suspicion, she wondered if she should just choose something from the locked drawer at home – except backing off now was cowardly, so steeling herself she pushed down the handle and walked brazenly in.

Hearing the bell the owner looked up, and seeing one of her more valued customers she welcomed Julia warmly, offering her coffee or wine, which Julia politely declined, before taking herself off to browse. To her relief the woman had not mentioned seeing Josh recently, had merely asked how he was, so Julia was able to relax as she made her choice, keeping his preferences in mind.

When it was time to pay the owner smiled benignly as she wrapped the transparent white negligee in tissue which she tied with a bow, then did the same with the hold-up stockings. 'I think your husband will like this very much,' she murmured, as she walked Julia to the door her assistant was holding open.

If only they knew, Julia was reflecting as she returned to the car. They think we've got it so together, but how deceiving appearances can be – and how was she going to appear to him in this exquisite lingerie tonight? Exactly as he would want her to, of course, ready for his lovemaking, and willing to give him everything he most desired. In the old days, if the children weren't around, she'd have greeted him at the door wearing the seductive outfit, then served him drinks and dinner, allowing him to touch her whenever he felt like it, until their need grew to such a pitch that they couldn't even make it to the bedroom. He'd take her right there in the kitchen, or the study, or the laundry room, in any position he pleased, and for as long as he could. If only she could work herself up to do that again, but right now the very idea was making her so tense inside that she had to put it out of her mind, or she knew she'd never stand a chance of going through with it.

Next stop was the Portobello market. As she headed over there, she was listening to the hardrock band on his CD player, not because she liked it, but because he did, and it made her feel closer to him. If he knew what she was doing now, it would make such a difference to his day, she was thinking, as she turned into a street close to Sylvia's. Finding a parking spot, she was just toying with the idea of dropping in to entertain Sylvia with an account of the lunch with Kincaid, when her mobile started to ring. Since the call came up as a private number, she clicked on and said, 'Hello, Julia Thayne speaking.'

'Mrs Thayne. My name is Fionnula Barrington,' a pleasantly cultured voice informed her. 'I'm calling from Sissons, Greene and Bower in Bodmin. I got your number from your answering machine. I hope I'm not disturbing you?'

Julia was half out of the car, but sank back into the driver's seat as she registered the official tone of the call. 'No, not at all,' she responded. 'What can I do for you?'

'Is it convenient to talk?' Fionnula Barrington enquired. 'I have news of some importance.'

Julia frowned, and felt a stirring of unease. 'Yes, it's fine,' she said.

There was a pause before Ms Barrington continued. 'Could I ask you to confirm whether you're the daughter of Douglas Henry Cowan?'

Julia's mouth turned dry, as her heartbeat seemed to slow. 'Yes, I am,' she answered, feeling absurdly inundated by surprise contact with her father, when in fact it amounted to only two calls in the space of six weeks. However, that was a hundred per cent more than there had been over the past twenty-four years.

'Then I'm afraid I have some bad news,' Fionnula Barrington was telling her. 'I'm extremely sorry to tell you that your father passed away last night.'

Julia blinked, took a breath, then felt everything around her starting to change. It was as though it was coming in on her, slowly, threateningly, with sound distorted and time dislodged.

'His instructions were to inform you as soon as it happened,' Fionnula Barrington continued. 'There is an inheritance, which we will go over with you in due course. Meanwhile, his request was to be cremated and his ashes buried with his wife's at their local church.'

Wife? It seemed bizarrely like a foreign word, something she didn't quite understand, or maybe she didn't want to.

'We can take care of everything. He specifically states that you must not feel obliged to attend his funeral . . .'

'Stop! Stop!' Julia cried, collecting herself. 'I'm sorry, this has come as a bit of a shock.'

'Of course. I know you haven't been in contact for many years. Would you like me to call back after you've had some time to assimilate, and maybe spoken to your family?'

Oh Christ. 'Does my mother know?' she asked.

'We were only instructed to inform you.'

Not knowing what she thought about that, Julia said, 'I think I . . . What did he die of? Where was he when it happened?'

'It was a stroke that took him in the end, but he'd had cancer for a while. He was at home, here in Cornwall. It was peaceful.'

Cornwall? Home? 'He would have been sixty-eight,' Julia said almost to herself, and put a hand to her head as something inside her seemed to fracture. 'I'm sorry, I think perhaps I do need a few minutes,' she said. 'Can I call you back?'

'Of course. I'll text my details to your mobile, including my home number. Please feel free to call me any time.'

Having rung off Julia continued to sit in the car, her feet on the pavement outside, her handbag in her lap, the phone still in her hand. She was trying to work out how to move from here, how to feel about what she'd heard, but for the moment nothing seemed to be coming through. It had to be shock, deadening her mind, while all the emotional wires tried to connect with the right responses.

She wasn't sure how long she sat there with people walking by, a traffic warden hovering and builders' debris roaring down a chute across the road. The phone bleeping brought her back to her senses. She opened the text and felt almost surprised to see Fionnula Barrington's details, for the past few minutes were starting to feel like a dream. Her father was dead. The man she'd loved with all her heart for the first sixteen years of her life, had gone. She'd never be able to speak to him now. Never be able to ask why he'd left, or if any of what she feared was true. She might never know now if she really had been the centre of his world once, as he had of hers.

Feeling herself starting to shake she quickly pressed Josh's number into the phone and waited for him to answer. To her frustration she was once again diverted to voicemail, so after leaving a message she tried Marina at the office to find out where he was, but got that answering machine too.

She clicked off the line, closed and locked the car door and started towards the market. She'd been about to shop for dinner, so that was what she would do. Life had to go on. After all, nothing had changed. The fact that her father was no longer in the world shouldn't make a difference, when she hadn't seen him for so long, so she'd put it aside for now, and deal with it later.

At the end of the street she merged into the crowd, but after a minute or two of walking she couldn't remember why she was there. She looked around and felt unnervingly detached from the noise and bustle. Then Fionnula Barrington's words started a strange echo in her head, as though forcing themselves out from the place where she was trying to hide them.

Turning away from the market, she walked

quickly to Sylvia's cobbled mews and to her relief found the workshop door open. There was no sign of Sylvia, so she walked in, past the wheel, and was about to start up the stairs when she registered the noises coming from above. Since there was no doubt about what was happening up there, she swallowed her frustration and went back outside to try Josh's number again. She was so agitated that it took her a moment to register the fact that while listening to the ringtone, she was also hearing the melody Daniel had downloaded a week ago somewhere behind her. Confused, she turned to look back into the workshop, half expecting Josh to be standing there, but that was absurd. Why would he be here? No, it must be Sylvia's phone, with the same ringtone as Josh's. Then the musical chime stopped at the same instant her call went through to messages.

As her hand fell to her side she stood staring at the jacket draped over a stool behind the wheel. She was trying to make herself accept what she was seeing, to make some sense of it, but everything in her was rejecting it. There had to be some mistake. It couldn't be Josh's, nor was it his phone she'd heard ringing – and the noises upstairs had nothing to do with him either. But even as she stood there, trying to make it all mean something else, it was as though everything inside her was breaking apart. She pressed a hand to her mouth and tried to force herself to think. This wasn't his jacket, or his phone. She was mistaken, misreading everything, and any second now she would understand how. She heard Sylvia laugh, then the familiar sound of Josh's voice as he neared a climax. She was wrong though, it wasn't him. She was imagining it. She tried to move and found she couldn't, because on some level, somewhere deep inside, she realised that hearing them was devastating enough, she didn't need to see them too.

With no real connection to what she was doing, she turned and walked out of the workshop. All she knew was that she needed some time to think, to absorb the horrible nightmare her life was suddenly becoming. Her father, then *Josh* ... She wasn't sure if she said his name out loud, or if it was screaming silently inside her. She was walking faster and faster, though she still had no idea where she was going, or what she should do. The loss of her father was beating a horrible tattoo. She wanted to run to him, as she had as a child, to have him make everything all right again, but he was gone now, she would never see him again, and the realisation of it made her stop suddenly as she started to gasp for air. Everything was coming in on her, the buildings, the noise, the smells, the people. It was too much, she had to break free ...

When she reached the car she tore open the door and once inside rested her head on the wheel, willing the panic to stop. OK, she'd been dealt two horrible blows in quick succession, but though it might feel as if the world was coming to an end, it wasn't. She could handle this. She wasn't going to allow it to drag her under, or let the terrible hollow opening up inside her to fill with fear. She had the strength to get through this, she would hold her life together and be there for her children, and for herself. The thought of losing Josh brought the panic flooding back. She'd rather die than live without him, but she hated him for this. She'd never be able to forgive him, for he knew how deep was her fear of betrayal and abandonment. It didn't matter that he had no way of knowing that her father had just died, the fact that he was back there screwing Sylvia was enough.

As the thought of them together burned painfully in her heart she heard herself cry out. It was as though she was only just registering it – Josh and Sylvia. Her husband and her best friend.

'Oh my God,' she gulped, pressing her hands to her face. 'It can't be true. It just can't.'

She didn't know what to do, or where to go. She had no way of understanding how they could do this to her. The lies, the deceit, everything they were doing was beyond her comprehension. She realised that all the time she'd been shopping for him, for tonight, he'd been with Sylvia. She felt herself becoming heavy and nauseous as she realised that the visitor who'd turned up while she and Sylvia were on the phone could easily have been him.

'No!' she gasped as the horror of it swept over her. 'Please no.'

Her mobile started to ring, but she couldn't talk to anyone now. Without checking who it was, she turned it off and let her head fall back against the seat. She wanted somehow to go back in time, to erase the awfulness of the past ten minutes, as if none of it had ever happened. Her life could never be the same again now, and she felt suddenly totally alone, isolated in a world that was seeming more remote with every second that passed. She wasn't sure which was scaring her more, her father's death, or Josh's betrayal, but it didn't matter. Both were intolerable, though the images of Josh with Sylvia, of their beautiful bodies entwined, and their passions aroused to a point where they lost control . . .

She couldn't bear it, she just couldn't. Not even in her worst nightmares had she ever imagined her husband was sleeping with her best friend. She wondered how long it had been going on, if they were in love, and desperate to be together, but couldn't because of her, and the children. The pain of the thought was so sharp that she pressed a hand to her chest to stop it, then she started violently, as someone tapped on the window to ask if she was leaving.

She nodded and turned on the ignition. She had to make herself think what to do now, for she couldn't just go on sitting here, as though by not moving she could stop the inevitable. She considered going back to confront them, but a hoot from an impatient driver forced her to put the car into gear and pull away.

She needed to go home now, she realised. She had to take some time to think and decide what she was going to do. Thank God the children weren't coming back till later, because she knew there was no way in the world she could pretend everything was normal after what she'd just found out, nor did she want them anywhere around when she finally came to deal with their father.

It was just after seven by the time Josh let himself in through the front door, to find the house unusually quiet. The unease he generally experienced after spending time with Sylvia immediately started to increase, particularly as he'd been trying to call Julia since he'd picked up her message earlier telling him to get back to her urgently. For some reason she hadn't answered her phone, so in the end he'd called Shannon and Dan to reassure himself there was no problem with them. The relief of finding out they were OK had been short-lived, for he'd then received a text from Julia telling him to ignore the message she'd left and that she'd see him later at home. She didn't usually text him. It was the children who did that.

Now, as he dropped his keys on the hall table, he tried to bolster himself by insisting there was no way she could know about Sylvia, but with the Porsche parked outside, telling him Julia was at home, and the house seeming so silent, it wasn't quite working.

'Julia!' he called.

No reply.

He went down to the kitchen, but there was no sign of her there, or the children. It didn't appear anything was cooking, either. He glanced into his study to see if anyone was using his computer, but there was no-one there, nor in the laundry room, nor the garden or downstairs loo.

Still carrying the carefully wrapped vase he'd bought from Sylvia, he returned to the hall and called out again. 'Hi, I'm home. Where is everyone?'

His voice echoed into the silent TV room, the drawing room and up over the stairs.

'Julia!' he shouted.

'I'm in here,' she finally answered.

Realising her voice had come from the drawing room, he pushed open the door and frowned, for at first it appeared empty. Then he saw her standing by the window, and he knew right away that something was horribly wrong, not only from the way her back was turned, but because she was wearing her winter coat.

'Is everything all right?' he asked, as though the lightness of his voice could make it so. 'What are you doing in here? Where are the kids?'

'They're out for the evening.' As she turned to look at him he was taken aback by the paleness of her face, and the blankness of her eyes. It was as though she'd turned herself into a shell.

'Are you going somewhere?' he asked, meaning the coat.

She didn't answer.

Feeling awkward, and even vaguely annoyed, he held up the parcel. 'I've got a surprise for you,' he told her, 'a peace offering, I suppose. I'm sorry for everything I said the other night.' The words seemed to echo inside his head and he suddenly wished he hadn't bought the vase, for if anything represented his guilt this had to be it.

'What is it?' she asked.

He took it to her and handed it over. 'Why don't you open it and find out?'

Dragging her eyes from his she lifted the parcel from the bag, unwound the bubble wrap and gazed down at the exquisite harp-shaped porcelain vase. 'Of course,' she said quietly.

She looked up at him and a thud of horror struck hard in his chest. She knew.

'How much did you pay for it?' she asked.

He found himself unable to answer.

'Two, three thousand pounds?' she prompted.

Anger suddenly galvanised his voice. 'What the hell has got into you?' he demanded. 'Don't you like it, or something?'

'I'm just wondering what the price of your conscience is,' she replied.

He stared at her hard, wondering how the hell she'd found out, and if there was any way he could deny it.

'I was at Sylvia's today,' she told him. 'I know you were there too, so please don't deny it, and please don't try telling me it was to get *this*, because if you do, I'll smash it over your head.'

'Of course it was to get that,' he cried, then his eyes widened in disbelief as she let the vase slip through her hands and smash to smithereens on the hardwood floor.

'Tell me, is that how you pay her for sex?' she asked. 'Or is it just to buy off your conscience?'

'Julia, for Christ's sake . . .'

'How much was this one?' she cut in, lifting a porcelain crescent moon from its plinth. 'Two thousand?' Without waiting for an answer she raised it over her head and flung it against the wall where it dissolved into a thousand pieces.

'Julia! Just stop . . .'

'What about this one?' She was picking up another. 'One thousand? Less?' She hurled it into the fireplace, then turned back to face him. 'Do we have one for every time you fucked her?' she asked tightly. 'Is that what our little art display is all about?'

'Have you completely lost your mind?' he cried.

'Not yet, but I'm getting there.'

'For Christ's sake stop,' he shouted, as she began destroying pieces that had nothing to do with Sylvia. Lalique. Baccarat. Natzler.

'Julia, pull yourself together,' he roared, trying to grab her.

'Don't touch me,' she hissed, pushing him away. Her eyes were blazing with fury now, her voice shredded with contempt as she laid into him. 'How could you? How fucking could you?' she raged. 'She was my best friend, *my best friend*, and you, you faithless bastard . . .' She slapped him so hard in the face that it cut his lip.

'You think every woman's on this earth just to part her legs for you, don't you?' she seethed. 'That's all that matters to you. *Sex*. We're not about anything else, you and me, and if you can't get it here, well that's all right, just as long as you don't go without. Am I right? Yes, of course I am. Forget about our marriage, forget about who you might be hurting, don't even bother to consider your children, just make sure *you* get what you want. Well you're a whore, Joshua! Do you know that? A filthy, disgusting whore who doesn't even come close to deserving the love of his family. You're even soiling our home just by being here.' Her lips were quivering, her chest heaving as she fought for air.

'Have you quite finished?' he asked tightly.

'Oh, I haven't even begun,' she spat. 'See this?' Tearing open her coat, she showed him the underwear she'd bought earlier. 'This was for you, because I know how much sex means to you, because I know you can't live without it, so tonight I was going to try again.'

Privately stunned by her choice, he said, 'And right there we have it, don't we? You keep trying, Julia, but it never damned well changes. You make all these promises, you lead me on to believe you've got it sorted, but you never deliver, and now you've got the fucking nerve to stand there accusing me of . . .'

'Don't you dare turn this around on me!'

'*I'm not a fucking monk,*' he yelled. 'And the hell am I going to apologise for wanting to have sex with my own wife. It happens to be because I love you . . .'

'Were you thinking about that while you were screwing Sylvia today?' she snarled. 'Were you saying to yourself, *I love Julia* . . .'

He made to answer, but she cut him off.

'I want to hear you admit it,' she challenged. 'Say the words Josh, go on, say them: I'm screwing your best friend . . .'

'All right, I'll own up to it,' he raged, 'and now tell me what you'd prefer, that I go out and screw a stranger, someone who might actually end up wanting me, even loving me, instead of constantly pushing me away, and behaving as though I repulse her? Think how that would be, Julia, if I started to fall in love with someone else, if I started to break up our home because I don't have a proper relationship with my wife. I went to Sylvia because she won't make any demands, and because I don't want to lose you. You and the kids mean everything to me, but I'm a man, for Christ's sake, I have my needs, whether you like it or not . . .'

'Don't tell me any more,' she cried, clasping her hands over her ears. 'I don't want to hear it. You've betrayed me in the worst possible way, Joshua, you both have . . .'

'We did it to protect you. To stop me looking elsewhere.'

'Just listen to yourself,' she yelled. 'Are you really so pathetic? Is that what you believe?'

'It's what I know to be true. It's just sex, Julia. It doesn't mean anything . . .'

'Maybe not to you, but to me it means you've lied and cheated and you're not the man I know . . .'

'What the hell was I supposed to do?' he demanded. 'You can hardly stand me near you. How do you think that makes me feel? What am I . . .'

'Stop blaming me!' she screamed. 'Take some responsibility here.'

'Then you take some too, because the real problem's inside *you* and you know it.'

'How dare you . . .'

'You're fucked up, Julia! Something's going on inside you and unless you face up to it, how the hell do you think we're ever going to work anything out?'

Temper was still flashing in her eyes, but now he'd raised the dreaded spectre he could already see her backing off.

'You've betrayed my trust, Joshua, you've thrown my love right back in my face . . .' Her voice was starting to fracture, and in frustration she turned sharply away.

'I'm sorry,' he said. 'I wish to God . . .'

'Don't!' She spun round again, her eyes bright

with tears. 'I needed you so much today,' she managed to tell him. 'I was trying to reach you ...' A sob of anguish broke through the words. 'Jesus Christ, what's the matter with me?' she seethed, furious that she was starting to cry.

He made to reach for her but she slapped him away.

'I don't want you to touch me. *Ever.* Do you hear me? Not ever again.'

He looked at her helplessly, then closed his eyes. 'I don't know how much more of this I can take, Julia,' he said quietly.

She stood where she was, hands clenching and unclenching at her sides, breath rasping raggedly from her lungs as tears spilled unchecked onto her cheeks. When he looked at her again she stared back, and he could almost feel the barrier she was putting between them.

'Don't do this,' he said softly.

She started to speak, but the air was trapped inside her. She tried again, but the only sound that emerged was a cry of torment that seemed to rip from the depths of her soul.

He went to her, and held her tightly in his arms while she sobbed as though her heart would break. 'I'm sorry,' he murmured, 'I'm so, so sorry.'

'No, you don't know,' she gasped. 'You ...'

'Ssh, it's all right.'

'No, Josh. You don't understand ...'

'It doesn't matter, just let me hold you.'

Keeping her head bowed, she pulled away and sank down on one of the sofas. She looked at her hands, then lifted them to her face as more tears spilled from her eyes.

'What is it?' he asked, finally realising there was more.

She glanced up at him, then used her fingers to wipe her cheeks as he sat down with her.

'What happened today?' he pressed gently. 'Why were you trying to reach me?'

She swallowed hard, and took a breath. 'I needed to talk to you,' she said, 'but I couldn't get you on the phone, so I went to Sylvia's instead. I had some news ...' She put a hand to her head and gulped in more air. 'I had a call from a solicitor. My father died last night ...'

'Oh my God,' he murmured. 'Oh Julia ... Jesus Christ, I'm so sorry.'

She drew back from him and again used her fingers to dry her tears.

'How did they find you?' he asked.

'I don't know. She just said he'd died and that he wanted me to know. I've got her number, but I wanted to talk to you before I rang back. Then I couldn't get hold of you, so I went to Sylvia's ...'

He made to hold her again, but she stood up to move out of his reach.

'What can I do?' he asked, standing up too.

Her back was turned as she shook her head. 'Nothing. Go to Sylvia if you have to. I can't live with you, knowing you want her ...'

'I don't. It's you ...'

'Please don't lie to me.'

He turned her round to face him. 'You're the only woman I've ever loved,' he told her fiercely.

For a while it was impossible to gauge what she was thinking, but when finally she spoke he felt only relief that she wasn't pressing the issue of him leaving. 'Apparently he's being cremated,' she said shakily. 'I need to find out when, and I have to tell my mother. I'll go down there tomorrow.'

'I'll come with you.'

She shook her head.

'But . . .'

'This has changed everything, Josh. You and Sylvia . . .'

'There is no me and Sylvia, not in the way you're thinking.'

'You've made love to her, that makes a you and Sylvia. Now tell me, how many times has it happened?'

'It doesn't matter . . .'

'It does to me.'

He didn't answer.

'Are you as besotted with her as all the other men she's known? Are you one of the crowd now, Josh, panting after her, willing to do anything for a minute of her time? I know how she operates, remember, I've seen what she does to men . . .'

'Stop it,' he said.

She continued to look at him, eyes bright with pain, breath still ragged in her throat, then wrapping her coat tightly around her she started towards the door. 'I'm going to bed,' she said. 'The children should be home soon. I don't want them to see me like this.'

'We have to talk.'

'We've said enough tonight.' She turned back, her eyes filling with more tears. 'I don't know where we go from here,' she said. 'All I know is I don't want to sleep in the same bed as you tonight, and I'm not sure I ever will again.'

He started to respond, but then let it go as she walked from the room. There was no point trying to reason with her now, she was still in shock, and clearly needed some time to come to terms with all that had happened today. Even so, his instinct was to go after her, to reassure her that he was there for her, but knowing she wouldn't welcome it, he stayed where he was.

For a long time he stared down at the shards of pottery and glass, until finally he began to collect up the larger pieces and prayed that they weren't going to prove symbolic of his marriage, because right now it felt as though everything was breaking apart.

But he wouldn't let it happen, he told himself firmly. They still loved each other, for Christ's sake, so no way was any of this going to come between them. Somehow he'd make it up to her over Sylvia. He'd think of something, though right now he had no idea how the hell he was going to put it right. He could hardly bear to think of how much he'd hurt her, or how deliberately he had shut himself off from her feelings, when no-one had ever mattered more to him than her. How could the insanity of his affair not have been clear to him before? What kind of man was he, that he could delude himself into believing he was doing it for her? The worst of it was that he had believed it at the time, and maybe a part of him still did. He couldn't say for certain, because he was hardly in a state to think straight, all he knew was that if he lost her over this, he wouldn't even want to go on.

Hearing her moving around upstairs he wondered again if he should go up there, but he could sense the wall she'd put between them, and knew very well it wouldn't come down tonight. She needed some time to think, to decide what she was going to do, and not only about him, but about her father too. His heart sank in dismay at the mere thought of the man who'd managed to cause so much havoc whilst alive – God only knew what power would be his in death. It was bizarre, for in every other way Julia was generally a strong and capable woman who could handle virtually anything life threw at her, yet where her father was concerned she was so emotionally fragile that even after twenty-four years he was still affecting her deeply. It made no sense to Josh, for having come from a loving and, for the most part, stable family, abandonment issues and the resulting psychological trauma meant almost nothing, but he could hardly deny their existence when they were so profoundly evident in his wife.

As he mulled it all over in his mind he wondered if he should have tried harder to find Douglas Cowan when he'd first attempted it, if he should have been firmer with Julia about making her deal with her problems. The trouble was, he'd been afraid to force it, because the last thing he wanted was to send her spinning off into some terrible breakdown. Even the therapist had agreed this was a possibility, considering the kind of horror she might be suppressing.

Not for the first time he could feel a build up of resentment towards his father-in-law, not only for still holding so much sway with his daughter, but for being the kind of man he despised. Of course he understood Julia's reluctance to believe the worst about him, what child would ever want to believe that of a parent, but the question had to be asked, what the hell had he done to her back then? Certainly she was still refusing to accept him as anything other than a gentle, devoted father who'd given her all the love her mother had denied her, but it wasn't her mother who'd walked out on her, was it? It was her hero, the man who could do no wrong, the man she simply couldn't let go of.

Sighing heavily to himself, he got up and went downstairs to the kitchen for a dustpan and brush. In any sane world Douglas Cowan's death should bring Julia the closure she needed now, and restore some kind of normalcy to their lives, but he knew instinctively that wasn't going to happen. If anything, he was very much afraid that events were conspiring to bring about the kind of crisis he most dreaded, for he'd sensed during that scene in the drawing room how close she was to the edge. His greatest fear now, thanks to the way he'd messed up so badly with Sylvia, was that he'd created the kind of gulf between them that would render him powerless to help her.

The thought had no time to plant its full horror in his mind before the front door suddenly slammed shut, and Dan came charging down to the kitchen yelling, 'Mum! Mum! I'm starving.'

'Ssh,' Josh said, putting a finger over his lips. 'She's asleep. Where's Shannon?'

Before Dan could answer the front door banged again and seconds later Shannon was descending into the kitchen, also calling for her mother.

'Where's Mum?' she demanded, looking accusingly at Josh as she dumped her bag on a counter top. 'What's wrong?' she added, registering his expression. 'I have to talk to Mum.'

'She's in bed,' Dan told her. 'Why?' he asked Josh. 'It's not even half past eight.'

'Come and sit down,' Josh answered, leading them to the breakfast niche.

'What is it, Dad?' Shannon urged, showing signs of panic. 'Is she all right? Can I go up there?'

'Yes, let's go up,' Dan said.

'She's fine,' Josh assured them. 'She's just had a bit of bad news.'

Their eyes grew big and round.

Josh looked at them and felt his insides tightening with the dread of them ever finding out how he'd betrayed their mother. Would Julia tell them? He hoped to God not, for their pain and bewilderment would almost be harder to bear than hers.

'Dad, what is it?' Shannon demanded. 'What's happened to Mum?'

Josh took her hand and squeezed it. 'She found out today that her father died,' he said gently.

Shannon's concern changed to confusion. 'I thought she didn't know where he was?' she protested.

'She had a phone call earlier, from a solicitor. It came as a bit of a shock, which is why she's having a lie-down. She'll be going to see Grandma Alice tomorrow, and then she'll probably go to the funeral.'

'Can we go too?' Dan asked, looking as upset as his sister.

'That depends where it is, and if she wants us to.'

They appeared baffled by that. Why wouldn't she want them to? She never did anything without them.

'You'll need to give her some time with this,' Josh said. 'Try to be understanding.'

Dan looked at Shannon as she said, 'I know how I'd feel if you died, Dad, so she must be very upset, even though she hasn't seen him for ages.'

Dan's eyes widened. 'You aren't going to die, are you Dad?'

'Of course not,' Josh answered, making his laugh light, for he was still mindful of what had happened the last time Dan had thought he might lose him. 'Shannon was only being empathetic. Now there's a word for you to look up.'

'Shall we do it now?'

'I don't see why not,' Josh answered, understanding his son's need to focus on the smaller issue.

'I know what it means,' Shannon said haughtily.

'Then you can write it down and we'll see if she's right, shall we?' Josh suggested.

'She's always right,' Dan grumbled, as they trudged off to Josh's study. 'I don't mind though, because her exams are coming up so she needs to be right.'

'Thanks for reminding me,' Shannon retorted. 'I've got like so much coursework to get through. You've got to help me with some of it, Dad, you said you would.'

Assuring her he'd keep his promise, Josh took the dictionary from a shelf and passed it to Dan. 'Aren't you writing it down?' he said, looking back at Shannon.

'No,' she answered, her mood clearly having taken a sharp descent.

Going to her, Josh tilted her chin up. 'What is it?' he asked.

'I really need to talk to Mum.'

'Girl things?'

Her mouth started to tremble, and remembering the teenage hormones raging around inside her, he pulled her against him. How lost they all seemed, he was thinking, even though Julia was only upstairs. The distance was far greater than that though, he could already feel it, and as the thought twisted his heart, he wanted more than anything to go upstairs and lie down with her. But he had to give her the space she needed, if only while she sorted things out with her mother and father. He was going to play this whichever way she wanted, for he had a lot of ground to make up now – and if he'd ever felt more anxious about his ability to handle things then he was at a loss to know when, because right now he wasn't even sure where to sleep tonight, never mind what he was going to do if she decided she really did want him to leave.

Chapter Five

The following morning, feeling as wretched as she looked, Julia accepted Josh's offer to take the children to school, and after clearing away the breakfast dishes, she made a fresh pot of coffee before going to call Fionnula Barrington. Having slept so badly, tormenting herself with all kinds of horrors in the early hours, only then to drift off with the dawn, she was now feeling oddly remote, as though much of yesterday was a bad dream she couldn't quite shake. It was perfectly real though, she was aware of that, and with her emotions so exhausted from their struggle through the night, she'd barely managed on autopilot this morning as she'd sorted out the children, discussed what she had to with Josh, and even, weirdly, kissed him before he left. Admittedly, she'd done that more for the children than him, but seeing how much it had surprised and pleased him, she'd almost instantly regretted it, because not for a minute did she want him to think that she was just going to forget what he'd done. However, nothing could be mentioned with the children around, for she certainly didn't want them to know anything, so she'd merely turned away as he looked at her, letting him know with her eyes that she was even more disgusted this morning than she'd been last night.

Glancing up at the clock, she wondered if it was still too early to ring the solicitor. She'd try anyway, and if she wasn't at her office there was always the mobile. Either way she wanted the call over before Josh came back. She wished he'd go straight into work, because she couldn't see what they'd achieve from being together right now – though she accepted he'd probably want to know the outcome of her call to Ms Barrington, as well as what her mother had said, should she get around to contacting her too.

After three rings Fionnula Barrington herself answered the office line, but since she had an early appointment they were only able to speak for a few minutes, during which Julia fell into calling her Fen, as she insisted, and managed to have most of her more pressing questions answered. In fact, the call turned out to be much less upsetting than Julia had feared, to the point, she realised as she put the phone down, that she was almost glad to have this to deal with rather than waste any precious energy thinking about how much she despised her so-called best friend for being needed now, for it had a power that just wasn't healthy.

Knowing a conversation with her mother would do nothing to improve her frame of mind, she put off dialling the Gloucestershire number and stood gazing out of the window into the garden. It was a dreary morning, with leaves scudding about the lawn and old rain dropping from the leaves onto the sodden patio. She pictured Josh and the children in the old Peugeot crawling through the morning traffic, arguing about which radio station to have on, or chatting about iPods, cricket, *EastEnders* or where to go skiing next year. Or maybe they were quiet, worrying about her and what would happen next. She knew Josh had told Shannon and Dan about her father, because they'd given her big hugs this morning and said how sorry they were, but had he told them anything about Sylvia? Of course not. It was absurd even to think it. She wondered if he'd been in touch with Sylvia, to let her know that their secret was out – and the very idea of them having any contact at all, never mind that it was in the form of a warning about her, filled her with such outrage and loathing that she pressed her hands to her head as though to stop it exploding.

Deciding that even speaking to her mother was preferable to tormenting herself like this, she picked up the phone again and dialled the number she'd known practically all her life. Inside her nerves were already starting to churn, making her wonder, not for the first time, what kind of mother could cause her to feel so intimidated. Actually, she knew very well what kind of mother she had, and she was too old now to be this nervous, particularly when she wasn't intending to raise the forbidden subject of her father just yet. She'd save that little treat for when they were face to face; right now all she needed was to make an appointment. *An appointment – with her own mother!*

'Mum? It's me, Julia.'

'Oh hello,' came the thin reply. 'How are you?'

'Fine. How are you?'

'Fine. What can I do for you?'

No, how are the children, or how's Josh? Just the implied: *I'm in a hurry, so please come to the point.* 'I was thinking of coming to see you,' Julia said.

There was a pause. 'Really? How nice. I think I should be free next Wednesday or Thursday. I'll check my diary . . .'

'Sooner than that,' Julia interrupted. 'Today, in fact.'

'I'm afraid that's out of the question. My schedule's quite full.'

'I need to talk to you, Mum. Something's happened you need to know about.'

Hostility crackled in Alice's voice as she said, 'Please don't tell me Josh has left you. Well, I can hardly say I blame him, you never were easy to live with . . .'

'He hasn't left me,' Julia cut in, almost shouting. Just imagine turning to such an icicle of a woman for comfort during this difficult time, she was thinking. The very idea was so preposterous it would be laughable if it weren't so bloody depressing.

'Then what is it?' Alice demanded. 'Really, Julia, why do you always have to be so mysterious?'

'I'm not. I just think what I have to tell you would be better said in person.'

'Then it'll have to wait. As I said, I'm busy today.'

'Find a slot, Mother. I'll leave here at lunchtime, so try to be there by the time I arrive. If you're not, I'll wait outside in the car.'

Before Alice could object again Julia abruptly rang off, and bit down hard on her anger. Many years had passed since she'd allowed her mother to push and boss her around, but she still ended up feeling shaky and anxious whenever she stood up to her. It made her wonder what on earth she'd done in a previous life to deserve such a monster of a parent. *Try to remember,* Josh had once said, back in the early days, *something must have happened to her to make her that way.* On the odd occasion that thought had actually managed to soften her towards her mother, though usually at a distance, for more often than not she detested her for being so cold and unyielding, and so bloody secretive about everything to do with her past.

Anyway, whatever had happened to her, it was clear her younger daughter was never going to make it any better, so Julia had long since stopped trying. And for Josh's voice to step in as mediator now was just plain outrageous, considering the situation they were in thanks to his 'marriage-saving' affair with Sylvia. That he could seriously have thought she'd even begin to find such deranged reasoning acceptable was so shocking it defied belief. Worse still, he actually seemed to believe this ludicrous suggestion himself.

Hearing the front door close and his footsteps on the stairs, she left the phone and went to refill her cup. 'Would you like some coffee?' she asked as he came into the kitchen.

'Sure.' He waited for her to pour, then took the cup as she passed it. 'So how did you get on with the solicitor?' he asked. 'Have you got hold of her yet?'

'The cremation's on Friday,' she answered. 'The ashes should be buried sometime next week, they're waiting for confirmation from the vicar.'

'Are you going down there?'

'Yes. I'll go today, after I've seen my mother.'

He sipped his coffee. 'Have you told her you're coming?'

'Yes, but she doesn't know what it's about yet.'

He nodded thoughtfully, but made no comment on the wisdom of her decision, even though she knew he'd have his doubts. 'So what about the children?' he asked. 'I take it you've thought about what's going to happen to them while you're away?'

Managing not to rise to it, she said, 'They break up for half-term tomorrow. I expect we can work something out till then.'

His eyes stayed on hers. 'I'm sure my mother will be happy to step in,' he said.

'I'm sure she will.'

Immediately his face darkened. 'You don't have to take that tone,' he snapped. 'In fact, you could try being grateful, since you're the one who's going off and leaving them.'

'For Christ's sake, my father's dead and I want to go to his funeral. Is that too much to ask?'

'No, of course not. I'm sorry.'

His contrition was so complete she couldn't bear to witness it, so turned away.

'And after tomorrow?' he said. 'Shall I drive them down to Cornwall so we can all be together? They've said they'd like to go to the funeral.'

'I don't want to be with you, Josh,' she said. 'Not right now.'

Though the hurt showed in his eyes, his voice was tight as he said, 'So what's new?'

'You've always got Sylvia,' she reminded him nastily.

'Oh, for God's sake.'

'Sorry, I'm forgetting, she won't be here, will she? Or maybe you've got plans to join her in New York.'

'I'm not even going to respond to that,' he said angrily.

'Tell me, when you left me and the children in France, back in the summer, to fly up to Edinburgh, was it to see her?'

'You know why I went.'

'But did you see her? Did she fly up too? And what about the other trips you've made lately? Paris, Amsterdam . . .'

'Julia, this isn't getting us anywhere.'

'You are such a bastard,' she told him, wanting to hit him again. 'You were with her, weren't you? No, don't answer, because I can't take any more of your lies.'

Clearly struggling with his own temper, he said, 'So how long are you planning to stay in Cornwall?'

Detesting him for not saying more to refute her suspicions, since it must mean she was right, she felt the pain of it churn in her heart, and wanted to do something desperate, even deranged, to hurt him too. 'I'm not sure,' she finally heard herself answer. There was no point in attacking him – it wasn't going to make his betrayal go away and would probably just end up somehow backfiring on her. 'Apparently my father's left his house to me, but I've no idea how big or small it is, all I know is it'll need to be cleared and probably sold. Unless I decide to keep it, of course.'

He looked at her hard, and she realised he was afraid she might not come back at all. Well, let him worry, because she sure as hell wasn't going to put his mind at rest, even though she'd never leave the children, nor would she force them to change schools, particularly not at such a critical time for Shannon.

'Why don't you take Shannon with you?' he suggested. 'The break will probably do her good before her mocks.'

Though the idea had already occurred to her, she didn't answer right away.

'I think she needs you at the moment,' Josh told her.

'She needs to be studying.'

'She can do that in Cornwall.'

'What about Dan?' she asked.

'I'll take some time off next week. We can go down to the boat, do some sailing. Hang out together. Unless you'd rather he was with you.'

She would, but Dan would love it, just him and his dad, so she made no objection. Then quite suddenly she didn't know if she could bear to let Dan go. She wanted him with her where he'd be safe, and no-one could hurt him. Realising she was turning into an emotional minefield, where anything could go off at any minute, she suppressed her moment of panic and drank more coffee.

'If you could delay going until tomorrow,' he said, 'you could take Shannon with you.'

She was shaking her head. 'I don't want her there when I talk to my mother. I'm not even sure I want her to be at the funeral, because frankly I don't know what I'm going to find once I get down there.'

'Then in that case, why don't I drive her down on Saturday, before taking Dan on to Chichester?'

At that moment the phone rang and they both made to answer, but Josh was the closest. He listened to the voice at the other end, then appearing decidedly uncomfortable he passed the receiver over. 'Pauline,' he said.

Taking the phone, Julia watched him go to pour himself more coffee. Neither of them had eaten any breakfast this morning, and she didn't imagine they'd manage much lunch either. What did she care about food, though, she knew it would turn to dust in her mouth, and what he ate was his business now, not hers. 'Hello,' she said to Pauline, wishing Josh had said she wasn't in.

'Julia. Hi. Is it OK to talk? I know he's there, but I heard what happened, so I had to call. You must be feeling awful. Do you want to come over? Or I can come there if you prefer. Whatever you want. I can cancel my day . . .'

Julia's blood was turning cold. So he had been in touch with Sylvia, and Sylvia had obviously got straight on the phone to Pauline.

'I'll call you back,' Julia said, and banging the

phone down she immediately rounded on him. 'So you've already spoken to Sylvia,' she seethed. 'Well, I hope you let her know that your ludicrous attempts to save our marriage by having sex with her have spectacularly failed. But I don't suppose you care very much about that, do you? In fact you're probably dying to get round there right now so you can shag her again, so please, don't let me stop you.'

'Julia, try and pull yourself together . . .'

'Don't you dare patronise me,' she seethed. 'And let me tell you this, Joshua Thayne, if I hear she's set as much as one foot in this house while I'm away, I swear to God you'll never see me back here again.'

'Stop making this about her,' he raged. 'It's about us, you and me, and if you threaten me again like that you'll find out how it feels when we both play that game.'

Her eyes widened with astonishment. 'What exactly is that supposed to mean?' she demanded.

'It means, if you don't start facing up to a few realities while you're down there in Cornwall you won't be welcome back,' and practically throwing his cup into the sink, he stormed up the stairs and slammed out of the front door.

By the time Julia turned off the M4 to start heading north towards Cirencester, she was aware that signs were passing her by that she was barely noticing, and for minutes at a stretch she actually forgot where she was going. She hadn't spoken to Josh again before leaving, nor did she want to, though after her anger had begun to lose some of its force a wretched insecurity had started to take root, making her wonder if she was insane to leave London now, while Sylvia was still there. She kept trying to reassure herself that he wouldn't dare to go and see her again, but she had no way of knowing that, for she still didn't have any clear idea of how serious their relationship was. All she knew was that so far he'd failed to promise to give her up.

As the tortuous image of them together threatened to close in on her again, she summoned what was left of her reserves to push it away, and decided she really must focus on something else for a while, or tiredness would continue to play cruel tricks on her mind and sap what was left of her energy. Picking up the mobile, she kept it hidden from view as she tried her sister's number, but the answering machine was still on, so she simply rang off. She'd already left a message asking Pam to be at their mother's around two, but had had no reply, so she had no idea if Pam was going to be there or not. Right now Julia wasn't even sure if she cared, and signalling to turn off the main road she began winding through familiar open countryside, until she finally arrived at the sleepy Cotswold backwater of Deakins.

To call the place a village would be overstating it, for it was more of a sprawling hamlet, with no shop, no pub or school, just a phone box, a medieval church and a monstrous water tower where a monstrous water tower should never be. Were it not for such an eyesore the place might be considered chocolate-box, particularly in summer, when plumbago and nasturtiums tumbled over the old stone walls and all the perfectly thatched roofs glistened in the afternoon sun. Today, it loomed out of the mizzle as a dismal, creepy enclave, tight with secrets and riven with ghouls – but then, she'd never liked it, so even on brighter days it failed to appear quaint or welcoming to her.

Passing her sister's gingerbread cottage, which was one of the smallest in a row behind the phone box, she drove the Porsche slowly along the narrow, winding road, past the twin pillars of Deakins Manor, and on to where the road split in front of the monster tower. As she gazed up at it she found herself being drawn into a memory of her father standing in her uncle's garden, not long after the offending object's arrival, and commenting, 'Mushrooms seem to be doing well, George.'

Her uncle had failed to see the funny side, while Julia and her father had laughed for weeks. Another remark about the very same tower, had caused them similar amusement whilst, as a family, they were sitting in her uncle's garden enjoying a sunny day. Her father had winked at her secretly, then innocently stated, 'You're a bit like a goblin with his own private toadstool sitting out here, George.'

Since her uncle was a veritable giant of a man, to her ten-year-old ears the comment had been hilarious, and was made even more so by George's thunderous expression as he'd glared at his brother-in-law. He'd looked so fearsome, though, that she'd been half afraid he might eat her father when he wasn't looking. Her parents had had a dreadful row that night, since her mother had never appreciated the way her husband took such delight in goading her brother.

As the echo of laughter receded back through the years Julia felt herself engulfed by a wave of sadness that, emotional as she already was, could easily have submerged her in a welter of grief, for she was suddenly missing her father more than ever before. However, she knew the sorrow was fuelled by self-pity, and that it wouldn't do to fall victim to any kind of weakness when she was about to face her mother. So pulling herself together, she slipped the car back into gear, and edged a few feet further on to turn in left through the five-bar gate that she'd never, as far as she could remember, seen closed. Strange that, for a family who was so stand-offish, but perhaps they were only like it with her – indeed, they probably were, because she couldn't recall her sister ever complaining of feeling shut out, or barely tolerated. On the contrary, Pam was so plainly at home here that Julia often wondered whether she might persuade her limp personality of a van-driver husband to close the fifty-yard gap that currently existed and move right into the house itself. And no-one, Julia knew, would be happier than Alice to have Pam's daughter, Rachel, under the same roof, because there could be no doubt of how besotted Alice was with the child. Admittedly, Rachel was completely adorable. Julia just wished that her mother would, once in a while, put herself out to show Shannon and Dan even a fraction of as much affection.

The grounds of their so-called family home were all smooth lawns, thrusting trees and immaculately tended beds, since gardening was her uncle's passion, along with hunting, shooting, model-making and God. Bridge was her mother's absorbing interest, and she didn't have the faintest idea what Aunt Rene's might be, because she'd never heard the mousy little creature express a preference for anything in her life. Julia wouldn't mind betting, however, that she'd rather not be sharing her home with her stridently bossy sister-in-law, but maybe that was just Julia projecting her own feelings onto the case again, for personally she could hardly think of anything worse than living with her mother.

The house itself was long and grey, with small, casement windows, several chimneys and a horribly forbidding front door. Once again she was allowing her prejudice to dictate, for most people would describe it as an extremely grand example of early-eighteenth-century craftsmanship. In those days the door was probably the gateway to an asylum for raving lunatics, which seemed suitable in view of its current location, she'd long ago decided.

By the time she got out of the car her mother was standing at the door, looking as primly immaculate as ever in a brown cashmere twinset and pearls, tweed skirt and brogues, though she was hardly frumpy. She was even taller than Julia, with immaculately styled salt-and-pepper hair, electric blue eyes that she'd passed on to Shannon, and a full-lipped mouth that was sexy on her younger daughter, and might once have been on her, before it had become pleated by a lifetime's disappointments and grudges. If she smiled more it would probably still be lovely, Julia had occasionally thought, and they might even get to see the dimples her sister had inherited, but they were almost as rare a sight as her mother's private parts, which Julia had *never* seen. Nor, she thought, as she went to greet her, would she want to, for a more chilling prospect was hard to imagine.

'Oh dear,' Alice Hope sighed, looking straight past Julia to the Porsche, 'I don't think Uncle George will want that parked where people can see it. Maybe you should take it round the back.'

Maybe you could greet me like a normal mother, starting with hello, Julia was thinking, as she turned back to look at the car. It made her feel suddenly protective of Josh, because he loved it, which was mindlessly stupid considering the fact it might have been bought to impress Sylvia, but how did she know her addled brain was going to react that way? 'I think it looks just fine where it is,' she replied, tilting her head to one side, as though assessing the Porsche's aesthetic value.

Alice sighed. 'Do you always have to be difficult?' she said, eyelids fluttering in exasperation.

Julia smiled benignly and waited to be invited inside.

'Have you put on weight?' Alice enquired, standing aside. 'Is that why you're wearing those ghastly clothes? It does no good. It shows in your face.'

'I'm wearing Nicole Farhi, actually, and I'm sorry if my face offends you.' Somehow she kept smiling, while inside, annoyingly, she wanted to cry. *Don't do this,* she scolded herself firmly. *If you let her get the upper hand now, you'll never get it back again.* 'So how are you?' she asked chirpily, as her mother closed the door. 'You're looking good. You definitely haven't put on weight, and your clothes are lovely. We must go shopping together.'

'We're all fine, thank you very much,' Alice responded, ignoring the sarcasm. 'Aunt Rene was delighted to receive the birthday card you sent. It was good of you to remember.'

'Did you have a party?' Julia asked, trying not to be cowed by the horribly gloomy entrance hall, with its grotesque animal trophies and borrowed family crests. She'd never felt comfortable in here, nor had her father, for they'd often wondered if her uncle was sizing them up for a spot over the mantel.

Alice didn't deign to reply. 'Come through to the drawing room,' she said. 'There's a fire in there. Have you eaten?'

'I'm fine, thank you. I wouldn't mind a triple whisky though.'

Ignoring her again, since she knew very well that her uncle strongly disapproved of alcohol, Alice pushed open a set of double doors and led the way into the only room in the house Julia had ever felt to be normal, possibly because it was the only one with furniture that wasn't an ordeal to sit on.

'Have you spoken to Pam?' Julia said. 'I left her a message asking her to meet me here.'

Alice's eyebrows arched. 'She's away visiting her father-in-law until tomorrow,' she responded.

Julia nodded, then to be polite, said, 'How are Uncle George and Aunt Rene? Are they here?'

'They should be home soon. They're attending a meeting of the agricultural committee for the local council. Now, what can possibly be so important that you've had to drive all this way to talk to me in person?'

'Aren't you worried?' Julia couldn't help asking. 'I mean, please don't think there's anything wrong with either of the children, because there isn't, provided we forget the seizure Daniel had a few weeks ago, of course . . .'

Alice's hostility cracked a little. 'How is he now?' she asked, exhibiting a trace of grand-motherly concern.

'OK. It was just a blip, we think.'

'He's a fine boy. We don't see enough of him.'

You wouldn't see anything of him at all, if it weren't for Josh, Julia was thinking.

'Or Shannon. How is she?'

'Growing up. Wanting a boyfriend. Being a handful. I suppose much like I was at her age.'

Alice's eyes narrowed suspiciously. 'I hope you're not here to start dredging all that up again,' she snapped.

Julia was about to deliver another biting response, when she decided to stop herself. The last thing she needed today was another harrowing scene, especially with her mother, and since she had no idea how Alice was going to respond to the news of her ex-husband's death, she could at least, if only for her own sake, try to break it to her gently. 'No, I'm not here for that,' she said. 'Not exactly.'

Alice stiffened. 'What does not exactly mean?' she demanded.

They were both still standing, so Julia said, 'Can we sit down? I think we should.'

Alice immediately dropped to the chair behind her, and sat ramrod straight. Julia took the furthest end of the sofa.

'I had a phone call yesterday,' she said, 'from a solicitor in Bodmin.'

Before Alice could respond the door opened and her brother came in. 'Ah, George,' she said. 'Julia's here. She was just telling me about a phone call she received yesterday.'

Julia rose to her feet and tried to stop her skin crawling, for though her uncle, enormous as he was, was a handsome, even congenial-looking man, with bushy grey hair and bright grey eyes, she'd never been able to forget the nightmare he'd once subjected her to following a particularly horrible showdown with her mother – over her father, of course. The humiliation and pain had been total, as he'd locked them both in her room and forced her to pray and pray until she'd been reduced to a gibbering wreck of subjugation and penitence. He'd then ordered her to remove her jeans and panties to receive her just punishment for a disobedience that could not be tolerated by him or his god. It was the only time it had ever happened, but even now, all these years later, it was impossible for her to look at him without remembering and hating. For his part, he seemed to have banished it completely from his mind, for when he wasn't spouting penitential psalms from his little *Treasury of Devotion*, or some other godly verse he had crowding his head, he generally treated her with a much greater warmth than her mother could muster, and had even, on occasion, taken her side when she and her mother fought. That had never happened when the issue was her father, of course, on that front brother and sister were fully united.

'Julia,' he said, reaching for her hand. 'What a pleasure. How are the children? And Josh?'

'They're all fine, thank you,' she answered, dutifully hugging him and trying not to cringe. 'And you?'

'Tip-top,' he chuckled. 'Yes, tip-top,' and removing his horn-rimmed specs he gave them a wipe with the bottom of his Fair Isle sweater.

'Is Aunt Rene joining us?' she asked, suddenly wishing Josh was with her, for he handled her family so much better than she ever did.

'She might, in a minute,' he answered. 'She hasn't been feeling too well lately. I've been quite worried about her actually.'

'Has she seen a doctor?'

'I wish she would. Maybe you can persuade her. Goodness knows, your mother and I have tried.' He looked at his sister and smiled warmly, reminding Julia of the bond they'd always shared, that had often seemed to exclude everyone else.

Unable to imagine why he thought she'd have more success in persuading her aunt, Julia merely smiled weakly and turned back to her mother.

'So where were we?' Alice said, and as she looked at Julia the softness in her eyes seemed to glaze over.

'I think something about a telephone call,' George prompted, gesturing for them to sit down.

'From a solicitor apparently,' Alice informed him. Then to Julia, 'I hope you're not here to tell us you've been trying to find your father again, because if you are, we're really not interested, and frankly, if he wanted to see you . . .'

'Mother, he's dead.'

Alice stopped mid-sentence, and for a moment she seemed so confounded that her mouth went slack, then quickly collecting herself, she turned to her brother and said, 'Well, thank goodness that's over.'

Julia's eyes rounded in amazement. 'What on earth's that supposed to mean?' she demanded.

Alice shot her a look, then looked away again.

'Answer me,' Julia cried.

'Are you becoming hysterical?' Alice enquired.

'For Christ's sake. I've just told you my father's dead, your ex-husband, the man you married all those years ago, whom you presumably once loved . . .' Alice's expression stopped her going any further with that. 'Well, whatever he was to you, he was my father,' Julia pressed on, 'and instead of offering some kind of sympathy, or asking how, or when he died, or anything any normal person might ask . . .'

'Julia, please keep your voice down,' her uncle cut in.

'Why?' she shouted. 'Who are you afraid's going to hear?'

'It's not a case of who's going to hear, it's that we don't need to be shouted at.'

'Then tell me the truth. He's dead now, so he can't hurt any of us . . .'

'My dear, I really do wish you'd let this go.'

'I want to know why he left,' she raged.

'Always the same,' he sighed irritably. 'You come here, upsetting yourself and your mother over matters that we've told you a hundred times are best left in the past . . .'

'*Why did he go*?' she almost screamed.

Her mother's voice was sharp as she said, 'If he wanted you to know, don't you think he'd have told you himself?'

'Maybe he didn't get the chance. Maybe you stopped him.'

'How could I? You've been an adult for a long time, though heaven knows you don't always behave like one.'

Julia leapt to her feet. 'This is my father we're talking about,' she stormed. 'I know that doesn't mean anything to you, but it does to me . . .'

'Do you always have to make such a drama out of things?' her mother interrupted. 'Now, please, calm down or we shall have to ask you to leave.'

Julia blinked with shock. 'Are you saying you'd throw me out? Right after I tell you my father's dead? Is that what you just said? Jesus, how can you call yourself a mother?'

George rose to his feet. 'We've put up with a lot from you over the years, Julia,' he said darkly. 'Your accusations, threats, paranoia . . .'

'*If you gave me some answers . . .*'

'We've tried, but you don't want to listen.'

'Well I'm listening now.'

'He didn't want to be with us any more,' her mother said. 'You have to make yourself face that.'

'Then why has he left his house to me? Why did he want me to know he'd died? And why did he call me six weeks ago?'

Alice shot a quick look at George. 'He called you?' she said, clearly troubled.

'So, did he explain why he left?' her uncle demanded.

Bitterly regretting having to admit it, Julia said, 'I didn't actually speak to him.'

Alice was starting to look flustered.

'For God's sake,' Julia implored. 'Why don't you just tell me the truth?'

Her uncle answered. 'Your father left for his own reasons. If he'd wanted you to know them, he'd have told you himself.'

'No! Something happened. They had a fight. I heard it . . .'

'As you've said on countless occasions, but as your mother's repeatedly told you, no such argument took place. It's all in your head.'

'Then why did she tell me it was my fault he left?'

Alice's colour deepened. 'I never said such a thing,' she declared. 'You have such a vivid imagination. It's . . .'

'You said it, Mother, and more than once. You even hit me . . .'

'Now you're just being offensive.'

Julia threw out her hands, lost for words.

'Why can't you be like your sister and just accept what happened?' her uncle barked. 'It's such a long way in the past, I really can't understand why you still can't let it go.'

'Because he was my father, and he loved me. I know he did.'

George's eyes were like granite as he said, 'I'm afraid, Julia, that you never saw him as he really was.'

'Isn't it enough that he abandoned you?' her mother added. 'That alone should tell you he wasn't the man you thought he was.'

'Then what was he? For Christ's sake, almost a quarter of a century has passed now, so surely to God you don't have to keep anything from me . . .'

'You're always assuming . . .'

'No!' she almost screamed. 'I won't let you put me off. I want to know. If he wasn't the man I thought he was, then *who was he? What did he do?'* Her eyes were livid as she threw down the challenge, but as she glared from one to the other she could see that neither of them was going to utter the one word that was now ticking like an unexploded bomb between them.

It was that moment that her aunt chose to walk into the room, all twittering apologies and aghast at discovering she'd intruded. 'I'm so sorry. I'll come back . . .'

'Stay,' George snapped. 'Julia is about to leave.'

Julia's eyes went to him 'So you are throwing me out?'

'I think you've caused your mother enough distress for one day, don't you?'

Julia shook her head in disgust. 'Believe me, it doesn't stop here,' she said in a voice full of warning. 'I'm going to get to the truth somehow, if it's the last thing I do.'

As she stalked across the room her aunt stepped out of her path, then watched with mournful eyes as the door closed behind her.

For several minutes no-one spoke, letting Julia's parting words reverberate around the room, until finally the sound of the Porsche roaring away seemed to rouse them.

As Alice walked over to the window George followed and put a comforting arm around her.

'She won't let it rest there,' she said, staring bleakly out at the empty drive. 'And now he's dead . . .'

'Hush, calm yourself,' George chided. 'You've done everything you can to protect her. If she can't accept that and she does manage to turn something up she'll only have herself to blame.'

Alice looked up at him, her eyes full of fear. 'How can you say that? You know what it'll do to her.'

Sounding exasperated, he said, 'She won't find anything, because there's nothing to find.'

'Shall I make us some tea?' Rene offered.

'But if she does,' Alice persisted, as though Rene hadn't spoken, 'it's not only her I'm worried about. You could go to prison, George.' The very idea seemed to make her feel faint.

'Oh, that won't happen,' Rene assured her. 'She'd never let it get that far.'

'We're talking about Julia,' Alice reminded her.

Rene backed down at that, and focused on George who was looking thoughtful.

'Do we know where this house of his is?' he

asked, steering Alice gently back to a sofa and sitting down with her.

Alice shook her head. 'He moved from the last address we had over fifteen years ago.'

'Pity,' he said, 'because if anything could cause us a problem, I rather think that will be it.'

Chapter Six

Fionnula Barrington – Fen – turned out to be something of a surprise to Julia, for on the phone she'd sounded much younger than her apparent forty-some years, and perhaps more glamorous. But she was certainly a pleasant-looking woman, Julia decided as they shook hands in Fen's small, but very lawyerly, reception. Her eyes, smile and handshake all conveyed a generous amount of warmth, while her long, crinkly auburn hair and random freckles appeared as lively as her spirit. Her attire was rather colourful for a solicitor, too – lime green polo neck with yellow chiffon scarf, tan jodhpurs and a snazzy pair of crocodile ankle boots, which she kicked off at the door of her office as she showed Julia through.

'Have you driven straight down from London?' she asked, padding in behind her and closing the door. 'You must have left extremely early.'

'Actually, just from Devon,' Julia replied. There was no reason to explain that after leaving her mother's she'd got only as far as Bristol before the whole horrible nightmare of the past twenty-four hours had forced her to pull into the motorway services. For some time she'd simply sat at the wheel, either sobbing uncontrollably, or staring at a grassy bank and wanting so desperately to call Josh she almost couldn't bear it. In the end, he'd called her, but she hadn't answered. She was still too angry to speak to him without mentioning Sylvia, and she really hadn't had the heart for another row.

After finally managing to pull herself together, she'd continued on down the M5 until, realising she couldn't turn up at the solicitor's in the middle of the evening, she'd checked into a small B & B near Cullompton. She'd called home from there, but had only spoken to Josh for a few minutes, mainly because the children would have found it odd if she hadn't. He'd been worried, he told her, sounding annoyed that she hadn't called earlier or answered her phone when he'd rung. Her tone had matched his as she'd cuttingly responded that no, the encounter with her mother hadn't gone well, thank you for asking, but he needn't concern himself about it, she could deal with it alone.

This morning's call hadn't been much friendlier either, since she'd asked if he planned to see Sylvia today, to which he'd replied that sarcasm didn't become her. Aware that it hadn't been an outright denial, she'd immediately started threatening him with divorce, total isolation from the children, and a devastating trip to the cleaners if he as much as went near the woman again. Somehow, and she still wasn't sure how, he'd managed to reassure her that it wouldn't happen, and even, to some degree, convince her he still loved her – which was considerably more than she'd been able to muster for him.

'Would you like some tea?' Fen asked cheerily, waving her towards a sofa next to an old stone fireplace. 'We've got quite an assortment.'

'No, I'm fine, thanks,' Julia assured her, regarding a portrait of an extremely distinguished-looking man that was hanging over the hearth.

'My father,' Fen told her. 'He's the Bower of Sissons, Greene and Bower. My husband's the Barrington, but he's a vet.'

Julia nodded and sat down. The office was quite typical of a country solicitor, she thought, slightly shabby furniture, haphazardly stacked files on every surface, and row upon row of dusty books, as well as the inevitable hi-tech installations, along with photographs of Mr Barrington and the Barrington offspring – two leggy, long-haired girls who both resembled their mother. The window behind Fen's desk looked out onto a small courtyard where benches were positioned under trees, and an ornamental pond claimed centre stage.

For some reason Julia already felt comfortable here, maybe because it was a very long way from Josh and her mother, remote enough even to feel like part of another world. It also had an atmosphere that was rather like Fen herself, friendly and slightly chaotic. She'd instantly warmed to Fen's staff too, whom she'd met in the front office where a bell had rung over the door as she'd let herself in. In fact, somewhere beyond the pain and bewilderment in her mind, she was aware of feeling buoyed by just about everything she'd so far seen of the town, with its meandering high street of old-fashioned shops and trendy cafés, Victorian lampposts with their late-blooming hanging baskets, and the grand Shire House where recreations of Bodmin's more notorious hangings were, apparently, regularly staged.

'I should begin by offering my condolences,' Fen said, sinking comfortably into an armchair. 'I ought to have done that on the phone, of course.'

'I appreciate you letting me know,' Julia told her. 'If you hadn't I might never have found out. Have you managed to speak to my sister? I know she's been away . . .'

Fen was shaking her head. 'We have no contact details for her,' she said. 'Only for you, though I understand neither of you have been in touch with him for some time.'

'Twenty-four years to be exact,' Julia replied. 'And believe me, it wasn't by choice – at least not on my part.'

Even though Fen's eyebrows rose, she didn't seem particularly surprised. 'So no news of him at all in that time, not even a spot of family gossip?'

Julia shook her head. 'Unless I brought it up, his name never got mentioned.'

Fen looked perplexed by that. 'So you don't really know much about him?'

'No. I'm afraid I don't.'

'Well, I can begin by telling you, he was a delightful man. We were all quite mad about him.'

More pleased to hear that than she wanted to show, Julia said, 'Did you know him well?'

'Oh yes. He and my father were great friends. His death has come as a bit of a blow to Dad, to us all, in fact, even though it was expected.'

'You mentioned he had cancer.'

'Yes, of the stomach. It was diagnosed over a year ago. He had all the treatment, but unfortunately . . .' Her lips flattened in a smile. 'I think he was rather ready to join his wife. He missed her a great deal after she died.'

Knowing it was absurd to feel shut out by a woman she'd never even met, and who was actually dead, Julia said, 'I didn't realise he'd married again.'

'Oh yes. He and Gwen were very close.'

'How long were they together?'

'I'm not sure. Certainly the whole time we knew them, which was probably around twenty years.'

'Did they have any children?'

'No. Gwen couldn't.'

But he had two, Julia was thinking. *And one of us at least would have liked to know Gwen.*

'I have to confess, you came as a bit of a surprise to us,' Fen told her. 'Until six weeks ago, when he got me to change his will, none of us even knew you existed.'

Unable not to feel hurt by that, Julia swallowed hard and tried to focus on the timing, rather than her reactions, for it was about six weeks ago that Shannon had taken the call.

'Why did he change it then?' she asked. 'Do you know?'

Fen nodded soberly. 'He'd just been given his countdown, as he put it. He wanted everything to be in order before he went. Mainly for you.' She smiled. 'He talked about you quite a lot during his last weeks.'

Again Julia felt herself being drawn into a quagmire of emotions. 'I wish you'd let me know he was so ill,' she said.

'Oh, believe me, I wanted to, but he wouldn't have it. "She hasn't seen me in all these years," he'd say to me, "I don't have the right to be a burden on her now."'

Julia's chest was starting to feel tight. 'He was my father,' she whispered. 'He wouldn't have been a burden.'

'I'm glad you think that, but he could be a stubborn old thing when he wanted to be. He wouldn't even tell us where we could find you. Your details were in a sealed envelope, not to be opened until after his death.'

Realising she was embarrassingly close to tears, Julia dug around for a tissue. 'I'm sorry,' she said. 'I just wish . . . I'd have liked the chance to know him, to find out why he left all those years ago.' She blew her nose, and took a deep breath. 'Did he tell you?'

Fen shook her head. 'I'm afraid not. Doesn't your mother know?'

'Probably, but she won't tell me.'

Fen frowned, apparently bemused by that.

'Something happened,' Julia found herself saying. 'I don't know what, but I'm determined to find out. My father and I were very close, you see, while I was growing up. It never made any sense to me that he would just go, without saying a word, or ever getting in touch. At first I was furious with him for just abandoning me, but all the time

I kept waiting and hoping, certain that one day he'd come back and explain. There had to be a reason behind him leaving like that, something more than I was being told.'

'Which was?'

Julia sighed a bitter laugh. 'More mixed messages than you can imagine,' she answered. 'They told me he was evil, that I didn't know him at all, only what I wanted to know ...' Her eyes moved to Fen's. 'The way you described him just now, that was the man I knew.'

Fen was looking vaguely miffed. 'Well, evil is certainly not a word any of us would use to describe Dougie Cowan,' she said tartly. 'That's a horrible thing to say about anyone, particularly someone who didn't have a bad bone in his body. However, something clearly did happen back then to break up your family, so I can understand your need to find out what it was. If I can be of any help, just say the word.'

'Thank you.'

'His papers should all be at the house, apart from those we have here, of course. Whether they contain anything to help you, well, I guess you won't know till you look. I've made copies of what we have, which includes the will. Essentially, there's not an enormous amount in the way of cash, though I dare say an insurance policy of twenty thousand won't be sniffed at, and of course the house is now yours.'

Julia was feeling slightly dazed. 'What about Pam?' she asked.

Fen shook her head. 'I'm afraid there's no provision for your sister. Only for you.'

Julia was confused. 'Why would he have left Pam out?' she asked.

Fen could only shake her head.

'But you were aware, before I got here, that he had another daughter?'

Fen nodded. 'He told us very little about her though.'

'What about Pam's daughter, Rachel? Did he ever mention her?'

'No. At least not to me.'

Julia looked away. He obviously couldn't have known about Rachel, because a man like her father would never have left a granddaughter with Down's out of his will.

'I've contacted the probate officer, and an independent valuer,' Fen was saying, 'but if you'd rather use someone . . .'

'I'm sure the person you've asked is fine.' She swallowed. 'I don't suppose he left a letter for me, or a tape, even a video?'

'There's nothing on file, but that's not to say you won't find anything at the house. Everything's as he left it.'

Julia's throat turned dry. 'Where is he now?' she asked, feeling dreadful for not having asked sooner.

'At Allston's, the funeral home. It's not far from here. You can see him whenever you're ready. If you want to, that is. I know not everyone . . .'

'I want to.' She glanced down at the balled-up tissue in her hand. 'Did he know he had grand-children?' she asked. 'Did he mention them at all?'

'Oh yes. I believe your children's names are Shannon and Daniel . . .'

'He knew that?' Yes, of course, he'd called Shannon by name when he rang.

Fen smiled. 'They're fifteen and eleven?'

Julia nodded. 'How did he know?'

'I can't answer that, I'm afraid, but it would appear he was much more aware of you and your life than you realised.' She got to her feet and started over to her desk. 'Now, I've put myself at your disposal today. I'll drive you around, show you where everything is, Allston's, the house, the church, then, once you've got your bearings, if you'd rather be alone just tell me to hop it. I won't mind, my skin's fairly thick. How long do you plan to be here?'

'I'm not sure. At least until the ashes are buried. I should probably contact my sister, to find out if she wants to come to the funeral.'

Fen made no comment on that. 'Will you stay at the house?' she asked.

Julia hadn't considered that.

'Wait till you see it,' Fen smiled. 'You're going to fall madly in love with it, so I think the answer will be yes. It's an old mill, actually, not big, but absolutely heavenly. Gwen had it updated not long before she died, so everything's in excellent condition.'

'How long ago did she die?'

'Five years. Dougie was rather lost without her, but he always managed to put up a good show. Rather typical of him, actually.'

Julia smiled. 'Is the house far from here?'

'About half an hour's drive if the Wadebridge road's not still up. Would you like to go over to Allston's now? Or would you prefer to wait until you've settled in a bit?'

'I think now,' Julia answered.

Seeming to sense her nerves, Fen said, 'It'll be fine. I'll be right there with you.'

Julia nodded. 'Maybe I'm more worried about what I might end up finding out once I get to the house.'

Fen's eyebrows went up. 'Well, whatever it is, let me attempt to put your mind at rest again – there was nothing evil or sinister about Dougie Cowan. He was the sweetest, kindest and most mischievous rogue ever to set foot in Cornwall.'

Grateful for the reassurance, but mindful of her need to try and stay objective, Julia said, 'Better things have been said about a lot worse people, before the truth was known.'

Fen seemed surprised. 'But I have no doubts about my old friend Dougie. You won't find anyone around here who has.'

Letting it go there, Julia followed her out of the office. The last thing she wanted was to destroy Fen's faith with the horrible suspicion that had haunted her for so many years. No, she'd much rather continue labouring under the same rosy delusions herself, at least for as long as she could.

The funeral home was probably no more than fifty paces from Fen's office, set a little back from the high street, inside a leafy garden full of cherubic statues and celestial fountains. By the time Julia and Fen reached it Fen had greeted at least half a dozen people, the last of whom was a sweet-looking old woman with wind-roughened cheeks and flat grey hair, who was just coming out of the gates as they approached.

'Hello Tilde,' Fen said, giving her a hug. 'Been in to see Dougie again?'

The old woman nodded and blinked her watery eyes. 'Thought he might want a bit of company,' she said, in a pronounced Cornish accent. 'Don't like to think of him lying in there on his own.'

Fen put an affectionate hand to the old lady's face and turned to Julia. 'This is Dougie's daughter, Julia,' she told her.

The woman's eyes shone with pleasure. 'Oh, my dear,' she said, clasping Julia's hands in both of hers. 'Your father told us all about you, come the end. I'm right glad you came, I am. He will be too. We said you would, didn't we?' she added to Fen.

Fen nodded. 'This is Tilde Reddy,' she explained to Julia. 'She helped your father keep house after Gwen went, and took extremely good care of him too, I'm here to tell you.'

Tilde was fixed on Julia, clearly quite transported by the delight of meeting Dougie's daughter. 'I'm sorry for your loss, my dear,' she said with feeling. 'We all are. Loved him dearly, I did. Going to miss him.' She dabbed away a tear. 'Going to miss him a lot, the old rascal that he was.'

'Thank you,' Julia responded. 'I'm sorry for your loss too.'

'There'll be a big turnout tomorrow,' Tilde assured her. 'And right pleased everyone'll be that you came.'

Julia was slightly taken aback, for she hadn't considered who might be at the funeral, or even what kind of affair it might be. One thing was certain though, even if she'd wanted it to be small and private, she had no right to deny a final farewell to these friends who'd taken her father so warmly to their hearts.

'Have you talked to Mum about the wake?' Fen was asking Tilde.

'Course I have. We got it all in hand.'

The wake. Julia turned to Fen. 'I hadn't thought . . . I . . .'

'My parents are taking care of it,' Fen told her. 'I hope that's all right.'

'Of course, but you must at least let me cover the cost.'

Fen's smile was wry. 'I'll let you discuss that with Daddy,' she responded, 'but I have a feeling you won't win.' Then to Tilde, 'We're just going to pay our respects.'

Tilde took Julia's hand again and squeezed it. 'Lovely meeting you,' she said warmly. 'If there's anything you need, anything at all, Fen here knows how to get hold of me.'

'Thank you,' Julia responded, and felt moved, once again, by the affection she was receiving just for being her father's daughter.

The reception of the funeral home was deserted as they walked in, until Fen chirped a 'Hello', and a stocky man in his mid-thirties with neat fair hair and a sober grey suit emerged from a back office.

'Reece, this is Julia Thayne,' Fen told him. 'Reece and his father will both be directing the funeral,' she explained to Julia, putting an emphasis on 'both' which seemed to suggest that normally only one person performed the role.

Reece Allston took Julia's hand in a firm grip. 'I'm sorry we meet under these circumstances,' he said in a gentle baritone. 'My condolences for your loss. Your father will be missed.'

Julia thanked him and added, 'I'm beginning to feel as though I'm the one who should be offering condolences. You all seemed to know him so well.'

Reece smiled. 'He was a generous man with a good soul and a wicked wit. The vicar's having a hard time deciding who should do the readings, he's had that many offers.'

Julia shook her head, lost for a response.

'I expect you'd like to see him,' Reece said, standing aside. 'The chapel of rest is through the door at the end of the corridor. I can come with you, or if you'd prefer to be alone . . .'

Julia glanced at Fen. 'I'll go alone, if you don't mind,' she replied.

As she walked the few steps towards the door Reece Allston had indicated, she found herself wishing with all her heart that Josh was with her now, for it had been a very long time since she'd done anything this momentous without him. However, being alone certainly would not stop her, for it was her father she was going to see, and this would be her last chance.

As she pushed open the door she felt herself becoming vaguely light-headed, as though she were slipping into a dream. The lights were respectfully low, casting half-moon shadows around the stone walls, and there was a scent of flowers mixed with sulphur in the air. Candles flickered on the altar that was against the opposite wall, lighting the granite cross over it, and a tasteful posy of flowers had dropped a few petals onto the pristine white cloth. The coffin was at the centre of the chapel, laid out on a long marble table and facing away from her towards the altar.

Closing the door she took a moment to collect herself, then walked quietly across the carpet, increasingly fearful now of how she was going to respond when she saw him again after all these years, and here, like this. As she drew near she closed her eyes, not quite ready yet. She wanted to recall him first as the younger man she'd known with lively blue eyes and a ready laugh, the loving father who'd taught her to ride a bike and play tennis, who'd read her stories at night and clapped the loudest at her little accomplishments. She wanted to think of him as the man his friends and neighbours spoke of with such affection, the parent she remembered and still missed so much, as though somehow her precious memories could destroy all the terrible doubts her mother had planted, that he hadn't loved her enough to stay.

She stood behind the coffin and let her eyes travel down it towards the altar. She was close enough now to see his hands, clasped lightly below his waist, pale and rugged against his navy velour robe. Her heart was so full that its beats felt cumbersome and heavy. It seemed hard to connect with the reality of why she was here, yet there was nothing else beyond it.

A few more steps and she was round at the side of the coffin. Her hands were clenched tightly together, her whole body was tensing so hard that she was barely able to breathe. Though she couldn't quite look yet, she was aware of a white silk cravat tucked into the neck of his robe, and the navy taffeta of the coffin lining with its matching frill. She listened to the tiny wisps of her breath, and the silence that surrounded her, then at last she forced her eyes to move to his face, and the rush of emotion as she saw him was so intense that her hands flew to her mouth to stifle the cry. He'd hardly changed. His long, slender cheekbones, his slightly crooked nose, the lines in his forehead and clean-shaven chin were just the same, hardly impaired by age. His hair was barely troubled by grey and his lips almost seemed to be smiling, and there was such an aura of peace around him that she wanted to lie down with him and become a part of it.

'Dad, oh Dad,' she whispered brokenly.

The temptation to hold him and try to make him put his arms around her was so strong she could barely fight it. She inhaled shakily and became aware of the tears falling onto her cheeks. 'I loved you so much,' she told him. 'I tried to understand, but I never could.' She put a hand on his and felt the coolness of his skin. 'Why did you go?' she whispered.

She gazed down at him, almost as though expecting a reply, but his secret, along with his laughter and love, had gone with him to another place now.

'Please be who I think you are,' she implored. 'Please don't be the man I'm so afraid of. That's not you, is it, Dad? Please tell me that's not you.'

Clearly sensing that Julia was in need of a restorative break after leaving the chapel of rest, Fen whisked her straight off to a nearby pub where she ordered them both a stiff drink, and collected a couple of menus from the bar.

Julia was grateful for her understanding, and relieved when she steered their conversation onto the safer territory of children, motherhood and careers, rather than pressing any more on her about her father right now. She soon realised she was finding Fen extremely easy to be with, supportive without being overwhelming, and interested without being intrusive. She was also discreet, for when Julia's mobile rang with calls from Shannon, then Dan, she made herself scarce, either by visiting the Ladies, or going to the bar and ordering some food.

Since she was still standing at the counter chatting when Julia rang off from Dan, Julia quickly dialled Josh's direct number at the office, and prayed he'd be there, for she certainly didn't want to call his mobile and start wondering where he was as they spoke.

'He's on the other line to New York, negotiating some film rights,' Marina told her, 'so he could be a while. Shall I ask him to call back?'

'If he has time,' Julia replied tartly, and was instantly sorry, for it was hardly Marina's fault that he wasn't free.

'How's it going down there?' Marina asked.

'OK. Everyone's very nice.'

'Is there anything I can do for you this end?'

'I don't think so, but thanks for the offer.'

As she rang off she was already regretting making the call, and wondered why she had. It was probably habit, for she was used to turning to Josh when she felt vulnerable and in need of a shoulder. However, she clearly wasn't thinking straight, for how on earth could he make her feel better, when he was such a big part of the reason she was feeling so bad?

'I ordered a bowl of chips on the side,' Fen confessed as she came to sit down again. 'A day for self-indulgence, methinks.'

Julia smiled. She wasn't going to argue with that, though she had virtually no appetite at all.

'Everything OK at home?' Fen enquired.

'Fine. The kids are a bit concerned about me, and how it's going down here. They were just checking up.'

'How adorable,' Fen commented, taking a sip of her drink. 'I'm not sure I could count on my two for such moral support.' She chuckled. 'Actually I do them a disservice, they're good girls really.'

'What age are they?'

'Fifteen and twelve. They're weekly borders at a school near Truro, and they're both horse-mad, which they get from their mother. Do either of yours ride?'

'Shannon's had a few lessons. Josh takes her when he has time.'

'Josh is your husband? Will he be coming for the funeral?'

Julia took a breath to say no, and to her surprise found she was on the brink of tears. Thankfully, she managed to pull herself back in time – Fen was dealing with enough of her family issues already, the last thing she needed was to have even more heaped on top. 'He'll be here on Saturday,' she said. 'He's bringing Shannon, then taking Daniel sailing.'

'Shannon's coming? Oh, what a pity my girls are going to miss her. My mother's taking them to Italy for the half-term break. She's Italian, you see. She still has family there, so she goes every year at this time, while Rico, her nephew, my cousin, generally comes here to help Dad with the farm and horses. You'll probably meet him over the next couple of days, and I should warn you, he'll probably turn your knees weak because he has that effect on most females who cross his path. He may be my cousin and twenty years younger, give or take, but they don't come much more gorgeous than him – and don't be taken in by his shyness, because it's all a ruse, or that's what I keep telling him.'

Julia was smiling. 'I'll look forward to meeting him,' she commented, glancing up as a barman came to put paper napkins and cutlery on their table. 'But it's a shame about the girls not being here.'

'I know, however, speaking purely selfishly, I wouldn't mind having their father to myself for a while, which I probably would have, if he weren't off to a conference in Salisbury for two days on Monday . . . Oh, that was quick, here's our lunch already.'

They continued to chat as Fen wolfed down a beef and horseradish baguette and all the chips, while Julia nibbled at a cheese sandwich, and felt the vodka going to her head.

'I was wondering,' she said, as they strolled back outside into a sudden blaze of autumn sunshine, 'if we could perhaps go to the house now. I need to decide if I'm going to stay there, because if I don't, I should book myself into a B & B.'

'If you don't, my parents will insist you stay with us,' Fen informed her. 'We're very close by. In fact the mill used to be on our land, until Daddy sold it, and half an acre, to your father.'

Julia was surprised, and curious. 'You live with your parents?' she said.

Fen's eyebrows made a comical rise. 'The house is big enough for half a dozen families,' she replied, 'but Bob and I only moved in a year ago, after Daddy's second heart attack. He wanted us to, in order to avoid inheritance tax when he and Mummy finally do pop off, otherwise David and I – that's my brother – would probably end up having to sell the place. David has an apartment in the east wing, but he spends most of his time over at Chapel Amble, where he has a scrummy restaurant and an even scrummier partner called Charles, who's a brilliant carpenter.'

Julia smiled. Everything sounded so idyllic about Fen's life and family that she could almost feel envious. 'I was wondering what my father did for a living?' she said, as they headed back towards Fen's office.

'He had a landscaping business that was quite successful actually. He had to give it up when he became ill, unfortunately, but we sold it for enough to make ends meet.'

'And Gwen? Did she work?'

'She taught at the village school. I think it kind of made up for not having children of her own.' Coming to a stop at her office door, she glanced at her watch and said, 'I guess the best thing to do now is for you to jump in your car and follow me to Shallard's Cross. Where did you park?'

'Over by the Shire Hall.'

'Excellent. My car's there too, so I'll just pop inside to pick up the file we prepared for you, and we'll be on our way.'

The drive to Shallard's Cross, the village closest to the mill and Bower family estate, ended up taking little more than twenty minutes, mostly on the main road, until they turned off down a narrow, winding lane that was bordered by high hedges and grassy banks for the last three miles. For a while they were trapped behind a tractor and, though she'd have preferred to absorb her surroundings, Julia found herself caught in the overriding fear that Josh might be with Sylvia right now, making love to her and planning how he was going to end his marriage. The dread of it was building to such a pitch inside her that she could feel herself starting to panic. Her chest was tight, her mind was entering a turmoil of horror and fear. Somehow she managed to draw herself back, but then she was thinking of her mother, and how she hadn't even called to check Julia was all right after she'd stormed off in a temper the day before. But what did she expect? Her mother had never shown much concern about her in the past, so she'd be some kind of fool to think she would now.

Fortunately, the blackness of her reveries was wiped away as the tractor turned off into a farm and she followed Fen over the brink of a hill to find herself faced with the most breathtaking vista of gently undulating fields and forests, spreading like a Utopian mirage throughout the valley before her. 'Oh my,' she murmured, feeling the beauty of it stirring inside her. Though the sun was weak and the sky colourless and low, the air was clear enough for her to see for miles, and the landscape was so graceful, yet rugged, so rousing, yet calming that already she could feel some of the knots inside her starting to unfurl.

She continued after Fen's Volvo, heading downhill towards a small village that clustered at the side of the valley. She found herself remembering a family holiday they'd once spent in Cornwall, when she was just fifteen, and her father had taken her on a tour of Daphne du Maurier's world. It had been so thrilling imagining all her favourite characters on the hilltops, in the creeks and valleys, galloping across the moors, climbing the cliffs and sailing over the horizon. She wondered how often he'd recalled those exhilarating days in the years since he'd left, and if he'd remembered them with as much emotion as she was feeling now.

Noticing that Fen was signalling to go left, Julia hit her indicator too, and looped around a giant horse chestnut to turn into an open driveway where they bumped over a cattle grid and stream. A winding dirt track led on to a rambling old farmhouse with late-blooming roses around the porch, and a roughly tended lawn at the front. There were a couple of cars in the yard, both being washed by a young lad in overalls and wellies, who turned at the sound of someone arriving.

Fen waved out, but kept on going, around the side of the house, past an old wooden barn and a field straggled with sheep, following the track as it snaked off into a small wood. Here it ran alongside the stream for a while, before crossing over a quaint little bridge and emerging into a sweeping grassy glade where the mill house and its garden nestled in a perfect pastoral setting.

As Julia drove towards it she felt her heart turn over, for she could hardly have imagined anything more picturesque or inviting than the sleepy-looking whitewashed mill with its grey stone walls and grey slate roof, and magnificent black wooden wheel that churned the water in the stream beside it. Behind was an extremely grand red maple, and a gently sloping lawn that blended into the fields beyond, which stretched on out to the horizon to meet a seemingly endless sky.

Fen came to a stop on a patch of gravel that was laid out in front of the house, where three white wooden steps rose to a white wooden deck with ivy-clad balustrades and brimming pots of pansies, leading to the mill's front door. Julia pulled up beside her, and feeling slightly dazed by the sheer magic of the place, sat where she was for a moment, drinking it all in.

'Gorgeous, isn't it?' Fen smiled, coming to join her as she got out of the car. 'I used to fantasise about living here as a child. I saw myself as Sleeping Beauty, with Prince Charming hacking his way through the woods to find me. Alas, it was only ever my brother David who made it, and as he had his own designs on the place that didn't include a stupid sister, my dreams were shattered at a very early age.'

Julia had to laugh.

'Come on, I have the keys,' Fen said, almost as though they were on an adventure. 'Let me show you around.'

As she trotted up the steps and across the

wooden deck to the French doors that served as an entrance, Julia went after her, looking around at the flower beds that surrounded the house, and then off to the far side where she spotted another barn-like building in the distance, and what was clearly an orchard in the next field.

'Those are the stables over there,' Fen told her, seeing her looking. 'Do you ride?'

'I've been known to.'

Fen seemed delighted. 'Well, if you fancy a bit of a hack while you're here, just say the word.'

Liking the idea of cantering out across the moors with Fen, Julia said, 'I take it the stables belong to the house we passed, which presumably is your parents'?'

'Absolutely. Mum's at the hairdressers this afternoon, and Dad's gone to Truro with Rico and David, but I'll take you over there later. They're absolutely dying to meet you, but don't worry if you're not up to it today . . .'

'No, I'd love to meet them.'

Clearly pleased with the answer, Fen jabbed a large, old-fashioned key in the lock and turned it. '*Et voilà!*' she declared, moving on ahead and sweeping her arms out for Julia to admire the spacious kitchen they'd entered.

Julia's eyes opened wide with surprise as she took in the immaculate peppermint green cabinets and dressers, with their flowery bone-china tea sets and shining beechwood counter tops. Though not exactly her taste, it was quaint beyond belief and she couldn't help loving it. In the middle of the room was a round pine table with a lavish bowl of fresh fruit at its centre, and a decorative old coach lamp hanging over it. The floor was laid with old flagstones, the ceiling was striped with gnarled oak beams, and across the back wall was a genuine inglenook fireplace with a cast-iron wood burner in the hearth.

'Amazing, isn't it?' Fen said admiringly. 'It was all Gwen's doing. She loved to cook, so Dougie splashed out on all this for her sixtieth birthday.' Her pleasure became edged with sadness as she added, 'At least she got a few years out of it before she went. Tilde's kept it up to scratch since, though Dougie always treated it gently. He used to say it was a part of Gwen, and she'd want him to keep it looking nice.'

'It sounds as though they were very happy together,' Julia said, wishing again that she could have been a part of it.

Fen nodded. 'Very. Can't you feel it?'

Julia looked around and after a while she thought that, yes, maybe she could.

Fen's eyes showed her delight. 'This place has always had good vibes, even before Dougie and Gwen lived here,' she said. 'They just made them better.'

Julia walked over to look through the cookery books in the deep-set window sill, and a bundle of opened letters that was stuffed inside an old-fashioned rack. Horse brasses and dried flowers hung from the walls, along with amateurish paintings of the spectacular views outside, and one of the mill itself. Everything about the place seemed so perfect that she could almost feel unnerved by it, though she guessed that probably had a lot more to do with her emotional state than any kind of reality.

'Mum said she'd get a few things in for you,' Fen was saying, as she pulled open one of the peppermint green doors to reveal a large fridge inside. 'Ah yes, she has. Milk, eggs, bread, wine, water, ham, cheese, fresh salad . . . She seems to have thought of most things, but if you need anything else there's a small shop in the village, or a supermarket about ten minutes away. I'll show you later how to get there. And of course there's always our kitchen to raid.'

Feeling slightly overwhelmed by so much generosity, Julia was about to thank her, when Fen took off along a narrow hallway to one side of the fireplace. 'On your right,' she announced, 'is the bathroom, on your left a study and at the end is a bedroom. We moved Dougie down here after his stroke. It was easier than having to keep negotiating the stairs.'

Julia stepped in behind her to find a room that was sunny and fresh, with pale lemon walls, mustard curtains, and a matching candlewick bedspread adorned with deep lavender cushions and a similar-colour throw. 'Tilde's changed all the sheets,' Fen assured her. 'Everything's nice and clean, even the carpets I think.' She looked down, and seeing a pair of slippers next to the bed she said, 'Oh dear, I don't think those should be there.'

Julia looked at the slippers too, and having detected the tremor in Fen's voice she put a comforting hand on her arm.

'It's OK,' Fen assured her. 'Silly me. I bought them for him, you see. A couple of Christmases ago. He told me they were horrible, then proceeded to wear them every day. I guess we should pop them away,' and picking them up, she dropped them inside a large hand-painted wardrobe and quickly closed the door. 'Going to miss him,' she said, 'but when you're ready, if you need a hand going through everything, I'll be happy to help.'

Running out of ways to say thank you, Julia merely smiled, and thought how lucky her father was to have known this woman, who must have been like a daughter to him.

'Sitting room,' Fen stated, and leading the way back into the kitchen, she began to mount the wooden staircase that rose across one wall.

The sitting room was another lovely surprise, with its high, vaulted ceiling and criss-cross beams, huge stone fireplace, and three comfy sofas. Clearly her father had used one end of it as a reading area, for beside the window where the mill wheel could be seen going round was a deep leather chair with an Anglepoise lamp behind, and bookshelves full of encyclopedias, gardening tomes, and, Julia noted with a poignant smile, the complete works of Daphne du Maurier. She wondered if she might find a copy of her own meagre effort tucked away somewhere, but there was no sign of it, which, though disappointing, was hardly surprising, when her father had never known her as Julia Thayne.

Spotting a clutch of photographs on a side table, she went to take a look. 'This must be Gwen,' she said, picking one up, and studying the round, open face, with bright, knowing eyes and a laughing mouth.

'Yes, that's her,' Fen confirmed, coming to peer over her shoulder.

'She gives the impression she's flirting with the photographer,' Julia commented.

Fen chuckled. 'That's because Dougie was holding the camera. They hardly ever stopped flirting with each other, those two. They were a treat to watch.'

Thinking that was how she and Josh had always been, Julia put the photo down and picked up another. It felt strange to see her father looking older in the picture than he had at the funeral home, but she knew that people often appeared younger in death than they had during the last years of their life.

'That was taken about six years ago, at a local wedding,' Fen informed her. 'He was one of the ushers. Looks very smart in his tails, doesn't he?'

Julia nodded.

The other pictures were of people she didn't recognise, except one of Fen with her children, and a few more of Gwen. Then her heart turned over as she glanced at another table and spotted a photograph she knew only too well. It had been taken not long after Daniel was born, and showed him being clutched in a four-year-old Shannon's arms.

'How did he get this?' she said, going to pick it up.

Fen shook her head. 'I haven't seen it before,' she answered. 'I take it they're yours?'

'Yes. But how did it get here?'

Fen was at a loss. 'Could your mother have sent it?' she ventured.

Julia's cynicism came out in a scoff. 'I don't think so. As far as I'm aware she doesn't even know where he lived. Besides, it's too nice a gesture for her. It wouldn't even enter her head that he might like a picture of his grandchildren.'

'What about another member of your family?'

'There's only my aunt and uncle, and they don't go in for nice gestures much either. Well, my aunt, possibly, but she doesn't even breathe without my uncle's approval.'

Fen was curious. 'So I wonder how he got it? It's not the kind of shot he could have taken himself, and anyway, I can't see him being that furtive.'

'It was done in a studio, as part of a set,' Julia told her. 'Josh and I are in the others.'

'So maybe he got it from the photographer – except how would he know it had been taken?'

'And how long has he had it? You say you haven't seen it before.'

'No, but I'm so used to the photos in here, I don't really notice them any more. He could have put it there last week, or last year.'

'I wonder if he has any others,' Julia said, looking around. Her eyes stopped at one of the deep window sills where several more photos were positioned around a big Chinese vase. 'Oh my God, there's a school photo of Shannon,' she murmured, going to pick it up. 'And one of Dan in his cricket gear. This is amazing, but how on earth did he get them?'

Fen was shaking her head.

Julia gazed down into her children's faces. 'Whatever the answer, I'm glad he had them,' she said. 'Actually, I'm glad he *wanted* them.' But even as she spoke the words her heart turned cold, for there could be a horribly sinister reason for them being here that she really didn't want to think about at all.

'I'm surprised he never pointed them out when he was telling me about you,' Fen remarked. 'He presumably had them then.'

Julia shrugged. 'Another mystery waiting to be solved,' she said quietly.

Fen waggled her eyebrows. 'Never could resist one of those,' she said, and they both smiled.

'So, do you want to see the main bedroom?' Fen said. 'It's in through here,' and going past the fireplace, she pulled a curtain back from a door, and walked on in. 'Oh, dear Tilde,' she murmured fondly, as Julia joined her. 'Fresh flowers and potpourri, and Gwen's best white lacy linens, because that's what Gwen would have wanted.'

'It's lovely,' Julia said, taking in the king-size wrought-iron bedstead, antique pine furniture, and plush burgundy carpet that matched the velvet curtains. 'I take it that opens into an attic,' she said, looking up at a small trapdoor.

'Correct. There's quite a bit up there, so it should keep you busy for a while.'

Julia gave her a look and once again they smiled.

'There's no bathroom up here, I'm afraid,' Fen said, 'which is mainly why we moved Dougie downstairs at the end. Obviously you can sleep down there too, if you'd prefer, but it's so beautifully cosy up here, don't you think?'

'Exactly where you'd want Prince Charming to find you,' Julia teased.

Fen laughed. 'I'll try to make sure it's not David who comes to the rescue,' she said, 'because I promise, that really would be a let-down since he's gay. He only came out a couple of years ago, actually, a bit of a blow for Mum and Dad, but they're slowly beginning to accept it now, and Charles, his partner, is an absolute sweetheart. He taught Dougie to surf last summer. You should have seen the pair of them, out there in the waves, struggling with the boards. Dougie never quite got the knack, but he was a star the way he tried. Put Daddy to shame, I can tell you, largely because Daddy didn't feel comfortable about being around someone like Charles without many clothes on. I ask you. As if anyone would fancy him, the great lump. Love him to bits, of course, but he's still a great lump.'

Julia was laughing.

Fen gave her a wink and started back into the sitting room. 'Shall I help you bring your things in?' she offered, apparently taking it for granted that Julia had decided to stay.

'I don't have much,' Julia told her. 'I might ask Josh to bring more when he comes on Saturday. Shannon has a ten-day half-term this time, and right now I'm thinking we'll probably spend the whole time here.' Quite what Josh would make of that when she told him she had no idea, nor was she certain that she really would stay for so long. All she knew for the moment was that she loved it here already, and since Sylvia was going to be in New York next week, and Josh would be sailing with Dan, there seemed no reason for her not to take at least a few days to try and recover from the blows of the past forty-eight hours.

After Fen left, half an hour or so later, Julia wandered back inside the house intending to go upstairs and take a nap before joining Fen's family for dinner. However, she found herself coming to a halt at the kitchen table where they'd spent the past half an hour chatting over a cup of tea and some digestive biscuits. As she stood there staring down at the delicate pieces of china and scattered crumbs, she was trying to recall what they'd discussed, but for some reason she couldn't. It didn't matter though. None of it had been important, except in the way she'd felt so comfortable with Fen. She wondered if she'd ever needed a friend more, but she wasn't about to saddle a stranger with her problems, no matter how kind and compassionate Fen clearly was. She thought of Pauline, but knew she'd never turn to her, she was far too close to Sylvia, and had very likely known about the affair all along, which, to Julia's mind, made her almost as guilty. And as for Sylvia … Even to think of her made Julia stiffen with loathing, and she could only feel thankful that the bitch hadn't had the guts to be in touch these past twenty-four hours, because Julia was a very long way from ready to deal with her yet, in fact were she to see Sylvia now, feeling as she did, she shuddered at the thought of what she might do.

She kept wondering which of them had started the affair, who'd actually had the gall to suggest it would be the best way to save Josh's marriage. Just to think of it stirred such a fury inside her that she wanted to lash out at Josh with all her might. How could he have been so stupid, or blind, or self-deceiving ever to think that screwing another woman would do anything but damage, or even destroy his marriage? And that he'd chosen Sylvia

Holland, her so-called best friend, the woman he'd always been so afraid would influence Julia away from him, was something that could drive her insane with rage.

Too exhausted to keep the anger going, she took herself upstairs to look at the photos of Shannon and Dan again, for right now, they felt like the only good and true part of her life. Picking them up from the window sill, she gazed down at their innocent young faces, a sublime mix of her and Josh, and felt such a build-up of love that the longing to hold them was hard to bear. How could he have done it, she kept asking herself. Hadn't he thought about the children? Did it matter so much to have sex that he'd put it before everything else? Or maybe he was so obsessed with Sylvia, the way so many men had been over the years, that he wouldn't let anything stand in the way. The fear of that tore so cruelly at her heart, that her eyes filled with tears. What if he couldn't give Sylvia up? What if it had gone so far now that he was willing to pay the ultimate price to have her?

Turning from the window, as though to escape her own torment, she carried the photographs to the sofa and sank wearily into it. For a moment she allowed her eyes to close, then quite suddenly they were open again. She kept seeing them together, bodies entwined in the throes of passion, Josh's mouth on Sylvia's, his hands on her skin. She knew how he looked at each moment, how he felt and touched, how he kissed and was able to give more pleasure than probably even Sylvia had ever known. She started to choke. She couldn't stand it, she just couldn't. She needed him to be here now, swearing it had meant nothing and that he'd already given her up. But even so, he'd never be able to erase the fact that it had happened, it would be with them for ever now. Though there was no doubt in her mind that she still loved him, this had changed things between them, and in a way that was frightening her almost as much as the dread of him leaving.

In another effort to put it from her mind, she reached for a photo of her father and sat staring into his softly twinkling eyes. The two most important men in her life, and both had let her down so badly that she couldn't even begin to think where that left her now. She was so tired that she soon gave up trying, and after a while she could feel herself sinking into the wonderfully soothing air of calm that seemed to exude from the walls of this house. If only she could stay here for ever and forget about everything, but just as she was drifting into the sublime release of sleep, her mobile started to ring downstairs. Suspecting it was Josh, she was tempted to ignore it, but if it was the children they'd only worry if she didn't answer, and since it probably wouldn't help to start avoiding Josh anyway, she pulled herself up and ran down the stairs.

'Hi, it's me,' he said when she answered.

'Hi,' she responded.

'How's it going down there?'

'OK.'

'Shannon tells me you went to the chapel of rest. Was that OK?'

'It was hard, but I didn't expect it to be easy. Did you negotiate a good film deal?'

'Still a few things to be ironed out, but it's not bad. Where are you now?'

'At my father's house. I'll be staying here. There's probably a phone, I'll give you the number when I find it.'

'What's it like?'

'The house? Very nice. You'll see it on Saturday, if you're still coming.'

'Of course I am, why wouldn't I be?'

'I just wondered if you might have plans to go to New York.'

He sighed. 'No, I don't have plans to go to New York, you know what I'm doing.'

Taking the phone with her, she walked back upstairs and returned to the sofa.

'You sound tired,' he told her.

'I am.'

'How did it go with the solicitor?'

'Fine.' She knew he was waiting for her to expand, but she didn't.

'This is like pulling teeth,' he said irritably.

'Well, I'm sorry if you're finding it difficult,' she replied, 'but frankly, I don't know what I want to say to you right now. I could have done with your support when I found out he was dead, and it would have helped if you'd been there with me today . . .'

'How the hell can both of us just take off and leave the children?'

'Don't speak to me like that, Josh. You don't have the right to be angry after what you've done.'

He fell silent, and as the seconds ticked on she

gazed at the rain on the window and felt a terrible sadness welling up inside her. 'Do you have any understanding at all of what I'm going through?' she asked him. 'You've lost your own father, so surely you can remember what that was like. And what great leap of imagination would it take to work out how you'd feel if I'd been sleeping with another man?'

'First, my father was a constant in my life,' he responded. 'Second . . .'

'So you think, because my father left me all those years ago, that it doesn't hurt as much to lose him? Is that what you're saying?'

'If I'm wrong, tell me.'

'You're wrong. You see, it's not only his death I'm mourning, it's all those lost years. The memories we'll never have.'

There was a note of contrition in his voice as he said, 'OK, I'm sorry.'

She let her eyes drift to her father's face, then on around the room as she tried to imagine him here, and even wondered if, on some other-worldly level, he was. What would he tell her to do now? Would he know how she should resolve this with Josh?

'The children are breaking up today,' Josh reminded her. 'They should be at home soon.'

'I'll call them. Is your mother there?'

'Yes.'

'Have you told her about Sylvia?'

'Don't be ridiculous.'

Anger flashed in her eyes. 'That's how it might seem to you,' she snapped, 'to me it seems like deceit and betrayal.'

His voice was equally as tight as he said, 'Do you think now's the right time to be having this conversation?'

'It's a shame we have to have it at all.'

'Jesus Christ, I don't know what to say to you, Julia. I'm sorry it happened, OK? I'm sorry you had to find out, and I'm even sorrier we got to a point where I needed to do it.'

Ordinarily she might have exploded at that, but right now she simply didn't have it in her, so in a coldly cutting voice she said, 'You're right, Josh, now isn't the time to be having this conversation, but let me tell you this, when we do finally talk we won't get anywhere if you don't start accepting that *you* are responsible for your actions, not me. It was *you* who screwed Sylvia, *you* who lied to me. There was nothing dishonest in my behaviour towards you. I couldn't help what was happening to me . . .'

'But you didn't even try to do anything about it.'

'That still doesn't make it my fault that you cheated on me. Anyway, we're not achieving anything here, so I'm going to ring off now.'

Without a word of objection he said a terse goodbye, and after hearing the line go dead, she clicked off her own phone and let her head fall back against the cushions. She could easily picture his face now, taut with anger, lips pale, struggling to keep his temper in check as he tried to get on with his work.

She hadn't told him anything about Fen, she realised, or about her father, or the will, or even the photographs of Shannon and Dan. Nor, she had to admit, did she want to. It wasn't that she was deliberately shutting him out, she just didn't know how to open up and let him in. It was scaring her to think that she'd started rejecting him on another level now, because she didn't want that to happen. She loved him, and was desperate not to lose him, but she was seeing him so differently now, for there was no doubt the deceit had somehow diminished him. He was no longer the man she'd always respected and looked up to, the man who'd never failed to put her and the children first, who'd been the very centre of their lives. Now what she saw was a stubborn and selfish man, who'd let his basic physical urges come before everything she'd always believed he valued most.

Chapter Seven

It was sunlight, streaming in through the curtains, that finally woke Julia the next morning, and the sound of voices outside. Having slept so deeply it took her a moment to recall where she was. As it came back to her she could only wish herself asleep again, for it seemed the more time that went by, the harder it was becoming to cope with what Josh had done. Then, remembering it was the funeral today, and that she owed the Bowers an apology for failing to make dinner last night after falling asleep on the sofa, she pushed back the covers and swung her feet to the floor.

For one alarming moment she thought she was going to faint, and dropped her head between her knees. She'd had virtually nothing to eat since the sandwich yesterday, and couldn't say she felt particularly hungry now, but she knew she should have something, for she certainly didn't want to black out at the funeral.

Wondering what the time was, she started out to the sitting room, and was just picking up her mobile when the sound of voices reached her again. Going to the window she opened the curtains a fraction and saw two men outside, standing next to the Porsche, apparently inspecting it, one quite elderly, the other much younger. Suspecting the older man was Fen's father, she quickly dragged on her jeans and a T-shirt and ran downstairs to introduce herself.

Her first attempts to get outside were hampered by the locked French doors. She looked around for the key, unable to think where she'd put it, for she didn't even remember locking up. Spotting it on the doormat, she snatched it up and let herself out onto the porch just as the two men approached the steps. The older man smiled at her.

'Hello,' she gasped, trying to tidy her hair with her fingers. 'You must be Mr Bower, Fen's father. I'm Julia Thayne. It's a pleasure to meet you.'

'Likewise,' he responded in a deep, plummy voice that managed to convey as much friendliness as his rich hazel eyes. He was tall and portly, and there was a sprightliness to his greying amber hair that made it the obvious forerunner to Fen's fiery crinkles. 'And please call me Peter,' he added, shaking her hand. 'This is my nephew, Mauricio, or Rico, as we call him. He's visiting us from Italy.'

'How do you do,' Rico said, leaning forward to take her hand. 'I am very pleased to meet Dougie's daughter.'

'Hello,' she said, seeing immediately what Fen had meant about how good-looking he was, for those dark brooding eyes would certainly get most women's pulses racing, as would that impossibly sensuous mouth. There was something about him, she realised, that was reminding her of Josh, though he was neither as tall nor as well built, so maybe it was just the darkness of the hair, or more likely the powerful aura of maleness that she knew so well in her husband. She even found herself faintly responding to it, and regretting the way she must look, which was absurd when he'd hardly be interested in someone her age, nor did she have the remotest wish to complicate her life to any greater degree than it already was.

Turning back to Peter Bower she said, 'I'm so sorry I didn't make it over last night. I dropped off, and it was so late when I woke . . .'

'Please, please,' he interrupted, waving her apology away. 'You were exhausted, which is quite understandable, so we guessed what had happened. Fen popped over around seven, just to check on you, and found you zizzing away peacefully on the sofa, so she locked the door and posted the key through. I trust you had a good night.'

'Very,' she replied. 'I don't even know what the time is now.'

He checked his watch. 'Almost ten,' he told her. 'Rico and I thought we'd stroll over to see if you need anything. Actually, my wife sent us, she wanted to get us out of the way, so if you've got a cup of coffee on offer . . .'

'Oh, yes, of course. Please come in.'

Once back inside she looked around the kitchen, wondering where everything was.

'Why don't you let me?' Peter suggested. 'I know this kitchen better than my own, since I've been allowed in it more often.'

Julia smiled and glanced at Rico, and as their

eyes met, she was aware of the shyness Fen had mentioned, for he seemed almost embarrassed to have been discovered looking at her.

'Dougie tried to arrange today,' Peter was telling her, as he filled the coffee-maker with water. 'He had it all planned out – a quiet ceremony, just family . . .' He broke off. 'I hope you don't mind that he thought of us that way.'

'No, of course not,' she assured him.

'He was the best friend I ever had,' he continued. 'Like a brother, in a way, but without all the nonsense that happens when blood's involved.' He shook his head, as though in wonderment at such an excellent relationship. Then his eyes came back to hers. 'Just can't work out why he never told me about you,' he said. 'In all the years we knew each other, he never once mentioned that he'd been married before, or had any children. Can't imagine why he kept it to himself. Keep asking myself if Gwen knew, but if she did she never mentioned it either.'

Realising how hurt he was by her father's failure to confide in him, and that he was hoping she'd be able to explain it, Julia said, 'I'm not sure what happened when he left my mother, but I think it was so painful that neither of them was ever really able to talk about it.'

'She never told you?'

Julia shook her head.

Looking more mystified than ever, he returned to his coffee-making, and without thinking Julia glanced at Rico again. This time it was her turn to feel embarrassed, for though he appeared to be reading the slogan on the front of her T-shirt which merely said St Tropez, she realised it must be perfectly apparent that she'd not taken the time to put on a bra. She turned quickly away, not wanting him to know that he'd been caught looking, or to see the way her nipples were automatically responding.

'As I was saying,' Peter continued, 'Dougie tried to plan it all out for today, a small affair, just us, and Tilde.' He chuckled as he spooned coffee grounds into a filter. 'I told him he didn't stand a chance of that, and it turns out I'm right. The crematorium is going to be packed, and Laura, my wife, is over there panicking about whether she's catered for enough people. The vicar's been on the phone already this morning, still not able to decide who should do the readings. He doesn't want to hurt anyone's feelings, but he's had so many requests if he grants them all we could find ourselves there until Monday, he informs me.'

Not knowing what to say, Julia merely smiled and started to search for some cups.

'I told Dougie it would be like this,' Peter went on, 'but he wouldn't listen. He'd have made our lives so much easier if he'd believed everyone would want to be there, and decided himself who he wanted to do the readings – and ride in the cars.' He turned around. 'Which reminds me, as his daughter, you'll be in the first one, naturally.'

'As his friend I hope you'll be there with me,' she responded.

Clearly very pleased with the invite, he said, 'It would be an honour, but maybe you'd like to ask Fen. It would mean a lot to her. And David, my son. Laura, Rico and I can travel in the car behind. Tilde will come with us.'

'Then, of course, that's what we'll do. Will we go from your house?'

'I hope that's all right.'

'Please, Peter, he was your friend, and from what I can tell you knew him probably better than anyone. I'm just glad to be here, to meet you all, and get to know him through you.'

Peter nodded, and let his eyes drop to the floor.

Seeming to realise he needed a moment to collect himself, Rico stepped forward saying, 'Please allow an Italian to finish the coffee.'

As Rico reached him Peter put a hand on his shoulder and gave him a squeeze of thanks. 'Dougie told me if he had anything to do with it,' Peter continued, 'the sun would shine today, so I think we can assume he has something to do with it, don't you?'

Julia looked outside and smiled. 'It really is glorious this morning,' she said, drinking in the sparkling autumnal colours, and feeling the crispness of the air as it drifted in through the open door. 'It could hardly be more perfect.'

At that moment her mobile rang, and seeing it was Josh she excused herself and quickly clicked on. 'Can I call you back?' she asked. 'In about an hour.'

'Of course. Are you OK?'

'Yes, I'm fine. Are you?'

'I miss you,' he said.

Though it pleased her to hear it, she didn't repeat it, because she was unwilling to give him anything of herself right now.

An hour and a half later she was in the bedroom, getting ready to leave, when he rang again. He made no comment about her failure to call him, merely said, 'I have to go into a meeting soon. Is it OK to talk now?'

'Yes, it's fine.'

'So are you feeling OK about the funeral?'

'I think so. I've been wondering if I should offer to do a reading. Do you think I should?'

'Do you want to?'

'I'm not sure. It doesn't really feel right. I hardly knew him, while these people clearly considered him one of their own.'

'Then I'd leave it to them. It'll probably mean something just to see you there.'

Julia felt a flutter of nerves and stopped applying her mascara. 'You know what's odd,' she said, watching her reflection in the mirror, 'no-one's mentioned my sister, and she hasn't bothered to get in touch either.'

'Do you think your mother's told her?'

'She's bound to have. Why would she keep it from her?'

'No idea, but you know Pam's never seemed particularly concerned about the way your father left, so maybe she feels it would be hypocritical to start pretending she cares now. Was she mentioned in the will, by the way?'

'No. That's the other thing that's odd. Everything goes to me, except a small bequest to his housekeeper and a backgammon set to his friend, Peter.'

'Well, if Pam's got wind of that, I doubt it'll have done anything to warm her towards him.'

'I don't know how she could have, unless there was some kind of communication between them before he died, which seems unlikely, don't you think? To tell the truth, I feel embarrassed for her, that she's not here. After all, everyone knows he had two daughters, even if they're not mentioning her, and it's not good, failing to turn up for your own father's funeral, is it?'

Josh's tone was sombre as he said, 'It suggests she knows something we don't.'

For Julia it was as though an ominous cloud had slipped into a clear sky, and all she wanted was to make it go away.

As though sensing it, Josh said, 'If I were you I'd try not to think about any of that today. Whatever went on between them, or whatever the truth is, he's dead now, and you're not going to change anything, so let his friends give him a decent send-off.'

'Of course,' she responded, and happy to let the shadows disperse, she turned from the mirror and shrugged off her robe to begin getting dressed. 'What time are you starting out tomorrow?' she asked.

'Early. I want to make sure Shannon's settled in down there before I take off with Dan.'

Julia blinked. 'She's coming to me,' she said. 'That hardly warrants her father having to make sure she's *settled in*.'

'You know what I mean. And Dan will want to spend some time with you before we leave.'

'I was thinking of inviting you to stay the night,' she told him, though it was the first time it had occurred to her.

'I see. I need an invitation now, do I?'

She was about to say no, of course not, when she realised that actually maybe he did. After all this was her house, something she owned without him, and though she'd never had a problem sharing everything with him before, considering their current difficulties maybe she wanted this to stay as her own. 'I'd rather we didn't get into a row this morning,' she said. 'I have to leave in a few minutes.'

'Of course. Would you like me to call later?'

'I expect the children will want to.'

'Then I'll talk to you at the same time. I hope everything goes well today.'

'Thank you.'

'You know where I am if you need me.'

Managing not to ask if that would be with Sylvia, she thanked him again, and rang off.

Her underwear was laid out neatly on the bed, and after stepping into her panties she picked up the bra. As she fastened it she turned back to the mirror and found herself remembering how she'd caught Rico staring at her earlier. Once again she felt embarrassed by how brazen she must have looked, but worse was knowing she'd greeted Peter Bower that way. Fortunately he hadn't seemed to notice, or was simply too polite to let it show if he had, and she could only wish that her nipples weren't quite so prominent, even when not aroused. Then for one heady moment she considered telling Josh about Rico, letting him know how handsome he was, and how captivated he'd seemed by her – or her breasts, anyway. But knowing Josh, he'd see straight through it, and besides, trying to make him jealous was hardly going to improve the situation they were in.

A few minutes later Fen called out from downstairs.

'Almost ready,' Julia called back, and taking a black cashmere jacket from a hanger she slipped it on over her matching knee-length dress and sheer black tights, and began stuffing make-up, tissues and money into her handbag. Then, feeling her nerves starting to churn, she quickly checked herself in the mirror, wanting to make sure she looked her best for her father. As usual, her lips appeared too full and red, so after applying a pale shade of lipstick in an attempt to tone them down, she ruffled her hair a little to bring more strands around her face and make her eyes seem bigger, then grabbing her phone she ran downstairs to join Fen and her brother, David, who'd driven over in the Land Rover to pick her up.

The funeral cars were already lined up outside the Bowers' farmhouse when they got there, two enormous black Mercedes, and the hearse bearing a coffin covered with flowers. Unwilling to make herself connect it with her father for the moment, she turned to greet the attractive older woman with lustrous brown eyes and an infectious smile who was coming towards her.

'I'm Laura Bower,' she said, taking Julia's hand and using it to pull her into an embrace. 'I'm very sorry we're meeting under these circumstances. You have my condolences, naturally, and I hope it will be some comfort to see how loved your father was.' Her voice was only faintly accented, while her tone was as warm as her eyes.

'Thank you,' Julia smiled. 'And thank you for organising everything.' She was looking at the marquee that was being set up on the lawn, and the caterers buzzing around it.

'Darling, I think we're ready to leave now,' Peter Bower said, coming to put a hand on his wife's arm.

'I hope we will have the chance to talk later,' Laura said, embracing Julia again. 'It will be a busy day, I think, but if it starts to feel too much . . .' She left the sentence unfinished, and allowed her husband to steer her towards the second Mercedes, while David, who greatly resembled his mother, escorted Julia and Fen to the first one where Reece Allston and his father, in top hats and tails, were holding the doors open for them all to get in.

They travelled slowly through the country lanes, a small but stately procession that grew by the mile as friends and neighbours fell in behind. Julia barely noticed, however, for she was keeping her eyes down, not wanting to look at the hearse in front. She was starting to feel strangely disconnected now, even slightly panicky, and in a way angry, for she didn't want it all to be over like this, to know that she'd never see her father again. She needed him here, in her life, not just to understand why he left, but to be a part of the love he'd shared with his wife Gwen and their friends.

As though sensing her turmoil, Fen slipped a hand in hers and gave it a squeeze, while David produced a most welcome hip flask.

The brandy burned her throat and fortified her, and when he nodded for her to have more, she did.

By the time they arrived at the crematorium so many were already there that they were spilling out of the doors, most of them dressed in black, some with hats, others with flowers in their lapels. Julia guessed they'd all be eager to catch a glimpse of her, and for one bewildering moment she felt like a movie star turning up for a premiere. It occurred to her how much her father would enjoy that, and she experienced a small surge of pleasure at the link it seemed to forge.

As she walked towards the crematorium with Fen beside her, she looked around at the faces watching her pass, and wondered who they all were. Was each one known to her father, or were there strangers present, men or women, or even children, who'd come from the past with sinister intent?

Forcing the ugly thoughts from her mind, she walked on into the building and was immediately assailed by the scent of flowers. For some reason she felt a strange coldness descending through her, followed by a sudden heat. She moved along the aisle, keeping her eyes lowered and listening to the recording of a Gluck sonata that was filling the hall with its gentle grandeur. She wondered if her father had chosen the music himself, and suspecting he had she found it easing some of the tension inside her.

The front row was empty, waiting for her and the Bowers to fill it. The vicar came over to greet her, offered his sympathies, and expressed a hope that she would find the service comforting and fitting. He'd known Dougie well, he said, so had been able to make his address personal, and, he hoped, as uplifting as Dougie himself.

Laura Bower arrived with Tilde and went to sit at the end of the row. Spaces were left for Peter and David to join them. The vicar returned to the altar, then the music stopped and everyone fell silent. Moments later the music began again. This time it was an aria from Salieri, so stirring and sublime that Julia knew the coffin was coming in now, riding on the shoulders of six of her father's closest friends. She didn't look round, but could hear people reaching into pockets and handbags for tissues. Next to her Fen's shoulder started to shake, and Julia reached for her hand.

They stayed that way throughout the service, not letting go of each other, needing the support of their new friendship and to share the link binding them to the man to whom they were saying goodbye. Though Julia listened to the readings, sang the hymns and closed her eyes for the prayers, she was starting to feel as though this was all being experienced by somebody else – a teenage girl, maybe, whose ghost had come to stand beside her beloved daddy's coffin. She could almost see herself there, gangly and dark-haired, head bowed as the core of her life was removed. How would she go on without him? He couldn't leave her again, he just couldn't.

They were moving the coffin now, sliding it towards a red curtain. The vicar was blessing it. The curtain glided back and Fen's grip became so hard it hurt. Julia's eyes stayed with the casket. He couldn't see the teenager following, or the grown woman watching. He was going to another world, a different place in time, and would never come back.

The coffin moved forward and the curtain started to close. Her chest was so tight she was barely able to breathe. The teenager didn't want to let go. She couldn't. It was all becoming tangled inside her now, voices, pain, fear. Somewhere in the darkest corners of her soul it was as though a raging current was coming to sweep her away. She could feel herself being swallowed into it, falling back and back . . .

She lifted her hands to her face and felt Fen's arm go round her. She needed Josh to be here, and Shannon and Dan. They were her life now, and she must hold onto them. Her father had gone. He couldn't come back, but even as she struggled to accept that, it was as though a terrible blackness was closing over her, sucking her into a void of endless loneliness and despair.

By the time they all filed out of the crematorium Julia had herself back under control, and was able to greet the people Fen was introducing with warm smiles and gratitude for their kind words. Never mind that she felt like an impostor, or someone who was taking credit for something she hadn't done, they all seemed more than happy to accept her as Dougie's daughter, and most of all pleased that she'd come. However, they didn't linger long, for everyone was returning to the house where the caterers, and a much-needed tipple, were waiting.

Though the reception started out as a sedate, dignified affair, with most sipping tea from bone-china cups, and nibbling sandwiches with no crusts, it wasn't long before champagne corks started to fly and balloons floated down from a net above, for it was a final request of her father's, she discovered, that everyone should have a thoroughly good time. And it didn't appear anyone had a problem with that, for the organ dirges were soon replaced by considerably more rousing music, and the laughter became much louder and more raucous. Toast after toast was drunk to Dougie and Gwen, who could almost have been there as newly-weds, rather than the dear departed.

Since she'd eaten nothing all day Julia soon felt the champagne going to her head, and as her glass was constantly being refilled, it wasn't long before her emotional pendulum was swinging around so erratically that she was barely aware of what she was thinking or feeling. All she knew was that she seemed to remain in the same spot as everyone jostled around her, each with a memory to share or an anecdote to relate. If they were curious about her, and they surely must be, today they appeared to be restraining it since no-one asked why Dougie had kept her a secret, or where the rest of her family was on this momentous occasion.

All the time she greeted new people, talked, laughed and listened, she was aware of Rico's moody eyes watching her, but though she felt flattered by the attention, she knew only too well what a dangerous combination alcohol and emotion could be, so deliberately kept her own gaze averted. It was hard, though, for as the day wore on and she drank even more, she was starting to feel reckless almost to the point of madness, and needy to a degree that could easily be shaming. More than anything she wanted Josh to be here, to be as close as they'd always been, with no Sylvia between them, no lies and no deceit. It was too late for that, she knew it was always going to be there now, but she mustn't let herself dwell on it. She should just go on enjoying being someone's cherished daughter for a change, instead of someone's mother or wife, because it felt liberating and stimulating and almost as intoxicating as the wine.

'Blimey, you're an 'ard one to get through to,' a florid-faced, stocky little man declared breathlessly, as he managed to elbow his way to the front of the crowd. 'Bin dying to meet you since we all got back here. Albert Granger, Gwen's second cousin. Everyone calls me Albie.'

'Nice to meet you, Albie,' Julia responded, shaking his hand.

'Don't mind telling you, I got the surprise of me life when I found out about you,' he confided. 'Who'd have thought old Dougie had such a stunner as you hidden away? Not me, that's for sure. Definitely got the better of me this time, he did. Mind you, I was always teasing him about his past. Reckoned he had a few too many secrets, that's what I always used to tell him. He'd say Albie, before I go I'll tell you where I buried the bodies.' He laughed loud and long, while Julia smiled politely and knew instinctively that her father hadn't much taken to this man.

'Course, I knows there's no bodies really,' he went on jovially. 'He just used to say that to get me going. Wouldn't hurt a fly, old Dougie, everyone knows that. Didn't have it in him, never mind the way he was when he first moved down here. Had a lot on his mind back then, our Gwen used to say. Had a right temper on him too, I can tell you, because I was one of the ones who copped it once. Could hardly say anything without him going off the handle in those days. Just thank God for our Gwen. She had the right influence on him. Never used to lose his temper and go off on his drunken rampages once he got settled with her, and thick with the Bowers.'

Realising they were coming dangerously close to a place she didn't want to go, especially today, Julia started to interrupt, but with her thoughts blurred by champagne she found an excuse maddeningly elusive.

'Course there was lots of rumours back then,' Albie continued, undeterred, 'but I never used to pay 'em much mind. It was his business if he'd been in trouble with the law, weren't it? Nothing to do with me.'

Julia's heartbeat was starting to slow. 'What kind of trouble?' she heard herself ask.

'Gwen never said, or not to me she didn't. She just told me once I had to stop getting on at him about things, because he found it painful to think about his past, and all what he'd done. Can see what she meant now, if he upped and left his family the way he did. Don't expect that made him feel very good about himself, did it?'

Julia could almost feel the paleness of her face as she stared at him, then suddenly Fen was at her side, gushing, 'There you are, you will excuse us won't you, Albie, but the vicar's looking for Julia,' and sliding an arm through Julia's she tugged her off towards the bar. 'Not really,' she murmured in

Julia's ear, 'you just looked as though you needed rescuing.'

'Yes, I think I did,' Julia responded. 'He's a bit . . .' She struggled for the word.

'Let's settle for drunk,' Fen suggested.

Julia smiled, and wondered whether to repeat anything Albie had told her, but the opportunity passed as Fen's husband, Bob, came bearing down on them with a freshly opened bottle of champagne.

'At last I get to meet you,' he declared, filling their glasses. 'Fen's been talking about nothing else since you arrived. You've made quite an impression.'

'Darling, you should be offering your sympathies,' Fen gently reminded him.

Bob immediately looked contrite.

'Oh no, really,' Julia protested. 'It's lovely to meet you, Bob.'

'I hope we're going to be seeing plenty of you while you're here,' he said, his smile making him seem boyish, while the thick lenses of his glasses and shock of grizzled hair lent him a distinctly professorial air. 'Fen tells me your husband arrives tomorrow.'

'Yes, but only to drop off my daughter. He's taking our son sailing over near Chichester.'

Bob's face lit up. 'He sails! Then he must be a splendid fellow.'

Fen rolled her eyes. 'Don't get him started, please,' she implored, as her mother joined them. 'Mummy, you've done a splendid job,' she told her, giving her a hug. 'Everyone's having a marvellous time, which is just what Dougie wanted.'

'It really is a wonderful party,' Julia assured her.

Laura Bower's face glowed with pleasure. 'Thank you,' she answered graciously. 'They're a very good catering company, we've used them before on a number of occasions.' She turned to Julia, and after checking no-one but close family was in earshot, she said, 'I hope it's not too indelicate to mention the photographs of your children in Dougie's house. Fen told me about them and we're positively agog with the mystery of how they got there. I don't suppose you've found out anything yet?'

Julia shook her head. 'No. I don't even know who to ask,' she confessed, 'except my mother, but I'm almost certain it wouldn't have been her.'

'Most curious,' Laura commented. 'I wonder how long he had them.'

Julia shrugged, and glanced up at Rico as he joined them.

'Ah, just the person,' Laura declared, and before he could utter a word of protest, she'd seized his arm and was marching him off into the crowd to only she knew where.

Laughing, Fen turned back to Julia. 'So what did Albie have to say for himself?' she asked.

Julia was on the point of answering when Peter Bower bundled up bringing a couple of Dougie's old chums with him, and by the time the introductions and condolences were over, Fen had been dragged away by someone else. Bob was eager for Julia to meet his parents, so ushered her over to where they were tucking into the best of the buffet.

The rest of the day continued in much the same vein, offering little or no opportunity for confidences, and by the time David drove her back to the mill it was so late, and she was so tired, that she'd virtually forgotten what Albie had said anyway.

It would come back to her, she decided as she climbed into bed, but she really didn't want to think about it now anyway, or about the way she and Josh had just been irritable with each other on the phone again, which she thought was probably her fault, but couldn't quite remember. She only wanted to snuggle down under the duvet now and fall fast asleep thinking of how relieved she was that Sylvia was off to New York tomorrow, and how eager she was to see the children in the morning, and Josh, damn him, and how much her father would have loved them all were he only here to meet them.

Chapter Eight

As Josh followed Julia's directions though the damp and tangled Cornish lanes, the prospect of seeing her was tightening the band of tension around his head to an almost intolerable degree. It wouldn't go well, he knew it already, not only because of their heated exchange on the phone last night, but because his conscience was giving him a seriously hard time this morning. In fact, since he was about to face her, knowing he'd screwed Sylvia again yesterday, he could only wonder that he hadn't turned the car around by now – except it would make matters a thousand times worse, which was difficult to imagine, considering how bad they already were.

He'd tried telling himself, before going over to Sylvia's, that his only purpose was to end the relationship, but he'd known very well what would happen when he got there, and in truth, it was exactly why he'd gone. He just wished he could stop himself wanting the damned woman, but even thinking about her now, and the way she'd opened the door to him, wearing nothing but spike-heeled shoes and a knowing smile, was making him hard. Just pray to God Julia never found out, because he didn't even want to think about what would happen if she did. At least he hadn't agreed to meet Sylvia in New York, in spite of how tempting she'd made it sound, because there was no doubt at all in his mind that if he succumbed it would be the end of his marriage.

Feeling the sharp bite of irritation dispel his lust, he changed down a gear and forced Patsy past a convoy of caravans. Fortunately both children were asleep now. The early morning start had made them fractious and bolshie so they'd been at each other, or him, almost the entire way, and since he was tired too, after working until gone midnight, and rising again at five to start packing, the journey had been far from fun. As if his conscience wasn't enough to be dealing with, he was having an extremely hard time being anything other than furious at having to take time out of the office next week when he could so ill afford it. Certainly he was sorry about Julia's father, and obviously sorrier still about Sylvia, but were it not for the fact that he'd already promised Dan, and that anything he did contrary to plans was going to be somehow connected to Sylvia, he'd leave both children with Julia today and head straight back to London.

However, he'd probably feel even worse if he let Dan down, and since Shannon was equally excited about having her mother to herself for a week, he had little choice but to go with the flow. It was just a pity Shannon had changed her tune so radically this morning, for last night she'd complained so bitterly about being torn away from her friends in London and everything they were planning for half-term, that he'd thought for a while that he had her on his side.

Glancing at his watch, he calculated another ten to fifteen minutes before they arrived. He could only hope that Julia had woken up in a better frame of mind this morning than the one she'd been in last night when she'd called sounding drunk or exhausted, or both, and extremely pissed off that he hadn't called her. If she'd checked her mobile she'd have known that he had, several times, but that information hadn't managed to appease her, if anything it had made her worse, which told him that she'd been determined to pick a fight, no matter what. So they'd had one, and out had spilled all her resentment that he hadn't been with her for the funeral, while he'd yelled back the reminder that they had two children to consider, and as far as he was concerned they came before a man who'd ducked out on his family and responsibilities a quarter of a century ago and was somehow still managing to create havoc in their lives now. It was at that point that the phone had gone down.

They hadn't spoken again since, not even during the calls she'd been making to the children this morning, charting their progress. Even that was annoying him, though not nearly as much as the certainty that she was going to throw Sylvia in his face the minute he arrived.

'Are we there yet?' Dan asked, sitting forward to rest his elbows on the two front seats.

Having been asked that question more times

than he'd ever want to hear it again, it was with profound relief that Josh was able to say, 'Yes, we're here, son,' and sweeping round a large horse chestnut tree, he accelerated gently over a cattle grid and started down a narrow, tree-lined drive.

Daniel's eyes grew round as an extremely grand farmhouse came into view. 'Is that it?' he asked, clearly impressed. 'Is that going to be ours now?'

'No, I think ours is behind this one,' Josh responded, feeling decidedly awkward about the possessive.

'But that's Mum,' Dan cried excitedly, as Julia broke away from a group of people standing in front of the house and started to wave.

'Are we here?' Shannon asked groggily as she came awake.

'There's Mum,' Dan told her, and as Josh brought the car to a stop Dan leapt out straight into his mother's arms.

'How are you?' Julia cried, holding him tight. 'Let me look at you. Oh my, you've grown so handsome.'

'It's only been two days,' Shannon remarked grumpily, as she pushed open the car door.

Julia regarded her with humorously narrowed eyes, until, unable to stop herself, Shannon broke into a smile, and next thing she was springing into her mother's arms too. 'Dad's in a vile mood,' she warned in Julia's ear. 'I'd give him a wide berth if I were you. I nearly killed him on the way down.'

Josh was coming round the car.

'Hello darling,' Julia said warmly, though they both knew it was an effort to keep up appearances. 'Did you have a good journey?'

'If you discount hiccups, car sickness, needing the toilet two minutes after we've left the services and a total inability to be civil to each other, I suppose you could say it was a good journey,' he responded.

Julia dutifully hugged him and winked at Shannon and Dan.

'Oh look!' Dan cried ecstatically as a couple of unruly border collies came bounding up to meet him.

'Sorry! Ottie let them out,' Fen shouted, running after them.

But Dan was in heaven, trying to get his arms round the dogs as they bounced about in delight and slobbered all over him.

'This is Fen who I've told you about,' Julia said, linking Josh's arm. 'She's not just the solicitor who broke the news, she's also a great family friend.'

Josh wondered which family, but refrained from asking, and allowed his inherent good manners to prevail as he shook Fen's hand. 'It's a pleasure to meet you,' he said. 'Julia's told me how supportive you've been.'

'Oh, we're happy to help in any way we can,' Fen assured him. 'Her father meant a lot to us. Anyway, welcome to Cornwall and Shallard's Cross. I hope you're going to like it here as much as Julia seems to.'

'I'm sure I will,' he responded politely, while turning to find out what the shriek coming from the boot was all about.

'Dad! You forgot to put my make-up case in. I asked you if it was there . . .'

'It's in the bag I brought for Mum,' he interrupted, as Shannon appeared. 'And you don't need it now.'

Smiling, Fen went forward. 'You must be Shannon,' she said, cupping the girl's face between her hands. 'How lovely you are. You have to meet Ottilie. She's your age and ... Ottie! Where are you?'

'Right here, Mum,' a lanky, freckle-faced teenager with a stunning mane of red hair and a sassy expression informed her.

Fen laughed. 'Sorry darling. This is Shannon, Julia's daughter. I'm sure you two will have a lot in common, so why don't you show her around?'

Though Shannon didn't appear exactly eager, it was clear to Josh that she was more impressed with the look of Ottie than she'd expected to be, so maybe now she'd accept that Orlando Bloom, Topshop and Notting Hill cool had managed to permeate as far as Cornwall, and have a good time.

'Right, let me introduce you to everyone else,' Fen said, as the others wandered over to join them. 'OK, father Peter, mother Laura, husband Bob, cousin Rico, and don't worry if you forget their names, they can generally be relied upon to remember them so can remind upon request.'

Smiling, Josh shook everyone's hands, and was just falling into step with Peter Bower, heading towards the house, when his mobile started to ring. Looking to see who it was, he quickly apologised and turned away to take it, feeling the cut of Julia's glare boring into his back. Well, what the hell was he supposed to do, forget he had any clients or loyalty to them just because she thought he was speaking to Sylvia?

By the time he'd finished the call everyone had gone inside except Dan who clearly couldn't tear himself away from the dogs, and the two girls, who'd apparently lost no time at all in bonding.

'Dad, can we get a dog?' Dan asked, looking up from where he was sitting with the delighted-looking beasts either side of him.

'Not today,' Josh answered. Then stooping down, he ruffled the dogs too, as he said, 'Would you rather stay here with Mum? We can always go sailing another time.'

Dan's face fell. 'But I want to go now, Dad. You said . . .'

'That's fine,' Josh assured him. 'I just thought you might prefer to be with the dogs.'

'Oh, Josh, there you are,' Fen said, coming out of the front door. 'Thought you might have trouble finding the way. A light lunch is being served in the conservatory, I do hope you're staying long enough to join us.'

'Of course,' he responded, standing up, and deciding he might as well resign himself to going with this for now, rather than create any more tension with Julia, he followed her inside.

As it turned out he found the Bowers to be rather good company, particularly Fen's husband, Bob, with whom he discovered he shared several interests, not least of which was sailing. This was a hobby he'd only got into during the past few years, while Bob was clearly an old hand. Yes, he could probably grow to like it here, he was reflecting as he accepted a second helping of the housekeeper's beef in cider stew. Certainly he could think of worse places to be leaving his wife and daughter for a week. Under any other circumstances he might even envy Julia and Shannon the break, for such idyllic surroundings certainly had their appeal – though his mind would be too full of what was going on at the office, and the mountain of work he had to get through, to allow himself to relax beyond the weekend.

'Lydia, our youngest, is over at a friend's house this afternoon,' Fen was explaining. 'She's off to Italy with Mummy tomorrow . . . Oh, by the way, Ottie's not going now, did I tell you?' she added to Julia.

Josh's eyes moved to his wife as she failed to answer. Her attention, it seemed, was focused on the paddock where Shannon and her new friend were watching the cousin Rico exercising a horse. 'Julia,' he said darkly.

Startled, she looked at him, and coloured slightly, as she said, 'Sorry, darling. Did you say something?'

'Fen did,' he told her.

'I'm so sorry,' she apologised, turning to Fen.

Fen smiled. 'It's OK. I was just saying that Ottie's decided to stay here this half-term instead of going to Italy, so Shannon will have some company after all.'

'Why, that's marvellous,' Julia exclaimed. 'Isn't it?' she said to Josh.

'If you say so,' he responded, not intending to sound rude, only to get under her skin the way she was getting under his.

Evidently sensing it, she said, 'Are you feeling all right, darling? Tired after the long drive?'

'I'm fine,' he retorted, wanting to ask, nastily,

how her hangover was today, but they were in company, so instead he asked if she'd like to show him her father's house before he left.

Twenty minutes later, having completed the guided tour, during which he agreed the place was as charming as she'd claimed, he followed her back out onto the porch where he refrained from expressing his true feelings about the mysterious presence of his children's photographs, as they stood watching Dan playing with the dogs. There was still no sign of Shannon, who was supposed to be walking over from the house with Ottilie.

'I've brought Kincaid's manuscript,' he told her, ducking as a ball whizzed past his ear, followed by Dan shouting sorry. 'It arrived yesterday, by hand.'

'Thanks,' she said. Then after a beat, 'I expect the car's full of them, isn't it?'

He looked puzzled, then realising she meant that he was incapable of making a trip without taking his work with him, he said, 'The world doesn't come to a stop just because you've decided to take some time out, you know.'

'I didn't mean that,' she retorted, 'and I'd hardly call sorting my father's affairs and editing a high-profile manuscript taking time out.'

A short, difficult silence followed as they watched Shannon and Ottilie emerge from the woods, escorted by Rico, who was leading a sleek, black mare saddled ready to ride. Josh was too preoccupied with his temper to notice the way Shannon was flirting and preening herself in front of the Italian, but Julia hadn't missed it at all. In fact, she was reflecting on how lucky it was for

Shannon that her father wasn't reading the signs, or it was highly unlikely he'd leave her here. He might not want to leave Julia here either, were he able to read some of the thoughts she'd been having about that particular young man lately, but fortunately he couldn't. Actually, considering his own behaviour, she decided he should be thankful that she had herself well under control. It was just a pity he couldn't say the same.

'So are you still seeing Sylvia?' she asked tartly.

'No,' he lied.

'But you'd like to.'

His jaw tightened. 'Stop trying to put words in my mouth.'

Noting that he hadn't denied it she turned incredulous, angry eyes to him, but before she could speak, he said, 'I knew you'd be unable to resist throwing it in my face when I got here, so please tell me exactly how you think it's helping.'

'Oh, I know you'd like it to just go away, to forget it ever happened,' she said tightly, 'but I'm afraid it doesn't work quite like that.'

Though his entire body stiffened, he said nothing, merely continued to stare out at Dan and the dogs.

'Whose idea was it?' she demanded. 'Which one of you came up with such a mind-numbingly stupid way of saving our marriage?'

'Does it really matter?'

'Oh yes, it matters, because I'd like to know just how deeply the treachery runs here, and on whose side. So was it you? Have you been lusting after her for years and saw this as your big opportunity?'

'She was the one who approached me,' he said truthfully.

Though she was relieved to hear that, it in no way exonerated him, nor was she going to allow him to think that it did. 'And you went for it?' she said, her lip curling with disgust.

'You know very well I wouldn't have if things had been different between us,' he muttered furiously. 'I've never wanted anyone else, not even for a minute.'

'And what about now? Do you still want her?'

'Even if I did I'm not going to admit it, am I, so it's a pointless question.'

'That must mean you do.'

'For God's sake,' he seethed. Then realising he was only making things worse, he reined in his temper with effort. 'Since it's obvious you're not going to believe anything I say, maybe we should change the subject,' he suggested.

Going along with this only because the children were nearby, she said, 'OK. Let's talk about my manuscript, shall we? The one that *I* wrote. I'm sure you've spent plenty of time discussing Sylvia's books with her, but you never mention mine now. So is there any more news on it?'

He looked at her in amazement. 'I thought you didn't want me to try anyone else,' he said.

She sighed impatiently and turned her head away.

'What the hell is that supposed to mean?' he demanded.

'You could have done it without me knowing,' she responded, in a tone that implied he should have realised that.

234

His face darkened. 'Just tell me what the hell it takes to please you,' he said angrily.

Her eyes flashed. 'You know very well you could have tried other publishers, or even pushed harder with McKenzies, but you didn't bother, did you? No, of course not, you were much too busy screwing Sylvia.'

'OK, you want the truth?' he retorted. 'I did try again, in fact I didn't only try again, I totally fucking humiliated myself with Harry Greenstock trying to get you a deal off the back of Moira Glaister . . .'

She turned round, eyes blazing. 'You did what?' she hissed.

His eyes closed as he realised his mistake.

'Please don't tell me you tried to *blackmail* him by threatening to take Moira elsewhere,' she said through her teeth.

'It didn't get that far, but it's how these things are done, you know that.'

'Not with me, they aren't. Jesus Christ, I wanted your support, yes, but now you've turned me into a laughing stock. Everyone must know . . .' She put her hands to her head, hardly able to believe what he'd done. 'How could you?' she demanded. 'I'll never be able to show my face again . . .'

'Harry gave me his word it would go no further,' he assured her. 'He's a good friend. You know we can trust him.'

Fury was still burning in her eyes. 'Frankly, I'm beginning to be less worried about him than I am about you,' she snapped, 'because I don't know who you are any more, though one thing's for certain, you're definitely not the man I married,' and turning abruptly away she glared across at Shannon, who was too distant to see, and too engrossed in Rico to care.

Josh stood where he was, still smarting at his own stupidity, and knowing he had to make this up to her somehow. God only knew how, when he was clearly incapable of putting a foot right anywhere, and when his conscience was throwing him around all over the place. In the end he opted for another change of subject.

'So the funeral passed off well,' he said, in a voice that was supposed to be friendly, but only just made it.

'Very well,' she confirmed.

'That's good.'

'I had too much to drink,' she confessed, 'but that doesn't mean I'm retracting anything I said last night, because it actually would have been nice if you'd been there with me. However, I will apologise for the tone I said it in.'

'Apology accepted,' he responded stiffly. Then, after a beat, 'So how are you feeling now?'

'Apart from a little hung-over, slightly apprehensive about going through his things.'

'Have you made a start?'

'Not yet.' She was watching Shannon again, whose arms were around Rico as he helped her up into the saddle. Then turning back into the house, as much to distract Josh as to dismiss the scene herself, she said, 'Now I've met some of his friends, I'm finding it very hard to believe anything bad about him, except . . .' She glanced up at him, then walked over to the table. 'I met one of his wife's cousins yesterday,' she said, confiding in him because she needed to, and because it was hard to change a lifetime's habits, even when there was so much pain and resentment simmering between them. 'He told me something . . . Well, let's just say it wasn't exactly in keeping with the image the others are painting.'

Josh looked down into her pale, tired face, and getting a fleeting sense of what an ordeal all this was for her, he almost gave in to an urge to gather her up in his arms. However, he guessed it probably wouldn't be welcome, so he merely listened as she repeated what Albie Granger had told her during the wake.

'I've no recollections whatsoever of Dad being a violent man,' she concluded. 'He didn't even have much of a temper, except during that last row with my mother. Several things got smashed then, and I've always assumed it was her who smashed them.'

'But you're doubting it now?'

'Let's just say I'm trying to keep an open mind. I asked Fen's father about Albie this morning. He more or less dismissed him as a troublemaker and a drunk.'

'Is that how he came across to you?'

'Yes, actually.'

'And did Fen's father know anything about any brushes with the law?'

'He says not, but he did admit his friend Dougie had a bit of a reputation for being hot-headed, back in the days before he met Gwen.'

'Which was when, exactly?'

'As far as I can make out, about four years after he left us.'

'So she wasn't the reason he left?'

'It doesn't seem so.'

As her gaze drifted Josh continued to look at her, sensing what was going through her mind now, but deciding he'd let her be the one to say it.

'He could have been in prison during that time,' she said quietly.

'It's possible,' he concurred.

Her eyes went down, and after a while she said, 'You don't think ... I mean, could I ... Would I be able to blot something out of my mind so completely that I have no recollection of it at all?'

'People have been known to.'

She nodded. 'Usually when it's something too terrible for the conscious mind to deal with.'

It wasn't a question, so he didn't offer an answer.

She put her hands over her face and breathed in deeply. 'Do I really want to go there?' she murmured. 'Is it just going to end up making everything even worse than it already is?' Her eyes moved to his, then away again. 'I'm not sure I have a choice,' she continued. 'Someone has to sort out his belongings, and he must have intended it to be me, or I wouldn't be here. So, are the answers in this house somewhere? Are they all set out in the pages of a diary, or a letter, or a file, waiting to be revealed in order to reassure me? Or has he got rid of everything that might incriminate him so that I'll never know?'

Josh didn't voice the third possibility, though he knew already what it would be.

'Or am I going to find some kind of confession, some kind of purging of the soul before he goes to meet his Maker?' Her eyes came back to his.

'Maybe the truth really is as horrible as we fear, and he just couldn't face me knowing it while he was still alive.'

Josh was barely back on the main road leading towards Bodmin when his mobile started to ring. Expecting it to be Julia, whom he'd still not managed to leave on the best of terms, he simply clicked on without looking at the display.

'Hi,' he said, trying to sound affectionate.

'Hi, yourself,' Sylvia responded. 'Is it OK to talk?'

Experiencing a jolt of anxiety, he glanced at Dan and said, 'No.'

'Is Julia there?'

'No.'

'One of the children?'

'Yes. I thought you'd be on the flight by now.'

'There's been a delay, so I decided to call and find out how you are.'

'Fine. Everything's fine.'

'How did it go with Julia today? Have you seen her yet?'

'Yes. It was OK.'

'Did you tell her about yesterday?'

'No, of course not.' He wanted to tell her it wouldn't happen again, but he was making a fool of himself now, over how many times he'd failed to keep his word.

There was a smile in her voice as she said, 'I'm going to miss you.'

He made no reply.

'I thought you might like to know that I took off my panties to call you,' she told him hoarsely.

The response struck like lightning in his groin, and glancing at Dan again, who appeared engrossed in his GameBoy, he said, 'That's nice.'

She laughed softly. 'I thought you might like it.'

'Who is it, Dad?' Dan suddenly asked.

'Uh, just a friend,' he answered. Then to Sylvia, 'I have to go.'

'I'll call you again when I get to New York,' she said.

'No, don't. I'm not going to be around this week. I told you, I'm sailing with my son.'

'I know you don't mean what you're saying,' she responded. 'Call me when you're alone and we'll have some fun on the phone.'

As he rang off, in spite of his erection, Josh was already telling himself the call would never happen, for the last thing he wanted was to duck and dive around his son for the next week, in an attempt to talk dirty with a woman he desperately needed to get out of his life, not invite even more deeply into it.

The phone didn't ring again until they were practically at the boat. This time it was Julia wanting his opinion on her decision to ring her aunt on Monday, to find out if she'd sent the photographs to her father. Sensing that she'd already made up her mind to do so, he did more listening than talking, and wished he'd made more of an effort while he was with her, because his conscience was giving him a really hard time now. He still loved her, there wasn't a single doubt in his mind about that, and there was no way in the world he'd ever give up his family for Sylvia. However, since speaking to Sylvia earlier, he'd finally admitted to himself that he was going to find it a lot harder to end their relationship than he'd ever want Julia to know.

Chapter Nine

Being the closest to the phone as it rang, Alice Hope – she had reverted to her maiden name immediately her divorce had come through – reached for the receiver, and tucked it into her shoulder to carry on zesting oranges, while her sister-in-law finished them off in a juicer.

'Hello,' she said pleasantly, expecting it to be Pam calling to say she was on her way over.

'Hello Mother.'

Alice's face immediately tightened. 'Julia,' she said, echoing her other daughter's chilly tone, and catching Rene's eye as she looked up. 'How are you?'

'I'm fine, thank you. How are you?'

'We're all fine thank you.'

'Good. Well, now that's established I'd like to speak to Aunt Rene please.'

Alice blinked in surprise. 'What for?' she asked. Julia didn't answer.

'Where are you?' Alice demanded irritably.

'Actually, I'm at Dad's house, sorting through his papers.'

Alice felt her mouth turn dry. 'So what have you found?' she asked, meeting Rene's eyes again.

'Oh, old bank statements, utility bills, letters from the council . . .'

'Don't be obtuse,' Alice snapped.

'Tell me what you think I might have found,' Julia countered.

'Oh for heaven's sake, you really are the most infuriating . . .'

'Please put Aunt Rene on. If she wants to tell you about our conversation after, it'll be up to her.'

Alice's features were pinched as she put a hand over the receiver and said to Rene, 'She wants to speak to you.'

Rene's surprise could hardly have been greater. 'Me?'

'That's what she said.'

After drying her hands on a tea towel, Rene took the receiver and put it tentatively to her ear. 'Julia? How are you, dear?'

'Very well, thank you,' Julia replied. 'There's something I'd like to ask you. If you'd prefer not to talk while my mother's there, I can give you the number here, so you can call me back when you're alone.'

Rene's face flooded with colour.

'What's she saying?' Alice hissed.

Rene held up a hand. 'I'm sure we can talk now, dear,' she said. 'Unless you'd rather I called back.'

Julia sounded vaguely disappointed as she said, 'No, it's OK. I just wanted to give you the opportunity to be more private.'

'That's very considerate of you, dear, but I'm

sure we don't need to be hiding anything from your mother. So what can I do for you?'

Julia took a breath. 'I'd like to know if you sent photographs of Shannon and Dan to my father.'

Rene frowned in confusion. 'Why on earth would you think I'd done such a thing?' she said. 'I haven't seen or spoken to him in years. I don't even know where he lived.'

'Are you sure? Because he has some, and you're the only person I can think of who might have removed them from the drawer my mother keeps them in and given them to him.'

Rene's expression was still one of bewilderment. 'Of course I'm sure,' she answered. 'I haven't had any contact with him since the day he left here. None of us has. Unless your mother . . .'

'What is it?' Alice demanded. 'What's she saying?'

'She wants to know if I sent photographs of her children to her father,' Rene replied.

Alice snatched the phone. 'If he has pictures of your children they didn't come from this house,' she snapped.

'Well, I certainly didn't think they'd come from you,' Julia retorted.

Alice struggled to hold onto her temper. 'Why don't you just leave this alone now?' she said coldly. 'He's dead, it's all over and frankly, you should be pleased.'

'Really? Why?'

'Because he can't hurt you now.'

Julia was silent.

'Are you still there?'

'What exactly do you mean by that?' Julia asked.

244

'Are you talking about the kind of hurt I felt when he left? Or was there something else?'

'For heaven's sake, why do you always have to assume there's a mystery, or a secret, or . . .'

'Because *there is*,' Julia cried. 'The very fact that you just made that comment proves it. And so do the photographs I'm holding in my hand. So how many more times do I have to ask you, Mother? What are you hiding?'

Alice turned round as the back door opened and her brother stomped in, carrying a shotgun under his arm and a couple of rabbits dripping with rain. 'Damn weather,' he muttered, dumping everything on a draining board and peeling off his saturated cap and Barbour.

'Alice is speaking to Julia,' Rene informed him. 'She's at her father's house, going through his papers.'

George's steely eyes moved to Alice.

'And how many more times do I have to ask *you*,' Alice was saying to Julia, while looking at George, 'to leave this alone and get on with your life?' Before Julia could reply George took the phone. 'Julia, dear,' he said, 'it's Uncle George. I'm sorry, but I really can't allow you to keep upsetting your mother like this. It's taken her until now to recover from your visit last week, and she really doesn't deserve to be treated this way.'

There was hardly a beat before Julia's fury exploded down the line. 'Are you talking about the mother who can hardly speak a civil word to me?' she yelled. 'The mother who's never shown me or my children a moment's affection in her life, and who made life so intolerable for my father that he couldn't bear to stay . . .'

'I'm not arguing with you, Julia,' he cut in. 'I've been most concerned about your mother since you were here, and you too, after the way you stormed off . . .'

'Which must be why you kept calling to make sure I hadn't driven off the road and ended up under a truck,' she spat.

George sighed. 'Your mother's right, always so dramatic,' he said. 'Now, you know you're always welcome here, but I have to ask you, for all our sakes, to stop bringing this up. It was for the best when your father left all those years ago, so perhaps we can all now say a prayer together that his soul will rest in peace . . .'

'Has anyone told Pam he's dead?' Julia interrupted.

'Yes, she's been informed, and like the rest of us, she's merely relieved to know there's finally an end to it.'

Julia's howl of frustration caused him to remove the phone from his ear. 'To *what*?' she demanded.

Again George sighed. 'I think we need to terminate this call in order to cool our tempers,' he responded. 'But before you go, I'd be interested to know where your father's been living all these years. What he's been doing?'

There was a pause before she said, 'If you seriously think, after the way you've treated me, that you're going to get one word out of me about anything to do with my father, then I have to inform you that something's horribly adrift inside your head.'

George's eyes showed a flash of annoyance as the line went dead, then reaching over to return the phone to its base, he said, 'Did she happen to tell you where he lives?'

'Lived,' Alice corrected. 'No, she didn't.'

Rene shook her head.

'Then I think we should find out.'

'What difference will it make?' Rene asked. 'He surely won't have kept anything.'

George drew Alice to him as she covered her face with her hands. 'It's all right,' he soothed, patting her shoulder. 'Rene's right, he won't have kept anything, so there's nothing to worry about.'

'But what if he's left her a letter, or a tape, something she hasn't found yet?' Alice protested.

'Why would he do that? What could he possibly gain?'

Her face was still white with fear as she looked up at him, her eyes full of doubt.

'He wouldn't want her to know, any more than we do,' George reminded her gently.

Though Rene was watching them, her mind was elsewhere. 'Yes, we really must try to stop her,' she said, almost to herself.

'And how are we going to do that, when she has as much right to be where she is, as she has to his papers?' Alice pointed out.

Rene was reaching for the phone. 'We can't, but I agree we should find out where he lived.' As she spoke she was dialling 1471. 'Mm,' she said as she jotted down the number, 'not a code I recognise, but it should be easy enough to trace.'

Alice's eyes closed as more dread engulfed her.

'Calm yourself,' George said shortly, and after

pressing a kiss to her forehead he started towards the boot room, only to turn back as Rene said, 'George, I've told you before about locking the guns away the minute you come in. Now please go and do it.'

Julia was still standing beside the phone, seething with temper and frustration. The call hadn't gone at all as she'd expected, since she'd hoped her aunt would admit to acting behind her husband's and sister-in-law's backs and come clean, saying something like, 'Yes dear, we all treated your father very shoddily back then, so I tried, in my own way, to make it up to him.' Or, 'He was a good man, so please don't believe anything you might hear about him.' But of course Rene wasn't going to admit to anything while the willowy witch was standing right there, any more than she was going to agree to call Julia back at a time when she couldn't be overheard. That wasn't to say she wouldn't, but Julia's instincts were already warning her not to hold out much hope on that score.

Turning back to the kitchen table, which was covered in bills, letters and bank statements, she sank down on a chair and propped her chin in her hands. If her aunt *hadn't* sent the photos, then how the heck had they got here? Had her father somehow managed to make contact with the photographer? Had he paid someone else to do so? Maybe he'd been having her watched all these years? She wasn't too sure how she felt about that, except it wasn't especially good. Of course, there was a chance she'd turn up some receipts or correspondence that could throw some light on the mystery, so she should keep on ploughing through, file after file, box after box. The study was stuffed so full of papers of one sort or another that she could be here for weeks.

Looking up at the sound of footsteps, she watched Shannon kicking off the riding boots Ottie had loaned her, while chatting on her mobile, presumably to Ottie, her new best friend. She looked so grown-up, Julia was thinking, with her sleek blonde hair caught up in a black net, and her long, slender thighs clad in tight ivory jodhpurs. She was evidently wearing a thong underneath, and despite the sunny day, it wasn't really warm enough to be in shirtsleeves with half the buttons undone, though Julia could easily guess the reason for it.

Boots off, and call over, Shannon came padding into the kitchen and headed straight for the fridge, saying, 'Hi Mum. How's it going?'

Julia smiled at the upbeat manner and happy flush in her cheeks, which, even if she'd not known already, would leave her in little doubt of where her daughter had been for the past two hours. 'Not bad,' she answered. 'Where are the others?'

'What do you mean, others? I was just with Ottie.'

'No Rico?'

'Oh yes, he was there too,' she answered, attempting to sound breezy as she filled a glass with juice.

Julia waited, and sure enough, a minute or two later, Shannon's eyes came to hers and she started to grin.

'Oh Mum, he's like so cool the way he's teaching me to ride,' she gushed. 'He's got this fantastic way with horses, and he says I'm doing really well already. He's taking us out again later, he said.' She drank deeply, then let go a long breath. 'Any news on the photos?' she asked, clearly deciding that was enough confiding for now. 'Was it Aunt Rene who sent them?'

Julia shook her head. 'She says not, and I don't think she's lying.'

Shannon's eyebrows went up. 'So who was it?'

Julia shrugged.

'Spoooky,' Shannon pronounced.

Julia flipped her bottom as she passed, then picked up a wad of bills to continue sifting through them. 'I thought you were supposed to be giving me a hand,' she said, before Shannon could disappear into the downstairs bedroom.

Shannon immediately protested. 'But I folded up all the clothes from the wardrobes this morning,' she cried. 'You didn't say I had to do any more than that.'

'But you do have your mocks coming up, and a mountain of coursework to get through, so what about some studying?'

'Honestly, I'm really cool with everything. I'm not behind, everyone says I'm doing really well, all the teachers . . .' Then, attempting a quick change of subject, 'Dad rang just now, sounds like they're having a really good time over there.'

Julia's eyes remained on what she was doing. 'What time did he ring?' she asked, trying not to mind that he hadn't called her.

'I don't know, about an hour ago, I suppose. I

told him how I'm getting on so great with my riding. He sounded really pleased.'

Clearly she hadn't mentioned Rico, Julia was thinking. 'How's Dan?' she asked. 'Did you speak to him?'

'Yeah, he's cool. He said he was sailing the boat single-handed this morning, without any help from Dad. Then he said if Dad doesn't behave himself, he'll sail away without him.'

Julia smiled, easily able to picture her son having the time of his life at the helm, and she imagined Josh was probably enjoying himself too, in spite of his irritation at being out of the office. He'd be careful not to let Daniel know about his work-related concerns, she was certain of it, for he loved him far too much to begrudge him his pleasure. He'd just take it out on her whenever he finally decided to ring.

'Did you know that Ottie's dad's got a boat too?' Shannon was gabbling on. 'We can go out in it whenever we like, apparently, but he's away until Wednesday, so Rico's agreed to take us if he has time. He's a really good sailor, Fen said. Oh yes, and Rico said he'll come over later to pick up the stuff you're sending to the charity shop. You just need to let him know if he should bring the pick-up or the estate. If he does come, shall we ask him if he'd like to have dinner with us one night? I don't mind doing the cooking.'

Only just managing to keep her eyebrows down, Julia said, 'It's a nice idea, but since when were you able to cook?'

'I can cook if I have to,' Shannon retorted indignantly.

Julia's eyes sparked with humour. 'Then we'll see,' she replied.

'Does that mean we'll see if I can cook, or we'll see if he can come?'

Julia looked into her lovely young face. 'He's a lot older than you, darling,' she said gently.

Shannon's cheeks turned scarlet. 'So what?' she said. 'It doesn't mean he doesn't eat. And anyway, he's only twenty-five.'

'Which means he's a lot more experienced than you, and you know very well Dad wouldn't approve.'

Shannon's eyes darkened with anger. 'But Dad's not here, and it's only dinner for heaven's sake. I'm not doing anything wrong. And you'll be there, so how risky is that?'

Julia had to laugh. 'All right, I'll think about it,' she said.

Shannon still wasn't satisfied. 'But what's there to think about?' she demanded. 'Why don't you ask him when he comes over later? Or you could ask when you ring to tell him what car to bring.'

'You're pushing too hard, Shannon, so stop now.'

Shannon's expression immediately turned sulky. 'It's not fair,' she mumbled, 'Ottie gets to see him all the time, and I'll be gone next week.'

Not surprised that some competition had arisen between them over Rico's affections, Julia said, 'He's her cousin, so it stands to reason . . .'

'Second cousin,' Shannon cut in. 'And she's already kissed him.'

Julia's eyes widened.

'You don't have to look at me like that.'

'And now you two are having some kind of contest about how long it's going to take you to kiss him?' Julia said, and knew immediately from Shannon's face that she'd guessed right. 'Shannon, you're playing with fire,' she warned. 'He's a man, not a boy, and you girls shouldn't be teasing him, trying to lead him on ... Apart from anything else, you could get *him* into trouble.'

Shannon threw out her hands in fury. 'That's the trouble with you,' she raged. 'You think everything's about sex, well no-one even mentioned it until you did ...'

'No, you did,' Julia corrected.

'I only said the word, whereas you ...'

'Listen, I might be prepared to tolerate more on the romance front than Dad, but it doesn't mean I'm going to look the other way while you throw yourself at Rico.'

'I'm not throwing myself,' Shannon shouted furiously. 'I only asked if he could come for dinner ...'

'Because you're on a mission to make him kiss you.'

'With you right there? I don't think so, and why do you have to take it out on me, just because you're having problems with Dad ...'

'That's got nothing to do with it.'

'Yes it has, and I think you're really mean to him. You didn't even kiss him when he left on Saturday, even though he tried to kiss you.'

Julia shook her head in despair. 'You don't miss a thing, do you?' she sighed. 'But you don't always understand everything you see, so before you start jumping to conclusions, let's get back to the main issue, which is you and Rico.'

Brightening at the sound of being paired with him, Shannon said, 'Rico and I are just friends, Mum. There's nothing else in it, except what's in your imagination.'

'If that's true, then you won't mind missing your ride with him this afternoon while you get on with some studying.'

Shannon's eyes bulged with fury. 'I've already told you, I know everything . . .'

'Discussion over, you're revising straight after lunch for three hours, and if you dare to backchat me again, I'll get Dad on the line.'

'You can do that, because he never makes me revise the way you do.'

'Don't force my hand over this, Shannon,' Julia warned. 'I'm not saying you can't see Rico, I'm just saying that your exams have to take precedence over learning to ride.'

'But Mum!'

'That's my final word. Now, go and wash your hands, then you can come and help me with lunch.'

As Shannon stomped off into her bedroom, Julia began tidying up the table, aware that she was far angrier than she'd shown, or than was probably warranted. Whether it was because Josh hadn't even attempted to speak to her since she'd called him on Saturday night – except through the children – or because she was concerned about Shannon's crush, she wasn't entirely sure. Actually, it undoubtedly had more to do with Josh, because she could barely think of him lately without becoming uptight and resentful over his failure to reassure her that he'd ended his affair with Sylvia. Though they obviously weren't together right now, they could easily be in touch by phone, and God only knew what kind of calls they might be having. Sylvia had often boasted about how good she was at phone sex, and the very idea that Josh had become one of the mindless idiots who drooled after her that way was so disgusting she could almost hate him.

She would hate him, she told herself, if she didn't love him so much, though God knew, she'd never felt less turned on by him than she had since finding out about Sylvia. However, she couldn't deny she was missing him, which in itself was extremely annoying when he clearly wasn't feeling the same way about her. Or, in typically perverse male fashion, he was punishing her with silence for making him feel guilty about something he damned well deserved to feel guilty about.

Chapter Ten

Josh was sitting on the aft deck checking email, while talking to Marina on the phone, and keeping an eye on Dan, who was helping hose down next door's catamaran. They'd long had the neighbouring berth to Brian Guest, a high-flying advertising executive, and his family, so they all knew each other well, and luckily Dan and Brian's son Gavin were around the same age.

Marina had a stack of messages, though fortunately there wasn't much she couldn't deal with herself, while this current batch of emails wasn't being quite so obliging. At least four needed answers immediately, which he couldn't provide without making several more calls, and three were from authors either demanding latest sales figures, or wanting to know why their books weren't in their local WHSmith. Some of the details Marina could handle, but the TLC and rockets-under-publishers were down to him.

Not until he rang off did he realise quite how far the temperature had dropped, for the wind coming into the marina had started to turn bitter now, and the way it was blowing up meant they could be in for a rocky night. Dan would love it – the wilder the better, as far as he was concerned. Watching him now, dashing about the other boat, taking orders from Brian and bossy Gavin like the good little crew he was, Josh felt his heart swell with pride. How could he be anything other than glad he'd brought Dan here, when the boy was clearly in seventh heaven? And when he, Josh, wasn't calming irate or insecure authors, courting new editors, living with the guilt of stealing into another berth in the dead of night to take a phone call from Sylvia, or dealing with his highly stressed teenage daughter who'd been on the phone earlier for over half an hour complaining about her mother, he was loving being here. It was just a pity Julia and Shannon didn't seem to be getting on so well, he reflected grimly to himself.

'It's not fair, Dad,' Shannon had wailed, 'I have to have a holiday too. I'm not a machine, and she's making me stay in to do all my coursework.'

'But your exams are coming up, sweetheart,' he'd pointed out. 'You need to study.'

'Yes, but not all day. I was doing really well with my riding, and I like need some relaxation in order to sit my exams, not to be all stressed and uptight, but now she's got me locked in my room and won't let me out. You've got to talk to her, Dad. Please.'

'Shannon . . .'

'No, don't take her side!' Shannon cried. 'I'm doing well at school, Dad, you know I am. So I should be allowed to go out, shouldn't I? Fen's not making Ottie study all the time, and she's got her mocks coming up too. Dad, please make her let me go out. Please, please, please. I'll love you for ever.'

In the end he'd agreed to have a word with Julia, as much to free up his hands to help Dan with the jib, as to placate Shannon. She probably wouldn't be feeling too happy with him by now though, for a couple of hours had passed since he'd promised to tackle her problem. He'd been up to his eyes coping with halyards and wind swings, not to mention phone calls, emails and a courier from Marina who'd been waiting when they'd returned to port, with documents in need of his signature.

He'd put Shannon out of her misery in the next few minutes though, for he really should call Julia anyway. She was probably assuming by now that he was deliberately avoiding her, and, in truth, she wasn't altogether wrong. However, he didn't want to risk another row before he'd dealt with these emails and vetted an urgent contract in order to FedEx it back to London tomorrow, so she and Shannon would just have to wait a little bit longer. Before he went any further, he needed to pop below to fetch a warm jacket for Dan, and make some kind of decision about what they were going to eat tonight.

After tossing Dan's fleece over to Brian he returned to his laptop, and was just getting stuck into the emails when his mobile burbled into life. With his eyes still on the computer screen he reached for it, expecting it to be Marina, or someone else related to work, but on hearing who it was all thoughts of everything else slipped from his mind.

'Hi,' she said. 'Can you talk?'

'Not really,' he answered, sounding deliberately cold, in spite of the intimacy of their more recent calls.

'OK. So just answer yes or no,' she said. 'Have you given any more thought to coming over here?'

'It's out of the question,' he told her. 'Julia knows you're there.'

'But you want to come.'

After checking to make sure Dan wasn't in earshot, he said, 'Look, there's no point me trying to pretend anything here, because we both know I'd be there if I could, but we agreed, when this started, that as soon as it needed to be over it would be, and it needs to be over.'

'How's Julia?' she said mildly. 'Has she found out anything about her father yet?'

He took a breath. 'Not really,' he answered. Then, trying again, he said, 'Sylvia, you have to stop calling me. I know it . . .'

'Josh, darling, I'm not asking you to marry me,' she said. 'I just want you to go on fucking me.'

His eyes closed as her bluntness had the desired effect. 'I have to go now,' he said gruffly.

She fell silent, but though he intended to ring off, for some reason he didn't.

'You know, I think I should call Julia,' she said finally. 'I'm very late with my condolences, which isn't good in a friend. Could you give me the number of where she is?'

Astonished that she was even suggesting it, he said, 'Sylvia, you must know there's no way in the world she wants to talk to you.'

'I can always call her mobile,' she went on, as

if he hadn't spoken. 'Or I could get the number from Shannon. Does she have her mobile with her? Yes, I'm sure she does . . .'

'Sylvia, what the hell is going on?' he cried.

'I just want the number of where Julia is,' she replied. 'So why don't you give it to me, and then I won't have to call Shannon, will I?'

Realising this was probably some kind of power play, to see how far she could push him, he was tempted just to ring off, but he sure as hell didn't want her calling Shannon, any more than he wanted her talking to Julia. However, he knew from experience that it wasn't wise to mess with her when she was intent on exerting control. It had only happened once before, when she'd wanted him to make love to her at his office and he'd refused. As far as he was concerned he wasn't prepared to conduct any part of their relationship on his territory. She'd clearly sensed it, so to show him that it would happen her way, she'd waltzed right in while Marina was there, chatted with her for a minute or two, then had unbelted her rain-coat, while turning her back so that only he could see, from where he was sitting, that she was stark naked underneath. He'd immediately ushered her into his office, closing the door firmly behind her, and had barely had time to send Marina out for coffee before he was fulfilling Sylvia's fantasy of being taken over his desk.

'Julia's your best friend,' he reminded her, after giving her the number of the mill house. 'Why would you want to hurt her?'

'She's your wife,' she countered, 'why would you?'

He took a breath, but before he could respond she said, 'The fact is, Josh, it's not about hurting her, it's about us not being able to get enough of each other. Now, I know you don't want to admit that, but we both know it's true. You're thinking about me all the time, even now you're imagining your cock going all the way inside me . . .'

'Sylvia stop . . .'

'Tell me it's not true.'

'It's not true.'

She laughed. 'You don't make a good liar,' she told him.

'Look, please don't call again,' he said, meaning it.

'If I thought you meant that, I wouldn't,' she responded. 'But I know you don't.'

As the line went dead he clicked off from his end and let his eyes drift to his computer screen, then on out across the marina, to where the clouds were gathering on a far horizon. But he was seeing nothing, he didn't even hear Dan calling out for him to look, because he was too appalled by how deep in this he seemed to be. Sylvia wasn't just going to go away as they'd agreed, that much was clear, but worse was the fact that he wasn't exactly trying to make her. Oh, he was saying the words, but he was convincing no-one, least of all her, because the truth was, he wanted to go on screwing her, and if he could get to New York, he knew he'd probably be on the next flight. He wished he knew what was drawing him to her, because he had no real feelings for her, and although she was great in bed, it didn't even come close to what he shared with Julia. So why the hell was he finding it so hard to let her go? It wasn't even easing his conscience to know that he was making no attempts to call her. She was doing all the running, letting him know that she wanted this affair to continue, and as far as she was concerned it was certainly going to.

Suddenly he was having visions of it turning into some kind of *Fatal Attraction* scenario, and knowing only too well where that had ended, his blood ran cold. But Sylvia was a successful woman with a public profile who greatly valued her reputation not only as an author, and an artist, but as someone who had her life totally together, particularly where men were concerned. So it was a ludicrous overreaction on his part to start thinking she posed some kind of danger, because there was just no way a woman in her position was going to start threatening Julia, or any of them . . . So what had the phone number been about? A little artful manipulation to see how far she could push him, or something much darker? With untold relief he decided it had to be the former, because she had Julia's mobile number, so if she really did want to be in touch, she'd use that . . .

His mobile started to bleep. It was another text from Shannon.

Pleeeez talk to Mum! Can I borro £20? Wl pay u bk. Promis.

'Dad!' Dan shouted, as though he were three moorings away.

'I can hear you,' Josh answered.

'Brian and Gavin are going to the pub tonight. Can we?'

'No problem.'

'*Yes!*' Dan cried, punching the air. 'I'll buy you a pint with my pocket money.'

Smiling, Josh looked at the text again, then putting the phone aside, he attempted to carry on with the message he'd been typing when Sylvia called. It didn't take long, but there were at least a dozen others that had to be written, and by the time he was halfway through them more had come in, all needing urgent attention. Then Marina called to warn him that one of his major, US-based clients had just sacked his publisher.

'But he can't do that,' Josh protested, 'he's in the middle of a contract.'

'Well apparently he thinks he can, and the publisher wants you over there PDQ to sort it out.'

Josh stared at the phone in horror. 'Marina, you've got to deal with this,' he told her urgently, 'because there's just no way in the world I can go to New York right now. If I do, I'll have a divorce on my hands.'

Marina's astonishment was audible. 'Are you asking me to go over there?' she replied. 'I don't think they'll accept that.'

'Then just stall. Next week maybe, but this week is absolutely out of the question.'

'Because of Dan, of course,' she said. 'OK, leave it with me, I'll see what I can do.'

Almost the minute he rang off another text came through from Shannon, begging him to ring Julia immediately.

Unable to face further entreaties, he punched in the mill-house number and as soon as Julia answered he said, 'What the hell's going on with

Shannon? She says you've got her locked up over there, and she's texting me every five minutes . . .'

Julia's voice came down the line like a whip. 'Just who the hell do you think you're talking to?' she seethed. 'I don't hear from you in over two days, and now you've got the nerve to . . .'

'All right, all right,' he cut in, accepting he could have started better. 'Just tell me what's going on. Why isn't she allowed out?'

'Of course she's allowed out, but in case you'd forgotten her mocks are coming up, so it can't be all play.'

'She says she's prepared and doesn't need to do any more revision.'

'Josh, I'm not arguing with you about this. You can take her side all you like, but she's still going to put in three hours a day, and that's an end to it. Jesus, if it were left to you, she'd never get anywhere.'

'And left to you she'd have no fun.'

'Excuse me?' Her tone of voice was so scathing, he could be in no doubt that he'd hit the wrong button again. 'Isn't it you who has a problem with the social life . . .'

'What does she need twenty pounds for?' he interrupted, attempting to get off the issue.

'Probably to go to the Eden Project with Ottie tomorrow. I said I'd lend it to her, so she's obviously planning to pay me back with another loan from you, who will no doubt extend the credit over a much longer term, such as eternity. Now, if that's Shannon dealt with, perhaps you could tell me how my son is.'

'Don't try pulling that one,' he said darkly.

'You've spoken to him at least twice this afternoon, so you know very well that he's perfectly all right. And can I remind you that he's *our* son?'

'If you feel it to be necessary.'

His jaw clenched, but he didn't take her up on it, since it was just plain absurd.

'I take it you're not at all interested to know how I am, or what's been happening here?' she said tightly.

Sighing, he sat back against the guard rail and closed his eyes. 'Of course I'm interested,' he said, wishing they were together right now, because they might at least find a way to stop this nonsense and even hold each other. 'So how are things going?'

'Fine, thank you.'

'Is that all?'

'It's all while you're in this kind of mood. I just hope you're not taking it out on Dan that you have to be with him instead of at the office.'

His temper was back through the roof. 'If you ever make a comment like that again,' he seethed, turning away from the other boat, 'you'll end up seriously regretting it.'

'And exactly what's that supposed to mean?' she snapped back.

'It means don't ever try to intimate again that I don't care about my son,' and before they could plunge to any further depths of stupidity he cut the call short.

Unable to concentrate after that, he swung in through the hatch and went to fix himself a stiff G & T. So what that it wasn't yet five o'clock, he needed something to calm his temper, and though he was sorry for the clumsy way he'd just handled the call to Julia, he was in no frame of mind to apologise. Nor was he going to take any more calls for at least the next ten minutes, so whoever was ringing now would just have to go through to voicemail, Julia included.

Carrying his glass to the map table, he sank down on a padded banquette and rested his head in his hands. The situation between them was getting out of control. They never seemed to exchange a civil word any more, and though he knew, and accepted, that he was to blame, he wanted to know what in God's name he was supposed to do with the cards she was handing him – no sex, no closeness, not wanting him with her . . . He didn't have the first idea how to play them, and the really frightening part of it was that he was starting not to care.

Taking a large sip of his drink, he let his head fall back against the wood panelling behind him and sighed deeply. Was this how marriages ended, he was asking himself, with two people who were still in love somehow managing to lose sight of each other and control of where they were going? He guessed it must be, though God forbid he and Julia were heading that way. He had to do something to change this, to get them back on the rails, though he had to admit, seeing her there in Cornwall, so cosily ensconced in her father's house with a ready-made family around her, had unnerved him a lot. He could all too easily imagine her wanting to stay, and would hardly be able to blame her. It was the perfect setting for a writer, or a freelance editor, or a mother with two children who really didn't need to be corrupted by the materialism of London. The kids probably wouldn't mind that much either, since there were obviously some good schools around, and if they were out in the country Dan could have a dog, while Shannon already had a best friend, and so, come to that, did Julia. The only one it wouldn't work for was him, because there was just no way he could run his business so far out of town.

Suddenly becoming aware of raised voices, he abandoned his drink and went up on deck to investigate. To his dismay he found Gavin laying into Dan like the monster bully he was, poking and pushing him around, and practically foaming at the mouth as he raged, 'You're just *stupid*, and thick and you don't know how to do anything properly. I should smash your head in for that . . .'

'I'm sorry,' Dan was saying, his little face pale with concern. 'I didn't mean to do it.'

'Yes you did! I know you did. Well you can get off my boat, because we don't want you on here. You stink and I hate you and everyone's right about you, you're just a weirdo . . .'

'Gavin, that's enough,' Brian snapped, appearing from below his own decks.

'What's going on?' Josh demanded.

'I got water on him by accident,' Dan explained. 'I was using the hose . . .'

'You did it on purpose,' Gavin yelled, purple in the face.

'No, I didn't, honestly,' Dan assured him. 'It really was an accident. It was, Dad,' he said, turning anxious eyes to his father. 'I never meant to do it.'

Suddenly Gavin was on him, rugby-tackling him to the deck, and as Dan's head hit a guard rail Josh leapt on board even before Brian could snatch his son from the fray.

'Are you OK?' Josh said, dropping down next to Dan.

Dan looked up at him with tear-filled eyes. 'I didn't mean to do it, Dad,' he said. 'Honest, Gavin, I didn't. Please be my friend again.'

'No fucking way!' came the response.

Josh's heart felt as though it would explode, as fighting down the urge to smash a fist into Gavin's fleshy white face, he helped Dan to his feet. He wouldn't carry him, because he didn't want Gavin jeering at him for being a baby, but one more word from that sorry-assed, overweight little bastard ... What the hell was the matter with him, for God's sake, going off like that over a drop of fucking water? And Dan apologised – though Josh was sorry he hadn't taken the hose and blasted the kid right off the deck. But it wasn't in Dan's nature to do anything like that. He almost always backed down, to the point of letting other people walk right over him, which never failed to make Josh love and worry about him even more.

Waiting until they were safely down in the cabin to lift his son in his arms, he held him tight, and rocked him back and forth. How was Dan ever going to survive in this world if he didn't learn to stand up for himself? He was too kind, too ready to admit he was wrong and too damned vulnerable physically for Josh to encourage him to get into a fight. *Just please God don't let that crack to the head have any adverse effects now,* he prayed, because he'd be holding that bully next door responsible if it did.

'Can we still go to the pub with them?' Dan asked.

Josh sighed and held him aloft to look into his face. 'Of course,' he said, managing to smile, for much as he didn't want to, he knew he had to put his own feelings aside and play this Dan's way. If he didn't Dan would only become agitated, which could lead to a seizure, and frankly he'd rather see his son bowing in humility than being thrown around by those terrible convulsions.

'Mum? Are you OK?' Shannon said, coming into the kitchen to find Julia sitting at the table and dabbing a tissue to her eyes.

'Yes, I'm fine,' Julia answered, inhaling deeply as she looked up.

'You're crying.'

'No. Well, a little. I had a bit of a row with Dad. Nothing serious.'

Shannon was immediately worried. 'It was my fault, wasn't it? I didn't mean to . . .'

'It's all right,' Julia assured her, slipping an arm round her waist. 'It was my fault really, but it'll be OK. Nothing to worry about.' She allowed a glimmer of irony to slip into her eyes as she looked up at her daughter. 'So I've been keeping you locked up, have I?'

Shannon's colour rose as she began twisting from side to side. 'It's really boring doing all that coursework, Mum, when I know it already.'

'Believe it or not, you'll thank me one day,' Julia told her, getting up to answer the phone. *If it's*

269

Josh, she was thinking, *I'm going to say sorry and make a special effort to be nice. I might even suggest Shannon and I drive over there for a couple of days to spend time with him and Dan.* 'Hello?' she said into the receiver.

'Julia? It's Rod Fuller,' a voice at the other end announced. 'I just got your message. What can I do for you?'

'Rod!' she exclaimed, having almost forgotten she'd tried to contact the ex-detective, now best-selling thriller writer, who, long ago, had been one of her star authors. 'Thanks for calling me back. I have a favour to ask.'

'As the woman who launched the ship of my success, I'd say just about anything goes,' he responded cheerily. 'So name it.'

Julia glanced at Shannon, who'd dropped down into a chair and was idly leafing through some papers on the table. 'I was hoping you could use your old contacts to help me trace someone,' she said. 'I mean someone who might have a criminal record.'

Shannon's head immediately came up.

'Shouldn't be a problem,' Fuller responded. 'Just give me what you have. Name, age, nature of crime, that sort of thing.'

'Douglas Henry Cowan, born 1936.'

After jotting it down and checking he had the spelling correct, he said, 'Nature of crime?'

Not wanting to put it into words, especially with Shannon in earshot, she said, 'I'd just like to know if his name comes up, and if it does, perhaps you could tell me what for.'

'Shouldn't be too much of a problem, but can

you give me some kind of time line? Last week, last year . . .'

Julia grimaced. 'Probably more like twenty-five years ago,' she confessed.

'OK,' he said slowly. 'Just as long as I know. I'll get back to you as soon as I have something.'

As Julia rang off Shannon was agog. 'Do you think he was a criminal?' she asked, excitedly.

Julia shook her head. 'Not really, but Grandma Alice said something once . . .' She shrugged. 'I just want to be sure.'

'What did she say?'

'Nothing specific.'

'What do you think it was? Oh my God, what if he murdered someone? Or robbed a bank, or he was a terrorist . . .'

'Stop it,' Julia chided.

Shannon was grinning. 'So have you found anything here?' she asked, ruffling her hands through the papers.

Julia sighed. 'Nothing but old bills, exercise books from the various courses he did, and a box of keys at the back of a drawer, which either fit his desk, the filing cabinets or the cupboard under the window, all of which I've now sorted through and emptied.'

'What about the key I found when I was folding his clothes? What does that belong to?'

Julia frowned. 'What key? You never mentioned it.'

'Yes I did. Well, I thought I did. It was in a rusty old tin, that was inside a pair of really raggedy trousers that looked as though they hadn't been worn for years. I found them stuffed in a carrier bag at the back of his wardrobe. I'll get it, shall I?'

Julia nodded, though she wasn't particularly excited, for by the sound of it, the key either belonged to the shed, which wasn't locked anyway, or to something that had long since been thrown away. When Shannon produced it, one look more or less confirmed her instincts. It was small and antiquated, and so rusty that even if it did have a home, it was doubtful it would work.

'Did you remember to call Rico about picking up the things for the charity shop?' Shannon asked, watching Julia drop the key into a drawer in the table.

'Yes, and he's going to delay until we've had time to go through the attic. He's bringing a ladder over any minute though, so if you want to go and make yourself presentable . . .'

Shannon gave her a wary look, then seeing she was smiling she jumped up to hug her, before zooming back into the bedroom to apply eye-liner, mascara and lip gloss, and possibly to change into something Rico might find really cool and sexy.

A few minutes later the Bowers' pickup truck, complete with Rico, Fen and stepladder, came crunching over the gravel outside.

'Hi,' Julia cried, going outside to greet them. 'What a surprise, I wasn't expecting to see you today.'

'Can't keep away,' Fen laughed, embracing her as she came down the steps. 'Daddy's out for the evening, so are Ottie and Rico, and as I imagine Shannon's going to the pub with them, I thought we could sink a bottle and have a bite together.'

'Sounds a wonderful idea,' Julia agreed. 'We just need to get some wine.'

'Already taken care of,' Fen declared, producing two bottles from inside the truck, and wasting no more time she sailed off into the kitchen to open one and chill the other.

'It's OK, I can do it,' Rico assured Julia as she started to help take down the ladder.

Their eyes met and she smiled before turning away, amused by the colour that had come into his cheeks. 'Ah ha,' she said, as Shannon appeared in the doorway. 'What's all this about a pub?'

'Oh yes, we're going to the one in the village tonight,' Shannon replied airily, as though she went to a pub every night. 'They've got a live band, and please don't say no alcohol, because I know that already.'

'Where would you like me to put it?' Rico asked, coming up behind them with the ladder on his shoulder.

'Oh, uh, would you mind carrying it to the upstairs bedroom?' Julia answered. She felt herself blush, simply for using the word bedroom, which was so ludicrous it almost made her laugh.

'I can help if you like,' Shannon offered, skimming round to the end Julia had tried to grab.

'Thank you,' he replied and after waiting for her to take it, he treated Julia to a brief, friendly smile before moving on.

Julia watched them, and tried not to feel anything as Shannon marched past positively glowing with pleasure.

'*Voilà!*' Fen proclaimed, holding up two full

glasses as Julia walked in. 'After the day I've had no-one could deserve it more.'

'That bad?' Julia asked, taking one.

'Don't ask.'

'Then here's to you,' and clinking glasses, they drank.

'What about you?' Fen asked. 'How did you get on here? Oh hell, sorry,' she groaned, as her mobile rang. 'This is probably the call I've been waiting for. Once over, I'm all yours,' and clicking on she started back outside to drag her briefcase from the truck.

Julia stood absently watching her, while listening to Shannon's and Rico's voices above, though she was thinking about Josh, and wondering how he was feeling after their call. Probably no better than she was, but now wasn't the time to ring back, with Fen having just arrived and the others around. She'd leave it until later, by which time, hopefully, they'd be ready to make up. Unless this was him ringing now, and feeling the tingle of anticipation she hadn't experienced since their early days together, she went to pick up the receiver.

'Julia? It's Pauline,' said the voice at the other end. 'How are you? I've been so worried about you. I wish you'd call, because honestly, honey, I really don't think it was serious between Josh and Sylvia, so you shouldn't . . .'

'I'm sorry, Pauline,' Julia interrupted tightly, 'I don't want to discuss it, so if you don't mind . . .'

'Oh, no, not at all. I know, it's perfectly ghastly when someone cheats on you. I've had it happen to me, and . . .'

'Just tell me this,' Julia said, deciding to go with it for the moment. 'Did you know before last week that they were seeing each other?'

'Hell, no. I mean, I ran into Josh coming out of there a while back, and I kind of had my suspicions, but I never actually *knew* it was going . . .'

'How long ago was a while back?'

'Oh, honey. I don't know. Three, four months, I guess.'

Julia's eyes closed as a terrible jealousy engulfed her. 'So it was going on for quite some time,' she said.

'I don't want to say that. I just want you to know I'm here for you, and if you need me to come down there . . .'

'No! Thank you. I really don't,' Julia assured her. 'But I would like to know how you got this number.'

'Why, Sylvia gave it me. She's been so concerned about you . . .'

Not even bothering to ask how Sylvia had got hold of it, since it could only have been from Josh, Julia said, 'I'm sorry, Pauline, I have to go now,' and without waiting for a response she hung up, just as Shannon bounced back into the kitchen with Rico at her heels.

'Everything OK?' Shannon asked, peering into her mother's face.

Julia forced a smile. 'Everything OK,' she confirmed, feeling acutely aware of Rico's eyes, and making sure not to meet them. 'Thanks for bringing the ladder,' she said, going to tidy up the table.

'It was my pleasure,' he assured her.

She smiled and nodded, and kept focused on what she was doing. 'Shannon and I were wondering if you'd like to have dinner with us one evening?' she said, surprising herself, as well as Shannon.

'Thank you,' he answered. 'I would like that very much.'

Shannon beamed, and gave Julia a bruising hug before announcing she was going to get her coat from the bedroom.

Julia and Rico watched her go, until Julia was forced to look at him as he said, 'I know this is a difficult time for you, so please, if there is anything I can do, you must ask me.'

'Thank you,' she said, having to clear her throat. 'You're very kind.'

His gaze didn't waver, even though hers did. 'I will wait outside,' he said, as though not wanting to bother her any more.

As he walked away she allowed her eyes to follow him, but in her mind she was seeing Josh and feeling her heart twisting so painfully in the betrayal of months rather than weeks, or even days, that she was at a total loss as to how to deal with it.

'OK, darling?' she said, finding Shannon's bedroom door open.

'Just coming,' Shannon responded, brushing her hair. 'Thanks, Mum,' she whispered in the mirror. 'You're the best.'

Remembering the dinner invitation, Julia's heart sank. Why had she done that, she wondered. But what did it matter? She'd be there to make sure nothing happened, and if she invited Fen and Ottie along too … 'If I give you twenty pounds from Dad,' she said, 'do you promise not to spend it on booze?'

'I swear. Ottie knows the landlord, and she says there's no way he'll give us a drink while we're still under age.'

Julia smiled. 'And no nonsense with Rico?' she said meaningfully as she drew a small wad of cash from her back pocket.

Shannon came to give her another hug. 'I promise, I won't do anything stupid,' she said, with all the sincerity she could muster as she took her loan.

Julia kissed her. 'Home by ten?'

Shannon pulled a face.

'OK, whatever time Ottie has to be home, same goes for you.'

Shannon couldn't have looked more delighted, and grabbing up her purse, she shoved it into a pocket and with a saucy, 'Don't get drunk, you girls,' she was gone.

After checking that Fen was still on the phone, Julia picked up her own mobile and carried it back into Shannon's room. Josh answered on the second ring.

'When did you last speak to Sylvia?' she asked.

She guessed it was surprise that prevented him from answering right away, so said, 'Please don't lie. I want to know when you last spoke to her.'

'She called about an hour ago,' he answered flatly.

Her heart turned over so harshly that she almost let the phone drop rather than go any further. 'And before that?' she said.

'I'm not sure. Sunday, Saturday. Look, I've tried telling her it's over . . .'

'So you're having phone sex with her?'

'No!'

'I know how she operates, Josh, and if you're too weak to resist her, or if you're so obsessed with her . . .'

'I'm trying to deal with it,' he cried. 'She's just not listening. Jesus Christ, if you can tell me how to stop her, I'll do it.'

Knowing very well that Sylvia wouldn't let go until Sylvia was ready, she said, 'How did she get this number?'

He didn't answer.

'Pauline just called me,' she almost shouted, 'and actually admitted that she got the number from Sylvia. So what the hell is going on, Joshua? Why did you give her this number?'

'Because she said she'd get it from Shannon if I didn't.'

Incensed by the very idea of her daughter being dragged into his tawdry affair, she said, 'Listen to me now, Joshua, and listen hard, because I mean every word I'm about to say. You either get her out of our lives, or you get out. The choice is yours,' and abruptly ending the call, she switched off the mobile and returned to the kitchen.

'Ah, there you are,' Fen said, looking up from an open newspaper on the table. 'So where were we? Maybe we should start with another toast.'

'To whatever you like,' Julia responded, reaching for her glass.

Fen frowned. 'Are you OK?' she said. 'You're looking a bit pale.'

'I'm fine. I just haven't eaten much today, but it's not going to stop me downing this entire bottle, and possibly even another.'

Fen smiled, though she still appeared concerned. 'So what shall we drink to?' she asked.

'To us,' Julia said decisively.

Seeming to like it, Fen clinked her glass, and they both drank.

'Are you seeing the probate officer tomorrow?' Fen asked, sitting down at the table.

Julia shook her head. 'No, on Thursday at eleven. Then we've got the ashes at three. Will you be there?'

'Of course.' Fen tilted her head to one side and peered into Julia's face again. 'I don't mean to pry,' she said, 'but I'm a good listener if you're feeling in need.'

Julia looked at her, then sighing heavily she stared down into her wine and wondered where to begin. In the end, it didn't prove too difficult, for she was soon confiding everything: Josh's affair, the problems they'd been having leading up to it, the appalling relationship with her mother, the call she'd just had from Pauline. She only stopped short at confessing her worst fears where her father was concerned, because that was something Fen really didn't need to know about.

When it had all finished spilling out she looked at Fen's bemused and kindly face and laughed dryly. 'Bet you wish you'd never asked,' she teased.

Fen smiled and emptying the bottle into their glasses, she went to open another.

'Please tell me that the perfection of your family

is real,' Julia said. 'You all seem so happy, and supportive of each other.'

Fen's expression was wry as she returned to the table. 'Believe me, there are plenty of cracks beneath our perfect surface,' she assured her. 'In fact, we've actually come through quite a lot, just in the last five years. Daddy's had two heart attacks, Mummy had a cancer scare, Ottie was almost killed in a school-bus crash. Then Bob had an affair -- not with my best friend, I have to say, but he actually left me for a while to go and live with her. He came back, as you can see, and he swears they have no contact now, but after something like that, how can you ever be sure?'

Julia's head was spinning at the very idea of how she would cope if Josh left to go and live with Sylvia. She wondered if she could ever take him back if he did, or if he would even want to come back. 'How on earth did you manage to forgive him?' she asked faintly.

Fen shrugged and let her eyes drift. 'It wasn't easy, but what choice did I have?' she answered. 'I still loved him, and I didn't want our marriage to be over, but even now, while he's supposed to be in Salisbury on this course, I'm wondering if he really is. I could check, of course, but I won't, because that way madness lies.' She sighed and smiled. 'We're getting there. It's a lot better now than when he first came back. I really didn't think it was going to work then.'

'I take it he was the one who ended the affair.'
'I think that's how it was. It's what he said.'
'Do you still love him now? I guess you must.'
'Yes, but there's no doubt, when your illusions

have been shattered and need repairing they never go back together quite the same way. It's different after, but you make it work, for the children, for the rest of your family and for yourselves, because ultimately it's what you want. You just have to accept that it won't be the same as it was before.' Her eyes moved to Julia's. 'I don't think your marriage is in any real trouble from what you've told me, at least I hope it's not, but you have to do something to get that woman off his back before she manages to do even more damage than she already has.'

Julia's heart turned over. 'Do you think it's serious between them?' she asked.

Fen grimaced and shook her head. 'It's hard to say.'

'What about his reasons for the affair?'

'You mean to save your marriage by stopping him looking elsewhere? Peculiarly warped though it is, to the male mind that would have some logic, and being such a skilled manipulator of men as Sylvia Holland obviously is, she would know that. So it's my guess that she's had her eye on him for a while.'

'So what do you think I should do?'

Fen took a breath. 'In the short term,' she said, 'I think you'll have to play it very carefully, and make sure Josh is totally aware of what he stands to lose if he goes any further with this. Obviously he already knows that, but women like Sylvia can be extremely persuasive.'

Feeling a shudder of dread run down her spine, Julia said, 'And in the long term?'

Fen looked at her meaningfully. 'I think you know the answer to that,' she said. 'You have to sort out the intimacy issue you're having, or you really might end up losing him.'

Though Julia's insides recoiled from the truth, she wasn't about to deny it. 'It's why I have to find out why my father left,' she said. 'It's the only piece of the puzzle that's missing, so as hard as I've tried to resist it, I have to accept that it must be connected to the way I am. If it's not, then I really don't know where we go from there.'

'And you really have no idea why he went?'

Hating lying to her, Julia shook her head. 'I've been over and over it,' she said, 'with Josh, with a therapist and on my own. I called my aunt, by the way, to find out if she'd sent the photos. She was the only one I could think of, simply on the basis that being a sister-in-law makes her one removed, so she might break ranks with my mother and uncle and do something decent for my father. I'm less of that opinion now I've spoken to her. What I do know, though, is that they're afraid of what I might discover. I have to confess, this is starting to scare me a bit too.'

Fen was looking pensive. 'I don't know if this means anything,' she said, 'but it only came back to me yesterday. Tilde mentioned something, just before Dougie had his second stroke, about a woman who'd visited him, here in the house, a couple of weeks before it happened, which would be about six or seven weeks ago now. She didn't have any idea who the woman was, said she'd never seen her before, and she didn't like to ask Dougie in case he thought she was prying.'

Julia's heart was starting to beat faster. 'Did she say what the woman looked like?' she asked.

'No, but we can ask,' Fen replied, picking up her mobile and speed-dialling Tilde's number.

A few minutes later, after some close quizzing and note-taking, Fen rang off and returned her gaze to Julia. 'Apparently she was quite young, fortyish, which is young to dear Tilde, plump, wore a purple-coloured dress that might have been brown, had short, dark hair, cut a bit like a pageboy, and drove a light blue or silver car. I can see this is ringing some bells.'

Julia's expression was incredulous. 'Apart from the car,' she said, 'the only person I know who comes close to fitting that description is my sister.'

Julia was still wide awake, staring into the moonlit darkness, when she heard Shannon coming in downstairs. She barely registered it, however, for her thoughts were entirely focused on Josh, and how much she was regretting the way she'd cut him short when he'd called, half an hour ago, to find out how she was. But she'd been too exhausted for another row, which she'd felt almost certain would happen, so she'd told him it was better that they both got some sleep and spoke in the morning.

Now, as the minutes ticked by, and the reality of his affair grew larger and larger in her mind, a desperate urgency was coming over her to call him, to make him swear that he still loved her, and that he despised Sylvia and regretted every moment he'd ever spent with her. But her mobile lay untouched, not only because she wouldn't allow herself to beg, but because she was afraid of finding his line busy. If it was, she knew she'd convince herself he was talking to Sylvia, and already she was imagining what they'd be saying to each other, how intimate they might be, and what form their masturbation might take. Denial and rage made her push her face into the pillow, as though she could block the hideous images from her mind, but she could still hear Josh's voice, see every part of him, and even feel how much he must be wishing he was in New York now. The pain of it rose up like a fire to engulf her, and in despair and fury she struggled hard not to scream. He couldn't be doing this, he just couldn't. She had to make him stop because the pain, the jealousy, and the fear of where it might lead was tearing her apart.

Dimly aware that her own imagination was tormenting her even more cruelly than the truth, she made herself sit up and take several deep breaths. She needed to regain some control, for she was becoming almost obsessed with the thought of them together, and if she carried on like this she was going to end up saying or doing something she'd bitterly regret. So in an attempt to blot it from her mind she tried focusing on her sister for a while, which brought no comfort, but it was still a welcome distraction.

Though she'd left several messages throughout the evening, Pam hadn't yet deigned to call back, and considering how little love was lost between them, Julia didn't imagine that even telling her it was urgent would particularly rouse her. So, for the time being at least, she was left wondering what might have brought Pam here six weeks ago – if indeed it was her whom Tilde had seen –

and if it was, how had she known where their father lived?

Finally accepting that no answers were going to present themselves tonight, about anything, she decided to try and let it all go till morning. God only knew what would happen when she spoke to Josh, but she could at least call Pam again, or hopefully Pam would call her. In the meantime, Shannon was knocking on the door.

'Are you awake Mum?' she whispered, putting her head round. 'Can I come in?'

Reaching out to turn on the lamp, Julia struggled up against the pillows, and grunted as Shannon all but threw herself on top of her.

'I had the most fantastic time,' she sighed ecstatically as she rolled back on the bed and spread out her arms. 'I absolutely love it here, Mum. It's so cool. Don't you love it here?'

In spite of the heaviness in her heart, Julia was regarding her with a knowing smile. 'So did you kiss him?' she asked, wishing her own life could be so uncomplicated and pure.

Shannon's head came up. 'No! I did not,' she cried. 'You told me I wasn't allowed to.'

'You're not,' Julia confirmed. 'But I take it you had a good time anyway?'

'The best. Ottie's friends are so cool. They're like really switched-on and they're into all the same kinds of things as me, like the same music, and stuff. Can I learn to play tennis, Mum? I mean, I know I didn't like it before, but everyone's going over there tomorrow, and I really want to go too. Please say I can. They've all got their mocks coming up, and their parents are allowing it.'

Julia was stroking her hair, and gazing into her lovely, fresh young face. 'OK,' she said.

Shannon could hardly believe she'd won without a fight. 'I love you, Mum,' she declared. 'You're the best mum in all the world. I told Dad that when he called me earlier.'

Julia's heart immediately reacted. 'You did?' she said. 'What did he say?'

'He said he knew.'

Feeling a surge of longing for him, Julia closed her eyes and let the warmth of it spread all the way through her. 'How's Dan?' she asked, looking at Shannon again. 'He'd had a row with Gavin the last time I spoke to him.'

'I think it's all sorted out now, but Dad really can't stand that boy. Nor can I. He's just a bully, and he doesn't deserve to have Dan as a friend.'

Julia winced, as Shannon shifted round to lie next to her. 'I thought you'd like what Dad said about you,' she said, settling her head on Julia's shoulder. 'He really loves you, Mum, I know he does. I think you've just got to be a bit nicer to him and then everything will be all right again.'

Julia was listening and smiling, and thinking that there was nothing quite like receiving advice on her love life from her teenage daughter, particularly when Shannon didn't know the half of what had gone on. Nor did Julia want her to, for there was nothing in the world to be gained from destroying Shannon's illusions where her father was concerned. 'So with all this talk of Ottie's friends, am I to understand that someone else has replaced Rico in your affections?' she asked hopefully.

Shannon sighed long and forlornly. 'No,' she replied, picking up Julia's hand and twisting her wedding ring. 'I really, really like him, Mum. I mean, I know he's too old for me now, but lots of people marry someone ten years older than them, don't they?'

'It might be a little early to be thinking about marriage,' Julia said softly.

'But I'll be sixteen soon. It'll be OK then.'

Easily able to understand her infatuation, and remembering just how intense it could be at that age, Julia gave her a squeeze, and said, 'Time for bed now. We can talk some more in the morning.'

Shannon got as far as the door before turning back with a worried look on her face. 'You're not going to stop me seeing him, now I've told you that, are you?' she asked.

Julia smiled. 'No, but I do want you to remember your promise that you won't do anything you shouldn't.'

Shannon brightened. 'I will remember and I won't, I promise,' she said. 'Love you, sweet dreams.'

'Love you too,' Julia responded, and reaching out to turn off the light, she closed her eyes, hoping that sleep might come quickly to release her from the ready torment of her conscious mind.

Chapter Eleven

Josh was laughing quietly into the phone as Sylvia regaled him with some of the more lurid details of a party she'd just left in New York. Since she was talking about several people he knew, he was easily able to picture the scene she was describing, and even hear the outrage in one publisher's voice as he'd publicly insulted another.

Though it was still only seven in the morning, making it two a.m. in New York, they'd already been on the line for over half an hour, and since Dan was still asleep below decks there didn't seem to be any reason to ring off yet. Besides, at some point he intended to try again to persuade her that she really did have to stop calling.

Twenty minutes later they were still talking, laughing as they discussed how to handle an awkward situation that had arisen between Sylvia and her American agent. He didn't imagine she couldn't negotiate it without his input, but since she seemed to be valuing it, he saw no reason not to advise her. And from there the conversation seemed to flow on quite naturally to various deals he'd pulled off in recent times, some of which she claimed to be impressed by, while she teased him playfully about others.

Ignoring the fact that someone had been trying to get through for some time, he continued to listen, occasionally chuckling as she applied her caustic wit to descriptions of people neither of them much cared for, and the various encounters she'd had with them, until finally she yawned sleepily and said, 'Well, as much as I'd love to spend the whole night lying here talking to you, my darling, I've got a breakfast meeting at eight, so I think it's time to ring off. I'll call again when I wake up.'

Though he started to protest about her calling later, he found himself lacking the words, since there had been nothing sexual, or even particularly intimate about this morning's call – they'd simply been chatting like old friends who had a lot in common, and who enjoyed each other's humour, so to make any objection to speaking again seemed inappropriate, and even petty.

After they'd said goodbye, he slipped back down through the hatch, and after looking in on Dan who was still fast asleep, he put on some coffee then checked his messages. He suspected there would be several, for the line had been almost constantly bleeping towards the end of his call. He wasn't surprised to find that one was from Julia, letting him know that she'd woken up early and just wanted to hear his voice, and another was from Marina asking him to get back to her the minute he could. There were also several more calls with no messages, two easily identified from Julia, the others only coming up as private numbers.

Already feeling wretched for having to lie to Julia about whom he'd been speaking to for so long, and so early in the morning, he decided to put it off for the moment, and call Marina first.

'What are you doing in the office at this hour?' he asked when she answered.

'I can get a lot done before the phones start,' she reminded him. 'I assume you've been on the line to Tim Roper all this time,' she added, referring to the American author who'd sacked his publisher the day before.

Taken aback, he said, 'It's three o'clock in the morning over there, he'd hardly be calling me now.' Then realising the unidentified numbers were probably Roper's, he said, 'What's happened?'

'I'm sure you won't be surprised to hear he's on one of his benders. I won't repeat what he intends to do to his publisher, his New York agent and the world's press, just suffice it to say, you're the only one he feels he can trust, and he wants you over there now!'

Josh stiffened, then immediately began shaking his head. 'It's just not possible,' he said. 'I told you yesterday . . .'

'And I told him, though I didn't mention the divorce bit, but he's absolutely insisting you go over there, or you're fired too.'

Though he wasn't at all sure he intended to go, Josh was already frantically searching his mind for a way to sell this to Julia, as if such a possibility actually existed. 'What time did you last speak to him?' he asked.

'About five minutes ago. He might well have passed out by now, because he certainly sounded on the verge of it.'

'We can always hope,' he responded, turning to pour himself a coffee. 'Look, I've got a big day on with Dan today. There's no way I can let him down, so let's give Roper some time to sleep things off, and I'll speak to him later, see if his problems can be dealt with over the phone.'

'Meanwhile, shall I go ahead and check out the availability of flights for tomorrow?' she asked.

Reminding himself that his conscience was clear over this, for Roper's drink problem was not in his control, he said, 'OK, but don't book anything yet, and if Roper calls you before me, remind him that other people have lives too.'

As he rang off he finished pouring his coffee, then turned to watch a bleary-eyed Dan climbing out of his berth.

'Who were you talking to?' Dan asked, yawning as he came into the cabin.

'Marina. Mum's called a couple of times, do you want to call her back?'

He nodded and yawned again as he took the mobile. 'Can I have some orange juice first?' he asked.

'Of course. Then I'll make you some porridge.'

It wasn't that he was avoiding speaking to Julia, exactly, he just wanted her to be fully mindful of the fact that Dan was around when he floated the possibility of having to dash over to New York.

*

Julia had no idea whether it was because she'd drunk too much wine last night, or because she was coming down with some kind of flu, but her stomach was rejecting everything this morning, even water, her head was pounding, she was cold, shivery and so numbingly tired that she'd already decided, once she'd spoken to Josh and Dan, she was going straight back to bed.

Since Shannon had dashed off early to go riding with Ottie, she'd been alone in the kitchen, tidying up from last night, and repeatedly trying to get hold of Josh. Though she dreaded the reason for how long his line had been busy, she'd somehow forced herself to stay calm, but as she carried a hot lemon drink to the table now, and sat down next to the phone, she was feeling so anxious and nervous that she was actually afraid to pick it up.

In the end she made herself, and this time after she dialled his number she managed to get through. Dan answered almost immediately, and even before she could say hello he launched into how he'd been just about to call her, so she must have read his mind, which made them telephonic. Hearing Josh correct him in the background she smiled and listened to him chatter on excitedly, telling her all about their plans for the day, how they were going to sail as far as the Isle of Wight, and might even go on to France, or even Jamaica, if they had the right wind.

Laughing softly she said, 'Just make sure you send me a postcard.'

'Oh I will,' he assured her. 'And I'll bring you back a present. And one for Shannon too. Do you want to speak to Dad now, because my porridge is ready?'

'Yes please,' she answered, and felt a horrible clenching of nerves again as she waited for Dan to pass over the phone.

'Hi darling,' he said, coming onto the line. 'So you were awake early and thinking of me?'

'You got my message.'

'Of course. I was just making Dan's breakfast, then I was going to call back.'

'So who were you talking to all that time?'

'Would you believe, Tim Roper's on another of his benders? He's trying to fire everyone, apparently.'

So he had been on the line to New York, and no she wouldn't believe Tim Roper was on another of his benders, because it was just too damned convenient. 'So I suppose you have to go over there,' she said, feeling such a weariness descend on her that for a moment she wasn't sure she had it in her to object.

'I'm trying to avoid it,' he assured her. 'He hasn't called back in the last twenty minutes, so with any luck that means he's out cold. I'll just have to see what kind of shape he's in when he comes round.'

She took a breath, and opened her eyes wide, trying to stay connected to this, for something strange seemed to be happening inside her head that was making her feel oddly remote. 'You know I want to believe you,' she said, 'but I can't.'

'Darling, it's the truth. Call Marina, she'll tell you . . .'

'I don't want to call Marina. I just want this to

be over, Josh.' She stared down at her cup and wondered when she'd ever felt so peculiar inside, or so afraid. 'When did you last speak to Sylvia?' she asked quietly.

He didn't reply, and her heart twisted with so much pain that she wanted to die.

'That's who you were talking to all that time, wasn't it?' she said.

'Look, she just needed some advice about her agent . . .'

'So she called you at two thirty in the morning?'

'She has a breakfast meeting and wanted to talk it through beforehand.'

The room seemed to be spinning now, making her feel faint. She took a deep breath and closed her eyes. 'I don't know what to do,' she murmured, realising how close she was to the edge. 'I'm not sure I can take any more.'

'Listen, I swear it's the truth about Tim Roper,' he told her. 'He wants me over there, and he's threatening to fire me too, if I don't go. I could fly out and come back and Sylvia wouldn't even have to know I was there.'

'Josh, please credit me with some intelligence,' she responded, unable to open her eyes.

'For Christ's sake, I didn't ask for this to happen now,' he cried. 'Tim Roper's on his own agenda. It's got nothing to do with me, or Sylvia, or anything else.'

She swallowed hard, and after a couple of deep breaths she finally started to feel a bit steadier. 'If you go, Josh,' she said, then stopped, not entirely sure what she wanted to say.

'He's one of my biggest clients, Julia,' he

reminded her. 'You know that. He's not someone I can afford to lose.'

'And what about your wife? Can you afford to lose her?'

Her question fell into such a terrible silence that she could almost feel herself drowning in it. In the end he said, 'Julia, listen . . .'

'No, you listen, Josh. I'm not going to threaten you, nor am I going to beg, I'm just going to ask you, if you still love me, please don't go to New York.'

'Of course I still love you,' he said.

'Then tell me you won't go.'

'But . . .'

'Josh.'

'OK. If that's how it has to be, I won't go.'

'No matter what?'

'No matter what.'

Relief unfurled some of the knots in her head, but they were soon tightening again, for she simply didn't trust him. 'Is that a promise?' she asked.

'Yes. It's a promise.'

She sat very still, hardly connecting with what she was feeling now beyond an overwhelming sense of longing that seemed to go so deep inside her, so far into her very soul that it might have no end. It made her think of her father, and his protective arms, then of Josh and his embrace, but as tears of self-pity came to her eyes she blinked them away.

'Are you OK?' he asked.

'I think so. Tell me this, Josh, do you want her more than you want me?'

'Oh God, no, of course not,' he groaned, only now seeming to grasp just how afraid she was. 'Don't ever think that. You're the only woman who's ever really mattered to me, and you still are.'

'I wish I could believe you.'

'It's true. Please don't ever doubt how much I love you.'

'How much is that?' she asked.

'Well, let's put it this way, if we weren't already married, I'd ask you to marry me now, because you're the only person in the world I want to spend my life with.'

She couldn't help but smile. 'You know how much I love you too, don't you?' she said.

'I think so, but I'm going to confess there have been times this past year when I haven't always been so sure.'

Emotion was locking her throat.

'It hasn't been easy,' he said softly. 'I miss how close we used to be.'

'So do I, but I'm trying with this, Josh. I swear. I want to be myself again, I want us back as we were.'

'That's all I want too,' he told her. 'Nothing else matters. Not Sylvia, nor Roper, nothing, just you.'

After she'd rung off she sat where she was for a while, staring into space as she wondered what to believe, for though he'd sounded sincere at the end, and she'd felt reassured while speaking to him, now she was here in silence she was aware of the fear starting to build all over again.

It was the thought of them speaking on the

phone for over an hour, discussing things that mattered, becoming involved in each other's lives that was scaring her so much, and as tears of desperation spilled onto her cheeks she felt herself starting to shake. She knew she should go to bed now, that if she sat here dwelling on it like this she'd only make it worse for herself, but the fact that Sylvia was out there, able to call Josh at any time, and that this Roper story was probably a ruse they'd cooked up to get him to New York, was paralysing her with dread. She had to do something to stop it. She couldn't just let it happen. He was her husband, the man she loved. He didn't belong to Sylvia. She was an intruder, a snake, a scheming bitch who didn't care who she hurt just as long as she got what she wanted. She had no right to come crashing into their marriage like this. She had to be got rid of, and if Josh wasn't doing it, then she must.

It would be almost four in the morning New York time now, but Julia wasn't even close to caring about that, her only concern was how capable she was of doing this while her energy was so depleted. Nevertheless, she pressed Sylvia's mobile number into the phone and waited for the connection.

Sylvia answered on the third ring.

'I know what you're trying to do,' Julia told her, 'and it's not going to work. He doesn't want you . . .'

'Julia,' Sylvia came in groggily. 'What a lovely surprise. How are you? I've been meaning to call . . .'

'Spare me the act, you're the last person I want to hear from, and you know it.'

'Gosh, is this some new line you've got going in wake-up calls?' Sylvia quipped.

'Josh was the only man who'd ever resisted you, wasn't he,' Julia raged, 'and you just couldn't stand it. You had to have him, if only to prove to yourself that you could, so the minute you knew I had problems, you struck, like the poisonous, pustulating viper that you are . . .'

'Ugh, how horrible you're making me sound,' Sylvia shuddered. 'But really darling, I thought Josh explained, we did it for you . . .'

'Don't even go there!' Julia cut in furiously. 'You did it because he was a challenge, because I had something you didn't. He never wanted you . . .'

'Oh dear Julia,' Sylvia sighed. 'You're very wrong about that, because the truth is he's wanted me for years, and I'm the one who's been turning him down. I can't say it's been easy, because he's pretty damned irresistible . . .'

'You're a liar!'

'If that's what you want to tell yourself, but you still have to accept that it takes two, Julia, and like it or not, Josh wanted me as much as I wanted him – and he still does.'

Julia was finding it hard to think now, as her mind started to clog with fury and fear. 'Just leave us alone, Sylvia,' she gasped. 'Get out of our lives.'

'I'm afraid you'll have to talk to Josh about that, because I don't think that's what he wants.'

'For Christ's sake, what's the matter with you?' Julia cried. 'Why are you doing this? You can have any man . . .'

'Now you're flattering me.'

'Sylvia, we go back so many years. I thought we were friends . . .'

'We are,' Sylvia assured her. 'Nothing's changed on that front, at least not for me. We're just going to share Josh for a while, that's all.'

The blood was pounding so hard in Julia's head now, she could barely see or think. She knew she had to end this call, to continue it when she was more in control, but she couldn't let her win. 'He's not coming to New York, so you can forget that right now,' she choked.

Sylvia sounded surprised. 'Why, did he say he was?' she said. 'How sweet of him to think of coming all this way, just for me, but we're very good together, so I probably shouldn't be surprised. Frankly, Julia, I don't know how you manage to resist him.'

Julia couldn't take much more. 'Just leave him alone,' she seethed. 'Don't ever go near him again or I'll make you sorrier than you've ever been in your life.'

'Oh really?' Sylvia responded, sounding intrigued. 'Now how would you do that?'

Cursing the fact that she had no real power, Julia clutched at what little she did have and said, 'I know everything there is to know about you, Sylvia. I can destroy your reputation. I can turn you into a social pariah, and believe me, I will if I hear you've even as much as picked up the phone to call him again.'

'But I'm dying to know what you'll actually do,' Sylvia prompted. 'Or do I have to screw him again to find out? It would be my pleasure, of course, and we both know it's going to happen anyway, though I'm getting the impression that's not what you want. You know, I just can't help wondering how you're going to cope with all this when he becomes my agent.'

Julia fell silent as a dark, deafening drone filled up her ears.

'He did tell you about that, didn't he?' Sylvia was saying. 'As you know, he's wanted to represent me for years, and . . .'

Unable to listen to any more Julia put down the phone, then immediately called Josh.

'What!' he cried when she repeated Sylvia's claim. 'That's absolutely not true. She's lying. The subject hasn't even come up, so I've got no idea why she's saying that.'

Julia started to respond, but all that came out were huge, racking sobs.

'Darling, stop, stop,' Josh soothed. 'It's going to be all right. I swear it. Don't listen to her, because none of it's true.'

'Are you sure?'

'Of course I am. Christ, do you really think I'd take her on as a client now, after what's happened? I'd have to be insane, and I'm not, I'm just madly in love with you and more sorry about the pain I've caused you than you can ever know.'

'I love you so much,' Julia gasped, her voice shredded by tears. 'I shouldn't have made that call now. I feel so dreadful. I've got a hangover, I think I'm coming down with flu . . .'

'Where's Shannon?' he said.

'Out riding.'

'Do you want me to come over there? I can pack up here . . .'

'No, it's OK, Dan's looking forward to today.' But she did want him to come, more than anything in the world she wanted him to be here now.

'Go back to bed,' he said gently. 'Let Shannon take care of you when she comes in, and if I can get a signal I'll call in a couple of hours to find out how you are.'

'OK,' she answered weakly. 'Have you set sail yet, you two?'

'We're just about to.'

She swallowed hard to try and prevent the next question, but in the end she couldn't. 'You won't call her now, will you?' she said.

'No, of course not,' he reassured her. 'I never call her, she always calls me, and I'm going to make sure that stops.'

Feeling slightly pacified, even though she'd heard it before, she told him she loved him again, then finally rang off. This time she forced herself up from the table, and carried the phone back to its base. She'd make no more calls this morning, not even to her sister, because she was feeling so ghastly now that it was going to take every ounce of the energy she had left to climb back up the stairs to bed.

Sylvia was still awake in her chic, minimalist hotel suite, lying on the king-size bed, and going back over her conversation with Julia. She had to confess, she was surprised she hadn't heard from her long before now, though she guessed Julia had had a lot on her plate, what with her father dying, and having to go down there to Cornwall to sort everything out. What terrible timing it had all been for her, finding out that Josh really was having an affair, only minutes after learning of her father's demise. Sylvia couldn't feel anything but sorry for Julia, because both men meant so much to her that it had to be heartbreaking losing them both at the same time – though the pain had to be somewhat muted with her father, considering how long it had been since she'd last seen him. Sylvia could only wonder now how long it was going to be before Julia accepted that she'd lost Josh too. With her history of taking twenty-five years to get over being abandoned, it didn't bode well, but at least in this instance she would know why Josh had gone. No mystery there, as there had been – still was – with her father.

Sighing gently to herself, Sylvia stretched out her long limbs and considered calling Josh again. In the end she decided not to, for she didn't want to appear too eager, and besides, he was probably out of range by now. Just thinking of him, on his boat, his hair blowing in the wind, his strong hands feeding the ropes, his muscular body moving about the deck, caused endless ripples of pleasure to float through her. It was a strange feeling, she was finding, being in love, and not altogether pleasant, actually, which was why she could empathise with Julia. For every degree of pleasure, there was a double degree of pain, she remembered reading somewhere once, and now she probably understood it. Not that Josh had hurt her at all, far from it, but it was certainly within his power to do so, which was more than she could say for any other man she'd known. Of course, she'd experienced deep affection with others, and certainly great passion, but with Josh there was everything there had been before – and so very much more. She felt a link to him, a connection that had her totally in his thrall. She just couldn't get enough of him, could hardly even stop thinking about him and was totally committed to finding out what it was like to make love to him when he was holding nothing of himself back.

Sighing again, she slid a hand down between her legs and imagined it was his. She knew now that he was everything she'd ever wanted in a man, for her life had changed completely since their affair had started, she'd felt so much more alive and fulfilled, such a sense of inner power and completeness, though even she had taken a while to realise just how profound an effect he was having.

For Josh the realisation was apparently going to take a while longer, but that was understandable when his life was so cluttered with other things. However, she was certain that on some level he did know, it was simply that he wasn't ready to confront it yet. But he would, provided she didn't rush him – and the discovery that he'd been intending to join her here in New York told her that he was possibly even closer to accepting the inevitable than she'd realised.

Chapter Twelve

The following morning, having slept right through the previous day, and all night, Julia was feeling almost human again, though perhaps a little groggy, but then she hadn't long woken up.

'Honestly, I'm fine,' she told Josh when he called, while snuggling back under the duvet with the phone. 'I think it must have been a combination of too much wine and not enough food, and maybe some kind of cold bug. Anyway, Tilde mixed me one of her magic potions last night, and it definitely seems to have done the trick, because I'm absolutely famished now, and our beautiful daughter is, as we speak, downstairs making me some breakfast.'

'I think you had her worried yesterday,' Josh informed her. 'In fact, we all were, and I'd probably be there by now, if Tilde hadn't insisted you needed to sleep.'

'Well, I'm touched that you care, and sorry that I turned into another person, because that's how it feels now, as though someone else took possession of me. So if I made a complete fool of myself, please don't remind me because I'd rather not know.'

He chuckled. 'You were adorable, and I loved you more than ever,' he assured her.

'You're not angry with me about calling Sylvia?'

'Not a bit. With any luck she'll listen to you, because she doesn't seem to be listening to me.'

Though she couldn't help wondering how many times Sylvia had called him since she'd warned her not to, she managed not to ask, saying instead, 'What about New York? Are you going to go?'

'No. Tim Roper can fire who the hell he damned well likes, me included, if it means I get to hold onto you.'

Feeling her heart swell, she said, 'So what are you going to do today?'

'I'm not sure yet. Dan's still asleep, so I'll probably get on with some work while it's quiet.'

'Does that mean I'm dismissed?'

'Don't take it personally. I'll call you again in an hour.'

Not long after they'd rung off Fen called to make sure she was still alive, and finding that she was they embarked upon a lengthy conversation, mostly about the call Julia had made to Sylvia, until Shannon finally trudged up the stairs with a half-burnt, half-uncooked breakfast, which Julia was hungry enough to demolish completely. Then Dan rang to say good morning, just before Tilde popped in to brew her another magic tea, and by the time she'd managed to get into the shower, reassure Shannon that she looked gorgeous in her riding gear, then dress herself, she was more or less ready to start making up for lost time.

She began by dialling her sister's number, and after informing her brother-in-law, somewhat tersely, that she would *still* like to speak to Pam, she carried the phone back upstairs, where she positioned the ladder ready to climb into the attic. Since she had the whole morning free now, thanks to the probate officer rescheduling their appointment, she was going to start uncovering whatever hidden treasures might be stored in the eaves, before joining Fen and her family for the burial of the ashes. Fortunately it would only be a small group of them today, clustered around Gwen's graveside to watch her husband's remains going to join hers. Julia could already feel how deeply it would touch them all, and was starting to wonder about the wisdom of allowing Shannon to come along.

Suddenly realising she'd been cut off, she glared meaningfully at the phone and was about to redial when it started to ring.

'Hi,' Josh said, 'just letting you know that Dan and I are heading back to London in about fifteen minutes.'

Julia blinked. 'That's a bit sudden, isn't it?' she said.

'There's so much going on, I have to be there.'

'But how does Dan feel about that? You promised him a week.'

'He's OK with it,' he assured her. 'Aren't you, son?' he said, clearly addressing Daniel.

'I'm fine, Mum,' Daniel shouted out.

'Of course he is,' Julia said curtly, 'anyone can talk him into anything.'

'Please don't give me a hard time over this, Julia. I'd stay if I could . . .'

'So what's the big deal, to create such a rush?'

'There's no one thing in particular, it's just getting too much for Marina to handle on her own, and there's a meeting I really ought to be at this afternoon. It's too important for the author to go alone, and my mother's going to be there for Dan when we arrive.'

Julia's face tightened. 'Really,' she responded.

He sighed. 'Julia.'

'OK, sorry, but you could have brought him here.'

'Why, when you're heading back to London yourself at the weekend?'

'Actually, I'm not. Shannon and I are going to stay here until she returns to school next Wednesday.'

Silence, which told her he was as unimpressed by that as she'd expected him to be, but at least it meant he wanted her home, which was pleasantly reassuring considering how insecure she was feeling.

'OK,' she said, 'here's the deal. I won't give you a hard time about cutting Daniel's holiday short, if you don't give me one about staying here longer than you thought. Anyway, I can't see the probate officer until next week now.'

More silence.

'Josh?'

'Well, what am I supposed to say?' he demanded.

'You could always feel glad I'm prepared to trust you, considering the fact that Sylvia's due back at the weekend.'

'OK, let's drop this now.'

'I thought you might say that, but it won't just go away, you know. We still have to discuss it . . .'

'We will, but not right now, eh?'

Realising he was reminding her about Dan she said, 'All right, I'll just hope I'm not making a big mistake. Now, do you think it'll be OK with your mother to stay until Tuesday? If not, I'll ask . . .'

'You know she'll do it, and don't even think about inflicting Maisie with the moustache on us, because we'll riot, won't we, son?'

'Definitely,' Dan shouted.

Julia smiled. 'OK, I'll talk to you later,' she said. 'I'm trying to get hold of my sister right now, so I'll let you know how it goes.'

After ringing off, she immediately redialled Pam's number. This time Pam herself answered, rather than the monosyllabic, flaccid personality she'd married.

'Julia, what can I do for you,' Pam said in an infuriatingly long-suffering tone.

Resisting the urge to say yes, I'm fine thank you, how are you, Julia decided to come straight to the point. 'Did you visit Dad around six weeks before he died?'

There was a moment's astonished silence before Pam said, '*What*? Why on earth would I have done that?'

'I'm asking you to tell me.'

'Julia, I didn't even know he was still alive, never mind where he lived.'

'Are you sure?'

'Of course I'm sure. What's the matter with you? Do you think I'm lying, or something?'

'I just needed to ask.'

'Well, now you know.'

Julia sat down on the edge of the bed and stared absently at some pots on the dressing table. 'Why haven't you returned any of my calls?' she asked.

'I've been busy.'

'Too busy to come to your own father's funeral?'

Pam sighed heavily. 'Frankly, as far as I'm concerned, he died twenty-five years ago,' she responded, 'so there seemed little point in putting myself to the bother of burying him now.'

Julia was shocked by the callousness, and genuinely perplexed. 'Don't you want to know anything about him?' she asked. 'Like where he's been all this time, what he's been doing, how he died.'

Pam's tone was still loaded with impatience as she answered, which made her sound exactly like their mother. 'I know everything I need to know, thank you very much.'

'And what would that be, exactly?'

'Don't be obtuse.'

Julia could feel herself becoming strangely hot. 'Aren't you at all sad that he's gone?' she asked. 'That there's no chance of ever seeing him again now?'

Pam's scoff was like a slap. 'Good riddance, is what I say,' she retorted. 'It's what you should be saying too.'

'But why?' Even as she asked the question she realised Pam was likely to blurt out the very words she never wanted to hear, and already she was preparing to hang up.

'Julia, you can't go on seeing him through

rose-coloured glasses,' Pam said sharply. 'Though I suppose now he's left everything to you, you'll want to. Just thank God he didn't leave any of it to me, is all I can say. I wouldn't have wanted it . . .'

'But what about Rachel? I'd like to give her the money he left . . .'

'No, thank you. You can keep it.'

Julia was stunned by the refusal, particularly when Pam didn't even know how much it was. 'Pam, tell me what he did to you,' she said quietly. 'He must have done something, so please, tell me what it was.'

'Oh no,' Pam responded with an acid laugh, 'you're not dragging me into one of your games, where I tell you and you refuse to believe me, and we end up having an almighty row.'

'When did that ever happen?' Julia asked. 'We've never discussed it. You always . . .'

'It's the way you operate,' Pam cut in. 'You never could believe anything bad about him. You were always his little princess, his favourite, the one he took everywhere and gave everything to, well I'm surprised the very thought of it doesn't make you want to vomit now. And as for him having pictures of Shannon and Daniel, let's just be thankful he's dead, shall we, and leave it at that.'

Realising her mother must have passed on the information about the photos, Julia stood up and walked over to the window, where a snapshot of her father and Gwen nestled cosily inside a hand-made frame. She picked it up and gazed down into his gentle grey-blue eyes, trying to see in him the

monster implied in Pam's words, but she felt no
sense of fear, no revulsion, nothing at all that could
connect him to the man Pam was describing.

'Before you go,' she said to Pam, 'what colour
car do you drive?'

'What?'

Julia waited.

'It's a green Audi. Why?'

'How long have you had it?'

'Terry and I aren't as well off as you and Josh ...'

'How long?'

'About six years, why?'

'Is it your only car?'

'What is this?'

'Nothing. I'll let you get back to whatever you
were doing now. Sorry to have taken up your
time.'

After ringing off she returned to the bed and sat
down heavily. She was trying to reach into the
darkness beyond her memories, seeking a place
where all the bad things lurked, and all the pain
was stored, but she could find no way through.
Had she blocked whatever had happened so
completely that nothing could release it? Had it
been trodden, compacted, buried like a corpse for
all these years? But even a corpse couldn't vanish
completely, there was always something there to
exhume, a tangible fragment, a scrap of reality, that
would prove it had once existed. She considered
the analogy and was unnerved by its similarity to
the quip Gwen's cousin had repeated at the funeral,
about her father telling him where the bodies were
buried. Was her mind merely echoing Albie's
words, or was some horrific memory stirring in her

deepest subconscious? With a shivering apprehension she thought of the way she'd been with Josh this past year. Was that proof she was hiding something from herself? Was her sudden coldness when making love the sign of a damaged and unhealed mind, and even body?

Looking down as the phone rang in her hand she clicked on without thinking and said, 'Hello?'

'Hi, it's Fen. Have you managed to speak to your sister yet?'

'Yes. Just. It wasn't her who came to see him.'

'Did she have any idea who it might have been?'

'I don't think so.'

'You sound upset.'

'A bit. It wasn't a pleasant call.'

'What are you doing now?'

'I was about to start sorting through the boxes in the attic.' She glanced up at the open trap door and felt a reluctance to go up there now. 'I keep thinking I'll lift a lid and a flurry of memories will come out to tell me everything I need to know,' she said, 'but I only want to see them if they're going to make everything all right again.'

There was a smile in Fen's voice as she said, 'There's always a chance they will.'

Julia's eyes were still on the open hatch, but even as she realised how little enthusiasm she had now for going any further, she accepted she had to, not only for her own sake, and possibly Josh's, but for her father's too. If he was the man she'd always believed him to be, that was how he deserved to be remembered. And if he wasn't, well, Pam was right, it was high time she made herself face it. So, as soon as she'd rung off from Fen, she ensured the ladder was safe, and started to climb.

Alice Hope's expression was pale and uncertain as she listened to the sounds of Rene saying goodbye to Pam at the front door. Her normal, implacable composure had been badly shaken by Pam's news, leaving her feeling raw and defence-less as the past continued its inexorable journey into the present.

George was standing with his back to the empty fireplace, his eyes dark hollows of intensity, his jowls quivering with unspoken words. He restrained himself until Rene came back into the room and closed the door.

'I've tried to resist bringing this up,' he said, his gaze sweeping from one to the other of them like a malevolent wind, 'indeed I had hoped that Julia would come to her senses by now, and leave well alone. From what Pam has just told us that clearly hasn't happened, so let's begin at the beginning, shall we? Someone gave Douglas those photo-graphs, and I don't find it unreasonable to assume it was the same person who paid him a visit six weeks ago. Very possibly, both events occurred at the same time. So, what I need to know is, which of you was it?'

Alice's hands were clasped tightly in her lap, her face showing a trace of anger, but most of all unease. 'You know very well it wouldn't have been me,' she replied tautly.

His eyes held hers, then moved to his wife.

Rene appeared more composed, though she too

was nervous. 'It wasn't me,' she assured him in a voice that rang with sincerity.

His head went down. 'Then how, ladies, do you suppose he got them?' he enquired, looking up again.

Neither of them answered.

He inhaled deeply and turned round to face his reflection in the mirror over the mantel. His cheeks were mottled, his eyes shone like bullets. 'I want the truth, and one of you has it,' he said, in a voice of quiet deliberation.

Again neither of them responded.

He nodded. 'Rene, fetch the number we have for Julia,' he said.

Obediently she rose to her feet and left the room. Silence prevailed until she came back, and put a small scrap of paper next to the phone.

After she'd returned to her chair he continued to stare into the fireplace, his hands stuffed inside his trouser pockets, his large frame rocking back and forth on his slippered feet.

Alice remained very still, saying nothing.

'For the last time, Alice,' he said, still with his back to her, 'was it you who visited Douglas and gave him the photographs?'

'No, George, it wasn't,' she replied.

Very slowly he turned to face her. She looked at his hands, then away again. Her own were clenched so hard they were white.

'Dial the number,' he said.

She pressed it into the phone and without checking if it had connected, handed it to him.

'Go to your room now,' he said, taking it, 'and select your prayers from the penitential devotions.

I will deal with Julia so you can put her out of your mind.'

Julia was sitting on a beam in the attic, the musty smell of old papers thickening the air, while the sound of rain pattered on the rafters that formed a tent around her. There was a large open box at her feet, its contents spread out across other boxes and over the floor. Though the light wasn't good, it was easy enough to recognise what she was looking at, because everything, without exception, belonged to her: an old Brownie card containing her attendance record and the motto long forgotten; a scruffy book of poems all written by her, aged eight; birthday cards she'd received over the years; her junior swimmer badge; old school reports; photographs from holidays and trips to the zoo; her old teddy with one eye and a missing leg; a broken record player that she remembered her father trying to mend; some of the records that had gone with it – Tina Charles, Abba, the Boomtown Rats; ribbons; hairslides; so much, right down to the first tooth she'd left for the fairies when she was five, to the glasses she'd had to wear until she was ten. There was even an old book of astrology that she remembered them consulting together to find out if she was compatible with David Bowie, her heartthrob at the time. It was all junk really, bric-a-brac, but to her – and it would appear to him too – they were treasures from her first sixteen years; one memento after another, after another, all stored in this big cardboard box, that, judging by the dust, hadn't been opened in years.

She wondered how he'd got it, if he'd taken it at the time he left, or if someone had collected it all up and given it to him later. She had no way of knowing, but what really mattered was the fact that he had it at all. If she believed what her mother and Pam wanted her to, this could chill her to the bone, but she was feeling only sadness and nostalgia, and less fear now at the prospect of knowing more.

Reaching out for a yellowing envelope, she folded back the flap and pulled out a small wad of stiff and crinkled sheets that turned out to be cheques. She frowned and looked more closely. The handwriting was blunt and style-less, making it easy to read. Then, realising what she was seeing, her heart slowed to an unsteady beat. Each cheque was made out to her father and signed by her uncle, and all were for the same amount: twenty-five thousand pounds.

Her head started to spin. The attic suddenly seemed airless and cramped. She gazed into the cobwebby shadows and tried to make some sense of it. Maybe her uncle had paid her father to stay away from her, but if he had, her father clearly hadn't taken the money, for none of the cheques had been cashed. So had her father been black-mailing her uncle, promising to stay away if he was paid enough? If so, then why not bank the money? She dug into the envelope again, hoping to find something that might explain the puzzle, but it was empty.

The phone was ringing down in the bedroom again, the third time in the past few minutes. The sound seemed to be coming from another world, another dimension, close to this one, but not quite attached. She ignored it. She was only interested in why her uncle would be writing cheques to her father for twenty-five thousand pounds. There were six of them, totalling one hundred and fifty thousand – a goodly sum today, back then, in the early Eighties, a staggering amount. She looked at the dates more closely. Each was six months apart, starting in July of 1982 – two years after he'd left – and ending in January of 1985. She racked her brains for some significance to the dates, but could find none. But they did tell her that there had been some contact with her father at a time when her mother had sworn she had no idea where he was. Then she realised it must have been around '85 that Gwen had come into his life, so did that have any relevance to why the cheques had stopped?

The phone started again. Obviously someone was keen to get hold of her. In case it was Shannon or Dan, she set everything aside and started carefully back down the ladder, reminding herself that one of the rungs near the bottom would rotate underfoot if she didn't hit it right.

The phone was still on the bed, where she'd left it after speaking to Pam.

'Ah, at last,' a gruff voice barked down the line when she answered. 'I thought you might be there.'

'Uncle George,' she said, feeling as disturbed by the timing as she was by the fact it was him. However, seizing the moment, she said, 'Actually you're just the person. Would you mind telling me why you sent my father six cheques for twenty-five thousand pounds back in the Eighties?'

Just as she'd expected, her request stopped him dead in his tracks.

'Are you still there?' she prompted, knowing he was.

There was a small growl that turned into, 'I want you to listen to me now, Julia, and I want you to listen well. You know that the bible teaches us to honour our mothers and fathers. Your father is dead, so it is your duty to honour your mother. She wants you to stop what you are doing, to burn all the papers you have there, and sell the house. Do you hear me? That is her wish, and it is my command. You will stop this nonsense now, or the consequences will be paid, most of all by you.'

The tone of his voice was reminding her of his ugly temper, but it was the threat at the end that almost took her breath away. 'You can't speak to me like that,' she responded, sounding much shakier than she'd like. 'I'm a grown woman now . . .'

'Julia, are you listening to me?' he said darkly. 'I want you to get down on your hands and knees and ask God to forgive you for your sins. I can do this with you on the phone. I can lead you in prayer. Are you kneeling, Julia? Are you down on your knees?'

She could hardly believe what she was hearing. He had to be insane if he thought she was going to obey him.

'Oh Lord Jesus Christ,' he chanted, 'pattern of humility, Who didst empty Thyself of Thy glory, and take upon Thee the form of a servant, root out of us all pride and swelling of heart . . .'

Julia was stupefied. He was quoting from his

Treasury of Devotion, the little black book she'd hoped never to see or hear of again in her life.

'We have tried to protect you, Julia,' he was saying. 'We have done everything in our power to do so, and still we try, but you are filled with the evils of pride and defiance. Now obey your mother. Let me hear meekness in your tone as you swear before Almighty God that you will honour your mother, who gave you life. Subjugate yourself before the Lord, and implore Him to forgive you.'

'Have you completely lost your mind?' she cried.

'Julia! Go down on your knees before God.'

Her head was spinning with memories of the only other time he'd ranted at her like this. It was over twenty years ago, but even so she could hear the whistle of leather in the air, the smack of it on her bare skin and her screams as he beat her. Nausea rose up in her, and anger such as she'd never known since came spouting from her lips.

'You are a sick, crazy old man,' she hissed, 'you should be locked away, and I'm going to see that you are,' and before he could respond she slammed down the phone and stood shaking, almost uncontrollably, with fury and shame. How could he seriously have thought she'd obey him? Just what kind of power did he believe he had over her? And what was all that rubbish about protecting her? He truly was deranged, and she could only thank God that she'd left home when she had, for she didn't even want to think about what might have happened if she hadn't.

She started to pace the floor, one hand clamped

about her waist, the other to her mouth. She would never forgive her mother for letting him do what he had to her that day. Alice had heard her cries, had seen the welts on her buttocks and legs afterwards, but had never uttered a word of comfort, or reproach. She'd merely shaken her head, as though Julia had received no more than she'd deserved, and carried on with whatever she'd been doing at the time.

So sickened by the call, and the way his ravings had reawakened that ugly memory, she decided to abandon her search for the moment and took herself downstairs to use the other phone. She found herself wondering what he was doing now, in the name of his god, but didn't really want to know. She was going to think only of the things that were beautiful and pure in her life, like Shannon and Dan, her new friendship with Fen, this house and all the years of happiness her father must have known here – and all those he'd shared with her before he'd left. If anyone was evil and twisted it was her uncle, not her father, who'd never laid one finger on her in violence, or any other deviant or obscene way. How dare her uncle start spouting off about protecting her, when she had far more to fear from him, than she'd ever had from someone as gentle and caring as her father?

'Of course I understand why you're angry,' Josh responded when she told him what had happened, 'but he's always been like that, going off about God when he's not getting his own way, you know that better than I do, so don't let it get to you.'

'That's easy for you to say when you don't have

to put up with it,' she retorted. 'And you're not the one who had the beating.'

'Twenty-odd years ago, and it happened once. Time to get over it.'

'Well, thanks for the sympathy.'

'This isn't exactly new, Julia. OK, it hasn't come up in a while . . .'

'Stop, stop,' she cried, not wanting to get into an argument about that, when right now it wasn't really relevant. 'Just tell me what you make of the cheques.'

There was a moment as he thought. 'Well, blackmail is obviously the first thing that comes to mind . . .'

'But he didn't bank them. Why?'

'If there's an answer to that, it's going to be down there with you.'

'And all those things belonging to me. What's that about?'

'He was your father. He wanted to hang onto stuff that was yours.'

'Would you do the same if it was you, with Shannon?'

'I guess so, but considering the circumstances, I'm not sure I like where this is going . . .'

'Try not to make it about you,' she retorted, and hearing him laugh she smiled. 'Just tell me you don't think it's anything sinister,' she said.

'Did it feel creepy when you found it all?'

'Not really. Actually, it was quite touching,' but even as she said it, she felt a shiver run through her. 'Well, maybe it is a bit odd,' she said, 'but that could be because everything's been tainted by that call from my uncle. He – and my mother, let's not forget her – are absolutely desperate to stop me going through this house, which is making me all the more determined to carry on.'

'Why doesn't that surprise me?' he commented. 'But listen, I have to go. I've got another call holding, and I'm due in a meeting in ten minutes.'

'Dan's OK, is he?'

'He's fine. Call and speak to him if you want to be sure. Now, I'm gone. I'll talk to you later,' and the line went dead.

'Well thanks for that,' she muttered, hanging up too. She was trying hard to understand that he had other priorities right now, important to him and his agency, as well as to their livelihood, but this was important to *her*, and she wanted his support. However, she clearly wasn't going to get it in the next half an hour, so to make sure that odious uncle of hers didn't get under her skin for a moment longer, she decided to give her mother-in-law the privilege instead. She would ring to find out how brilliantly the old dear was coping with her beloved son and grandson in her selfish and neglectful daughter-in-law's absence.

After finishing his call with Julia, Josh was now speaking forcefully to a bewildered editor at a major publishing house, whilst keeping a regular check on the time. 'But what the hell happened?' he was demanding. 'A week ago the woman was all ready to sign the contract, now, after a lunch with you, she's refusing to go near it. So what was said, for God's sake?'

'I swear, I've got no idea,' the editor replied. 'It all seemed to go well . . . Christ, I've known her 'for six years, we've never had a problem before.'

'Well, it looks like you've got one now, so may I respectfully suggest that you get on the phone and find out exactly what went wrong, or there'll be no deal, which isn't what either of us wants.'

As the editor rang off Josh clicked over to take another call. 'Can you hold please for Janet Greene,' a perky young voice requested.

He immediately returned to his open agenda, checking what was on for the rest of the day, but as his eyes skimmed down the page his thoughts were returning to Julia, immediately stirring the wretchedness inside him for the way he was deceiving her. He pictured her down there in Cornwall, so beautiful and capable, and yet so alone in her search for answers to her father's desertion. He wanted to be there with her, to protect her from any more pain, even though right now he was its greatest source. He didn't understand how he could do this to her, it made no sense when he loved her so much, and recalling the way she'd broken down on the phone yesterday he felt such an over-whelming surge of self-loathing that it seemed almost to choke him. He had to make this up to her, and he would, just as soon as he'd worked out how.

Making a mental note to call her back once he'd finished with Janet Greene, he then instantly reversed it, since the next hour or so probably wouldn't be the best time to be talking to her.

'Josh, how are you?' Janet Greene enquired, in her honeyed Scots tones. 'I'm surprised you're not at some glossy West End restaurant having an expensive lunch on my account. That's what you agents do in the middle of the day, isn't it?'

Ignoring the jibe he'd heard a hundred times before, and from a hundred different authors, he said, 'You want to know about the royalty cock-up. I'm on it, so don't worry, it'll get sorted. How's the new book coming along?'

As she regaled him with far more information than he needed, he waved out to Marina as she went off to lunch, then going to close the door between their two offices he started to wind up the call.

When finally he was free, he switched the main phones through to the answering machine and took out his mobile. For several long minutes he merely stared down at it, turning it over in his hand as doubt and indecision clouded the purpose in his mind. In the end, reminding himself he could ring off at any second, he began to press in the number.

As he waited for the call to connect he walked over to the window, his thumb still poised ready to cut the line. He thought he would, he was sure he would, but when it started to ring at the other end, he just let it.

'Hi,' he said, when Sylvia's voice finally came down the line. 'Did I wake you?'

'No, I was just dozing,' she responded sleepily. 'This is a nice surprise.'

'Are you jet-lagged?'

'Maybe just a little.' She yawned and stretched. 'Where are you?'

'At the office.'

There was a pause before she said, 'You're back in London already?'

'I was on my way here when I got your message.'

'Then it seems we're both back early,' she said, sounding sultry and pleased.

'I'd like to see you,' he told her.

'Well, I imagine that can be arranged. When?'

'I can come now.'

'Then I'll be waiting.'

After ringing off he grabbed his coat, dropped the mobile in his pocket and went outside to hail a cab. He wasn't thinking about anything now beyond his reason for going there. He wanted nothing to distract him, nor would he consider the nightmare of Julia finding out that Sylvia was already back in London, for never in a million years would she believe that it had nothing to do with his own early return. But it didn't, because he hadn't even known Sylvia had left New York until he'd picked up her message telling him that her plane had just landed at Heathrow. By then he'd been at home, dropping Dan off, and though she'd rung two or three times since, he'd been careful not to call her back until a few minutes ago, when no-one else was around.

By the time the cab pulled up outside her mews house he was so bound up in guilt and apprehension that he almost told the driver to keep going. He was crazy to come here and he knew it, since he barely trusted himself any more than he did her, but she was ringing so often now, and was starting to sound so serious and even possessive that he needed to make her understand that their relationship really was over. What was more, he needed to do it in a way that left neither of them in any doubt that he meant it.

As the cab pulled away and he turned to the door, he had to concede that allowing her to think he couldn't wait to see her had probably not been a good move, for even he was now seriously doubting his true motive for coming.

She didn't speak into the entryphone, merely buzzed to release the door, then hung up again. As he walked through her workshop he was wondering how he would handle it if she was naked when she opened the door, or dressed in such a way that she might as well be. The mere thought of it was starting to turn him on, and as he pictured it he found himself thinking, *maybe one last time – a kind of goodbye. No-one would ever know, and what difference would it make when it had already happened so many times before*?

The answer, he knew, was that Julia would be absolutely devastated if she knew he was here, never mind his purpose, so he must keep reminding himself of that: he'd only come because he didn't want to go on hurting and deceiving her the way he had been.

Sylvia was waiting at the door, wearing, to his relief, a silk, cream-coloured suit that was quite modest in its cut, though the shortness of the skirt showed off her bare legs to perfection, and not all the jacket buttons were fastened, but at least she was dressed.

'Hi,' she murmured, raking him with her ice-blue eyes, before lifting her mouth for a kiss.

Pressing his lips briefly to hers, he walked on into the room where her suitcase was in the middle of the floor, and a freshly opened bottle of wine was on a table in front of the window.

'I can't stay long,' he said, turning as she closed the door.

Her eyebrows went up, but she made no comment as she sauntered past him to go and pour the wine.

'Not for me,' he said, as she made to fill the second glass.

Her hand paused, but then continued to pour. 'So is there something else you would like?' she enquired, picking up her own wine and turning round to lean back against the table.

For a moment he was able to look into her eyes, but then his own moved away as he said, 'We have to talk.'

She arched her eyebrows and sipped her wine. 'Considering how much we've done of that lately, I rather thought you might be ready for something a little more . . . *physical*, by now.'

He swallowed hard and dug his hands into his coat pockets. 'You know what I'm saying. We have to end this.'

For several seconds she seemed to have no reaction at all, until finally she started to smile. 'Poor Josh,' she said, 'you're clearly having a dreadful struggle with your conscience again. I can't say I'm surprised, though I am a little disappointed, because I was so looking forward to our reunion. I've missed you, my darling, and I don't think you can deny that you've missed me too.'

'Sylvia, please,' he said. 'We had an agreement. As soon as one of us wanted out . . .'

'I do remember,' she assured him, 'but a lot's happened in the past few months, things have changed between us, you know that as well as I do.'

'No, not for me.'

'I think it has,' she corrected. 'And I've become extremely attached to you too.'

A thud of alarm beat in his heart. 'But you know Julia means everything to me,' he said, trying to keep his voice calm. 'I've never tried to pretend otherwise, and it hasn't changed. It was only because . . . Well, you know why this affair started, and it was never meant to last.'

Sylvia nodded thoughtfully and took another sip of wine. 'Are you sleeping with her again?' she asked.

His eyes didn't meet hers as, wishing he could say yes, he replied, 'That's not the point. I love her, she's the only woman I want . . .'

Sylvia laughed softly. 'Now we both know that's not true,' she chided. 'You want me too, Joshua. Very much in fact, and look at me, I'm not resisting, am I? I'm right here, and you know you can do anything you want to me.'

His groin tightened at the words, and he could only feel glad she was unable to see it.

'You know, I'm prepared to make a lot of changes in my life for you . . .'

'No!' he cut in. 'Don't. Christ, it's the last thing I want.'

She regarded him sceptically.

He dashed a hand through his hair and started to pace. 'Look, I'm not denying it was good between us,' he said, 'or that I haven't enjoyed our times together, but it has to end, Julia . . .'

Her eyes narrowed as she registered the wrong name.

'Don't read anything into that,' he told her sharply. 'Just don't.'

She took another sip of wine, watching him intently over the rim of the glass. 'Tell me why you're really here,' she said finally.

'I'm trying to,' he answered. 'I need you to understand that you have to stop calling me . . .'

'But you didn't have to come here in person for that, you could have told me on the phone.'

'I've tried,' he said, 'OK, maybe not hard enough, but that's why I'm here now, to make sure you understand that we can't be in touch any more.'

Turning to put down her glass, she folded her arms across her waist, then regarded him again. 'The trouble with you, Josh,' she told him, 'is that you say one thing and mean another.'

'I mean what I'm saying.'

She was shaking her head. 'But your actions aren't bearing it out,' she said, sitting up on the table and resting her feet on a chair. 'First, you try to find a way to see me in New York, then you come straight up to London the minute you hear I'm back . . . You're here now because you couldn't wait to see me . . .'

Appalled by how she'd misread everything, he said, 'Sylvia, I promise, you've got totally the wrong end . . .'

'Darling, it's fine by me if you don't want to admit it,' she cut in, 'I'm not going to force you – why would I, when I know the truth without having to be told? And the truth is, we both know you won't be leaving here today until you've had what you came for. So really, all this talking now is nothing more than a waste of time.'

Aware of how much ground he seemed to be losing, he said, 'Look, I swear that's not why I'm here. I came because I just didn't feel that I was getting through to you . . . Oh Christ,' he groaned, as she opened her legs to show that she wore nothing under her skirt.

'Can you tell me now that it's not why you came?' she murmured.

'Sylvia, please don't do this,' he said, looking away.

'Tell me you're not hard,' she challenged.

He turned his back and put a hand to his head. He needed to leave. He had to make his feet move, and carry him to the door. And he would, as soon as he'd got the message across – it was over, she had to stop calling him, he was never coming here again – he just wished to God he knew how he was going to convince her when he was so close, so very close to turning around now and taking her straight to the stars.

'Josh,' she said softly.

He didn't reply.

Her voice lilted with amusement as she said, 'Everything's hidden now. I promise.'

Feeling foolish he turned around and wasn't entirely sure whether he was sorry or relieved to discover that she was telling the truth.

'Come here,' she said, holding out a hand.

He looked at it, knowing it would be a big mistake to take it. 'If Julia were ever to find out I was here . . .' he said.

'But how is she going to find out? I won't tell her, and we know you won't.' She smiled and leaned forward to take his hand. 'You see, it was easy,' she said, as she drew him to her. 'And this,' she added, pressing a hand to his cock, 'is very hard indeed.'

His eyes closed, and as she started to rub him to his shame he did nothing to stop her. He knew he should, and he would, it just felt so good . . .

She opened her legs again, and though he didn't look, he didn't have to, because he could see her in his mind's eye, as ready for him as he was for her. His hand fell to his side as she let go, then he felt her unfastening his belt. Somewhere inside he was still resisting her, though nothing in him was moving. His zip went down and he knew if he didn't stop her now, then within seconds he'd be inside her. He didn't know if he could prevent it, or even if he wanted to . . .

She was reaching inside his trousers, searching for the opening in his shorts, then a moan escaped him as her fingers touched him. He raised a hand, not sure what he intended to do. Would he stroke her hair, reach into her jacket for her breasts, or touch her between the legs?

Her eyes came up to his and he stared down at her, watching her lips curve in a slow, triumphant smile. She knew she had him, that any second now she'd free his cock completely and he'd be plunging deep inside her, making a total mockery of everything he'd said. He touched her face, and felt her fingers wrapping around him. He continued to gaze into her eyes, then as she started to free him he lowered his hand and clamped it hard around her wrist.

Their eyes remained locked. He knew she was waiting for him to pull her hand away, and he would . . . He meant to, but seconds were ticking by . . .

She started to smile again, but as she tightened her grip on his penis, so he tightened his on her wrist.

Then suddenly his mobile started to ring, and without even considering who it might be, he grabbed it from his pocket and clicked on.

'Josh Thayne,' he barked, turning abruptly away.

'All sorted,' a voice at the other end announced. It was the editor he'd spoken to earlier. 'Big mistake on my part, I talked about another author while we were having lunch. After all these years, I should have known better.'

'As long as it's all straightened out now,' Josh said, refastening his trousers.

'Plenty of ego-massaging did the trick. You know what these authors are like. I'll look forward to receiving the signed contract.'

After ringing off, Josh turned back to Sylvia, his eyes hard with contempt – though much more for himself than for her. 'I have to go,' he said roughly. 'I'm sorry if you've misread some of the things I've said, or done. I hold myself entirely responsible, because I was a fool ever to get into this. That isn't meant to hurt you, or to try and claim that I wasn't willing, because I was, and maybe, if things had been different, we could find out where this might lead. But it can't happen. I'm a happily married man. I love my wife and my children, and nothing in the world is ever going to make me give them up. So please understand that it's over between us now. I won't be coming here again, nor can I take any more of your calls.'

As he turned and walked to the door he could feel her eyes burning into him, but not until he'd reached the door did she say, 'The only person you're fooling is yourself.'

He kept on going. It made no difference what she thought, she was out of his life now, and there wasn't even any point in tormenting himself over how far he might have gone had the phone not rung, because it hadn't happened, and that was all that mattered.

Not until he was back at the office did he answer his mobile again. Seeing it was Shannon he immediately clicked on, wanting very much to submerge himself in his family as though it could in some way cleanse him of the past hour. 'Hi darling,' he said, shrugging off his coat and returning to his desk. 'How's it going down there?'

'Everything's cool,' she answered chirpily. 'We just buried the ashes. Mum let me go with her, and now she wishes she hadn't, because you'll never guess what, Dad, we had this really terrible fit of the giggles. We just couldn't stop, because the undertaker turned up with this little miniature coffin under his arm, like Granddad was now some sort of Mini-Me, you know, like from *Austin Powers* . . . I swear I wasn't the first one to laugh, it was Mum. She let out this really terrible snort. Then Fen started, and her brother . . . Mum said it was exactly the sort of thing Granddad would have laughed at too, if he'd been there, which he was, I suppose . . . *Stop it, Mum*. She's still laughing, Dad, and she's the one who's saying we have to go back and try to be a bit more respectful tomorrow, but if you could see her now . . . I think she's going a bit hysterical, actually.'

Josh was smiling, for he knew the black side of Julia's humour only too well, and as he pictured the scene down there, he wished with all his soul that he could be with them.

'Shall I put her on?' Shannon asked.

'No, tell her I'll call in an hour,' he said, 'I've only just got back to the office and there's a stack of messages waiting.'

'OK, you probably won't get any sense out of her anyway, I know I can't.'

He was about to ring off when suddenly he changed his mind and said, 'Shannon?'

'Yes?'

'Tell her I love her.'

'Oh gross!' Shannon blurted. 'I can't say that. You're my parents, for God's sake.'

He laughed. 'All right, then put her on.'

'I would, but she's just gone into the bathroom to try and pull herself together.'

Still smiling he said, 'OK, it can wait,' and after ringing off he put the phone aside and sat down in front of a small pile of contracts to start checking them over. It was a while before they had his full attention though, because he was still thinking about Julia, and how much he wanted to tell her that it was over with Sylvia now. But he knew he couldn't, because it would mean admitting Sylvia was back in London, and that he'd been over there. So dismissing it, he turned his thoughts instead to the hope that Julia would find something soon to help her overcome whatever ghosts she needed to overcome. He felt certain that once she did, they'd be able to return to the kind of intimacy they'd always shared, the only intimacy he'd ever really wanted, and once they did he knew that any lingering desire he might have for Sylvia would simply cease to exist.

Chapter Thirteen

The truth is finally out. Life can never be the same now. Afraid I will lose everything.

Julia was seated at the kitchen table, staring down at the entry in an old pocket diary she'd found in the attic. The year was 1980, the date was 24th June, three weeks before her father had left.

She read the words again, her heart thudding, her thoughts racing in too many directions. What truth? And why would it mean he'd lose everything?

Recoiling from the first answers, she quickly flipped over the page, but there was no more until 10th September, when he'd written,

they still won't let me have any contact with her.

And on 23rd September,

The need is growing stronger instead of weaker. God, help me, I want them to die.

A horrible, suffocating feeling was coming over her, as she considered the possible meanings of what she was reading. Had he asked to be in touch with her, and 'they' – her mother and uncle – had refused? And what was the need that was growing so strong? *Please God don't let it be that, please,* though what else could it be? And who did he want to die? Again, her mother and uncle?

The rest of the diary was empty, no more entries to throw light on those she'd read, and nothing to direct her to any kind of answers. Putting it down, she stared out through the open kitchen door to where a couple of robins were pecking about in the leaf-covered grass. The world was splashed in autumn sunlight, yet seemed oddly out of kilter now, as though it had taken a step back, pausing a moment to keep watch from a distance as she struggled between denial and dread. But no matter what was going on inside her, how horrific her thoughts, or intense the effort to stir her own memories, she just couldn't make herself connect the monster she was imagining with the father she remembered and loved.

She picked up the diary again and checked to make sure she'd missed nothing, but the only entries were those she'd read. So all she had to go on was her own instinct and guesswork, neither of which was helped by adding the conundrum of the uncashed cheques. Had they been to finance the start of a new life? Payment to stay away from his children? Or blackmail? *I'll do as you want and stay away, but you have to pay me to.* To her mind it couldn't have sounded less like her father, and the fact that he'd never used the money . . .

Reaching for the tatty shoebox she'd carried down from the attic, she rummaged through again and found a diary for the following year. 1981.

Again not many entries, and most turned out to be utterly prosaic.

8th February *Started new job.*

12th February *spent day in library*

16th April *changed job*

17th April *take away this murdherin' hate, an' give us thine own eternal love!*

This was clearly a quote, but she had no idea what from, though it was almost certainly a desire to die.

29th April *I miss her so much. Does she miss me? What have they told her?*

She stopped there and read the entry again. There was no mention of her name, but she felt certain he was writing about her.

Then . . .

15th July *One year has passed since I last saw her. They won't even let me write to her. Maybe it's best for her if I don't.*

10th August *They told me to forget she exists. It's what I have to do. My precious girl . . . Julia, my Julia . . .*

As her heart turned over in the echo of his pain, she stared down at her name and watched it become blurred by tears. This last entry had been made on her seventeenth birthday; the previous one marked the anniversary of the day he'd left. She read the words over and over until her heart was so full she could take no more. So he had loved her, there had been no pretence, despite what her mother had said, and only now did she realise just how terrified she'd been that it would all turn out to be false. But it wasn't, because in his own words he was telling her that he'd missed her every bit as much as she had him, had felt the severing of their bond as brutally, so why had he never gone against them and got in touch?

She tried again with her memory, searching for something, a moment's terror or revulsion, a stifled scream, a shudder of guilt or shame, but she could find no nightmare buried inside her, no dark secrets too horrific to reveal. Because none were there. He'd only ever loved her as any father loves his daughter, perhaps more than some, but that didn't make it wrong. Her mother and uncle had kept him away from her out of jealousy and vindictiveness, but even as she thought it, she realised with a horrible sinking sensation that it could as easily have been some kind of legal authority that had stood in his way.

She continued turning the pages to the end of the year, but there were only two more entries, one chronicling the start of another new job and the other a reminder for the dentist. There was no mention of what kind of work he was doing, or where he was living during that time. Until he'd left home he'd been the manager at a local engineering factory, but from the cursory nature of the entries she got the impression these jobs were more menial, temporary, a means of earning money in order simply to exist. Though bleak, it was a scenario she preferred over the other one that fitted equally as well – that he'd been in prison.

She was so engrossed that she didn't hear a car pulling up outside, or the sound of footsteps on the deck. It was only when Rico said, 'I am sorry if I am interrupting,' that she realised he was there.

'Oh no, no,' she said hurriedly, getting to her feet. 'Not at all. I didn't hear you. Please, come in.'

He took a couple of steps in through the open door. 'I am going into the town,' he explained, 'so I thought maybe I take some boxes to the charity shop now, if they are ready?'

'Uh, yes, of course,' she responded, feeling oddly flustered. 'There are quite a lot actually. Mainly clothes. I'm still going through all the books and papers.'

'I can see,' he said.

She looked down at the table.

'Is it helping? Are you finding him?' he asked.

Managing to clear a path through the muddle in her head, she said, 'Perhaps. I'm not sure. There's still a lot to go through.' She looked at him and managed a smile. 'Did you know him well?' she asked, wondering if her cheeks had turned red from the sudden heat in her body.

'I see him every year for most of my life, maybe only for a few weeks, but I spend some of it with him and Gwen. He liked the sea, and to do things a little crazy.' He smiled. 'He did roller skates and surfboards and one day he go in a parachute from a helicopter and injure his ankle when he land on the ground.' His eyes grew mischievous. 'You know, I think you are like him.'

To her confusion she heard herself stammer. 'You – you mean I look like him?' she said.

'No, I mean in the special way. My family take him to their hearts, and now they do same with you.'

She looked away, thrown by the way she was

responding, but maybe he'd just caught her in a vulnerable state after reading her father's diaries.

'It is sad for you,' he said, 'to find him again this way. After he has gone.'

She moved her gaze to the diaries, and feeling a strange sort of connection to him, she heard herself saying, 'Would you like a drink? I think the coffee's gone cold, but I can make more.'

He didn't answer, so without looking at him she went to check the pot. 'Cold,' she confirmed.

He stayed where he was, watching her, still saying nothing.

As she crossed to the sink she was aware of the oddest sensations moving through her, as though her mind was floating in a liquid world, somewhere apart from who she was and where they were. She found herself wondering what he was thinking, and hoping he found her attractive, because after what Josh had done her confidence was in pieces. But he was so much younger, and she was looking so far from her best ... For one giddy moment she wanted to flirt with him, to feel that charge of adrenaline as the chemistry kicked in, but she knew she wouldn't, not only because it would be wrong to use him to flatter her ego, but because she was so out of practice she'd probably end up embarrassing them both.

After refilling the coffee machine she turned back to face him, and caught the jolt of a response as their eyes connected. 'Shall we go and fetch the boxes?' she said, feeling as though she might actually float into the bedroom.

'Yes, of course,' he answered.

She started to move, then registering the fact

that they were about to go into a bedroom together, she felt suddenly sober, and was on the point of blurting out an excuse to do it later, when the phone rang. Not sure whether she wanted to laugh at how ridiculous she was being, or feel relieved that she'd been saved from disgracing herself, she reached out to pick it up.

'Julia?' a voice boomed down the line. 'Rod Fuller. I've got some news. Is this a good time?'

'Uh, yes, now's fine,' she said, her eyes going to Rico. 'Just give me a second.' She put a hand over the mouthpiece and said, 'I'm sorry, I have to take this. Can we ... Can you ...?'

'I'll get the boxes,' he said.

'They're through there,' she told him, pointing past the fireplace, then added, 'I was wondering about dinner. Would tomorrow night work for you?'

As he looked at her she felt the heat coming back to her cheeks. Had she made it sound as though it would be just the two of them? 'I would like that very much,' he said. 'Thank you.'

Feeling the need to make sure he understood, she said, playfully, 'Shannon's threatening to cook.'

After allowing his eyes to linger a moment longer than necessary, he started towards the hall.

Waiting until he'd disappeared, she took a deep, steadying breath and returned to her call. 'Rod, sorry. I'm with you now,' she said, refocusing. 'So what do you have?'

'Would you believe eight Douglas Cowans, but fortunately only one who fits the full picture. So, I'm going to run with this one being yours.'

She braced herself, for after what she'd read in

the diaries she was certain he was about to confirm the worst.

'Right, we begin with three arrests for assault and battery,' he said. 'The first couple of occasions it turns out the charges were dropped, but on the third he received a suspended sentence.'

She felt stunned. It had to be a mistake, her father had never been a violent man, in spite of what Gwen's cousin Albie had said. 'When?' she asked.

'All three back in the Eighties. Two in '81, the third in '83.'

After he'd left home. 'Nothing before that?'

'Not that I could find, so the answer has to be no.'

'And he didn't serve any time?'

'No. No prison record at all.'

Room then for some relief.

'There are a few other court appearances,' he went on, 'nothing serious, all resulting in fines – drunk and disorderly, disturbing the peace, threatening behaviour. Sounds a proper charmer, if you ask me – or he was back then. So who is he? If I'm allowed to ask.'

She looked round as Rico emerged with a stack of boxes. 'He was my father,' she heard herself answer.

'I see,' Fuller responded, drawing out the words in a tone that didn't sound pleased. 'If I'd known that, I'd have come at you a bit differently.'

'It's OK,' she assured him. 'Is there anything else?'

There was a pause, before he said, 'No, I guess that's it.'

She frowned. 'Are you sure?'

'I'm sure, but if more comes up, I'll let you know.'

After he'd rung off she continued standing where she was, her hand still on the phone as a hundred different thoughts chased each other round in her mind. She watched Rico slam down the tailgate of the car and slip into the driver's seat. Then as the Volvo disappeared into the trees, she let go of the phone and went to sit down again.

So it seemed the stories about her father being violent were true. Three arrests for assault and battery, all in the early Eighties. It was a serious enough crime, and one that often resulted in a prison term, but on two occasions the charges had been dropped, and on the third he'd clearly been let off lightly. Why? Without the court records it was impossible to know. What really mattered, though, was that the worst of all imaginable crimes had not come up attached to his name. Surely that had to be cause for some kind of celebration.

A few minutes later Shannon appeared from the woods, laughing into her mobile phone while throwing sticks for the dogs, who'd followed her over. 'Hi,' she said brightly, as clicking off the line she came in the door. 'Everything OK?'

'Everything's great,' Julia replied. 'You look happy. Who were you talking to?'

'Oh that was just Dad, being Dad. You know what he's like when he's in a good mood. What's all this?' she said, picking up one of the diaries.

'I found them in the attic. I haven't read many of

them yet, but I've just had a phone call confirming that he did *not* have a criminal record.' Well, at least not the one she'd feared.

Shannon's eyes were brimming with laughter as she said, 'You were really afraid that he did, weren't you?'

'Well how would you feel, if it were Dad?' Julia countered.

Shannon wrinkled her nose. 'He should have one the way he dances,' she retorted, 'he is like so embarrassing when he gets up at parties and things.'

Julia had to laugh. 'He does it to wind you up, you know that. When he's with me, he's Mr Cool.' Did he ever dance with Sylvia, she found herself wondering.

Shannon's eyebrows arched. 'He likes to think he's that all the time,' she declared. 'So, what have we got to eat?'

'Whatever's in the fridge, which won't be much. We need to go to the supermarket. Correction, you need to go, because if you're serious about cooking for Rico, I've set a date for tomorrow night.'

Shannon's eyes grew round as her cheeks flooded with colour. 'Really?' she said, clearly not sure whether she was allowed to burst with excitement or not.

'Really,' Julia confirmed, still trying to escape the image of Josh and Sylvia dancing.

'Oh my God,' Shannon cried, clapping her hands to her face. 'Oh my God. That is like, so cool. Oh Mum, you're the best. What shall I cook? You've got to help me. We'll have to get some candles, and find some decent music. What do you think he's into? Oh Mum, I am just going to die. I've got to call Ottie and tell her.'

'I think we should invite her and Fen too, don't you?' Julia said. 'It'll seem rather odd if we don't, particularly when we're going over there tonight.'

'We are? You mean I'm going to see him tonight as well? I think I'm going to faint.'

Laughing, Julia threw a tea towel at her. 'Just make sure you remember your promise,' she said.

'If anything happens, I mean anything at all, I promise to tell you,' Shannon declared. 'Anyway, how can it, while you're right there?'

Julia walked over and tilted up her chin. 'Nothing's going to happen,' she told her firmly, then experiencing an uncomfortable moment as she wondered whether she was talking to herself or her daughter, she pressed a kiss to Shannon's forehead and went to the phone to find out what Josh was in such a good mood about.

'Does it have to be anything in particular?' he responded when she asked.

'No, of course not. I just wondered if something had happened. A new deal. A new author . . .'

'I was just sharing a joke with Shannon, that's all.'

She frowned at his defensiveness. 'Josh, I asked an innocent question, and now you're behaving as though I've accused you of something.'

'Are you?'

She felt her face start to drain as she wondered if accusation was needed.

'Don't argue, Mum,' Shannon whispered from behind. 'I hate it when you argue.'

Julia held up a hand to reassure her, and said

to Josh, 'Shall I call back? This is obviously a bad time . . .'

'No, we can speak now, but you'll have to make it quick . . .'

'Then pardon me for interrupting,' she snapped, and banged down the phone.

'Oh Mum,' Shannon groaned. 'Why did you have to do that? He was in a really good mood just now . . .'

'With you, maybe, obviously not with me. Now stop arguing his case, and get revising.'

Shannon looked mutinous.

'OK, then answer the phone.'

'It'll be him calling back.'

'Just answer it, Shannon.'

'What do I say if it's him?'

'Try hello.'

Shooting her a withering look, Shannon grabbed up the phone and said, 'Hello.'

'Put her on.'

'It's Dad,' she said to Julia.

Grudgingly Julia took the phone. 'Yes?'

'I'm sorry. I was out of order.'

'You were, but I'll forgive you if you're going to be nice to me now.'

'I miss you,' he said sharply.

'Is that your excuse?'

'Yes.'

'Then maybe it would improve your temper to come down here at the weekend, because I'm missing you too.'

There was a pause before he said, 'Dan's got a couple of things on, and I promised my mother I'd take her to Harrods.'

As the coldness of suspicion came over her again, she said, 'Well, she has to come first.'

'Julia, she's helping us out.'

She sighed. 'I know, I'm sorry.'

After a pause he said, 'I love you.'

'I love you too.'

'*Yes!*' Shannon whispered in the background, and grinning happily she skipped off to her room.

'So what was all that about just now?' Julia asked, after hearing Shannon's door close.

'I don't know,' he answered, sounding tired. 'I just feel kind of irritable today, and I guess I thought you were starting to read something into my good mood with Shannon, which was actually a bit of an act, because frankly I feel about ready to murder the world.'

'Why? What's irritating you so much?'

'I don't know – and please don't start reading anything into it.'

He kept being so defensive. 'Like what?' she asked.

'Like nothing. Look, let's drop this, shall we?'

'I'm not sure I've got hold of anything to drop,' she replied, 'but I can tell you this, you're beginning to sound like someone with a guilty conscience.'

'Oh for God's sake. I've got nothing to feel guilty about.'

'Are you sure?'

'Of course I'm sure.'

She remained silent, trying to make herself believe him, but her instincts were warning her not to. 'She's back, isn't she?' she said, feeling the heat of fear starting to burn through her.

'What do you mean? Who?'

'Oh Josh, that response alone . . . Please tell me it's not why you went back to London early.'

'Of course it's not. I didn't even know she was back in the country . . .'

'So she is there.'

'Yes, but . . .'

'And you've seen her.'

He didn't answer.

'Oh my God!' she gasped, putting a hand to her mouth as all her fears and suspicions started to explode.

'OK, I have seen her, but not in the way you're thinking.'

Her eyes were darting wildly around. She didn't want this to be happening. Somehow she had to make it stop . . .

'I went round there to tell her it was over,' he was saying. 'She kept calling me, she wasn't listening . . .'

'You could have told her on the phone,' she cried. 'You didn't have to see her. Oh my God, I can't believe what you're doing, Josh. Are you really so obsessed with her? Tell me now if you are . . .'

'No! For Christ's sake, I've just told you, it's over.'

She tried desperately to believe him, but it just wasn't happening. 'Did you fuck her?' she heard herself say bitterly. 'While you were there, did you . . . ?'

'I never laid a finger on her.'

She was shaking her head. 'You're lying.'

'I'm telling you the truth.'

'She won't let you go, will she? But maybe you don't want her to.'

'Julia stop this. She knows it's over. I couldn't have made it any clearer, and she's out of my life now.'

She lowered her head as though to escape the horror of the new realisation dawning in her mind. 'That's why you're angry with me, isn't it?' she said. 'You still want her, and now you resent me for making you give her up.'

'That is just ridiculous,' he almost shouted.

'Ridiculous or not, it's true.'

'For Christ's sake, what do I have to say to convince you? I don't want her. I want you.'

She was staring at nothing, knowing she'd be wrong to believe him, yet almost desperate to, for everything would be so much easier if she could . . .

'Look, I have to go now,' he said, 'but I'll come at the weekend.'

She didn't protest, saying nothing as she rang off and turned to gaze at the mill wheel, going round in front of the window. She barely knew what she was thinking, or even feeling, beyond the dread of being drawn further and deeper into the pain of his betrayal. She'd thwarted his plan to go to New York, so unable to stand being apart any longer, Sylvia had flown back early, and he'd rushed up to London to be with her. She could feel herself almost buckling as she envisaged their passion at the moment they saw each other again, him sweeping her straight into bed, or taking her right there, against the wall. She knew Josh, the way he operated, and how he could make a woman feel. A barrier of denial rose up around her mind, as though to block out the images, but she couldn't let them go.

'Revision can wait,' Shannon suddenly declared, bouncing back into the kitchen, 'let's look through some of those books, shall we, decide what we're going to cook tomorrow night.'

Julia turned to watch her as she carried a small pile over to the table and cleared a space.

'Do you think we should do pasta, or will he get enough of that at home?' Shannon was chattering on as she sorted through the books. 'It has to be something easy, whatever it is, because I'm definitely going to do this myself, and I want to impress him so he'll know he'll be getting a wife who's as good in the kitchen as she is in the bedroom.'

It took Julia a moment to realise a reaction was required, then registering what Shannon had said, she narrowed her eyes and treated her to a menacing look.

Shannon giggled delightedly, and moved up to make room as Julia went to sit down with her.

'You're incorrigible,' Julia told her, taking one of the books to start leafing through the recipes. She had to force herself to act normally now, because she desperately didn't want Shannon to know what was going on. It would break her heart to think that her father was involved with another woman, for she'd grown up with such a solid belief in her parents' love that it had never even entered her head to doubt it. Were she ever to find out about Sylvia, the foundations of her world would totally fall apart. She could well end up hating him for being false and a hypocrite when he'd been so strict with her over romance and boyfriends, while all the time he was betraying her mother . . .

Feeling a powerful need to protect her daughter, she slipped an arm around Shannon's shoulders and pressed her lips to her hair. She couldn't let anything hurt or damage her precious girl, particularly not while she was at such a vulnerable age. She must do everything she could to prevent it, she just wished Josh felt that way too. Once she would never have doubted it, but now she could only wonder how he could put his own sexual urges before his children, before everything they'd built together. All the lies, the deceit, the running after a woman who would only toss him aside when she was done with him – how could Josh have come to this?

Aware that her thoughts were starting to diminish him as a man, she tried to push them aside. She didn't want to despise or hate him, she wanted them to be as they always had, together, complete, trusting each other and above all loving each other. But this weakness for Sylvia, this inability to understand the pain it was going to cause to those he loved most, was making her question whether she could ever truly love or respect him again.

Three o'clock in the morning was a cruel time to be lying awake, remembering the mistakes she'd made, the people she'd hurt, and the damage she'd caused. Overwhelmed by it all, Alice could only clutch her bible and beg forgiveness from the good

Lord, who, in His mercy, had guarded their terrible secret all these years.

Since learning of Douglas's death she'd lived in morbid dread of it being revealed. Not a minute of the day passed when it wasn't there in her mind, burying itself deeper and deeper, entwining itself around her, like roots. Julia would never understand, which was why they'd never told her. It would have destroyed her young life, and would even now, were she to find out what they'd been hiding. Douglas would never have wanted that. Throughout all these years he hadn't attempted to tell her, so surely he wouldn't reveal in death what he'd been unable to communicate to her in life. It would be no easier for Julia to deal with now, in many ways it would be even harder.

Alice's eyes moved gingerly through the darkness, as though expecting to see his ghost. Was he there, watching her, accusing, damning, hating? But he'd agreed it was for the best, and how could he argue it? He'd had to leave, they'd had to make him go, for once the truth was out there was simply no way he could stay. He'd fought them, of course, but he couldn't win, they wouldn't allow it, and they'd done everything possible to help him start a new life. He'd refused it all, except the lawyers George had paid to defend him when times had become so hard he'd been unable to stop himself lashing out. She'd heard that he'd been questioned several times in connection with child sex offences, but she'd never wanted to learn the details. George knew them, because for years he'd kept a close eye on Douglas's comings and goings, until finally Douglas had seemed to settle down with a woman in Cornwall and start rebuilding his life. Apparently he'd stayed there all this time, integrating with the community, probably barely even aware of all George had done. Alice was as thankful for that as she was for how simply Pam had accepted his desertion. It was only Julia who'd been unable to let go – and now, considering his will, it seemed that Douglas had been unable to, either.

Hearing her bedroom door open, she closed her eyes and held on more tightly to the Good Book. There was the creak of a floorboard as George crossed the room, then the dip of the bed as he pulled back the sheets and slid in next to her. He was a stern man, principled and God-fearing, but with a kind and loving heart that Julia had never understood. He'd sensed his sister needed comfort in these darkest hours of the night, so he was here, holding her to him and lending her his strength, while sharing the terrible angst in her heart, the way he always had throughout their lives.

But there were so many lies, so much heartache and deception. How could God ever forgive any of them for what they'd done?

Just over two hundred miles away, Julia was unable to sleep either, as the thought of Josh and Sylvia, rushing back to London to be together, kept going round and round in her mind. Beside her on the bed were her father's notebooks and diaries. She'd been using them to distract herself with a search for answers she felt certain were there, but nothing had yielded itself up, and her concentration had been so poor as her mind constantly struggled to return to the greatest source of her pain that in the end she'd set them aside and turned out the light.

Now she lay in the darkness, listening to the mill wheel swishing the water, and the call of night birds warbling through the woods. For a while she found herself thinking about her conversation with Rod Fuller earlier, and the feeling she'd had at the end that he'd kept something back. She regretted telling him now that Douglas Cowan was her father, for if she hadn't, she felt sure he'd have said more. Then, aware that the hour was starting to play its devilish tricks on her mind, she tried to move her thoughts elsewhere, but found no comfort in how quickly they returned to Josh. When she'd called after dinner his mother had told her he was out for the evening, and hadn't said where. Though it wasn't unusual for him to have dinner meetings when she wasn't around, how could she be anything other than suspicious now? However, when she'd called him, he had been at a restaurant, and the author he was with had spoken to her himself to say hi.

Trying to take reassurance from that, she turned over and pulled the sheet up around her face. She felt so weary, yet her mind remained restless, skipping from Josh, to her father, to her mother, to Shannon and Dan, to Fen . . . Dinner had been fun this evening. Bob was back, and clearly in good spirits, though she could tell that Fen hadn't been able to help wondering where he'd really been. Knowing the torment of those feelings, her heart went out to her friend. How difficult, maybe even impossible, it was to rebuild love without trust. It was like trying to create a life with no dreams.

As they'd eaten she'd been aware of Rico, but had been careful not to look at him, nor would she think about him now, for the idea of using him to punish Josh was the kind of insanity that only held good in the dead of night. Even so, she couldn't deny being attracted to him, for those moments in the kitchen earlier would make her a liar if she tried, though it baffled her that she could even think of another man that way when she was so afraid of losing Josh. But there was no fear of her going astray, because if she couldn't get it together with Josh, she certainly wouldn't be able to with anyone else.

Hearing the bedroom door open, she pushed back the covers, and made room for Shannon to cuddle in next to her. Whether she'd sensed her mother's need, or had come to gain comfort for her own, wasn't possible to say, for neither of them spoke. Julia guessed it was both, since she knew Shannon was worried that her mother wasn't seeming like herself, and hurt that Rico had hardly talked to her tonight. There had been a few tears on the way back through the woods, and a very long chat before Julia had turned out her light. Teenage crushes could be every bit as painful as adult angst, though mercifully much more short-lived, but since this was Shannon's first she was finding it particularly hard. It was such a pity the evening had been spoiled for her, because she'd been so excited to see Rico and so sure that he was becoming interested in her now. And she'd looked lovely, her naturally red mouth so full and enticing, her flawless peachy skin so young and smooth. How could Rico resist her? He must know how she felt, for she was too inexperienced to hide it, and too infatuated to care. Julia couldn't help wondering if one kiss between them would be so wrong, but knew she'd do nothing to encourage it, for Rico was a man, while Shannon was still a child.

Chapter Fourteen

The following morning Julia was back in the attic, hauling suitcases to the hatch ready to lower down the ladder. Shannon had vanished first thing for a tennis lesson, and from there she was going on to the supermarket with Ottie and Tilde to shop for this evening's dinner. It seemed last night's hiccup with Rico had been magically forgotten, since she'd been bubbling with excitement earlier as they'd jotted down her shopping list, having finally decided on something nice and simple so she could claim to have made it herself – though Julia had agreed to keep an eye on things while Shannon prepared herself for the big event. Quite what she was planning to wear Julia had yet to find out, though if last night's outfit was anything to go by, it was probably a good thing Josh wasn't around, for he certainly wouldn't be happy about jeans that were so low-cut her hip bones showed. She'd looked pretty sensational though, and with her long slim legs, shining blonde hair and pert little breasts, Josh was very soon going to have to accept the fact that she was growing up fast.

Julia had spoken to him about an hour ago, though only briefly for he'd had another call coming in, but at least they'd managed to have a reasonable conversation without him sounding defensive, or irritable, or her becoming suspicious or needy, or any of the negative emotions she was actually feeling. Nor had she found herself tormented by doubt after they'd rung off, though she was still extremely uneasy about his visit to Sylvia. However, since he was due to arrive tomorrow, when hopefully he could go at least some way to convincing her that nothing had happened and it really was over, she'd resigned herself to putting it all on hold until they could talk, in order to get on with things here. *Just please don't let anything happen today to send my suspicions into overdrive again*, she thought, because she was actually daring to have high hopes for the weekend.

Having dragged three suitcases out from under the eaves, she was returning for the last, when her foot kicked against something hard. She looked down, but in the dim light couldn't quite make out what it was. It certainly hadn't been there before, or she'd have noticed it, so it must have been jammed under one of the suitcases and worked itself free en route to the hatch. Stooping to pick it up, she tilted it towards the dim overhead bulb and saw that it was a large metal cash box, which, judging by its weight, contained something, though a good shake produced no sound of coins. She tried opening it, but the lid wouldn't budge, and despite being rusted, the hinges seemed pretty solid too.

Wondering if the key Shannon had found might fit, she set it down on top of an old sewing machine and went back for the one remaining case.

'Hello! Is anyone up there?' a voice called out from downstairs.

Immediately recognising it as Rico's, she felt a jolt of surprise. 'I'm in the attic,' she called back.

Seconds later she heard his footsteps on the stairs and frowned, for she'd been about to go down and join him, but since she could do with his help, it probably made more sense for him to come up.

'Hi,' he said, arriving at the foot of the ladder.

'Hi,' she responded, hoping she didn't look too ghoulish or bat-like, gazing down at him from this shadowy above.

'Can I do something to help?'

'Yes, as a matter of fact you can,' she answered, making ready to pass him the first case. 'They aren't especially heavy, but they're awkward to carry down on my own.'

'It is no problem,' he assured her, climbing the first few rungs to take it. 'Where would you like me to put it?'

'In the sitting room will be fine. I can go through them in there. Careful, there's a rotating rung at the bottom.'

Avoiding it, he stepped down to the floor and deposited the case next door, and by the time he came back she was ready with the second one. Once the cases were dealt with, she passed down the cash box, but before he could take it she felt it slipping from her hands. 'Oh my God, look out,' she gasped, as it plunged towards him.

He ducked. It missed and went crashing to the ground.

'Are you OK?' she cried.

He was laughing. 'I'm fine,' he answered, going to pick it up.

'Are you sure?'

'Sure.' He turned it over in his hands, checking to see what it was.

'Is it broken?' she asked. 'Did it come open?'

'It doesn't look like it,' he answered. 'It is very rusted.' He shook it. 'Do you know what is in here?'

'No idea. I've only just found it.'

'Is there a key?'

'Unless it's one Shannon found the other day I'll have to bring a torch up here to look,' she replied.

Shrugging, he put the box on the pine chest next to him, and held the ladder steady as she started to descend.

Aware of coming at him from the most unflattering angle, she tried to avoid the comedy and focus on why he might be here, because she hadn't been expecting him, and he presumably knew where Shannon was, so maybe he'd come to say he couldn't make it for dinner ... She hoped it wasn't that, because it would devastate poor Shannon. Although, it could be for the best, since he really was too old for her, and she was almost bound to end up with a broken heart. Maybe he had a message from Fen, or had just popped in on the off chance she might need help ... There was so much going round in her head that she totally forgot about the bottom rung and as her foot went down on it, it rolled and she staggered and the next thing she knew she was falling against him.

'Oh gosh, I'm sorry,' she gasped.

He steadied her, hands under her elbows, chest on her back. 'Are you OK?' he asked.

'Yes. Fine.'

He didn't let go, and unable to believe she was doing it, she stayed where she was. She could hear him breathing, smell the masculine scent of him mingled with horses and fresh air. Her breath locked inside her as her senses began to swirl.

Still neither of them moved. Then his hands slipped round in front of her and he began to rub her waist and her breasts. She wasn't allowing herself to think, or move, or do anything except feel his hands. His mouth touched her neck, and she turned so weak with longing that her head fell back on his shoulder. She would stop him in a moment, she would have to, but it had been so long since she'd felt like this . . .

He was murmuring in Italian, still rubbing her breasts, and his mouth was so gentle, yet insistent, and as he began raising her top she merely lifted her arms to let him remove it completely. Then he was unfastening her bra, and the need to feel his hands on her skin was so intense that she still didn't stop him. He peeled the bra away and she gasped as he scooped her breasts in his hands. Her nipples were so aroused that they were throbbing between his fingers, and she wanted more and more – but only of this, no more than this . . .

Her tracksuit bottoms slid down easily to her thighs, exposing her completely to his hands, and the sensations pulsing through her became so commanding that she could do nothing but give in to them. He was easing her trousers on down to her ankles, and as she stepped out of them he turned her to face him. She thought of Josh and Sylvia, of how they'd betrayed her, then she looked down at Rico's tousled dark head, as he pushed his tongue between her legs.

'Oh my God,' she choked, putting her hands against the wall to steady herself. The suddenness of the sensations was too powerful, she had been so long without them that she was helpless to control them – and she was almost afraid to breathe in case any movement snatched them away.

Then he was standing up, and resting his hands on her waist as he gazed into her eyes.

'We can't do this,' she mumbled, but even as she said it she was allowing his mouth to come to hers. Then she was helping him to take off his own clothes and moving to him as he wrapped her in his arms. The feel of his skin against hers was so erotic that she had to have more, and as they lay down on the bed she opened her legs to take him.

As he began to move in and out of her she became so dazed by the pleasure that she was barely even aware of gripping her legs around him and urging him to go faster and harder. In some disconnected part of herself she could still hardly believe it was happening, but she was too immersed in their mounting passion to care, or even to wonder why there was no creeping cold-ness of fear coming in to stop her. There was only the need for more and yet more. He was pumping her so hard now that the bed was slamming against the wall. She grabbed the rail overhead, and urged him on and on. She could feel a climax beginning to build, and nothing in her wanted him to stop. She was so close to the ultimate release, he was taking her there, this stranger, this boy, and as she looked up into his face she felt such a surge of emotion that tears burned in her eyes.

'Are you OK?' he whispered.

'Yes. Oh God, yes.'

In some vague other world the phone seemed to be ringing downstairs, but she barely heard it. She was almost there. He was taking her so close now . . . And then suddenly it began . . .

'Oh my God!' she gasped, as the first waves broke so forcefully inside her she could hardly bear it. She raised her hips higher, needing to take him deeper, and the release kept on coming and coming. The power of it was so overwhelming that it reverberated like shocks through her entire body. She shuddered and convulsed, cried out and clung to him harder than ever. There was no coldness, no dark vacuum, or fear, no suffocating terror – there was only this, a raging torrent of sensation made so much more intense by having been stifled for so long. She wanted it to go on and on. She wanted to rejoice and cry, for it had been so easy, so clear of the shadows inside her. She felt free and euphoric, delirious and triumphant. Then he was coming too, and she held him tight, urging him to let go, to give her everything he had.

Finally he collapsed over her and buried his face in her neck. She kept her arms around him and stroked his hair and his back. His skin was smooth, his muscles hard and taut. Her eyes were closed, her breath still ragged, and her body weak from having been unlocked so suddenly and exquisitely. How had she managed this with him, when she couldn't with Josh? It made no sense, but for the moment it was enough that it had happened at all, there would be time later for the guilt and confusion.

The phone was ringing again, but she just went on holding him. Whoever it was could wait, because she wanted to lie here like this for a very long time, letting the dying throes of her climax pulse around him, as his mouth sought hers and kissed her so deeply and tenderly it brought tears to her eyes.

At last he rolled over onto his side and propped his head on one arm to gaze down at her. She smiled at his look of uncertainty, and reached up to touch his mouth.

He kissed her fingers and said, 'I want to make love to you since the first time I see you.'

Her heart responded to the pleasure of his words and she felt such an affection for him that she brought his mouth back to hers to kiss him.

'You look at me with your beautiful eyes,' he said, touching his fingers gently to her nipples, 'and then you stand there with your T-shirt and I can see you in a way that makes me want you so much. I want to kiss you and make your sadness go away.'

She frowned in surprise. 'My sadness?' Then she smiled as she realised he meant her father, and because of the last few minutes, she said, 'I think you've done that.'

He continued to gaze down at her, as though

drinking in every part of her, wanting to absorb himself in these moments, which was how she felt too, though she knew she should get dressed now and start trying to come to terms with what she'd done.

'I will do anything you want me to,' he said gruffly.

She regarded him curiously, not sure what he meant.

'I wish you to be mine, but I know this is not possible,' he explained. 'So if you want that I am your lover, or that I go away and never see you again . . .'

'Ssh,' she said, pressing her finger to his lips. 'This was wonderful, beautiful . . .' Her eyes fluttered closed as he lowered his mouth to cover her words.

By the time he raised his head again they were both ready for more, and though her conscience was stirring, she made no protest as he rolled onto her, for if she could have one more climax, just one, to prove it wasn't a fluke . . .

Though he wasn't as well endowed as Josh, and his physique was much slighter, he still felt good as he entered her, as did the rawness of his skill. Everything about him was different to Josh, in a way that made what they were doing feel unencumbered by intimacy and need, and she wondered if that was why she was able to let go. She had no fear of Rico leaving her, no dread of abandonment that prevented her from being able to trust.

As he started to move in and out of her she gave herself willingly to the mounting sensations, moaning and closing her eyes, then opening them again and watching his face.

'"Already you are mine. Rest with your dream inside my dream,"' he whispered softly.

She smiled.

'You know Pablo Neruda?' he asked.

She shook her head.

'I know no more in English,' he confessed.

'Tell me in Italian.'

'I know it in Spanish.'

As he started to recite, she lifted her hands to his face and pushed her fingers into his hair. He moved with the gentle rhythm of the words, watching her and filling her with their emotion. She wanted to understand them, but the sound of his voice, and the feel of his body, were enough. Then the poem ended and his mouth returned to hers.

Very soon she could feel herself becoming lost in the power of his movements. They were taking her relentlessly towards where she longed to go. It felt so sublime that she didn't want him to hurry, she wanted him to take her slowly, tantalisingly and with the same excruciating intensity that Josh could create as he carried her from one orgasm to the next, and to the next, never coming himself, always staying hard, never letting go until she could take no more . . . She wanted that now. She wanted Josh, who knew her body even better than she knew it herself . . .

She opened her eyes and looked up at Rico's face.

'Is this OK?' he asked.

She nodded, because it was, and she wouldn't

stop him, even though he was the wrong man. It made her wonder how Josh felt when he looked at Sylvia. Was she the wrong woman? But he kept going back for more, so did he make love to her as knowledgeably and skilfully as he did to his wife? Had Sylvia experienced the full power of his technique, the way he could tease a woman to madness, whilst taking her to oblivion? Had he allowed Sylvia to know the unsurpassable rapture he had given so readily and so often to his wife?

She moaned softly and let her head fall to one side. She needed to believe that he had no desire to understand Sylvia's body the way he did hers, that he used Sylvia only for sex and a quick, ultimate release, as she was doing now with Rico. She wanted to think of making love with Josh tomorrow night, of how they might finally end their physical estrangement. Hope and excitement stirred in her heart, and as she looked at the open door she was barely aware of who she was with now, for in her mind it was Josh, and that was all that mattered.

Then suddenly to her horror she realised she was looking at Shannon. 'Oh my God!' she gasped, shoving Rico aside and grabbing for her clothes. 'Shannon, wait, don't go,' but Shannon was already turning away.

Rico leapt up, but by the time he'd dressed Julia was in her clothes and racing downstairs.

'Shannon!' she shouted. 'Shannon, wait,' but as she dashed outside there was no sign of her.

Assuming she'd run back through the woods Julia started in that direction, hearing Rico running behind her.

'Go the other way,' she shouted. 'She might have gone towards the village.'

She ran on, dashing through the trees, plunging from sunlight to shadow, over the stream, through a broken fence, around a hollow, until minutes later she was behind the Bowers' house. She paused, looked around, then spotted Shannon disappearing into the stables.

'No!' she screamed. 'Shannon, no.'

She'd barely covered half the distance before Shannon rode out on one of the mares, no saddle, only reins and nowhere near enough experience to handle her.

'Shannon! Please!' Julia cried.

But Shannon was wheeling the horse round, struggling to stay on and spurring her towards another part of the woods.

Julia charged after her. There was no way she could keep up, but she had to try. She could hear the mare's hooves thudding into the ground, the beat of terror in her ears. She could see the branch that would knock her daughter senseless or worse, the pothole that would bring the horse down and crush her.

'Shannon. Shannon,' she gasped, stumbling on.

She couldn't see her now, she'd been swallowed up by the trees, sucked deeper and deeper into a danger she was too shocked, too traumatised to see.

'Please God, please,' Julia begged, tears streaming down her cheeks. She pressed on, hardly aware of the branches ripping at her clothes and skin, or the mud and brambles underfoot. She reached a clearing, stopped and spun round.

Which way? She tried to listen, but could only hear the pounding of her heart.

'Shannon!' she cried. 'Shannon!'

Had she already fallen? Was she lying somewhere, dazed and broken, or, heaven help her, lifeless? 'Shannon, please!'

She thought of Josh, and what he would do if he ever found out about this ... She couldn't let the fear of it go any further, she just had to find Shannon.

Seeing a pathway she ran to it, calling Shannon's name over and over, but there was no reply.

'Please God, please,' she sobbed, stumbling on a twisted root.

She forced herself on, scratched and bleeding, twisting and turning, colliding with branches and slipping in the mire. She wrenched an ankle, but limped on, wincing with pain, still calling, still pleading. 'Shannon, come back. Shannon please.'

Finally she emerged from the woods to find herself on the bank of a stream. Fields rose up in front of her, wide and empty – no rider, no horse, no sign of life. She dropped to her knees, lungs burning, nightmare descending. She didn't know what to do, she'd lost all power in her body, all reason in her mind. She tried to catch her breath. Her chest was on fire. Her limbs shook uncontrollably. She felt the trickle of semen on her leg and wanted only to die.

Then she heard a horse whinny.

She looked up and listened. Everything was still. Only the bubble of the brook, and ragged gasps of her breath. She peered back into the trees, and on along the path to where it descended out of sight. Quickly she staggered towards it. Please God, let her be there. Please. Please.

She reached the hollow, looked down and her heart turned inside out. There was the horse, but no sign of Shannon. She clasped her hands to her face and tried not to panic. Oh God, no. Please, please no.

She stumbled towards the horse and grabbed the reins.

'Where is she?' she begged. 'Please show me where she is.'

The horse sidestepped and nickered. Julia watched her eyes but they told her nothing. She was crazy to think they would. Dropping the reins, she looked along the stream and back into the woods. Her eyes probed every nook and shadow, every bush and branch. There could be no fear greater than this, no dread more intense, no conscience more unforgiving. She stared out at the emptiness of the fields and felt an emptiness that was far greater, and much less benign. Where was her girl? Somewhere beneath this grey-blue sky her child was alone, frightened, angry, confused – or injured, or worse. She had to find her. Nothing could ever matter more.

And then she saw her, sitting against a tree, her face turned to its trunk.

'Shannon,' she gasped, and felt the relief so profoundly that it heaved in her stomach, and turning aside she put a hand to her throat as she retched. 'Shannon,' she said again, as she wiped her mouth. 'Darling, are you all right?'

Shannon put out a hand to block her. 'Go away!' she seethed, keeping her face hidden.

'But darling, are you . . .'

'I said go away!' She turned round and her lovely young face was ravaged with hate and tears and so much pain it almost broke Julia's heart. 'Don't come near me,' she spat. 'I hate you. *I hate you.*'

'Darling, I understand how you're feeling . . .'

Shannon covered her face with her hands and let out a scream of rage. 'I don't want to look at you. I never want to see you again.'

'Shannon, please let me try to explain . . .'

'*Nooooo!* I don't want you to. I hate you. You took him away from me. He was mine! *Mine!*'

'Darling, it's not how you're seeing it. It wasn't meant to hurt you . . .'

'How could you?' Shannon shrieked, pushing her face up. 'You're my mother. *My mother!* You're so disgusting . . .'

'Please listen . . .'

'What about Daddy? How could you do it to him?'

'It wasn't like that. It . . .'

'I want Dad!' Shannon sobbed. 'I want to go home and be with Daddy.'

'Listen, we have to talk . . .'

'No! I never want to talk to you again. I just want Dad. He loves me! Not like you. You hate me, but I don't care. I hate you.'

'Shannon, you know I love you.'

'No I don't, just go away and leave me alone.'

'I can't leave you here, so let me take you back . . .'

'No. I'm going home to Dad. I don't want to be with you.'

'All right. Whatever you say. Just let's take the horse back now.'

After a while Shannon started to get up, but as Julia made to help her she violently recoiled. 'Don't touch me!' she snarled.

Julia stepped back. 'I'll get the horse,' she said, feeling more guilt and wretchedness than she'd ever known in her life – and so much fear of the future now that her mind was going blank rather than think of it.

They walked back through the woods in silence, Julia one side of the horse, Shannon the other. Julia was praying that Rico wouldn't come along, trying to find them, for his presence now would be too much for Shannon to bear. But he didn't, and after leaving the horse in the stables, they started in silence back to the mill.

Julia was thinking of Josh now and how he was going to take this, and as her heart folded around the dread of it, she wanted to bury herself under a mountain of denial, but all she found was layer upon layer of bitter recrimination. How could she have been such a fool? What had she thought it would achieve, beyond the kind of nightmare she was in now? A momentary madness allowed her to think that she could keep it from him, but it was soon gone, because she couldn't ask Shannon to share such a secret, any more than she could expect her forgiveness. She would have to tell Josh herself. She'd drive Shannon back to London today, and confess what had happened, then God only knew what he would do. The fact that she'd made love with another man would be bad enough, that she'd allowed Shannon to see it would be so intolerable that she knew already he would never forgive her.

The next hour passed like a slow-motion nightmare. Shannon still refused to talk, except to tell Julia that there was no way she was travelling back to London with her, she wanted to go on the train and take the tube at the other end. Julia tried to argue, but Shannon went into her room and slammed the door. Seconds later her music went on to drown out anything else Julia might say.

Never having felt so helpless, Julia took herself into the bathroom to shower, keeping the door locked in case Shannon came in. The last thing she'd want now was to see her mother naked, it would be too horrendous a reminder.

When she came out she heard Shannon talking to someone on the phone and immediately froze, in case it was Josh. She stood where she was, listening, but it soon became clear she was talking to Ottie, letting her know that she wouldn't be going to the supermarket, or cooking dinner tonight, because something had come up and she had to go back to London.

Despising herself, and steeped in guilt, Julia slipped upstairs to dress, then came down again a few minutes later to find Shannon in the kitchen looking through the Yellow Pages.

'What are you doing?' Julia asked.

'I need a taxi to take me to the station.'

'I'll take you.'

'I'm not going anywhere with you.'

'Shannon, please.'

Shannon picked up the phone and started to dial.

Julia pressed down the connectors and took the receiver. 'Don't leave like this,' she said softly.

Shannon turned abruptly away, and started to pick up her luggage. 'I want Dad,' she said coldly.

Wishing she knew how to handle this, Julia tried to take her bags, but was only pushed aside. 'You can't walk to the station,' she said. 'It's too far.'

'It's none of your business what I do.'

'Put it in the car and I'll drive you,' Julia said. 'Do you have any money for a ticket?'

Shannon didn't answer, merely walked outside to the car and dumped her bags in the boot.

All the way to the station she remained plugged into her iPod, while Julia tried desperately to find a way to explain what she'd done, even though she knew that in Shannon's eyes no excuse in the world would ever be good enough. She hadn't only betrayed Shannon, she'd betrayed her beloved father too.

When they finally got out of the car Shannon waited while Julia bought a ticket, then refusing to allow Julia to help her over to the platform, she picked up her bags and struggled up the steps to cross the footbridge. Julia stayed where she was, watching as she descended onto the opposite platform and feeling such an ache in her heart that it surpassed any kind of pain she'd known before. She'd done this to her daughter, she was the one who'd devastated her dream and cast her adrift in a cold, harsh world of loneliness, confusion, anger and hate.

As they waited, Shannon wouldn't look across,

though she would know Julia was still there. Julia could see the paleness of her face, and stiffness of her body, just as she could feel the anguish in her heart. Then at last the train came, blocking them from each other's view, until a few minutes later Julia saw her enter a carriage, then set down her luggage before choosing a seat. She sat the other side of the train and turned her head away. When the train pulled out of the station, Julia lifted a hand to wave, but Shannon wasn't looking. Then she was left facing an empty platform and as she stared at it, she knew she'd never been so afraid of losing those she loved.

As she drove back to the house she felt numb. It was strange, even unsettling, to realise that she was still in the same day she'd been in a mere two hours ago, the same world even, for it was all so different now and she had no idea how she was going to continue – except as soon as she got back she knew she'd have to call Josh. She tried over and over to form the words in her mind, to find the right way to break this to him, but the mere thought of it filled her with so much dread that she had to pull over because she thought she was going to be sick. In the end she wasn't, so she drove on, her heart pounding, her eyes stinging, almost as though she had thrown up. She kept picturing Shannon sitting alone in that carriage, trying to hold herself together as she broke apart inside, and as the tears coursed down Julia's cheeks, blinding her, she knew she had never felt so connected to her daughter's pain.

Thankfully there was no-one around as she

drove past the Bowers' house, nor when she reached her own. She hoped Rico would stay away, because she truly couldn't face him now.

After dabbing her face in cold water, she went to stand beside the phone, but it was a long time before she could make herself pick it up. She was going to push Josh straight into Sylvia's arms now, and she knew it, but as devastated as she was by that, and as hard as she was still fighting it, she couldn't think about herself when Shannon was all that mattered. So, finally, afraid that Shannon might already have called him from the train, she forced herself to dial his number.

'He's not here,' Marina answered. 'He's at home.'

Julia frowned, but not wanting to get into anything with Marina, she thanked her, rang off and dialled again.

'Josh? What are you doing at home?' she asked when he answered.

'Where the hell have you been?' he replied sharply. 'We've been trying to get hold of you.'

She felt a thud of alarm as her mind went instantly to Dan. 'Is everything all right?' she demanded.

'No, it's not. Dan had an attack . . .'

'Where is he?' she cried. 'Is he OK?'

'He's sleeping, but you should have been here, Julia. You're his mother. It shouldn't be falling to mine to deal with these things. Just thank God I wasn't in a meeting, or somewhere she couldn't get hold of me. But you were, and it's just not good enough. I want you back here, Julia. Today. Shannon too. I've had as much as I can take of this trawling through your past. He left, he's dead, time to get over it.'

She flinched at the harshness. 'Josh, listen,' she said, 'I have something to tell you.'

'Tell me when you get here.'

'No. Don't ring off. Please, I have to tell you now. Shannon's already on her way back.'

There was a pause before he said, 'What do you mean? Why aren't you with her?'

'She's on the train . . .'

'Alone? Jesus Christ Julia, what's the matter with you?'

'She's fifteen, Josh. That makes her old enough . . .'

'In your book, maybe. Not in mine. So why the hell aren't you bringing her?'

'That's what I need to talk to you about. Are you alone at the moment?'

Again there was a pause and she could almost feel his confusion. 'My mother's upstairs, sitting with Dan,' he said. 'Why? What the hell's going on?'

Julia swallowed, and put a hand to her head. 'Shannon's had a bit of a shock. She's very upset . . .'

'What kind of shock? She was fine when I last spoke to her.'

'You should meet her at Paddington. The train gets in at ten to seven.'

'Julia, what's happened?' he growled darkly.

She took a breath, then knowing she had no choice but to go through with it, she braced herself and said, 'She found me in bed with Rico, Fen's cousin.'

For a long time there was only silence, and the longer it went on the more she could feel her future slipping away. Finally, in a voice that was so bitter that she flinched at every word, he said, 'So while our son was having a seizure and needed his mother, while we were trying to get hold of you, you were too busy fucking another man to answer the phone? Is that what you're telling me?'

'Josh – I . . .'

'Not only were you fucking another man, you were doing it in a place where your own daughter could walk right in and find you. Is that what you're saying? I want to get this right Julia, because if my wife has turned into some kind of brainless, self-involved fucking whore, I need to know.'

Wincing at the words, she said, 'You can't make me feel any worse than I already do.'

'Oh, I haven't even started,' he snarled.

'Josh, please. Shannon needs our help now . . .'

'Are you out of your mind? I think you've done enough where she's concerned, don't you? And frankly, if she never wants to see you again, that'll be fine by me.'

'Listen, I'm going to pack up this house today . . .'

'No, *you* listen. You just stay right where you are. We don't want you here.'

'But you said yourself, Dan needs me,' she cried. 'I have to come home. We have to deal with Shannon together.'

'Just stay away from her,' he raged. 'You're not fit to call yourself a mother, or a wife . . .'

'Josh . . .'

'Just tell me this,' he cut in savagely, 'did you go the whole way? Did he make you come?'

She should lie, and she was going to, but her hesitation told him the truth.

'Jesus Christ,' he seethed, and she heard the slam of his fist against something hard. 'I could kill you for this.'

Unable to stop herself she said, 'Then now you know how I feel about you and Sylvia.'

'Don't even go there!' he yelled. 'It's not the same thing. I wasn't refusing to have sex with you . . . I didn't find you repulsive . . .'

'I never found you repulsive . . .'

'You were all I needed, everything I wanted, but it wasn't enough for you, was it? You had to create problems where none existed. You thought you were drowning, or suffocating, or whatever other crap you could come up with. Well it doesn't sound as though you had any trouble with *Rico*, does it? No, it was all fine with him, until our daughter happened to walk into the room. How fucking inconvenient. Well she's out of the way now . . .'

'OK, the moral high ground's yours,' she shouted, 'but it still doesn't change the fact that you've been deceiving me with my own best friend, and probably still are for all I know.'

'Well, maybe I am. At least she wants me in her bed . . .'

'I've always wanted you, you know that. I still do. I love you . . .'

'Spare me the bullshit. It's too late now, Julia. It's finished. We're never going to get past this, so stay where you are, because we sure as hell don't need you here.'

She flinched as the line went dead, and knowing there would be no point trying to call back yet, she hung up too. She didn't blame him for the way he'd reacted, she more than deserved it. She'd hurt him in the worst possible way, while at the same time she'd traumatised and devastated their daughter, as well as failing to answer the phone when their son needed her. Her crimes were piling up, and never mind that there was nothing she could have done for Dan from this far away, Josh was right, she should have been there, not here, neglecting her motherly duties, and making love with another man.

Though she wanted nothing more than to get in the car and drive straight to Dan, she'd had enough experience of his seizures to know that he was likely to be fully recovered by now and probably didn't need her at all. Nevertheless, she still felt the urge to be with him. He was her boy, her own flesh and blood, nothing mattered more than him. So why didn't she just go? Why was she just standing here, staring at nothing? She felt so drained that maybe all she really wanted was to go and lie down. However, she knew that as soon as her head hit the pillow, the self-loathing and fear would keep her awake. She looked around, unable to think what to do. She lacked the heart now to continue clearing the house, and the strength to go outside and walk. She thought of calling Fen, but how could she possibly tell her what had happened? She'd be as appalled as she ought to be, and probably even ashamed to call her a friend. Then, hearing footsteps on the deck, she looked up and her heart twisted to see Rico standing at the open door.

'I can go away,' he said

She shook her head. 'No, it's OK,' she answered, then without even knowing she was going to do it, she put her hands over her face and started to sob.

He came to her, held her in his arms and rocked her as she cried. He murmured gently in Italian, stroking her hair, and letting the tears soak through his shirt to his skin. 'It'll be all right,' he told her softly. 'She will get over it.'

Julia couldn't see how, nor could she envisage a scene where Josh would forgive her. She didn't tell Rico that though, she was too distraught, too racked with tears to find a voice.

After a while she lifted her head and tried to break free. He held onto her and tilted her face to his. She looked up at him, and saw so much concern in his eyes that she felt her own fill with tears again. He wiped them away with his fingers, and continued to look at her. Then his mouth was touching hers, lightly, tentatively, in a way that was tender and undemanding, and craving the affection she kissed him back, feeling herself warming to the comfort and relaxing into his arms. His hand moved to her neck, stroking it gently, and after a while her mouth came open, allowing his kiss to become stronger and deeper. She lifted her hands to his face and held it as their tongues met and their passion grew.

He took her right there, and she clung to him desperately, needing him to help her block out the pain. She wanted him to hurt and punish her and force her to keep going so she would never have to think of anything else ever again.

'Julia,' he murmured across her open mouth. 'Julia.'

Suddenly her head fell back and she cried out as she started to come. It was breaking in harsh, unrelenting waves, pulling so savagely at her it was as though her own body was trying to destroy her. She cried out again and again, holding onto him and letting the tears run down her cheeks as he came too and whispered that he loved her.

For a long time afterwards they stayed where they were, arms around each other, their bodies still joined. It was almost as though she was afraid to let go. Somewhere at a distance she was aware of Josh and the children, but she couldn't let them in now. Her shame would be great enough when it came, so it could wait. She wanted only to go on holding Rico, feeling the strength of his body supporting hers, and the tenderness of his heart as it beat against her own. For these few precious moments the world was standing still, and nothing in her was willing for it to move forward again.

Chapter Fifteen

Sylvia was sitting in the production gallery of a national radio station, waiting to go into the studio. Robin, her publicist, was with her, a short, wiry man with a serious frown and an infectious smile, and an impressive record of getting maximum exposure for his authors at the time of publication. In Sylvia's case, drumming up interest was rarely difficult, for she was a regular top-seller, a beautiful woman, and a totally dedicated singleton – a term Robin was never allowed to use in her presence, since she utterly loathed it. However, the fact that she remained so resolutely unattached when she was clearly highly desirable on just about every front was a source of fascination to many. She must surely be inundated with offers, so who, it was often asked, was finally going to capture this elusive ice queen?

Sylvia never denied having lovers, though she guarded their identities as jealously as her own reputation, however that didn't stop her teasing interviewers with the occasional exotic or sensual detail of her life. It all added to her air of mystique, and the image she enjoyed most of all, of the irresistible woman who broke hearts, never the other way around.

Robin, of course, knew who many of her lovers were, but he was as discreet as he was trustworthy, mainly because if he weren't, he knew he'd be out of a job. On the other hand, she also had to tread a little carefully with him, for should he ever be of a mind to, he could probably make a small fortune by selling her story. This was not because she herself was of any great value to tabloid readers, but several of the men she'd had affairs with most definitely were.

Now, as they updated her schedule for the next two weeks, she could sense Robin's excitement building, and smiling she squeezed his hand, for he almost always got more worked up about her going on air than she did. It was one of the little idiosyncrasies she enjoyed most about him, though he'd obviously forgotten that this particular interview was due to be recorded, rather than transmitted live, so didn't really warrant many nerves. However, it was to be the first of the dozen or so he had lined up, so perhaps that was good enough cause for his giddy anticipation.

'Sorry to keep you waiting,' a researcher said, popping her head round the studio door. 'We're having a technical problem, but it shouldn't be long now.'

'No rush,' Sylvia assured her pleasantly, and went back to reviewing the schedule.

'The really big event, obviously,' Robin said, 'is the launch party tomorrow night. We've got loads of media lined up, and celebs and other authors, and the venue's a big publicity draw in itself, being Marcello Diego's new restaurant-cum-nightclub. There'll be about seventy for a four-course dinner, and they'll be expecting you to give a talk after, obviously, so I've prepared a few notes, but you're much better at it than I am, so feel free to chuck mine. Oh God, who's this calling now,' he groaned, picking up his mobile. 'Ah, it's our two o'clock. Better make sure it's still happening.'

As he took the call, Sylvia continued to glance over the schedule, though she wasn't paying it any detailed attention, for she was already familiar with its most salient points. Since Robin could always be relied upon to inform her immediately anything new had been added, she was happy to let her thoughts drift in a completely different direction, and as they did she could feel the warmth of pleasure closing around her heart. Though she'd been certain when Josh had left last week that he would contact her again, she wasn't sure she'd expected it to be quite this soon, and knowing that he hadn't even lasted four days sent frissons of lust shivering through her. How pleasing it was to realise he couldn't give her up, that his conscience, in the end, couldn't overcome his need. He had to have her, and she had to have him too, and though she hadn't actually seen him yet, she'd got the feeling when they'd spoken, yesterday, and again this morning, that he was finally ready to start letting Julia go.

Were it possible to feel more thrilled by that, she didn't know how, though she was aware that she still needed to play it carefully. Having found the man for whom she was willing to give up her precious freedom, it would be an absolute disaster if she did anything to mess it up now. However, the fact that he'd agreed to be her escort tomorrow night, in full view of all their publishing colleagues, as well as the media of course, went to prove how much closer he was to accepting the inevitable. Where that left Julia and the children she had no idea – she guessed she'd find out when she saw him. For a fleeting moment the wait till tomorrow night seemed almost intolerable. She just hoped he'd come early enough to allow some private time together before they left for the party.

'OK, everything's fine for this afternoon,' Robin declared, ringing off. 'They just want a couple hundred more books for you to sign, if you can bear it. I'll get onto it while you're working the magic in there.'

Sylvia's chill blue eyes sparkled, for she loved giving interviews, and being on such a high today, she was really looking forward to making a start. What a pity she couldn't mention anything about Josh yet. It would be quite a scoop for this particular show's host to be told that the famously single Sylvia Holland had finally met her man, but she'd need Josh's permission for that so, alas, it would have to wait. However, just for the sheer pleasure of it, she decided to run with the idea of going public for a while. She imagined what it would be like to tell the world how she felt, watching Josh as he dealt with the envy and admiration he would receive when the famously aloof author revealed she had finally fallen for him. The images and pride delighted her so much that she almost laughed to think of how Robin would react once he found out, not only for the publicity value, but because, like her, he'd never imagined her succumbing to the tired old temptation of wedded bliss. However, she was getting ahead of herself now, for though she'd love their first holiday to be a honeymoon, there was a considerable amount to sort out before that could happen, not least of all Josh's divorce. This hadn't even come up as a topic yet, never mind a possibility, so she really should start reining in her imagination now.

An hour later she was in the back of a chauffeur-driven Mercedes with Robin and wanting very much to laugh out loud, for he'd obviously been so tied up on the phone during her interview that he hadn't heard a word she'd said. But he would, tomorrow, when the programme was aired – and once again she fought the urge to laugh, for she could already hear his screech of disbelief, hotly followed by a reminder that as one of her closest friends, her publicist and chief guardian of secrets, he had an absolute right to know before anyone else who this amazing man was.

As Julia gazed down at the viscous green surface of the river she had no clear idea of why she was here, except it was a beautiful and tranquil place to be, in amongst the rushes, and sheltered from the sky by a vast canopy of red and gold branches. It seemed so remote from the rest of the world, and after another dreadful row with Josh this morning, that was how she wanted to be, remote, separate, no longer attached to all the pain she had caused. Except in her heart she wanted to be with him, in London, trying in some way to repair the damage, but he wouldn't allow it.

'You can't keep me from my children,' she'd shouted at him when he'd refused again to let her come home.

'As far as I'm concerned we play this Shannon's way,' he'd shouted back, 'and right now she doesn't want to see you.'

'But what about Dan? You can't tell me . . .'

'Dan's fine. The minute he's not, I'll let you know.'

'Josh, don't ring off,' she'd cried, certain he'd been about to. 'We need to talk. We can't let everything fall apart like this.'

'What we need, Julia, is a break,' he said coldly.

'But for how long?'

'I don't know.'

She'd tried not to say it, but in the end it had just blurted from her. 'So that you can carry on seeing Sylvia?'

'Oh for Christ's sake.'

'Are you still seeing her?'

'If I am, I don't have to answer to you.'

'Yes you do,' she'd almost screamed. 'I'm your wife, whether you like it or not. And they're *my* children. Josh please, don't do this . . . I'm sorry for what I did . . .'

'I have to go,' he said, and cut her off.

Feeling the dampness of the air starting to seep through her clothes, she wrapped her coat more tightly around her and watched a rabbit skirting across the opposite bank. Apart from her, the wildlife and Rico, there wasn't another living soul around, and the only sounds were those of the trees creaking, birds twittering or squawking, or an occasional splash as something plopped into the water. She'd been here once before, many years ago with her father, after reading the book she'd loved above all others at the time, *Frenchman's Creek*. She'd wanted to see the place for herself and had secretly hoped to discover that Dona and her pirate lover were still there, even if only in ghost form now, fishing and building fires and sailing *La Mouette* into the sun. She remembered being so distraught at the end of the book that Dona hadn't gone with her Frenchman, that her father had encouraged her to write a small sequel, just for them, which would see Dona and her lover together again. So she had, and – not wanting to alter anything her idol Daphne du Maurier had set down – she'd made it so that Dona had given birth to her lover's child nine months after letting him go, and then her horrid fat slob of a husband was killed falling from a horse. Jean-Benoit Aubéry, her dashing pirate lover who was a wealthy Frenchman really, was then able to marry her and take care of all her children, including his own.

What wouldn't she give to be able to write her way out of the heartache she was suffering now, making everything different and right again, with her father, with Josh, with Shannon? She wasn't sure what kind of story she would create, though her father would certainly still be alive, and Josh wouldn't be sleeping with another woman, and she wouldn't be standing in one of the most romantic spots she knew with a young man who had no place in her life, and for whom there was really no room in her heart.

Smiling as he slipped an arm around her, she leaned into his shoulder, and let him hold her as they turned to start back. Yesterday, after the probate officer had given her yet more bad news, Rico had driven her to Fowey to cheer her up, and had wanted to walk like this with her there, but she wouldn't allow it, not only because she didn't want to encourage him, but because she'd felt foolish, a woman her age with a man so young. However, in the privacy of the creek it was different, there was no-one to see them here, and she liked the feeling of warmth he gave her, but once they returned to the car she'd have to tell him that this kind of closeness must end now. The fact that she'd continued to make love with him after Shannon had gone was as mystifying to her as it was shaming, yet she didn't want to think of it that way, for she knew how much it had meant to him, and, in truth, it had meant a great deal to her too.

'Will you come to Italy with me?' he asked, as he drove them back to Shallard's Cross.

She turned to look at him and resisted the impulse to touch him. He'd asked her this question many times over the last few days, but only now was she seeing the similarity between her story and Dona's – neither of them could go with their foreign lovers because of their children. However, the similarity ended there, because she didn't love him the way Dona had loved her pirate, nor did she want to write a sequel that had him taking Josh's place.

'It is a very beautiful country, and we could be very happy there,' he told her, earnestly. 'I will take care of you, and your children can come . . .'

'You know it can't happen,' she said gently, 'but I'll always treasure the time we've had together.'

He looked so downcast as he said, 'It has been very special for me. The most special in all my life. I have never been in love before.'

Whether or not that was true she had no idea. If it were, the bitter irony of it wasn't escaping her, that she should be his first love, while he was her daughter's. 'If I don't go back to London yet,' she said, 'will you do something for me?'

'Of course, anything.'

She took a breath, knowing she wasn't going to say what he wanted to hear. 'Will you leave here and go back to Italy?'

He glanced over at her in confusion. 'With you?'

'No, not with me. Rico, you mean a great deal to me, but my children, my marriage . . . They have to come first, and while you're here . . . It's not right, what we're doing.'

'But how can it be wrong when I love you?' he protested.

Knowing he already knew the answer to that, she turned to look at the passing countryside, and let her thoughts drift away from him to Josh. She presumed he'd be at the office now, but he could be at a meeting somewhere, or just finishing lunch with a client – or was he with Sylvia, using her to blot out the pain, the way she'd been using Rico? She had far more to fear from Sylvia than he did from Rico though, because he'd already proved how hard he'd found it to give her up, and remembering that Sylvia's new book was out tomorrow, she wondered if there would be a party, and if there was, whether he'd go.

'I think,' Fen said later, 'if you do go rushing back to London now, you're likely to make things a whole lot worse. It needs time to settle, you all do, so I'm inclined to agree with Josh that you should stay here, at least for a few more days.'

Shuddering at the very idea of how bitter the scenes could be if she forced her way into the house now, Julia lowered her eyes to cover the pain. 'But the children are back at school,' she said after a while. 'I should be there for them.'

'Of course, but they're not babies any more, they can manage.'

It was true, thanks to Josh's mother they could, but it was tearing her apart to think of what Shannon was going through, and to know that there was nothing she could do to make it any better. 'Shannon won't speak to me, or answer my texts,' she confessed. 'I don't even know if she reads them, or if she even discusses it with Josh.'

Since Fen knew the whole story now, she was able to say, 'Obviously it was a shock, and a pretty profound one, but she'll get over it, I promise – and so will he. Once again, we're back to giving it time.'

Hoping with all her heart that Fen was right, Julia gazed down at the small fire she'd made in the kitchen hearth, and tried to think what to do next. 'If I do stay . . .' She looked up at Fen. 'I've asked Rico to leave.'

Fen nodded reassuringly. 'That's probably a good idea,' she said. 'He's clearly besotted with you, which we've all known from the beginning, but as big a confidence boost as it might be, it's not the kind of complication you need right now.'

How right she was, Julia thought, and sighing she pushed her hands through her hair. 'I've been getting these awful feelings of panic,' she said. 'Sometimes I feel so convinced I'm going to lose him, and the children, and everything we have that I just want to scream and scream to blot it all out. It's reminding me of how I felt when my father left, utterly desperate and needy and terrified I'd never see him again. I know that's not going to happen here, because obviously they're not all just going to disappear, but I remember the biggest fear I had when my father went was that he'd never really loved me at all, that it was just a pretence.'

Her eyes moved briefly to Fen's, and seeing how intently she was listening, she smiled weakly. 'I think that's what started happening with Josh,' she said, 'that as time went on, I became more and more convinced that he didn't really love me either, and that sooner or later he would leave me too, so to protect myself I started to withdraw.' She was shaking her head, as though baffled by the disconnect with her own psyche. 'I guess you could say that on some unconscious level I was actually making it happen,' she said, and gave a dry empty laugh. 'It seems I'm succeeding pretty well, wouldn't you say?'

Fen was smiling. 'Only in understanding what you're doing, not in pushing your family away. They love you too much to allow you to do that.'

'The children, maybe, I'm just not sure about Josh. I think he's fallen much harder for Sylvia than he's admitting, or maybe even realises . . .'

'You don't know that,' Fen chided, 'and actually the evidence isn't bearing it out at all, because before all this happened, didn't he tell you he'd ended it with her?'

Julia's eyes reflected the irony in her tone as she said, 'Considering the circumstances he probably doesn't see why he should give her up, and besides, I don't know for certain that he did.'

'But all he's said is that you need a break, not that he doesn't want you back, and you have to agree, it's not such a bad idea, because while you're feeling this afraid and insecure you'd probably end up stifling him.'

Julia nodded slowly as she considered that, and let her eyes drift off to the middle distance.

'You know what I think?' Fen said. 'I think there's a strange sort of serendipity going on here, that it should be your father who's providing you with sanctuary while you sort yourself out.'

Julia smiled. 'It's a nice thought,' she said. 'And God knows I need to do that – and where else would I go?' Then, after a pause, 'I have to be honest though, I don't think I can face going through any more of his things just yet. There's so much else going on with Josh and Shannon . . .'

'There's no rush,' Fen reminded her. 'It's your house now. It all belongs to you, so you can go back to it whenever you feel ready.'

'I wish that were true,' Julia responded grimly, 'but now I know what the inheritance tax is going to be, I'll probably have to sell.'

'Surely it won't come to that?'

'It's over eighty thousand pounds, and the only

way I can afford that is either to sell the house, or to ask Josh for the money.'

'Have you mentioned it to him?'

'Not yet, because right now the most likely answer will either be a resounding no, or yes, but as part of a divorce settlement. Anyway, I don't even want to think about it, I just need to work out how I'm going to sort out the unholy mess my life is in, and get Hamish Kincaid's manuscript back to him by the end of the month.'

'That soon? Have you made a start yet?'

Julia almost laughed. 'I haven't even opened the parcel,' she admitted, 'but don't for God's sake tell him that, because he's called twice in the last few days wanting to know how I'm getting on.'

'So what are you telling him?'

'I explained that I was prevented from making an early start by my father's death, which he grudgingly accepted, and now he's waiting to hear back from me after I've completed the first read.'

'Which will be when?'

'He thinks by the end of the day tomorrow.'

Fen regarded her sceptically. 'Is that possible?'

Julia nodded. 'Provided I can restrain myself from visiting any more disasters on my own head, then yes, it should be,' she answered. 'In fact, it could prove an absolute godsend of a distraction if Josh continues to insist we have a break – plus, I've started to have some ideas for a book of my own.'

Fen's eyebrows rose with interest. 'Can I ask what it's about?'

Julia laughed wryly. 'Would you believe a woman who's spent most of her life cultivating an image of cool sophistication, total self-confidence and unshakable calm, while underneath it all she's a hot-blooded whore who's shagged more married men than she's sold hardback copies.'

Fen laughed. 'You're basing it on Sylvia?'

Julia's eyes rounded in innocence. 'Did her name cross my lips?' she challenged. Then, 'Actually it started out as a plan to make her leave Josh alone – I thought if I threatened to go public with some of the high-profile men she's had affairs with, she might just disappear into the ether, but then I asked myself, why would I do that to their wives? Then the more I thought about it, the more I could see what a pathetic little character she really is, hiding behind her ice-queen image, pretending she's above wanting what other women want, parading her success, using her sexuality, befriending women just to seduce their husbands – can you believe I was so stupid as to think she'd never use that technique on me? It's all a power trip, a game, a charade, because underneath it all she's just a sad and lonely forty-year-old bitch who hasn't found what she's really looking for, what we're all looking for, which is to be loved and appreciated, and to feel that we matter to the one person we love as much as they matter to you.'

Fen was regarding her curiously, though her eyes were starting to narrow as she said, 'As your lawyer, as well as your friend, I hope you're planning to weave in enough fiction to avoid a lawsuit.'

Julia smiled. 'Actually, I'm not really a vengeful sort of person,' she sighed. 'Sometimes I wish I were, but as much as I'd like to give that bitch everything she deserves, when it comes right down to it I have to ask myself, do I really want to spend the next year focusing so intensely on her? The answer has to be no, but even if I did, would I really let it be known that the main character is based on her, in order to make sure it was published?'

'Well, definitely hold onto the thought,' Fen advised, 'because it would be great publicity if you did, which would guarantee sales, and go quite some way towards settling the score.'

'Only if she doesn't have Josh,' Julia responded quietly. 'If she has him, then the score will never be settled.'

The following morning, having already spoken to Dan on the phone twice, on his way to school and again at break, Julia finally settled down to make a start on Hamish Kincaid's manuscript. Since she always worked best when there was some kind of music or chatter in the background, she had the radio on low, which together with the sound of the rain outside should have lulled her smoothly into the story, but this morning it wasn't happening. Her head was simply too full of Josh and Shannon, and the fact that neither of them had spoken to her when she'd called Dan first thing, even though they'd both been in the car, nor had Shannon answered her text. Though she couldn't claim to be surprised, the hurt and worry were increasing to a point now where she kept tormenting herself with visions of rifts that went on for years, and resentments that could never be healed.

However, eventually, after reading the first few

pages several times, she found herself starting to let go of her turmoil and even registering some of what she was reading, until finally she became so engrossed that it was gone midday by the time she looked up again. Almost immediately she wished she hadn't, for suddenly reconnecting with reality caused a painful twist in her heart. Since there still hadn't been a call from Josh, she gave up reading for the moment and went to make herself a coffee while she decided whether or not to call him. The trouble was, she had nothing in particular to talk to him about, and she desperately didn't want to get into another row, or be any more hurt by the coldness of his manner, but nor did she want this silence to drag on for much longer.

In the end, though it was against her better judgement, she decided she had to call him because she couldn't stand this waiting any more, but even as she turned towards the phone it started to ring. Hoping and praying it would be him she quickly put down her coffee and reached for it.

'Hi, it's me,' Rico said.

Her disappointment was so intense that it sent a flash of anger through her. 'Hi, how are you?' she said, somehow managing to sound friendly, though she was already preparing an excuse to ring off.

'I am fine,' he answered. 'I am ringing to let you know that I will fly back to Italy tonight.'

Her relief was quickly swamped by a horrible surge of guilt. Brief as their love affair had been, it had clearly affected him deeply, and now he was doing this for her, even though he obviously didn't want to. 'I'm really sorry,' she said softly. 'I didn't mean to hurt you, I just – it's . . . If things had been different, if I weren't married and perhaps a little closer to your age . . .'

'Please don't say those things. I care nothing for them. I love you and I want you to come with me, so that we can always be together.'

'You know I can't,' she responded gently.

'Not now, but maybe later you change your mind.'

Feeling for him in his despair, while not wanting to lend him false hope she said, 'You must try to forget me now, Rico . . .'

'Please let me come to say goodbye,' he interrupted. 'I want to look at you and hold you and kiss you one more time.'

'No, you mustn't do that,' she said. 'It'll only make it harder, for us both.'

'You can't stop me coming,' he said stubbornly.

'I know, but I'm asking you not to.'

There was a long pause, then she heard the terrible anguish in his voice as he said, 'I will not give up hope, Julia. In my heart I know you are mine. You have made me so happy and so sad, maybe soon you will make me happy again.'

'No, someone else will do that,' she said softly. 'A beautiful Italian girl . . .'

'I don't want to hear you say those things. Please, don't say them, just tell me that you love me a little too.'

'It would be wrong of me to do that,' she replied.

'I will call you again when I get to my home,' he said abruptly. 'Please don't tell me not to, because I must.'

'OK,' she answered, not having the heart to refuse him, even though she knew she should.

'I go now,' he said, and before she could respond he'd put the phone down.

As she rang off too, she was imagining him in his room over at the house, packing and crying and knowing all the torment she was feeling in herself, and a very strong part of her wanted to go and comfort him. But it was for the best that he left now, without them seeing each other again, and before his feelings became any deeper, because there really never could be a future for them. She had much to thank him for though, not least the way he'd accepted her need for him to go.

If only Sylvia were so easily removed from Josh's life, she was thinking, as she continued to stare down at the phone. As the dread of what might be happening between them, even right now, this minute, took hold, an overwhelming panic started to seize her. It was so black and despairing and consuming that she could feel herself being sucked in deeper and deeper, so that it was hard to breathe and her whole body was shaking. *Josh, please, please,* she was crying inside. *Don't do this. Don't leave me.*

It took a while to steady herself, to make herself accept that she was creating scenarios that had no basis in reality. She had no idea where he was now, he might not be with Sylvia at all, and he could well be feeling just as bad about what was happening as she was. She wondered if it would make her feel any better if he asked about Rico, even if only to demand she gave him up, or to find out if he was still there, but since the day

Shannon had gone back, Rico's name hadn't been mentioned between them again – and now she was unable to stop reading all sorts of things into that.

Deciding that it really wouldn't be a good idea to call him while she was still so on edge, she started back to the table, telling herself that he might call first if she left it a while longer. She gazed down at the manuscript, trying to find the will to go on, then registering the voice on the radio behind her she quickly spun round, intending to cut the programme dead. Instead she froze as she heard Sylvia laugh airily and say, 'Oh yes, he's very special. Very special indeed.'

'Have you known him long?' the interviewer asked.

'Actually yes, but it's only recently that we started to fall in love.'

Julia stared at the radio in horror.

'So if you won't tell us who he is, what will you tell us about him?' the interviewer probed.

'Oh, let me see. Well, he's very handsome, and very successful, and he knows exactly how to handle me.' She laughed playfully.

'What does he do exactly? I mean as a profession. I take it he is a professional man?'

'He is, but right now I'll go no further than that.'

'Then when can we expect the big announcement?'

'But you've just had it,' Sylvia protested with a laugh, 'I'm in love with the most wonderful man, and he's in love with me. Isn't that enough?'

'But at some point, if, as you say, you're going to settle down with him, we'll have to know who he is, so why not now?'

'You're rushing me,' Sylvia chided.

'Then I have to ask if he's married.'

'To which I have to reply, he might be. Actually he is, but not for much longer . . .'

Julia snatched up the phone and, hands shaking, somehow punched in Josh's number.

'Is she talking about you?' she demanded breathlessly when he answered.

'What?'

'Sylvia's on the radio and I need to know she's not talking about you.'

'I don't even know what she's saying,' he retorted furiously.

'She's telling everyone about the married man she's in love with, who's in love with her, and . . .'

'Then of course she's not talking about me,' he cut in, 'now calm down, will you?'

'What do you mean calm down?' she almost screamed. 'She's just announced to the fucking world that you're not going to be married much longer . . .'

'I'm not getting into this.'

'Don't you dare ring off. I want to know why that bitch is on the radio talking about the break-up of my marriage when you haven't even discussed it with me?'

'And nor have I discussed it with her. So whoever she's talking about, it's not me.'

'Then who is it?'

'How the hell do I know?

'You know what games she plays, and the timing of this . . . Josh, what else am I supposed to think?'

'You can think what you like, it doesn't make it a fact.'

'Then I want to know if you've seen her.'

'You're in no position to be asking that question,' he said coldly.

'*Tell me*,' she shouted.

'I'm ending this call now, we'll speak again later when you've got yourself under control.'

'You bastard!' she screamed as he rang off. 'You bastard, you bastard,' and dropping the phone, she doubled over in anguish and despair. 'I'm going to kill you, or her, or somebody, because I can't take any more of this,' she sobbed, and suddenly grabbing the phone again she jabbed in Sylvia's mobile number.

'I want you to listen to this,' she raged as Sylvia answered, 'and I want you to listen hard, because these are the names that are going public if you go anywhere near my husband again.' Then in a voice shaking with fury she listed two top-level government officials, three senior publishing executives, one media mogul and several sportsmen, all married and all still very much in the public eye. She then rounded it off by saying, 'You're a slut, Sylvia, a sad, sorry, pretentious little slut who preys on other women's husbands because she can't get a man of her own. I know, better than anyone, how you got to where you are, because you shagged Jack McKenzie – *an eighty-seven-year-old man* who was your boss and mine – when you were only twenty-three, and then you promised him more if he did the right thing with your book. And he got more, didn't he, because you'll turn it on for anyone, as long as you get what you want out of it. Oh, I'm not saying you don't have talent, but you're even better as a whore. And now you're trying to get your claws into Josh, thinking you'll be able to take from me the one thing I've always had that you never have, a man who totally loves you. Well, dream on, Sylvia, because it's not going to happen. You don't have what it takes to hold onto a man – if you did, you'd have done it by now. You think the whole world finds you fascinating and mysterious and sexy, but you're nothing but a waste of space. No-one has any real time for you, so why don't you do us all a favour and drive a stake through your own heart?'

She was about to hang up when Sylvia said, 'Pretty speech, darling, but I have to wonder what you're getting so worked up about if you're so certain Josh still loves you,' and before Julia could respond she cut the line dead.

'Who was that?' Robin asked as Sylvia dropped her mobile back into her bag.

'Oh just some hysterical wife,' she responded, not meeting his eyes. 'You know how they come crawling out of the woodwork every time I've got a book out.'

Robin regarded her carefully, while refilling their glasses with sparkling water. 'Correct me if I'm wrong,' he said, 'but this one seems to have got under your skin a tad.'

Sylvia cocked an eyebrow. 'Not a bit,' she replied, waving a dismissive hand. 'No, I was just thinking about this evening, and the speech I have to give.'

Robin looked sceptical, then with a mischievous grin he said, 'So it wasn't Julia Thayne?'

Sylvia's eyes narrowed, but since he'd heard the interview she'd recorded yesterday and witnessed the fuss she'd made about ensuring Josh was sitting at the top table with her tonight, she saw no point in denying it. 'Actually, it was her,' she said. 'And before you start getting on my case about betraying a friend, I already feel bad enough, thank you very much. But what are Josh and I supposed to do? We didn't ask for this to happen. God knows, it was the last thing we wanted, but we're so completely mad about each other that neither of us wants to go on hiding it, and tonight's a special night for me, so obviously he wants to be there.'

Robin was shaking his head incredulously. 'So I am right,' he said. 'Shit, I never thought I'd see the day when those two broke up. They've always been so close.'

Sylvia looked mournful as she said, 'I know that's how it seems to outsiders, but like most marriages there's a whole lot that goes on behind the scenes you never get to see. Theirs has been falling apart for quite some time, and I swear it had nothing to do with me. Josh and I have only been together for a few months . . .'

'But Julia's obviously not taking it well.'

'We never thought she would. Obviously, it's going to be a difficult time for her, which is why Josh and I need to be patient and do everything we can to lessen her pain.'

'And to do that you're going to flaunt your relationship at the party tonight?'

Sylvia shrugged. 'She has to get used to the idea we're together now,' she replied smoothly. 'Of course it's going to be hard, but Josh and I have our lives too.'

Robin looked at her closely, but remembering who was paying for lunch, he only said, 'You sure do, and who am I to criticise? If you're in love, you're in love, so good luck to you. I just need to know what to say when everyone starts asking me tonight if he's the one you talked about in the interview.'

Sylvia's eyes glowed. 'You can tell them that he is,' she replied. 'In fact, you can even tip a couple of them off in advance, because it might be quite nice to have some shots of us arriving. A new book, a new love, and a new life.' Liking the sound of that, she said it again, while taking out her mobile to call and make sure Josh hadn't forgotten his promise to come early tonight. And maybe, while she was at it, she'd suggest he stayed the entire night, because it would be too awful if he got up to go home – and it wasn't as if the children were that young any more, or even on their own.

Finding herself going straight through to voice-mail, she left him a message, then looked at Robin who was already on the line tipping off one of his major diary contacts. As she listened Sylvia couldn't help being impressed.

'I'm telling you, Sylvia would go utterly ballistic if she knew I was giving you this,' he informed the person at the other end. 'It's top, top secret, not supposed to be out for weeks yet, so officially, tonight, they're just friends. But I owe you, mate, so I'm letting you have it now. Just remember, you never heard it from me.' He paused, then winked at Sylvia as he said, 'That's right. They're completely mad about each other, that's why he's going to be there for her tonight.'

Josh was already dressed in his dinner suit, and wearing a black cashmere overcoat with a pale silk scarf around the collar, as he knocked on Shannon's open door to let her know he was there. 'Everything OK?' he asked, going to stand behind her at the computer.

'Yeah, I'm fine,' she answered, keeping her eyes on the screen. 'Just got a lot of revising to do.'

'Anything I can help with?'

'No, it's OK.'

As he looked down at the work she was doing, he was wondering whether or not to broach the subject of Julia, and in the end decided he ought at least to attempt it. 'Have you spoken to Mum today?' he asked.

'No, and please don't try and make me, because I really, really don't want to.'

He put his hands on her shoulders, as though to stop her becoming angry. 'But you know, what happened down there . . .'

'I *don't* want to talk about it,' she cut in.

Since he didn't either he was happy to let it go, though he knew it wasn't good for Shannon to prolong her refusal to speak to her mother. However, now was hardly the time to try and force matters, when he was on his way out, and since she seemed OK for the moment, he dropped a kiss on her head and was just going through the door, when she said, 'You look nice. Where are you going?'

'To a launch party,' he answered, turning back.

'Must be a posh one, if it's black tie.'

'Sort of,' he responded, finding himself thinking of the many times he'd left the house dressed like this, with Julia looking absolutely stunning beside him. 'Do you mind me going out?' he asked.

She shrugged. 'No, it's fine. Have a nice time.'

He smiled, then came back to kiss her again.

This time she tilted her face to look up at him. 'I really love you, Dad,' she said, gazing earnestly into his eyes.

Knowing it was her way of trying to make him feel better about what had happened between Julia and Rico, he said, 'I know, and I really love you too.'

Seeming satisfied with that, she returned to the keyboard and began typing again. Leaving her to it, he went to check on Dan who was teaching his grandmother how to download music, then after making sure he had his wallet and keys, he let himself quietly out of the front door.

It was a cold, blustery night, with early fireworks squealing and exploding overhead, and the usual logjam of traffic leading from Holland Park up to Notting Hill. It shouldn't take him long to get there though, for it was hardly any distance, and even if he stopped for flowers he should still make it on time.

As he turned out onto the main road his mobile started to ring, but seeing it was Julia he let it go through to voicemail. He didn't want to speak to her now, he hardly wanted to speak to her at all, though obviously he had to for the children's sake, and he guessed sooner or later they'd have to discuss what had happened and where they went now. The trouble was, he was still so damned angry about what she'd done, and the way she'd allowed Shannon to walk in on it, that he couldn't trust himself to hold onto his temper long enough to achieve anything worthwhile when they did speak. As it was, every communication they'd had after she'd screwed the Italian had turned into an almighty row and the boy's name hadn't even been mentioned since then, so God only knew what would happen when it was.

Remembering how distraught she'd sounded earlier, when she'd called about Sylvia's radio interview, started him wondering again what Sylvia had actually said. Since he'd been in meetings all afternoon he hadn't had the opportunity to ask her, though she'd called him plenty of times, leaving messages that made it abundantly clear what she was expecting the minute he walked in the door tonight. Oddly, the thought of it didn't seem to be turning him on the way it normally did, in fact, he was almost beginning to wish he'd arranged to meet her there, rather than pick her up at home. However, it was too late now, he was already on his way, and as long as she got it out of her head that he'd be staying the night, there didn't seem any reason why they shouldn't have a good time catching up with colleagues and old friends at the party.

Coming to a stop at the Notting Hill traffic lights, he reached for his mobile to see if Julia had left a message, but, unusually, she hadn't. He wasn't quite sure what to make of that, he only knew that going to a function like this without her was starting to feel uncomfortably strange. He hardly ever socialised unless she was with him, and knowing everyone was bound to ask where she was, he was almost regretting his decision to go. He wondered what she was doing down there now, if she was still tearing herself apart over Sylvia's interview, or maybe she was so busy fucking the Italian she'd forgotten all about it.

Just to think of her with another man pierced him to his very soul, while doubly hardening his resolve not to let her come back to London until things had had time to cool down considerably. The fact that she hadn't just defied him over that and got in the car anyway – which would be much more like her – went to prove that she was too wrapped up in the boy to care. Though he admitted that subconsciously he knew that probably wasn't true, all he was allowing himself to see right now was the total fucking bullshit she'd been spinning him about some kind of mental block on being able to make love with him, because she'd clearly got it on with the Italian no problem at all. And since, by her own admission, he'd taken her to the stars, then she could fucking well stay there, orbiting the planet in an orgasmic fucking frenzy, until she couldn't take any more – and if she thought he was going to be there to catch her when she decided she'd had enough, she was going to be in for one big fucking surprise.

The lights turned green and he pulled away far too fast, only narrowly missing a young woman who was running to get clear. After accepting her storm of abuse, and mouthing an apology, he made a more careful left turn and drove on to the flower stall. God only knew what kind of flowers Sylvia liked, but since it was her publication day, he guessed he should take some. After allowing the vendor to do the choosing, he carried them back to the car and continued his journey, finding himself troubled again by exactly what might have been said in that interview. But if she'd been going on about some great love and a marriage breaking up, she couldn't have been talking about him. It was just plain absurd to think it, when nothing like it had ever entered his head, never mind crossed his lips. Except Julia might have a point about the timing, and when he considered the different tone of Sylvia's messages since his last call, and this kind-of-date situation he was in tonight, he started to feel more than a little uneasy, and wished he'd thought more carefully before accepting her invite.

Surely she couldn't be telling herself that there was something serious between them, when she knew very well that the most they'd ever amounted to was an occasional good screw? Yet even as he was thinking it, his gut was responding in a way he didn't like at all, because he could see that maybe there *was* a chance she'd been talking about him, and if she had, he now had to start wondering what tonight was really all about. As far as he was concerned, he'd only called her again because he'd wanted to screw her as some kind of revenge on Julia. Obviously she hadn't known that, so, as usual, she'd told him to come right away, but then something had come up with Dan, and when he'd called to rearrange she'd suggested he might like to be her escort at the party tonight –

and without giving it any particular thought, he'd agreed.

Only now were the repercussions of his knee-jerk response to Julia's betrayal dawning on him, for he was beginning to see how Sylvia might have read much more than he'd ever intended into the fact that he'd called her so soon after insisting it was all over. And that he was amenable to attending an event that was so significant for her, not merely as a guest – which was more or less as he'd seen himself – but as an escort, could, without a doubt, have sent all the wrong signals.

Realising he had to sort this out in his head before he went any further, he pulled over to the side of the road and turned off the engine. It didn't matter if he was late, because he had no intention of screwing her when he got there anyway. Right at this moment, he wasn't entirely sure he was even going to go. It would be hard on her if he let her down at this late hour, but insane with jealousy as he was over Julia and her Italian, to go flaunting Sylvia in Julia's face like this wasn't the kind of payback she deserved. Considering his own miserable show of fidelity, he couldn't even say what she did deserve, but as he stared out at the dark, windy night, with its constantly moving headlights and scurrying pedestrians, he simply couldn't escape the fact that he was in the wrong place, heading in the wrong direction, towards the wrong woman.

Picking up his mobile, he pressed in Sylvia's number, and waited for her to answer.

'Hi, darling,' she said, apparently already knowing it was him on the line. 'Are you almost here? I've got champagne on ice, and nothing on me . . .'

'Sylvia, I won't be coming,' he said.

For a moment there was only a stunned silence, until she said, 'But darling, you have to. Everything's all arranged . . .'

'I'm sorry, I know this is very short notice, but I'm sure you'll find someone else to step in.'

'Like who?' she said icily.

'Maybe the man you were talking about on the radio today.'

She laughed incredulously. 'Well, surely you realised that was you,' she responded. Then, in a gentler, more affectionate tone, 'Did you like what I said about you being handsome . . . ?'

'Sylvia, we've been to bed together a few times and it was good, but that's all there is between us, so to go on the radio . . .'

'Darling, I don't think you understand what I'm saying. I'm completely, madly and incurably in love with you, which is something that has never happened to me before. Isn't that amazing? Don't you realise how many men there are out there who'd give their eye teeth to have me feel that way about them?'

'Then you need to be with them,' he replied.

There was a startled moment before she said, 'What do you mean? Didn't you hear what I just said?'

'Yes, I did, and I can see now what a big mistake I made in calling you the other night . . .'

'You called because you just had to see me,' she reminded him. 'Those were your words, Joshua, "Sylvia, I have to see you."' She took a breath, and softened her tone as she said, 'Josh, please don't go back on this now. I'm sorry if I jumped the gun today, but I was just so excited about seeing you tonight, and I'm being completely honest when I say I've never felt this way before. God, you must know that. I mean, when have you ever heard me talking like this? I love you, and I can't pretend I don't, not to you, but if you don't want to go public with anything yet, that's fine . . .'

'There's nothing to go public with . . .'

'OK, OK, I'll play it whichever way you want,' she went on, clearly not listening. 'Just say you'll come tonight, please. Everyone's expecting to see you at the party. You're on the top table, next to me.'

He said nothing, only knew that it wasn't going to happen.

'Josh, please. The evening will be totally ruined if you're not there.'

Still he said nothing.

'Or, if you prefer, I'll cancel it, and you can come here,' she said. 'We can be just the two of us, the way we normally are, if that's what you'd prefer.'

'Sylvia,' he said, more baffled than anything else now, 'I feel like I'm talking to another woman. This just doesn't sound like you.'

'Maybe that's because I don't feel like me,' she responded, her voice catching with emotion. 'I thought you really cared for me, Josh. I truly believed I meant as much to you as you do to me.'

'But we've never discussed our feelings, not in any real sense.'

'So are you saying I've made it all up, that I imagined our times together, the things we did and said?'

'No, of course not, but you're letting it get way out of hand.'

'Josh, you have to come tonight, please. I'll be a laughing stock, if you don't.'

'I'm sorry,' he said.

'But you have to,' she cried. 'I've just told you how I feel about you, what I'm prepared to do for you, so how can you turn me down?'

'Sylvia, I don't know if this is how you behave in all your relationships, but I've got to tell you, if you get as clingy and self-delusional as this . . .'

'How dare you say that to me?' she yelled. 'It's never me who wants them, it's always them who want me.'

'OK,' he said, going with it.

'It *is*,' she insisted.

'I'm not arguing,' he replied. 'You've still got time to get yourself together before going to the party. Tell them what you want about why I couldn't make it . . .'

'Josh . . .'

'Let it go, Sylvia.'

She took a breath. 'Will you see me tomorrow?' she asked.

'I'm going to ring off now,' he told her, and ending the call, he started the engine and began edging back out into the traffic.

Even before he'd managed to turn around his mobile was ringing, but seeing it was her he just left it. There was nothing to be gained from talking to her again, and he could only feel relieved that he'd come to his senses before reaching her house, because after that bizarre conversation he shuddered to think where the evening might have gone.

How many men, he wondered, had gone through the same unnerving experience of having her cling on like that? He guessed only she knew the answer, and he should no doubt consider himself lucky that at least it had been on the phone, rather than face to face, for the very idea of watching her plead like that turned him stone cold.

He was driving back into Holland Park when the phone started to ring again. Were it not for Shannon and Dan he'd have turned it off by now, but just in case, he checked the display and seeing it was Julia, he decided that this time he'd answer.

'Where are you?' she asked, sounding angry and stressed and ready for another row.

'In the car,' he answered.

'I've just spoken to Dan, he tells me you're going to be out very late tonight. Does that mean you're going to her launch?'

'No,' he said.

'Then where are you going?'

'Nowhere.'

'But he said you're wearing your DJ.'

'I am, but as we speak I'm pulling up outside the house.'

She was quiet then, leaving him to imagine what she was thinking, though he guessed she'd assume he'd been on his way and had changed his mind before getting there. What she'd deduce from that was entirely up to her, he certainly wasn't going to discuss it.

In the end, in a tone that was much more conciliatory than before, she said, 'You haven't asked once if I'm still seeing Rico. Does that mean you don't care?'

'It means I presume you are.'
'Then you're wrong.'
He didn't respond.
'I said, you're wrong.'
'It makes no difference,' he said coldly, 'you've still sullied your relationship with your own daughter, and at the same time you've killed something in me,' and ending the call, he turned off the phone and went to let himself back into the house.

Chapter Sixteen

Fen was half-walking, half-running to her car, her mind full of the meeting she'd just come from with a local councillor who was having the devil of a time gaining access to his children. His wife's claims that he beat them were untrue – Fen knew that, and the wife's lawyer probably did too. The problem was going to be persuading the judge, when the man in question had claimed his fifteen minutes a couple of years back, for thumping a member of the public who hadn't been especially impressed with his politics.

Still, she'd worry about that tomorrow, right now she was rushing towels, brandies, thick sweaters and padded coats to the mad surfers – her brother David, his partner, Charles, Julia and Dan – who'd taken to the waves a couple of hours ago, so they must be freezing their whatsits off by now. Of course, it was her fault that David didn't have the Volvo which contained all the necessary, because she should have realised this morning, when she'd left home with it, that he'd need it later. The fact that he hadn't checked the boot of the Renault to make sure it was stocked up as usual was also her fault, because he'd said so. How male was that? And how anyone could go surfing in this weather anyway, when it was blowing a gale, and the rain was fancying its chances with a horizontal flow, was totally beyond her. However, each to his own. There were probably those who considered her nuts for riding in all winds and weathers – and sorry souls they must be, for until you'd galloped across the moors in a powerful storm, you simply hadn't lived.

As she drove out of Bodmin, heading towards Polzeath, she was wondering if she should alert Julia to the surprise she had in store. Considering the ghastliness of the past few weeks, first Shannon catching her in flagrante with Rico and then Josh serving her with papers for a legal separation, she was more than due for an uplift, but there were no guarantees the surprise was going to turn out the way Fen hoped, so maybe she should keep it to herself for now and let events take their course.

What a terrible blow that had been for Julia, receiving the order for a separation. She'd had no idea it was coming – how could she, when Josh hadn't mentioned a word? Just thank God it had turned up after the rather gratifying piece in a diary column about Sylvia Holland taking off on an extended book tour of Australia after being dumped by the mysterious Mr Right, or even Fen might have gone into a spin. As it was, it had been all she could do to prevent Julia charging straight back to London, if only to stop her from killing herself in the car.

Once she'd calmed down, and they'd had an opportunity to discuss it, Fen's advice had been for her to play it the same way Josh had. This was to say nothing, just to see if he pushed it any further, in other words test out how serious he was. So far, there was still a resounding silence, which, in Fen's book, definitely wasn't a bad thing. However, it would be much better all round if they were talking, and not just about the children and usual domestic trivia which was inevitable, but since Julia's pride had kicked in big time, she was proving every bit as stubborn as her husband.

So, basically, it was still all a dreadful mess, which Julia had more or less blocked out by sinking herself into the Hamish Kincaid manuscript these past weeks. Her work was complete now, and after taking it to London last Thursday to embark upon some fairly gruelling (though highly entertaining in the retelling) episodes with the author, she'd picked up Dan and driven him back here to Cornwall. Since he had two in-service days he'd been able to stay for a nice long weekend, but she was due to take him home again tomorrow, which was going to be hard, for she obviously missed her children terribly. And who could blame her for that? Any mother would, and it remained to be seen when she got there if enough time had yet passed for Josh's temper to mellow and Shannon's shock to heal, for only her mother-in-law had been at the house when she'd called in to collect Dan at the start of the weekend.

It was all such a terrible shame, Fen was thinking, as she drove onto Polzeath beach to park the car, because for two people who'd clearly loved each other very much once, and actually still did, it seemed every turn they took to get back to each other was a wrong one. Admittedly, it might help if they were taking any turns at all, but who could say, the winds were apt to change at any moment, and absolutely anything could blow in.

No matter how many times Fen came to this beach, or what time of year, it never failed to take her breath away. Today was no exception, for its vast grey expanse of sea, foaming and roaring to the shore, beneath a wrathful achromatic sky shot through with stark rays of sunlight, was so powerfully dramatic it seemed to swirl right through the senses. Only the dullest of minds could resist the timeless scenarios it conjured, of pirates and smugglers, shipwrecks and lovers' trysts amongst the rocks. Heaven and the stars knew she and Bob had had many such trysts back in the early days, and even since their reconciliation, time and tide permitting, they'd occasionally sneaked out to steal some private, romantic time together in the cave where they'd first made love.

Spotting three windswept figures down at the water's edge, with one much smaller one, she honked the horn to let them know she'd arrived, then dashed round to the boot to grab jackets, towels, flasks and sweaters. The cove was partly protected by two giant headlands which blocked at least some of the wind, and for the moment the sun was staging a bit of a breakthrough. However, they must be iced to the bone by now, and close to exhausted.

Hearing the sound of the horn, Julia spun round and waved, then checking Dan was safely ashore, she began squelching across the sand to meet Fen halfway.

'Mum, I'm drowning,' Dan called after her.

She turned to walk backwards, hair and voice being whipped about by the wind as she shouted, 'Not funny,' and a great surge of love rose up in her to see the mischief in his grin. He'd yelled the same SOS earlier, whilst out in the waves, and like a fool she'd gone plunging in to try and save him, before realising he'd never have been able to shout it if it were true, and besides, Charles had been right there. So it had been a deliberate wind-up, which had proved so successful he was dying to make it work again. 'You're not even in the water,' she pointed out.

His grin grew wider, then he looked round as David and Charles waded out of the surf, boards under their arms and goggles dangling from their hands. She couldn't hear what they were saying, but it soon became apparent that they were going to take him out for one more ride of the waves.

'How do you stand it?' Fen cried, as she reached her. 'Any normal human being would be blue or dead by now.'

Julia laughed and took one of the towels. 'He's had the time of his life,' she declared. 'They're so good with him. So patient. He can actually get up and stay on now. You wait and see.'

'What about you?' Fen asked, as they trudged back down the beach. 'Will you be auditioning for *Baywatch* any time soon?'

Julia slanted her a look. 'Too old, too fat, not blonde . . .'

'*Fat!*' Fen exclaimed. 'I don't think so. Have you

seen yourself in that wetsuit? All boobs and no hips. I wouldn't be surprised if David and Charles are rethinking their orientation by now.'

Julia laughed again. 'I can't tell you how wonderful it is having him here,' she said, watching Dan. 'I'm dreading taking him back.'

'I'm guessing he doesn't want to go either.'

'No, but he'll be fine once he sees Josh.' She swallowed hard, and continued to watch him, feeling his thrills as though they were her own. 'He looks so happy,' she said. 'He's so easy-going. Whatever we all want, it's OK by him, but I can't help worrying what kind of toll this separation might be taking.'

'Josh must be concerned too,' Fen ventured.

Julia nodded. 'He is, which is why I'm going to insist we talk when I get there tomorrow. We can't go on like this. We have to sort something out, even if it does mean splitting up.' The very idea of that was so awful that she couldn't bear to think of it now, so changing the subject she said, 'Charles is going to take that old cash box to his workshop to see if he can open it. You remember, the one I found in the attic?'

'Sure. So does that mean you're going to start your search again?'

Julia turned to her. 'I have to know the truth,' she said. 'I mean, I know my father loved me now, and that it wasn't anything I did that made him go, but I have to find out what it was.'

Fen sighed and stared out towards the colourless horizon. 'It won't be that,' she said, being party now to Julia's worst nightmare. 'I know it won't.'

Wishing all the evidence wasn't pointing so

strongly to it, Julia said, 'I'm sorry I told you now. If I hadn't, your memories would always remain intact.'

'No, I'm glad you did. I knew something wasn't right, that you were more nervous about what you were going to find than you were admitting to – and he was your father, not mine, so I don't have a right to . . .'

'You have every right,' Julia assured her. 'You knew him for over twenty years, and considered him family.'

Fen was about to respond when an exuberant scream erupted from the waves, and they both turned to watch Dan gleefully wobbling about on his board, before crashing back into the surf.

An hour later, after changing in the cars with the heaters up high, they were all seated around the fire at the Oyster Catcher up on one of the headlands, sipping hot toddies, or, in Dan's case, a grandfather mug of thick, frothy cocoa. Outside rain was lashing the windows, and the sea was churning up ready for a mighty storm.

'You're going to sleep well tonight,' Julia said, ruffling Dan's hair as he yawned.

He nodded and let his head drop against her.

'You did good today,' David told him. 'He was up on the second go,' he informed Fen.

Julia smiled at his kindly face, and was just asking him about the times he'd taken her father surfing, when Fen's mobile rang.

Glancing at the readout Fen clicked on and said, 'Hi. Where are you?' After listening to the reply, she said, 'That's right . . . No, I haven't. You weren't too sure when we last spoke, so I thought . . . Yes, we're here. You're virtually outside, so why don't you come and join us?' There were several seconds during which she didn't appear to be receiving the response she expected, then excusing herself she got up and walked away from the table. 'I'll have fish and chips when you order,' she called back over her shoulder to David.

'Consider it done,' David saluted, and turned back to the others. 'Must be Bob having a difficult time over something. So where were we?'

'You were going to tell Mum about taking Grandpa surfing,' Dan reminded him, but before he could answer Dan suddenly remembered the high spot of his own day, when he'd stayed up longer than David, and leaping forward he began excitedly to recount it.

Chuckling, Charles leaned in to Julia and said, 'Did you know David and I are trying to adopt? If we could have one like him . . .'

Julia gazed at her son adoringly. 'I confess there's no-one else in the world I'd surf for in the middle of November,' she responded, 'and as for having sand in places where there shouldn't be sand, the last time that happened . . .' Was with Josh on a moonlit beach in Barbados. She smiled weakly. 'You probably won't want to hear about that,' she said.

Charles's eyes were twinkling. 'I think I get the picture,' he said. 'So now, when would you like me to pick up this box?'

'Oh, I don't want to put you to any trouble. I can bring it to you. I'd like to see your workshop anyway.'

'You're on, but it's a bit of a mess. We carpenters aren't known for our orderliness. Well, not this one anyway. So, if you don't mind that, pop it along any time.'

'Thanks. It'll have to be when I get back from London now. We're leaving first thing.' She glanced up as Fen came back round the corner, then suddenly her smile drained and her heart stood still.

There was a long moment as she and Josh looked at each other, then Dan spotted him and yelled, 'Dad!' and charged into Josh's arms. 'I've been surfing today,' he told him, 'and I was really good. I got up on the second go, and I even beat David, who's really experienced and has been doing it all his life . . .'

Josh was smiling, and sweeping Dan's hair back from his face. 'Sounds like you've been having a good time,' he commented.

'Oh yes, the best. And Mum's really good too. Well, not like David and Charles, but she manages to stay up sometimes, don't you Mum?'

Julia attempted a nod, but her insides were in freefall as she looked at Josh, who now seemed to be avoiding her – however, if she'd been in any doubt of how much she loved him, which she hadn't, it would have been swept away in these few seconds. The force of her reaction to his familiar face, and the pull inside her that seemed to connect her straight to him, were so overpowering that her entire body seemed to be locked in its might. 'I didn't realise you were coming,' she said, getting up.

'I wasn't sure if I'd be able to make it,' he replied, his eyes still on Dan. David was on his feet. 'Hi, it's good to see you again,' he said, reaching for Josh's hand. 'I don't think you met Charles the last time you were here.'

'No, it's a pleasure,' Josh said, shaking Charles's hand.

'Likewise,' Charles responded. 'I was just remarking to Julia what a great boy you have.'

Josh smiled and tilted Dan's face up to his. 'He's not bad,' he responded.

'I'm a champion surfer,' Dan informed him.

'With two new heroes, by the sound of it.'

'Oh, they're the best,' Dan assured him. Then to David and Charles, 'But you should see my dad when he skis. He goes down all the black slopes, and he's really, really good. Mum does it too, and sometimes they have a race and he lets her win.'

Julia laughed. 'Rubbish, I beat him every time,' she declared, wishing Josh would look at her.

Josh's smile was wry, but he added nothing to the banter.

'Can I get you a drink?' David offered.

'Just a beer, thanks,' Josh answered.

'Tell you what,' Fen piped up, 'if you two want to go somewhere else, we'll be happy to take care of Dan and bring him home.'

Julia looked at Josh, and felt her heart twist at the signs of strain on his face.

'No, here's fine,' he said, settling in next to Dan.

Struggling to hide her disappointment, Julia gave Fen a look to convey appreciation for the thoughtfulness, to which Fen could do no more than shrug until they went to the bar to order the food.

'He called me earlier,' she said. 'Apparently he

was seeing an author down this way, and thought he might come over. He didn't want me to tell you in case he couldn't make it.'

Though Julia knew Josh had an author in Launceston, she was doubtful that was the reason he'd come all this way, since he didn't normally make personal visits to clients who earned him less than ten thousand a year. So she could only conclude that he wanted to talk. She'd like to think it was about her going back, but if it were, he'd surely have waited until she was in London, which meant he could be here to discuss making their separation official.

'So how are you feeling now you've seen him?' Fen asked.

Julia's eyes closed as she took a breath. 'A moment ago I was nervous as hell,' she confessed. 'Now I almost want to go out and shoot myself.'

Fen's eyebrows rose, but there was no time for Julia to explain what she meant, as Dan turned up to make a last-minute change to his order.

Considering how awkward the evening could have been with so much tension between them, it somehow managed to pass quite smoothly, though Julia was horribly aware of how little contact Josh was making with her, and how her every attempt to engage with him was being politely, though effectively blocked. Whether anyone else noticed was impossible to tell, for they were certainly far too well mannered to let it show, though Fen's whispered remark as they left the pub was still resonating with Julia when she got back to the house.

'He's here, it's a start,' she'd said.

Julia only wished she could feel the optimism the words were meant to convey, but her heart was tight with foreboding as Josh carried a sleeping Dan into the house and together they struggled to undress him and put him to bed.

'I would have brought him back,' she said, watching him gaze down at Dan's face. 'I wasn't planning on keeping him.'

Josh made no comment as he stooped to kiss Dan's forehead.

'That's why you came, isn't it?' she said, trying to keep her voice steady. 'You were afraid I . . .'

'Do we have to have this conversation with him in the room?' Josh interrupted.

Refraining from pointing out that he was asleep, she kissed Dan too, then left Josh to turn out the light.

'Can I get you anything?' she offered when he joined her in the kitchen.

He shook his head.

For several moments they stood in silence, until he said, in answer to her earlier remark, 'It's not why I came.'

A faint flicker of relief stirred inside her, but soon died when his eyes failed to meet hers, and then the dread that she'd managed to keep in check all evening began to grow into a terrible burn of fear. He'd come because he, or Shannon, or both, didn't want her in the house tomorrow – or because he wanted her to respond to the papers his solicitor had sent. He could even be suing for full custody of the children . . . Her heart was beating too fast, her mind was in turmoil, and in a futile attempt to stall whatever it was, she said,

'Are you planning to stay here tonight? I can always sleep on the sofa. It converts into . . .'

'I've booked into a B & B just up the road,' he cut in.

Feeling the jolt of that as if it were a blow, she turned away and for something to do put on the kettle.

'I wanted to see you,' he told her, 'because I needed to find out how I'd feel when I did.' He took a breath. 'Shannon still insists she doesn't want you to come back, but I think she says it more for me now.'

Hardly daring to hope, she kept her back to him as she said, 'Does that mean you do?'

'I don't know. '

She turned round and wondered if she'd ever wanted to hold him more.

'I miss you, I'm not going to deny that,' he said. 'I just don't know if it can work.'

'Neither of us will know unless we try.'

His head went down as he slid his hands into his pockets. 'The problem is, I'm not sure I feel the same way about you now.'

Though her heart shrank from the words, she forced herself not to respond, and merely said, 'I wish you'd stay here tonight, for Dan's sake, if not for mine.'

His eyes narrowed, and for a moment he seemed to be considering it, but then he shook his head and said, 'No, it's best this way.'

She continued to look at him, willing him to bring his eyes back to hers, but he wouldn't. In the end, deciding to throw caution to the wind and just be truthful, she said, 'I want us to get back together, Josh. I love you, I've always loved you and I've never stopped wanting you. Even now . . .'

His hands went up as though to block her, though it was several seconds before he said, 'I never thought I'd hear myself saying this, but for the first time in my life I feel nothing when I look at you, so if you were about to try and talk me into bed, please spare us both the embarrassment, because it's not going to happen.'

Her eyes flashed with hurt. 'Actually, I was going to say, even now, after all we've been through, I still love you more than I've ever loved anyone,' she replied.

A look of cynicism came into his eyes. 'Of course, it's young Italians you want to go to bed with, isn't it?' he said. 'Forgive my conceit.'

'Josh, don't do this,' she cried. 'Please just try to understand that the only reason it worked with him was because I wasn't afraid he was going to leave me. All my abandonment issues, the locked-in terror, the fear of really letting go, it's because I was afraid you were going to leave me, reject me the way my father did. But I don't think I have that fear any more. I can't say for certain . . .'

'No-one's asking you to.'

'For heaven's sake, let's stop making this all about sex. We've got two children, a whole life, a history . . . You can't just want to throw it all away. It has to mean something. It has to be worth fighting for. If we can just give it a try. Josh listen,' she urged as his eyes moved sharply away. 'I've had to forgive you for Sylvia . . .'

'It's not the same thing, and you know it,' he cut in angrily. 'I wasn't rejecting you . . .'

'I know, I understand that . . .'

' . . . it was you I'd have been with, if you'd let me. I'd never even have looked at another woman if you hadn't kept turning me away, but there clearly wasn't any problem for you when it came to Rico, was there? In fact, you were obviously so rampant for him that you didn't even give a thought for your own daughter.'

'I'm not going to attempt to make excuses for what I did,' she responded, trying to keep her voice down, 'it was wrong and I fully admit that, but it still has to be said, if you hadn't been sleeping with Sylvia, it would never have happened.'

'Oh for Christ's sake, make it my fault . . .'

'It was both our faults, but that's not what matters now, is it? What matters is not allowing it to do any more damage than it already has. Please Josh, let's try to find each other again. It's what I want, and I don't care what you say, I can't believe you don't want it too.'

His eyes stayed on her, harsh and impenetrable, as though still fully determined not to let her back in, even resenting the fact she was trying. Finally he looked away and at least some of his anger seemed to abate. 'What about this place?' he asked abruptly. 'What are you going to do with it?'

'I can have it cleared in a couple of days,' she answered, 'then I can sell up, if that's what you want.'

He was looking around, seeming to take it all in, the hearth with its logs, the dressers with their photographs, the cupboards, the windows, the shadow of the mill turning outside. As she watched him she could only guess at what he was thinking, though he knew how much it all meant to her, how desperately she wanted to hold onto it if she could.

In the end he said, 'Where did it happen? You and the Italian. Which room?'

'Upstairs. In the bedroom,' she replied. She didn't have to tell him about the other times, because it was over now, and there was no reason for him to know.

The coldness was back in his eyes as he said, 'I think you should keep it.'

Realising he could be about to offer it as a settlement she quickly said, 'But if it's not somewhere we can share . . .'

'That's not what I'm saying. I don't know what's in the future for us, but I do know, if I ever spend time with you here, I won't want to sleep in that bed.'

'Then I'll get rid of it,' she said, without hesitation.

He nodded briefly. 'It'll be a start,' and picking up his keys he turned to the door, saying, 'I'll be back in the morning for Dan.'

The following morning, after a tearful goodbye to Daniel, and a difficult embrace with Josh, which was more for Dan's benefit than either of theirs, Julia went straight over to the Bowers to see if she could find Tilde. If anyone would know who to call about removing a bed, she would, and since that was what Josh wanted, Julia was more than happy to comply. No matter that it had belonged to her father and Gwen, there was no room for sentimentality in this scenario, for if the situation were reversed and Josh was asking her to sleep on a bed he'd shared with Sylvia, she knew only too well what her reaction would be. Even to think of it caused a sickening twist in her heart, for she was still a very long way from being over either the jealousy or the pain, and though she knew Sylvia was in Australia now, it didn't mean she'd stopped tormenting herself with images of them together.

She had never found out what had really happened the night of Sylvia's launch, but for now, at least, it was enough that Josh hadn't gone, and that Sylvia had been utterly humiliated over the next few days in the press. Many of the diarists had gone to town with how she'd been stood up, proving she wasn't quite as popular with journalists as she'd liked to think. Julia had savoured every word, and might even have called to gloat had she not been afraid it would backfire. In the end, she'd just been thankful for the way Josh had claimed to be mystified as to why anyone had thought he was going to the party, and as for his marriage being in trouble, that was plain absurd.

As usual, Tilde was delighted to be asked for help. Since the bed wasn't very old, and was extremely handy with its built-in drawers, she immediately proposed selling it, nice and cheap, to a young couple she knew who were just setting up home. If she wondered why Julia wanted rid of it, she never asked, which led Julia to suspect that she probably knew, for very little ever made it past Tilde.

'I'll get onto 'em right away,' she said, bustling across the big old farmhouse kitchen to the phone. 'I know they don't have a bed yet, because I saw them last night, and they happened to mention it. So I reckon Providence is having a bit of a hand in here, don't you?'

Relieved that it was proving so easy, Julia waited for Tilde to arrange a viewing for the couple, then returned to the mill to unpack the blankets and linens stored in the bed's drawers. After piling them on one of the sofas, she went back to the bedroom for the cash box, which was still on the pine chest where Rico had put it on that fateful morning. Though she didn't want to relive what had happened then, she couldn't help wondering how Rico was now, for it had been almost two weeks since he was last in touch. Hopefully, that was a sign he was starting to get over it. When he'd first gone back he'd been calling at least twice a day, wanting to make absolutely sure she understood how much he still loved her, and to find out if maybe she had changed her mind.

Feeling guilty even as she dismissed him from her thoughts, she carried the box downstairs and got into the car to drive over to Chapel Amble where David and Charles lived and Charles had his workshop.

As she wove through the picturesque lanes and byways, she was so focused on Josh and the future, and how determined she was to bring her family back together, that she wasn't really thinking about what the box might contain. But even when it did finally penetrate her thoughts, she knew in her heart that whatever its secrets might be, no matter how terrible or dark, nothing, but nothing could be worse than losing Josh and her children.

Chapter Seventeen

Josh's face was tight with anger as he glared at Shannon across the kitchen. 'Do you really have to be so selfish?' he demanded. 'Are you the only person living in this house who counts? Is that how it's working with you? Invite in whoever you like, turn the place into a pigsty, leave nothing for anyone else.'

Shannon's cheeks were hot with colour, her eyes blazing with fury at the way he was embarrassing her in front of her friends. 'We have to eat!' she cried. 'And you knew everyone was coming.'

'There's nothing left in the damned fridge,' he shouted. 'It was full this morning, and this kitchen was clean. Now look at it. What the hell's the matter with you? You're supposed to be helping your grandmother, not making her life ten times harder. Now send everyone home.'

'But they're here to . . .'

'Don't argue,' he raged.

'I'm sorry,' Shannon mumbled to her friends, who were already sidling towards the stairs. 'I didn't know this was going to happen. He's not normally so mean . . .'

'Can it, Shannon,' he snapped, and going to dump his briefcase and a heavy manuscript in his study, he took out his mobile to turn it off mid-ring. He'd had enough of that particular instrument today, for it had seemed to bring nothing but one problem after another, not least of all the call from his mother letting him know that she would be having a lie-down when he came in, because Shannon had a few friends over, who were a little noisy and boisterous for her, and heavens, what appetites they had. Virtually the entire contents of a recent supermarket haul had been demolished, and there was nothing left in the fridge for dinner, but she was sure they'd manage.

As the front door slammed Josh went back into the kitchen, and hearing Shannon starting upstairs to her room he shouted, 'Back down here please!'

When she appeared her face was mutinous, her eyes glittering with anger. 'You really showed me up . . .'

'You deserve to be shown up. Christ, I've got enough on my plate without coming in to find the place stuffed full of your friends who can't be bothered to pick up after themselves.'

'You said they could come over,' she yelled. 'I asked you this morning, and you . . .'

'I didn't say they could eat us out of house and home and send your grandmother upstairs to lie down because she can't take any more. You were supposed to be doing homework, and if any one of those cans contains alcohol- or caffeine-charged liquids you are going to find yourself grounded for a month.'

'Then ground me. I don't care. It's like living in a prison anyway, with you. I'm never allowed to do anything. At least Mum never minded my friends coming over, and she never showed me up the way you do. She'd let us eat what we wanted ...'

'But your mother's not here, is she? And she never will be if it goes on like this.'

Shannon's angry expression showed a trace of unease. 'What do you mean?' she demanded.

'I mean you won't even speak to her on the phone, so to be holding her up as some kind of icon now is a bit rich, isn't it?'

'I was just saying ...'

'I'm not interested in what you're saying. Just quit arguing and start tidying up this mess. I have to pick Dan up in ten minutes, and now, thanks to you, I'll have to go to the supermarket so the rest of us can eat tonight.'

'There's stuff in the freezer.'

'Well, thank you.'

As he snatched up his keys and started to leave Shannon broke down in tears. 'You're always taking it out on me,' she sobbed, 'and it's not my fault. I didn't make her do that, so it's not fair to keep picking on me, and being horrible to me ...'

Taking a deep breath, he stopped and turned back. 'I'm just pointing out that your behaviour is not very helpful when Grandma is trying so hard to take care of us,' he said, softening his tone a little.

Shannon's distress was growing to a point where she could barely catch her breath. 'Mum never had a problem with my friends,' she cried, 'and I could always talk to her about anything. You're just mean to me, and I want to go away and never have to see any of you again.'

'Come on,' he said, pulling her into his arms. 'I'm sorry I shouted, and I'm sorry if I showed you up.'

Allowing him to draw her down onto his lap, she put her arms round his neck and wept into his collar. 'I really wish Mum hadn't done what she did,' she said. 'It's messed up everything, and we're all really unhappy now. Why did she have to do it, Dad?'

As he tried to think how to answer, she said, 'It was wrong and really bad of her to do that to you, and I understand why it's made you in a bad mood all the time, but I just hate it when you keep picking on me.'

'I'm sorry if that's how it seems,' he said, stroking her hair. 'I don't mean to. I guess we're all a bit stressed and we need to sort out what we're going to do, because poor Grandma can't cope much longer.'

For a while they sat quietly amidst the debris of her teenage feast, their thoughts inevitably focused on Julia, though neither of them knew quite how to proceed from here. In the end, Shannon said, 'Is she living with him now?'

He frowned. 'Do you mean is Mum living with Rico?'

She nodded.

'No, of course not,' he answered. 'She's on her own down there, and, actually, she really wants to come home.'

Shannon sat up and looked into his face. 'Do you want her to?' she asked, her watery eyes searching his for guidance.

He nodded. 'I think so,' he answered. 'Do you?'

Her gaze moved away, then tightening her arms around his neck, she said, 'I really love you Dad and I don't want her to hurt you again.'

He laughed sadly, and held her close. 'I don't think she wants to do that,' he said, feeling wretched for letting Julia take all the blame. However, confessing his own guilt was hardly going to help Shannon to understand things any better – if anything, it would be too much for her to bear.

'But how are you going to forgive her?' Shannon asked.

'Oh, I think I can manage it,' he answered, realising that she might be waiting for such a signal to allow herself to forgive too. To his surprise though, she started to cry again.

'He would have been my boyfriend, but she took him away,' she wailed.

'Don't be silly now. He was far too old for you . . .'

'I'm not being silly! You never understand . . . I really liked him, but she knew you'd be angry because he was so much older, so that's why she did it, to stop me from getting into trouble with you.'

His eyes closed at her tortured teenage logic, and the guilt that he hadn't realised she'd been carrying. 'That's not why she did it, sweetheart,' he said.

'Then why?'

Knowing he didn't have an answer that would be suitable for her ears, or that he could even think about giving without seeking Julia's advice first, he said, 'Maybe we need to ask her why.'

Immediately Shannon shook her head. 'I don't want to. I don't want to talk to her about it *ever*.'

'But you would like her to come home?'

'No. I want it to be just us, like we are now.'

He smiled. 'You know that's not true, and besides, it's not really working very well, is it? You said yourself, I'm always in a bad mood, and it's because I miss her.'

'But you can't still love her after what she did.'

Taking her face between his hands, he looked deeply into her eyes. 'One day,' he said, 'you'll understand why things aren't quite as straightforward as you're seeing them now. I've done things that have hurt Mum, and she's tried her best to forgive me, which is why I'm trying to do the same now. That's how it happens sometimes in relationships. We don't mean to hurt the people we love, but one way or another we almost always do.'

He watched her struggling to take that on board, then felt his heart sink with dismay at the sound of his mother coming down the stairs. He loved her very much and was deeply indebted to her for the way she'd bailed them out these past weeks, but it was driving him insane having her here, when the only person he wanted walking into the kitchen right now, or at any other time, was his wife.

'Ah, I thought I heard voices,' Emma said, spotting them over by the table. 'Where's Dan? Shouldn't you have picked him up by now?'

443

'Shannon and I were just having a bit of a chat before I go,' Josh said, still holding Shannon on his lap.

'Oh my, what's the matter with you?' Emma exclaimed, noticing Shannon's tear-stained cheeks. Then her eyes rounded with knowing. 'I expect you're crying about all this mess,' she declared. 'Dad told you off, did he? Well, I can't say I blame him. I really don't know how you manage it . . .'

'She's about to clear it up,' Josh interrupted. 'And I've been explaining to her, that it's time her mother came home so that you can go home too. You've got your own life . . .'

'Oh, now that's nonsense,' Emma told him. 'I'm more than happy to be here. Keeps me busy, and you know how much I love being with you all.'

'But it's still time Julia came home,' he persisted.

Emma's lips pursed. 'Well, I'd say the question is, does she want to?' she sniped nastily.

Josh sighed and eased Shannon to her feet as he got up. 'I don't have time for this now,' he said. 'We can talk later, when Dan's here too.'

'No,' Shannon protested. 'He always gets his own way and he's bound to want her to come home.'

Josh looked at her sadly. 'And you don't?'

She turned away. 'No, I don't,' she muttered.

'You can't blame her,' Emma piped up. 'After what she's been through . . .'

'Mum, you're not being helpful.'

'I'm just saying, the poor child had a very unpleasant experience . . .'

'Leave it!' Josh barked. 'Now, I'm going to pick

up Dan, then we'll all go out for dinner, so make sure you're ready when I get back.'

After he'd gone Shannon and Emma stood in silence, neither of them quite knowing what to say. In the end Emma spoke first.

'It's all right, sweetie, I'll clear all this up, and I'll be here as long as you need me, so you don't have to let Dad push you into a decision you'd rather not make.'

Shannon kept her eyes lowered.

'I wouldn't find it very easy to forgive either, if I were you,' Emma said sympathetically. 'It was a dreadful thing to see. It would have been bad enough if it was strangers, but your own mother!' She was shaking her head in disgust. 'It's enough to scar you for life. Probably has.'

'It was really horrible,' Shannon said brokenly.

Emma went to hug her. 'Of course it was, horrible and appalling, but it's good that you're talking about it now. It doesn't help to keep it bottled up, and you know you can say anything to me.'

Though Shannon leaned in to her for a moment, she was soon moving away again. 'Dad really wants her to come back,' she said, staring down at the debris on the table.

'But what you want is important too,' Emma told her.

Shannon said nothing.

'Do you want her to come back?'

Shannon shook her head.

'Then that's that,' Emma said crisply. 'We'll tell Dad when he comes home, and . . .'

'I meant I don't know,' Shannon cried. 'Sometimes I do and sometimes I don't.'

'Then in that case, dear, I think we should abide by an old northern maxim, when in doubt, do nowt.'

'What does that mean?'

'It means don't do anything until you're sure it's what you want – and don't worry about Dan, he's not going through the same trauma you are, so in this instance what he thinks doesn't really count.'

'But he's had two fits, and I know Dad thinks it's because he's upset about Mum not being here.'

'Oh now,' Emma tutted. 'There's no way of knowing what brings them on. It might have nothing at all to do with your mother.'

'But what if it does? It'll be my fault if he has another, because I wouldn't let her come home.'

'Now you just put that nonsense out of your head, young lady. You're not to blame for anything, do you hear me? It's your mother who's at fault, utterly and completely, and don't you forget it.'

Alice was sitting in the darkness, staring at the dying embers in the hearth. Every now and again they shifted and hissed, or a spark would fly upwards and fade. The clock on the mantel had a loud, lolloping tick, the rain on the leaves outside was a flat, pattering sound that harmonised comfortably with the sough of the wind. The window was open to let in air. She'd close it again before going up to bed. George had said goodnight over an hour ago, though he'd probably be listening for her to come up, needing to know she'd settled, so he could too. She wasn't sure Rene cared about her as much as George, though considering how loyal Rene had been over the years Alice had no reason to doubt her. Rene's first concern would always be for George though, which was right. She'd want to protect him, but most of all they needed to protect Julia. They'd agreed that all those years ago, when Douglas had left, and had never questioned it since, mainly because it wasn't something anyone ever discussed more than once. It was simply understood that it was for Julia's own good to be kept in the dark, and none of them had ever wavered from that in spite of Julia's threats and rantings, because the truth would no more set her free than it would restore her father to life.

More than a month had gone by now since Douglas's death, and they hadn't heard from Julia since the day George had rung her. Alice had known Julia would pay him no heed, would probably consider him half-demented or delusional, the way she always had when he'd attempted to apply the word of the Lord. She just didn't understand, had never been able to see good in any of them except her beloved father, who'd deserted her, had never contacted her again, and who, she seemed conveniently to have forgotten, had never enjoyed the same adulation from Pam. Had Julia ever questioned herself about that? Did she ever wonder why Pam had never regretted him going? Or why he'd left nothing to Pam in his will? She was an intelligent, insightful and analytical woman, so how had she reconciled these omissions to herself? Was she still breezing over them, as though they didn't exist, the way she always had? Or had she by now learned the truth behind them?

Alice shivered and folded her arms more tightly around her. Julia had been in Cornwall long enough to have gone through Douglas's papers by now, so had he really left nothing, or was she so shattered by discovering the reality of her life that she was unable to face them? Knowing her daughter as she did, Alice felt certain Julia still hadn't found out. If she had, it would be unlike her to keep silent, even over something such as this. True, she probably wouldn't shout it from the rooftops, but her mother was the last person she'd be likely to spare. It was why Alice was finding it so difficult to sleep at night, for she was constantly expecting her daughter to arrive on the doorstep, and when she did . . . Dear God Almighty, please save them all when she did.

Chapter Eighteen

The phone was ringing as Julia dashed through the rain and up over the wooden deck into the house. Desperately hoping it was Josh, she threw open the door, dropped the elastic-bound cash box on the table and grabbed the receiver.

'Julia? Hi, it's Fen. Is this a bad time?'

'No, not at all,' Julia replied breathlessly. Though disappointed it wasn't Josh, she was always happy to hear from Fen. 'I was just coming in the door.'

'Ghastly weather,' Fen commented. 'No leaks in the roof, I hope.'

'Not that I've noticed.'

'Well if you find anything, do let me know. We've got a wonderful chap who takes care of things like that.'

'Thanks, I will. Everything OK with you?'

'Everything's great. I was calling to find out what you're doing for dinner. Bob and I have a table booked over at David's place, and thought you might like to come with us.'

Sorely tempted, Julia said, 'Normally I'd love to, he's such a great chef, but I've just collected the cash box from Charles, so I thought . . .'

'Did he manage to open it?' Fen cut in excitedly.

'Yes. And it contains two journals, one of which appears to cover the time my father left.'

'You're kidding! That's excellent news. I hope. So you're going to spend the evening going through them?'

'That's the plan.'

'Well, you know where I'll be if you need me.'

'Thanks. I appreciate it.'

'Before you go, any news from Josh?'

Julia's nerves fluttered in a way that seemed to accompany every mention of him lately. 'We spoke earlier,' she said, shrugging off her raincoat, 'but he didn't mention anything about me coming back. I'm still aiming to go the day after tomorrow though.'

'What about Shannon?'

'Josh says she's started talking about what happened now. Not in any big way, but it's a breakthrough of sorts. He'd rather I dealt with it though, he feels I'd be better at it than he is.'

'Typically male . . . Oh, hang on.'

While waiting for Fen to speak to whoever had popped into her office, Julia spotted a note propped up against the kettle and after hanging up her coat walked over to read it.

'Still there?' Fen said, coming back on the line.

'Mm,' Julia responded. 'Apparently the young couple want the bed, Tilde says, so they'll come over with a van to pick it up tomorrow.' She put the note down. 'Well, at least that's some good news I can pass on to Josh when I next speak to him. Do you think that insisting I get rid of the bed could mean he's considering paying the inheritance tax so we can keep the house?'

'I'm daring to hope so,' Fen confessed.

Julia felt herself turning light-headed with her own flurry of hopes. 'I was wondering if I should broach the subject of a proper reunion,' she said.

'You feel ready for that?'

'I think so. I guess I won't know till I try, and that's not going to happen until I get back to London, so the quicker I sort things out here . . .' She paused as her eyes came to rest on the cash box again, and a wave of apprehension coasted through her. 'I wonder what these journals contain?' she said, almost glad they were still sealed inside the box.

'I'm not sure whether I'm any more, or less, keen than you to find out,' Fen replied, 'but it's going to be fine. This is Dougie we're talking about, it can't not be. Anyway, I'm sorry, I have to go, my six o'clock's outside waiting.'

After ringing off Julia remained standing where she was, staring down at the box as she braced herself to open it. If the journals were going to confirm her worst nightmares, she had no idea how she would handle it. It was horrible enough to think of her father as one of society's most reviled offenders, worse still would be to find out that she'd been blocking her own abusive treatment to the point that she was still telling herself she loved him.

Taking a breath, she lifted her head and looked around. Everything was silent in the house, a small pocket of stillness, calm and almost gracious, like the eye of a storm, while the wind outside howled and whirled, sweeping the rain in thick, misty torrents through the woods and fields. Her eyes travelled from a camera on a worktop, to the toaster, to a fruit bowl, to bottles of olive oil and sauces. The chairs around the table were haphazardly placed, a vase of greenery and berries was slightly off centre, the rattan mats were unevenly stacked. She was totally alone, and yet strangely didn't feel it. She wondered if the dead could see, if her father was watching her now. She pictured him standing against the sink with his arms folded, eyes twinkling merrily as he surveyed her; or sitting at the table, frowning as though listening to something she was saying, or coming down the stairs to find out what was bothering her. She was certain she could sense his presence, not in a creepy or threatening kind of way, just in a curious, cautious way that made her feel both confident and unnerved.

She started as the phone suddenly rang.

Expecting it to be Josh she quickly snatched it up, but it was the voice of her ex-detective contact that came down the line.

'Julia? Rod Fuller. Sorry I've taken a couple of days to get back to you, I've been fishing, and only just got your message. Is there something else I can do?'

'Oh, yes, yes,' she answered, collecting her thoughts. 'I just wanted to ask you, when we last spoke, I got the feeling you might be holding something back.'

'Really?' he said, sounding more wary than surprised.

'You were, weren't you?' she pressed. 'Once I'd told you Douglas Cowan was my father, I think you didn't want to go any further. So I need to know, is there something you were trying to spare my feelings about?'

When he didn't answer right away her insides turned cold, for it was confirmation enough. 'I was really, really hoping you weren't going to ask me that,' he said finally.

Almost wishing she hadn't now, she took a breath and said, 'Just tell me.'

'Are you sure? I mean, if he's your father . . .'

'I'm sure,' she interrupted.

'OK. Well, there's nothing to prove anything, no actual charges or . . .'

'Bottom line,' she said, unable to go through the preamble.

'Right. Well, it seems he was pulled in a few times for questioning in child sex-abuse cases. Like I said, he was never charged. Nothing ever went to trial, and he's definitely not on any sex-offenders list.'

Julia's skin was prickling with sweat. Her insides were churning, and her hand was barely holding onto the phone as images began flashing bizarrely in her mind: her father laughing and swinging her up in the air, the blood on his face the night he'd fought with her mother, the day they'd walked at Frenchman's Creek, the photographs he had of Shannon and Dan, the way he'd always seemed so sad about Pam . . . But what was it all adding up to? 'When . . . How long ago?' she asked. 'I mean, is there anything recent?'

'No. It's all early Eighties. Just like the other stuff. After that, nothing.'

'What about before?'

'Not that's coming up.'

She was still trying to assimilate, forcing her mind to accept the words, even as she was struggling to reject them. 'And you're not holding anything else back?' she finally said.

'No. That's it.'

'OK. Thanks for calling me back.'

'No problem. I'm just sorry it had to be anything like that. But listen, so's you know, it's normal for petty offenders, vagrant types to be pulled in when those kinds of crimes are committed, and since he was obviously down on his uppers around then, and was never charged, it's only proving he was in the wrong place at the wrong time. Nothing else.'

Julia attempted a smile. 'Thanks for that,' she said.

After putting the phone down she turned to the box on the table. Feeling slightly shaky, as well as oddly suspended from her emotions now, she slipped off the elastic and lifted the battered lid.

Both books were old, their hardback covers peeling, and the spines weakening, though neither was particularly thick. From glancing through them earlier, she knew that all the pages were ruled, with margins at the side, though she'd seen no annotations or jottings. Some entries were written in blue biro, others in black ink, and while a few had appeared to run for several pages, others were little more than a paragraph or two. The dates had all been written in by hand and underlined, the first being April of 1979, the last August of 1984.

Deciding to fortify herself with a glass of wine, she went to take a bottle from the fridge, and a corkscrew from the drawer next to it. It was pitch dark outside. No glimmer of moonlight, or sighting of a star. The wind was still pelting the trees, whipping them into a frenzy of branches and leaves. The mill wheel churned the stream, oblivious to the copious downpour of rain. She considered lighting a fire up in the sitting room, but knew it was only stalling, because the heating was on and it was far from cold inside – except her hands were like ice and her blood felt chill as she tugged the cork from the bottle and filled a glass with wine.

After taking a sip, she carried the books up the staircase and settled herself down in a corner of one of the big comfy sofas, next to a table and under a lamp. Impatience was driving her to begin at the same date he'd entered in his pocket diary that he'd found out something that explained everything, but to her disappointment and, to a degree, relief, he'd written nothing on that day. There was nothing for the weeks after that either, so deciding she should start at the beginning and diligently read through, she set aside the second book, and turned to the opening entry of the first. It wasn't long, nor did it turn out to be particularly informative, merely a few lines on what had been happening at work that week, and some plans he had for the garden.

It went on in much the same vein, the occasional frustration with his boss, relief when the man was fired and surprise when he was promoted to take over the position. A celebration dinner with Alice, Pam and Julia followed, during which Alice had made him laugh by doing a splendid imitation of one of their neighbours. For several entries after that he sounded rather gloomy and fed up, the weather wasn't good and he wasn't enjoying being a manager as much as he'd hoped. Then came a prideful entry all about Julia's school report, which prompted another celebration, this time a trip to the cinema, which was her choice, to see Roman Polanski's *Tess*. Pam hadn't come because she hated films, and Alice hadn't wanted her to feel left out, so she'd stayed at home with her. No mention of Pam's school report, or of the row that had erupted, when they'd returned home, that Julia suddenly remembered now, though couldn't recall precisely what had caused it.

In March of 1980 he commented on his dislike of visiting George and Rene. He didn't say why exactly, just that, unlike Alice, he never felt comfortable in the house, though she obviously would, having grown up there. Later that month he wrote at some length about George's passion for the bible and how he, Douglas, resented being preached at down the phone, as though he were some recalcitrant schoolboy who needed to be swatted by hellfire and damnation to bring him back to God. Julia smiled as she read on, for he'd followed it up with how they, she and her father, would secretly laugh at God's Boy George, as they'd dubbed him, and he'd even added the silly rhyme they'd made up about him when she was probably no older than eight. *Humpity Grumpity sat on a pew, Humpity Grumpity needed a poo*, at which point she used to collapse into such helpless laughter that they could never get any further. It had clearly given him a lot of pleasure to remember that all those years later, and the rhyme was having a similar effect on her now.

The following month, April of 1980, contained a delighted entry all about her first crush on a boy, and how thrilled her father was that she'd confided in him, so he'd bought a book of horoscopes to see how well she and the boy were suited, but they'd had to check out David Bowie too, because he was her real great love of the moment. He went on to write of how he felt she'd have little trouble in attracting boys, because she was clearly going to be an even greater beauty than her mother, whose looks, sadly, seemed to be marred by too many frown lines these days, and whose mouth had taken on a permanent curve of disapproval. *I often wonder why Alice is so unhappy,* he wrote, *but my enquiries seem as unwelcome as my concern. I think I know, because for years it's been there at the back of my mind, but I never broach the subject and nor does she. I hope she never does, but I feel I have to be solicitous in asking, from time to time, if there's anything I can do to make her feel better. There never is.*

Julia was frowning herself as she read the last part of the entry again. What was her mother so unhappy about, she wondered. It seemed that her father had probably known, but had chosen neither to discuss it, nor commit it to his journal. Of course, he could be the cause of it, which might explain his reticence, but his words seemed not to display a burden of guilt, merely an unwillingness to confront an issue that might have lain dormant for years.

She turned a page and read on. More accounts of her and what she was up to, either at school, or with friends. A little about Pam and how worried he was that she seemed to be taking after her mother in the way she was shunning him. He gave no reason for why it might be happening, or what could have triggered it, until the final paragraph, when he'd written, *Alice tells me I love Julia too much. She makes it sound like a failing, rather than a father's natural affection and pride in a child who is, in truth, the greatest love of my life. I quite simply adore her, and will make no apology for it. As for Pam, who Alice accuses me of loving less, I try to deny it, but I know it's true. Alice says I am wicked and sinful in my neglect of her, but how can it be wrong for a father to love his own child more?*

Julia blinked as her heart skipped a beat. She read the last line again and felt everything slipping out of kilter. Was he saying she and Pam had different fathers? Well, yes, that was exactly what he seemed to be saying, and as the meaning of it slid into her mind she thought of the way her mother had always sided with Pam; how different Pam looked to her; Pam's unwillingness to be close as sisters; her father's struggle to make Pam sit with him or even tell him about her school day. Then there was Pam's failure to care when he left; her refusal to come to the funeral; her father's neglect of Pam in his will. So did that mean Pam knew he wasn't her father? It certainly seemed to suggest that, but why keep it a secret?

Julia lowered the book and stared across the room at the rain-spattered window. Why had no-one ever told her? It wasn't so terrible these days to have a child before marriage. Even when Pam was born, back in the mid-Sixties, illegitimacy hadn't carried anything like the kind of stigma it had a decade before – unless, of course, you had George Hope as a brother, and Julia shuddered to think of how her uncle would have viewed the disgrace his own sister was bringing upon his God-fearing family. She could see the manic gleam in his eye and the foam on his lips as he spouted his biblical damnation, shaming his sister and imploring God to visit all manner of suffering upon her for her sins. She could almost hear the Acts of Devotion he'd have forced her mother to learn by heart and recite at his will. *Oh Gracious Lord Jesu Christ, I a sinner . . . Trusting in thy mercy and goodness with fear and trembling . . . My heart and body are stained with many sins . . .*

The scene at the time must have been terrible, even terrifying, for her mother, he might even have thrashed her, the way he had Julia, and locked her up refusing to let her see her lover ever again. The man was probably married, or wholly unsuitable, or Catholic, but whoever Pam's father was, and whatever George had put her mother through, Julia had to concede that he'd stood by her in the end, and never once had she seen him treat Pam with anything other than the same awkward fondness with which he'd tried to treat her.

It was only then that she realised her parents had probably not been married as long as she thought. Either that, or her mother had become pregnant by someone else whilst already married to her father. It would perhaps account more easily for why her father had found it so hard to bond with Pam, if his wife had cheated on him then asked him to treat the child as his. A hole seemed to open up inside Julia as she considered her own late period and how Josh would react if confronted with the same nightmare dilemma – but she'd been under a lot of stress lately, and had never been particularly reliable in that department anyway, so she wasn't going to start scaring herself with that. Her body would undoubtedly kick back to normal any minute, and when, like now, she was attempting to deal with something else entirely.

It took very little time for her to decide that she didn't mind at all about Pam not being a full sister – if anything she was relieved, for it helped alleviate some of the guilt she'd always felt that her father had so clearly loved her more. On the other hand, a much more terrible spectre began to take shape. If Pam wasn't his daughter, might he have found it more acceptable to subject her young body to sexual abuse?

The next shock came in the entry for 18th October 1980.

I am renting a small bedsit in Edgware now. I had to take the money from George, though I hated doing it. If I hadn't, I could have found myself in a lot worse trouble than I've already been in lately. I'm so full of hate and anger that I want to keep lashing out at the world around me. I don't understand why God would do this to me? Maybe because there is no God, and this proves it.

I wrote to Julia, but they won't pass the letter on. I want to go to her school, kidnap her and run away with her, but I can't. I miss her as I'd miss a limb of my body or even my soul were it to be torn out. George has offered me very large sums of money to stay away from her. I won't touch it, but they have nothing to fear from me. I am no more desirous of her learning the truth than they are.

The police questioned me two days ago about the abduction and rape of a young boy from Ealing back in March. I wasn't even in the vicinity. My life hadn't fallen apart by then. I suspect George of giving my name to the police. It's a warning to stay away from Julia. Julia, my Julia. Life is so empty without her.

As the despair in his words seemed to lift up from the page, Julia's heart filled with the same emotion. Why were they going to such extremes to keep him away from her? What the hell had he done, except the unthinkable of course? However, that particular answer seemed less obvious than it might have done a few minutes ago. To her mind at least, his lack of concern about being questioned over such a heinous crime was giving rise to doubt now, rather than suspicion.

She continued reading, page after page of almost illegible scrawl, evidently written by a man who was drunk most of the time, enraged beyond reason and so emotionally wrung out it was hard to make sense of it all. All she could really deduce was that this journal was probably his only companion during that time.

Then finally his writing started to become

legible again. He seemed much more sober and able to wield a pen as he made sporadic comments about finding himself a job, spending hours in a library just reading, and holding onto George's cheques so that George would never know what he planned to do with them. There was an element of glee to those particular entries that intrigued her, for he seemed to be experiencing a sense of power that had been eluding him before. It could be blackmail, though clearly not in the conventional sense, because he hadn't cashed the cheques, in spite of needing the money. There was no record of him asking for payment either. So what were those entries really about? For the moment she was left guessing, as there was no more mention of George's money for a while. In fact nothing at all about George, her mother or her, until she reached the entry for 21st June 1981. It was a date that was later to remain indelibly stamped on her mind, though in itself it had no real significance – it was merely the day her father had chosen to reveal the true horror behind the events that had changed his life so completely.

It's been a whole year now since I found them together, and not a day goes by that I don't regret walking into that room. I'd long had my suspicions, but I continually ignored them, and I would sell my soul to go back to that happy state, for I know now that ignorance truly can be bliss. The truth has been the worst kind of hell to live with, because in this case it has robbed me of the most precious part of my life. Julia, my Julia. Where is she now? What is she doing? Does she wonder why I left? Does it break her heart as it breaks mine for us to be apart? No father could love his child more, and even knowing she isn't mine hasn't changed that. I just pray that the worst she has to live with is my desertion, because learning who her real father is would surely destroy her young life, and I'd rather destroy my own than ever have that happen.

What I saw that day still sickens me to my stomach, and always will. Alice and George . . .

Julia leapt to her feet and held the book away as though it might contaminate her. She could hardly breathe. Horror and revulsion were pulsing thickly through her veins. Please God this wasn't going where she thought it was. It couldn't. It was unthinkable, unbearable . . . She must find out though, she had to force herself to read on. Still on her feet, and keeping the book at a distance, she made her eyes look at the words.

I'd thought myself depraved for even thinking it, but that day I discovered I was right. All these years, all his bible-thumping hypocrisy, all her deceit . . . Their perversion has robbed me of everything, but nothing matters more than Julia. They have allowed me to think of her as my own. I know now that isn't true, which is why I can't take her from them. I have no right to her, and even though I fool myself sometimes into believing she's still mine, to prove it would be to put her through the worst imaginable hell, and should I turn out to be wrong, it is far better that she never learns the truth.

Julia could read no more. Her stomach was churning so badly that she cast the book aside, and ran downstairs to the bathroom. Vomit spewed out of her, over and over and over, until there was nothing but dry, heaving sobs to wrench the disgust from her body and horror from her mind. But it was still there. It would never go away now, and as the sheer enormity of it washed over her again, she began to tear at her hair and scream from the very depths of her soul.

George had fathered her. That warped, evil bastard she so hated . . . It couldn't be true. It just couldn't. She put her hands to her burning cheeks and pressed in hard. Her blood was tainted. She was the product of incest . . . She thought of Josh and then Dan, and her entire world collapsed. George and her mother and their ugly, filthy, despicable depravity were the cause of Dan's problems. Oh dear God, how was she ever going to tell Josh? How could he possibly look at her the same way again? He'd never be able to live with something like this, any more than she could. She thought of Pam and her own dear little daughter, Rachel, with Down's and epilepsy. Julia had no idea how much Pam knew, but it surely couldn't be the whole truth, because not even Pam could forgive the perversion that had resulted in such afflictions on her own precious child.

Rage was boiling so fast through her gut now that to reach out for the phone was nowhere near enough. She was going to confront her mother and that abomination she called a brother, and when she did, God help them all. They were going to regret the day they'd conceived her, even more than she did, and right now that regret was profound enough for her to wish herself stone-cold dead.

Rene had not long turned out the light when she heard a car pulling into the drive, and glanced at the digital clock beside her. Ten fifty-one. Instinct told her who it would be, and as a car horn started to blast, her suspicions were confirmed.

Slipping out of bed, she went to peer through the curtains and seeing that indeed it was Julia's car, a small smile passed over her lips, for retribution was clearly at hand. It should have been Douglas himself, but Julia would do just as well.

Though Alice's room was at the back of the house, Rene knew she couldn't fail to hear the din, and Rene took a moment's delight in the justice that had led George to his sister's room this night, instead of his own. Like Rene, they would know instantly it was Julia outside causing the commotion, and Rene could almost feel the fear creeping through Alice's incestuous bones. George would probably be out of bed by now, ludicrously stumbling into his pyjamas, wrapping his robe around his girth, and ordering Alice to stay where she was.

From behind her curtains Rene watched Julia striding to the front door and starting to hammer with all her might. She felt sorry for her, but there was nothing she could do to alter the tragedy now, it was all far too late for that. Events would have to take their course, though she, Rene, had given them a hand the day she'd sent someone to see Douglas with photographs, and the real version of the truth. It hadn't quite worked out the way she'd expected then, but she had more confidence that it would now, and going to the phone next to her bed, she picked it up and dialled 999. It would take the police a while to get here, but never mind, it was always best to report an intruder.

*

Not even the long drive, or the virtual three hours it had taken, had lessened Julia's horror or subdued her rage. If anything, her fury had intensified, and as she banged on her mother's front door it was as though she was trying to push her fist straight through it.

'Open this door!' she raged. 'Open it now or the whole neighbourhood's going to know what's going on in there.' She thumped and kicked it again, and stood back to look up at the windows.

'For heaven's sake, control yourself,' George snapped, pulling the door open. 'Do you know what time of night it is . . .'

'Get out of my way,' she snarled, and shoving him aside she stormed into the hall. 'Where is she? *Where are you*, you fucking bitch. Come down here and face me . . .'

'How dare you,' George growled behind her. 'I won't have that sort of language in this house . . .'

'Language!' Julia spat incredulously. 'You're worried about language, when you've been fucking your own sister! What kind of man are you? No, don't even speak to me,' she cried, blocking her ears with her hands.

George's face was white. 'Come into the sitting room,' he said. 'We need to talk, and you . . .'

'I have nothing to discuss with you. I don't want you ever to come anywhere near me, but I'm not leaving here until *she shows her face*.'

'Julia,' her mother said from the top of the stairs, 'please try to calm down.'

Julia spun round and only fury kept her heart from breaking into a thousand pieces. 'How could you?' she screamed. 'I know what you've done, what you are ...'

'Julia, please, come into the sitting room,' George persisted.

'Don't touch me!' she hissed, jerking away as he tried to take her arm. 'Don't you ever touch me, you disgusting ...'

'Julia, stop it!' Alice snapped, starting down the stairs. 'All this rage isn't going to get us anywhere, now pull yourself together.'

'Don't you dare say that to me. After what you've done ...'

'Always the drama queen,' Alice cut in sharply. 'Always over-exaggerating a situation ...'

Julia stared at her in shock. 'Mother, that just isn't possible,' she told her scathingly. 'Don't you have any understanding of what you've done? Doesn't it make you feel ashamed ...'

'If you'd let someone else speak ...'

'You think I want the details of your sordid little life, or to hear any more of your lies? What you've done to me, to my father ... And please don't try to tell me that sick monster there is my father, because I'll never accept it. Do you hear me, *never*! Douglas Cowan is the only father I've ever had, or will ever have.'

'Douglas Cowan was ...'

'Don't you dare! If you go even one word towards trying to tell me he was a paedophile, so help me God I'll kill you.'

'I wasn't going to say any such thing,' Alice objected.

Julia was barely listening. 'All these years, when you knew how much I loved him,' she seethed, 'how devastated I was when he left . . . How *could* you? What kind of woman are you? You even set him up to be questioned by the police . . . I've read it all. I know what you did. Do you have no conscience, no shame? How can you live with yourself?'

'We need to talk,' Alice said, glancing towards George. 'Let's please try to do it in a calm and adult manner.' She was already moving towards the sitting room, where George was opening the double doors.

'I hope you're not going to try and deny it,' Julia shouted, as she went after them, 'because he's written it all down, how he found you together . . . How do you look at yourself in a mirror? How can you show your faces in a church? You're such hypocrites. It's a sin, you know that, don't you?'

'For heaven's sake, stop,' Alice barked.

'I think we should pray,' George said.

Julia gaped at him. 'Are you out of your mind?' she cried. 'He's not going to help you now. Frankly, I'm amazed you can even suggest such a thing, knowing what you've done.' She spun back to her mother. 'You know it's not normal. Christ, it's not even legal. Do you ever think about how much damage you've caused? Aren't you tormented by your own conscience? How do you bring yourself to look at Rachel, or Dan?' Saying her son's name brought a sob from her throat. 'I don't know how I'm ever going to live with this,' she cried. 'I've passed my tainted genes on to my son. How do you think Josh will feel when I tell him? He'll want to kill you.'

'Julia, will you please listen,' George broke in, going to stand closer to Alice.

'Not to you. Never to you . . . Does Pam know?' she shot at her mother. 'She can't, because surely to God . . .'

'All Pam knows is that Douglas isn't her father,' Alice said quietly, 'and we'd prefer it if you didn't tell her the truth.'

Julia was about to yell again when George shouted over her, '*Oh most meek Jesus, implant in our hearts the virtues of gentleness and patience . . .*'

'Stop it! *Stop!*' Julia shrieked. 'God's not listening to you. No-one is. You lost that right the day you screwed your own sister.'

'Julia, please try to understand,' Alice said. 'George and I . . . It's not something we wanted to happen. All our young lives we tried to fight it, because we knew it was wrong. But it never felt that way . . .'

Julia was recoiling. 'Don't go any further,' she warned. 'I'm perfectly clear about what's been happening and why my son's the way he is . . .'

'You're jumping to conclusions again,' Alice cried. 'You did the same with Douglas. No-one ever told you he was a paedophile . . .'

'You led me to it,' Julia screamed in despair. 'You tried to make me think he was the lowest of the low, the scum of the earth, but do you know what, it never really worked, because I always knew something was wrong about it. I knew he wasn't like that. He was good and kind and pure. He loved me, and you stole me from him.' Emotion was locking her throat. 'He was my father,' she sobbed helplessly. 'Whatever you say, Douglas Cowan was my father.'

'Yes, he was,' Alice said calmly.

It took a moment for Julia to register the words.

'Douglas was your father,' her mother repeated.

Julia stared at her, unable to make sense of this sudden change. 'But he wrote in his diary . . . He said you'd told him . . .'

'That's what we told him, but it wasn't true,' Alice confessed. 'Not of you. Only of Pam. I just didn't want him to take you away, so we lied to him.'

Julia's heart twisted with pain and as a new understanding began to dawn she shook uncontrollably. 'Oh my God!' she murmured, hardly able to take it in. 'You let him believe I wasn't his. You told him . . . You let him think . . . Oh my God, how could you have done that? You broke his heart. You virtually destroyed him . . .' Hate filled up her heart. 'How could you have taken me from him?' she flung at her mother. 'You never wanted me, you bitch! Oh God, I can't bear it. All he went through. The years you stole from him.' Tears were streaming down her face, too much pain was crushing her heart. '*I want to kill you for this!*' she screamed. 'Do you know that? I want to kill you for how much you made him suffer.'

'Here, Julia. Take this,' Rene said from behind her.

Julia spun round.

'Rene, in the name of the Lord,' George cried, lunging forward, but he stopped as Rene raised the barrel of the shotgun.

'Do not invoke God one more time in this house,' she snarled. 'Your sins are beyond numbering, and beyond redemption. For what you've done to Julia, to Douglas, and most of all to Pam and her dear little child, you deserve to die. Julia, take the gun, and shoot them like the animals they are.'

Hardly knowing what she was doing, Julia took the gun. Somewhere in the back of her mind she knew she had to get it away from Rene, but once it was in her hands she felt an intoxicating surge of power that dizzied and disoriented her.

'Your father knew the truth in the end,' Rene told her gently. 'I sent someone to see him. I couldn't bear the lie to go on any longer. He was a good man. The man you always believed in. They should never have lied to him the way they did, and I should never have kept silent. We are all sinners, but no-one has sinned as much or as heinously as they have.'

'Rene, you don't know what you're saying,' George growled.

'Don't be a fool, George,' she responded. 'It's over now, can't you see that? Julia was always going to find out one day, and I blame myself for letting it go on so long. But at least I allowed Douglas to die knowing his daughter was his. What you did to him was beyond forgiveness. The lies you told, the money you tried to buy him off with, and for what?' She turned to Alice, her pale eyes gleaming with hatred. 'For *her*! Your own flesh and blood. You're not fit to tread God's earth, either of you, and condoning it the way I have makes me almost as bad as you. But I can't live with my conscience any longer. I need to cleanse my soul of my sins before I die, but for you there is only hell and eternal damnation.'

'Oh Lord Jesus Christ, draw Thou near to Thy suffering servant Rene in her trouble of mind . . '

Ignoring him, Rene said to Alice, 'You've never been a mother to Julia. You've always resented her for loving her father more, so you repaid her by making her think he was a criminal of the very worst sort. You convinced Pam. She truly believes it, but think how much worse the truth is for her, because she really is George's daughter.'

'Julia, give me that gun,' George barked.

Dazed by the past few minutes, Julia asserted it and pointed it at him. 'Don't come near me,' she warned.

'Julia,' Alice pleaded. 'We've told you the truth, and of course we were wrong to do what we did to your father, but it was because I loved you and wanted to keep you . . .'

'You liar!' Julia spat. 'What you wanted was to make sure he never breathed a word of what was really going on in this house, that's why you kept me. It was to guard your disgusting little secret, and the only way you could do that was to make him believe he wasn't my father.'

'No, Julia,' Alice implored.

'Yes, Julia,' Rene confirmed.

'But you know Douglas was your father now,' Alice cried, 'so there's no need to harm George. He hasn't done anything to hurt you . . .'

Julia regarded her with loathing. 'He was behind it all,' she snarled. 'He lied to the police, he wrote the cheques . . .'

'At my behest. I told him to do it, because I didn't want to lose you . . . It's true, I swear it. I knew once Douglas found out the truth he'd take you away ...'

'She's a liar,' Rene muttered in Julia's ear.

'If he thought you weren't his,' Alice ran on, 'he'd have no rights. He couldn't take you from me then ...'

'*O Gracious Lord Jesus, who didst vouchsafe to die on the cross ...*'

'They stole you from him, Julia. He loved you ...'

'Julia, please. Put the gun down ...'

'They don't deserve to live.'

'*... hear our prayers for all such as sin against Thee ...*'

'There are two bullets.'

'Julia, please. I know it was wrong ...'

'It was more than wrong. It was evil. He's dead now. You'll never see him again.'

'Don't listen to her, Julia.'

'He'd have been so proud of your children. I sent him the photos ...'

'*Almighty and Everlasting God, who willest not the death of a sinner ...*'

Julia's finger tightened on the trigger.

'No!' Alice cried.

Her voice was drowned by the sound of the shot blasting from the barrels. Julia was knocked back into Rene who kept her upright, while almost in slow-motion, George crashed against the table behind him, and slumped to the floor.

'Again,' Rene hissed. 'She's right there. Right there.'

Alice's face was ashen. 'Julia please,' she begged, dropping to her knees.

'Do it!' Rene urged. 'There's one more. Do it. She deserves it.'

Julia fired again and as the room filled with gunsmoke, and dust tumbled around them, an armed response unit skidded to a halt outside in the drive.

Chapter Nineteen

It was the dead of night as Fen sped along the motorway, swallowing up the miles and dangerously defying the limit. The torrential rain that was flooding Devon and Somerset was finally starting to ease now, improving visibility, and as the flickering lights of a city appeared in the distance she glanced at the clock. Two twenty-five. With any luck she'd be there by three.

Pressing down hard to overtake a lone lorry she watched the needle approach ninety, then hit a button on the dash to answer her mobile.

'Where are you?' Bob asked.

'Just outside Bristol.'

'You've made good time, but don't go killing yourself to get there.'

'I won't. Tell me, do you think I should ring Josh?'

'She asked you not to.'

'I know, but you heard the state she was in, and the more I think about it, the more convinced I'm becoming that I should.'

'Then let me do it. That way you won't be quite so in breach of your lawyer–client relationship . . . I just need to know what to tell him.'

As Fen searched for the right words, her heart was already going out to Josh for the terrible shock this would be. 'I think, until I've got the full details,' she said in the end, 'you should just tell him there's been a shooting at her mother's house, and that she's at Stroud police station. We don't actually know much more than that right now, anyway.'

'He'll want to call you.'

'Tell him I'm almost there, so I'll be in touch the minute I know any more.'

An hour later, having broken the speed limit the entire way, Fen circled a mini-roundabout near the centre of Stroud and headed up Corn Hill towards the police station and courts. Drizzle was misting the air, while lampposts pooled a yellow glow into puddles and over slick, wet walls that rose up around the official buildings. There was absolutely no-one around, not even another moving vehicle, or luckless tramp.

Turning left after the courts, she drove round to the back of the station, and finding a space at the top of a grassy bank, she stopped the car, grabbed her briefcase and coat, and following instructions, virtually ran round to the van dock. As she pressed the bell she turned her face to the security camera for the benefit of those within, and seconds later the iron shutters began a clattering rise to allow her in.

Having skirted the police van, and entered

through the rear security doors, she found herself in the brightly lit custody area. Sergeant Holmes, whom she'd spoken to on the phone, was seated behind his semicircular barricade-cum-reception desk making notes on a pad in front of him, and occasionally glancing at a CCTV.

'You must be Mrs Thayne's solicitor,' he said, looking up as she approached.

'Fionnula Barrington,' she reminded him, setting down her briefcase. 'Can I see the custody record?'

Following form, he turned it towards her. 'We got a 999 reporting an intruder,' he told her, as she read, 'lucky there was an armed response team in the area, you know, with us being close to the royal households and that . . .'

Fen was still scanning the record. 'Possession of firearm with intent to endanger life,' she read aloud, feeling faintly dizzied by the offence, though immeasurably relieved that it wasn't showing any of the worst-case scenarios she'd been imagining all the way here – at least not yet. 'Has anyone been hurt?' she asked.

'The old man's in hospital,' he answered.

Fen's mouth was turning dry. 'What are his injuries?' she demanded.

The sergeant was looking at her in a way that seemed both curious and hostile. 'He hasn't been shot, if that's what you're thinking,' he replied.

'Then why's he there?'

'He got a crack to the head, I'm told. Concussion.'

'Was anyone else hurt?'

His eyes bored hard into hers. 'Not that we know

of,' he answered, as though suspecting her of already knowing more. 'Officers are still at the scene. Apparently she shot the place up a bit, and the old woman's a gibbering wreck, if you'll excuse . . .'

'What old woman?'

He glanced down at his records. 'Rene Hope,' he said. 'The family solicitor's already been in to see her. Ranting and raving she was. Couldn't get any sense out of her. The lads brought her in because they didn't know what else to do with her.'

'Where is she now?'

'We let her go on police bail. I think the solicitor took her back to his house, if you want to be in touch. He left his card.'

Fen took it, saying, 'Thank you. I'd like to see my client now, please.'

He rose to his feet. 'Solicitor's interview room's along that corridor,' he said, pointing behind her.

Fen remained where she was, watching him draw a long key chain from his pocket as he came round the barricade. 'If you ask me, she's still in shock,' he confided as he passed, 'but she's calmer than when they brought her in. Couldn't stop crying then, or shaking. Beside herself, she was.'

Having heard her on the phone, Fen said nothing, merely waited as he entered a small corridor of cells, and stopped at the first one to check the hatch. 'Solicitor's here,' he announced, then slamming the hatch closed again, he unlocked the door and swung it open.

From where she was standing Fen could see Julia sitting on the bunk at the back of the cell, hugging her knees to her chest, face buried in her arms. She didn't look up as the door opened, nor did she immediately respond when Fen said her name.

Fen glanced at the sergeant. 'Julia,' she said again.

This time Julia lifted her head, and seeing Fen she finally seemed to come to her senses. 'Oh thank God,' she murmured, getting to her feet. 'I'm sorry to call you like this ...'

'There's nothing to be sorry for, you did the right thing.'

Before Julia could respond the sergeant was ushering her out of the cell, and along the corridor to the interview room. 'Shout if you need anything,' he told Fen as he pushed open the door.

The room stank of old sweat, and was hardly any bigger than a king-size bed, with two chairs and a table, all bolted to the floor, no windows and a notice Sellotaped to one wall declaring it a no-smoking zone.

As Fen closed the door, Julia sank down on one of the chairs and pushed her hands into her hair.

'First tell me if you're OK?' Fen said, sitting down too. 'Are you hurt? Do you need a doctor?'

Julia shook her head, and forced herself to look up. Her face was drained of all colour, her eyes flat and cold.

'You need to tell me what happened,' Fen said gently.

Julia nodded, then wiped her hands over her face. 'I had the gun,' she said shakily. 'They kept talking, all of them. My mother was shouting, Rene was whispering in my ear, George was chanting his bloody prayers ... It was like a nightmare where the sounds swoop in on you ... In and in ... In and in ... I had to make them stop, or they were going to drive me crazy.' She swallowed.

'So you fired the gun?' Fen prompted.

Julia nodded.

'You know no-one's been shot, don't you?'

Julia merely looked at her.

'No-one's been hurt,' Fen assured her.

Though Julia seemed to register the words, she showed no emotion. 'I thought he was dead,' she said dully. 'I wanted him to be ...' She took a breath and pressed her hands to her face again. 'When he fell, he must have been throwing himself out of the way. It happened so fast, I thought the bullet had ricocheted off the wall and hit him.'

'So you didn't aim the gun at him?' Fen said.

Julia's eyes came back to hers.

'When you pulled the trigger, you were deliberately firing at the wall,' Fen pressed.

Julia seemed confused. 'I wanted to kill him,' she said.

'But you didn't. You fired at the wall.'

Julia nodded.

Having enough reassurance regarding intent for now, Fen said, 'OK, so tell me where you got the gun.'

'Rene gave it to me. She just appeared out of nowhere, then she was urging me to shoot them, and I was so angry, believe me, I wanted to ... I wanted to so badly ...'

Trying to keep her focused, Fen said, 'How many times did you fire the gun?'

'Twice.'

'Once at the wall, and once . . . Where did you aim the other shot?'

'I'm not sure. It was meant for her . . .'

'But where was the gun pointing when you fired?'

'I don't know. At the ceiling, I think.'

'Then what happened?'

Julia covered her face with her hands, still so shaken by the fact that she'd been involved in such a scene that even now she couldn't make it seem real. 'The police came in,' she said. 'They had helmets and guns . . . They were shouting at me to put the gun down . . . Rene was screaming, I think my mother was too . . . I dropped the gun, then suddenly I was being shoved to the floor, face down with someone's foot on my back . . .' She shook her head in bewilderment. 'Everyone was still shouting. It was insane. There was dust and debris all over the place, all over George. I was trying to tell them he was dead, but no-one seemed to be listening. Then an ambulance came . . .'

'What was your mother doing?'

Julia's expression changed. 'She was kneeling next to George and screaming that she hated me and always had, and if anything happened to him she'd make sure I paid.'

Though Fen knew there had never been much love lost between them, she could see what a terrible impact her mother's words had made.

'I told her I wished she was dead,' Julia went on, 'that I should have blown her to bits, because the world would be a better place without her.'

'And Rene? What was she doing?'

'She was jabbering away to the police, telling

them that she'd tried to get the gun away from me, but I'd threatened to kill her. She was spouting so much rubbish . . .'

'Did you threaten to kill her?'

'No. She was the one who gave me the gun.' Her eyes came to Fen's, seeming to ask for an understanding she could barely grasp herself.

'It's OK,' Fen assured her. 'We'll need to go through it all from the beginning, but from what I've heard so far it's not looking as bad as I feared. Do you know whose gun it was?'

'George's, I suppose. He keeps them for hunting.' Suddenly her eyes closed and she averted her head, seeming to deal with a different kind of pain. 'What they've done, Fen,' she said brokenly, 'who they are . . .'

Sensing her nearing the edge, Fen took her hands and tried to will her some strength. 'The last time we spoke you were about to go through the journals,' she said. 'I take it you found something, so can you talk me through it from there?'

Julia inhaled deeply, and looked down at their hands. 'It's a horrible story,' she said. 'I don't know if I can bear to retell it. The very idea that I'm related to them, though thank God not in the way I first thought.' Her eyes moved to Fen's, and realising she wasn't making much sense, she said, 'Sorry, the journals . . . God, it seems so long ago . . .'

Fen listened quietly as Julia was finally able to recount what she'd read, how appalled she'd been and ashamed – and so full of hate that even now she couldn't feel sorry they weren't dead. 'To think they cheated him like that,' she said brokenly at the end. 'All these years when we could have been a part of each other's lives ...'

Hardly able to comprehend how devastated she must feel, or indeed how to express the disgust she was experiencing herself, Fen simply held onto her hands and tried to convey as much empathy as she could.

'Are they going to keep me here?' Julia asked, seeming to come out of a reverie.

'I don't know. They've let Rene go on police bail, so maybe we can work the same for you. It'll probably depend on the duty inspector. Have you seen him?'

Julia nodded, but her attention was obviously elsewhere. 'I meant to kill them,' she stated quietly. Her eyes came up to Fen's. 'I wanted to kill them.'

'If that were true, you'd have done it.'

Julia looked away. 'Can you believe that my own mother ... ?' She shuddered. 'It's so horrible, so ...'

'Try not to go there. Just focus on the fact that Douglas was your father, and the man we all knew and loved. It's all that matters.'

As Julia's eyes came back to hers, Fen caught a glimpse of the dreadful pain inside her. 'But to have lied to him like that,' she whispered. Then, swallowing hard, she made a visible effort to get past it. 'I'm so glad he found Gwen, and you,' she said, her voice thick with emotion.

'We could never have replaced you,' Fen said softly, 'but we loved him very much.'

'That at least gives me some comfort, but for what they did to him, to both of us, they deserved to die.'

Not arguing with that, Fen rose to her feet. 'I'll go and see if there's any way I can get you out of here now,' she said.

Julia nodded, then her focus seemed to shift again as she said, 'It all feels like a dream. I keep thinking I'll wake up in a minute . . .'

'You're still in shock,' Fen told her. 'You need some time to recover,' and dropping a kiss on her forehead she left the room.

Outside in the custody area she waited for the sergeant to finish on the phone, then boldly said, 'There doesn't seem to be any reason to keep her here, so I'd like to take her home now.'

The sergeant pulled an astonished face. 'Well, as it so happens that was Inspector Bradley on the phone,' he told her. 'He's been at the hospital talking to Mr Hope and his sister, your client's mother. Apparently they don't want to press charges, and by the sound of it the inspector don't seem inclined to either, but I'll have to clear it with him before I can release her – and then it'll only be on police bail.'

'I understand that,' Fen responded.

Realising she was waiting for him to make the call right away he grunted, then picked up the phone and started to dial. 'Just one thing that bothers me,' he remarked, as he waited for the connection. 'Why did Mrs Hope, your client's aunt, call to report an intruder, then end up handing the gun to her niece?'

'You'll have to ask Mrs Hope that,' Fen replied.

'She's claiming that your client smashed the gun cabinet and helped herself.'

'What do Mr Hope and his sister say?'

'The same as your client, by all accounts.'

'Then where's the problem?'

He shrugged. 'Just that I get the feeling something's being covered up here,' he said. 'I don't reckon we're getting the whole picture.'

'Even if that were true, and I'm not saying it is, you're still only facing a domestic dispute, because there are no bodies, no injuries, no break-ins.'

He was just reminding her that firearms were involved, when he made his connection, so letting it go, he began speaking to the inspector.

Leaving him to it, Fen returned to the interview room and beckoned Julia to come out into the corridor. 'I think we're in with a chance,' she whispered. 'Apparently no-one's pressing charges.'

Julia looked at her with strangely clouded eyes, then suddenly she started to retch.

'It's OK, it's OK,' Fen said, going to her.

Julia took a breath. Nothing had come up, but the nausea was still there and a cold sweat was breaking out on her skin.

'Do you need to sit down?' Fen asked.

'No, I'm fine,' Julia was finally able to answer. 'It's passed now.'

Fen was watching her closely. 'It's part of the shock,' she said gently. 'You've been through quite an ordeal.'

Julia looked past her as the custody sergeant came to find out where they were. 'You'll need to leave details of where you're taking her,' he told Fen, 'and fill in the relevant forms.'

Knowing the forms inside out Fen had them completed in next to no time, and five minutes later, after waiting for Julia's few personal effects to be returned, they walked out of the station into the cold, clammy drizzle that was drifting across the yard.

'The car's just around here,' Fen said as they exited the van-dock door. 'I should have brought an extra coat and umbrella.'

'I'll be fine,' Julia assured her.

As they reached the Volvo Julia was about to get in when a set of headlights swept in from the road and across the lower car park, to come to a stop at the foot of the grassy bank directly below them.

Even before the lights went out Fen realised it was the Porsche, and as Josh got out she heard a small sob catch in Julia's throat.

For what seemed a strangely long time husband and wife merely stood looking at each other in the darkness. Josh's face was pale in the lamplight, his eyes lost in shadow, but in those moments even Fen could sense the power of the feelings that connected them. Finally Julia started to move towards him, walking, then breaking into a run, and as she reached the bottom of the bank he caught her hard in his arms.

As Fen went down to join them they continued to cling to each other, making no attempt to speak, simply yielding to the need to be close. Fen could only feel glad she had instinctively agreed that Bob should alert Josh to what was happening.

'She'll be fine,' she said quietly, as Josh looked at her over Julia's shoulder. 'Still quite shaken up . . .'

'Can I take her home?'

Fen nodded. 'I gave them my address, but I can go back inside to change it.'

'We need to collect my car,' Julia said, pulling back to look at him. 'It's still at the house.'

'We can do it another time,' he told her gently.

'No, I want it over with tonight,' she insisted. 'Then I'll never have to go there again.'

'You won't have to. I'll pick it up.'

As she gazed into his eyes it was as though she still couldn't quite believe he was here, then putting her hands either side of his face, she looked at him with so much love that in spite of Fen's presence, he had to kiss her. 'Let's go now,' he said. 'You can tell me what happened on the way back in the car.'

She was still holding his face, and gazing into his eyes as though unable to make herself stop, then turning to Fen she said, 'Do you mind if we use your car for a moment?'

Fen frowned curiously and looked at Josh, who appeared equally as baffled. 'Of course,' she said, shrugging.

After making sure Fen had the keys to the Porsche so she could wait in the warm, Julia linked Josh's arm and they climbed the bank, to the Volvo. 'Sit in the back with me,' she said, as he unlocked it. 'I want to be close to you, and I can't in the Porsche.'

Still not quite understanding, he held the door open for her to slide in first, then slipped in next to her and drew her back into his arms. 'Are you OK?' he whispered against her hair.

She nodded. After a while she said, 'I love you so much.'

He kissed her head. 'I love you too.' Then, with a note of irony in his voice, 'Tell me, how the hell did we get here?'

'I don't know, but as long as we're together . . .' She tilted her face up and kept her eyes on his as he touched his lips to hers.

'Do you want to tell me what this is about?' he murmured.

She nodded, but then found herself almost overcome by the urge to cry. 'I'm sorry,' she said shakily. 'I'll have myself together in a minute.'

'Why don't you let it wait?' he suggested. 'Let's just go home now.'

'No, I need to tell you,' she insisted.

Letting her do it her way, he listened in silence as the nightmare of the past eight hours finally began to unfold. All the time she spoke he gazed intently into her lovely face, watching the tremble of her lips and occasionally wiping the tears from her cheeks. He understood completely the horror and rage that had driven her to confront her mother and uncle, because he was feeling it himself, though in her shoes he doubted he'd have been so circumspect with the gun.

'But he *was* my father,' she said forcefully at the end. 'He was, and I'm so happy for that, not just because of what it would mean if he wasn't, but because he was so special.'

'So's his daughter,' he said, 'and I can't tell you how glad I am you're sitting here now. Not that they don't deserve worse, but I couldn't bear to lose you.'

Lifting a hand to his face, she ran it over the hard stubble on his chin and on into his hair. 'I kept thinking about Daniel and his seizures,' she said.

'Epilepsy happens to thousands of children,' he said gently. 'It doesn't mean . . .'

'I know, but when I first read that . . .'

'Don't torment yourself. It's not the reality and that's all that matters.'

'It is for Pam though.'

'Yes. We'll have to decide what to do about that.'

She rested her cheek against him then and felt the comforting warmth of his arms, as his words reminded her that she wasn't alone.

'Do you feel ready to deal with Shannon?' he asked after a while.

Her heart contracted, and there was a pause before she could bring herself to answer. 'Not really, not yet,' she confessed.

'Then I'll come to Cornwall with you. My mother can probably cope for a couple of days.'

She sat up to look at him, and loved him so much for his offer, that it could almost surpass everything she'd felt before. How could she allow herself to come first, though, when they had two children who even now were at home without them? 'The kids need you more than I do right now,' she said. 'I'll get over this. It'll just take me a day or two, then I'll come home – if you're sure you want me.'

'Don't ever doubt it,' he murmured, and as his eyes gazed more deeply into hers, she could feel the familiar longing for him starting to stir. The sensation became so forceful that she pushed herself harder against him. 'I've been such a fool,' he said, his lips almost on hers. 'I'm sorry for all the pain I've caused you. I swear, I'll never let anything come between us again.'

She started to respond, but her throat was locked with emotion, and as his mouth covered hers all she would allow herself to think about was this precious, beautiful moment, because as much as she'd like to tell herself it was all behind them now, she knew in her heart that this was far from true.

Though it was against Fen's better judgement, she agreed to take Julia to her car so that she could drive it back to Cornwall, since she would need it when she got there. When they arrived at her uncle's house lights were blazing from most of the windows, and a small police unit was guarding the scene, preventing any contamination before forensics turned up. After some to-ing and fro-ing, which involved several calls to the station and even one to Alice who was still at the hospital with George, Fen managed to persuade the officer in charge to let the car go. After filling up with petrol at the first garage they came to, she led the way back to the motorway, where she set a much more sedate pace than either of them had taken on their northward journey.

By the time they got back to the mill it was just after nine a.m. and Julia was clearly exhausted.

'Get some sleep, we'll talk later,' Fen said, walking as far as the front steps with her.

Julia turned to look around, needing to absorb the sense of calm and welcome that exuded from her surroundings, the feeling of rightness and normalcy that separated it so completely from the world from which she'd just emerged. Drawing her mind back from those shadows, she let her eyes settle on Fen. 'Thanks for coming,' she said, wishing the words didn't sound so inadequate.

'I'm glad you called,' Fen responded. 'Are you going to be OK?'

Julia nodded, though she wished now that she'd let Josh come, for she wanted nothing more than to lie down with him and feel his arms around her. 'I'll be fine,' she said. 'I imagine you're pretty shattered too.'

'I'll probably grab a couple of hours before going to the office,' Fen admitted. 'You know where I am if you need me.'

After thanking her again, and embracing her, Julia stood watching as she turned her car round and drove back to the woods. Once she was out of sight, Julia pushed open the door, and without even removing her coat went straight upstairs. When she got to the sitting room her heart twisted to see the journal she'd thrown across the room last night. It was spread out on a rug in front of the fireplace, and feeling a terrible sadness starting to weigh her down she went to pick it up. Her father's words were one of her most precious possessions now, the link that would always bind them together, and after gazing down at the writing for a while, not reading it, just needing to see it, she closed the book and hugged it to her. She knew that soon the grieving for him would begin in earnest, but it would be a normal, healing process of mourning, unclouded by doubt and suspicion, unburdened by lies and despair.

Deciding to take the book with her, she walked into the bedroom and was about to take off her coat when she came to a surprised stop. For a moment she thought her eyes were playing her tricks, so she blinked and looked again, but there really was no bed. Then she remembered Tilde's young friends had arranged to take it today, so having no alternative, she went back downstairs to use the bedroom down there.

On her way through the kitchen she spotted a note, propped up against the kettle, and stopped to read it.

'Sally and Jeremy have bin to take bed. Hope that was all right. They left a cheque, which I've kept hold of for safekeeping. Found this book under the bed, didn't read none of it, but reckon it's your Dad's. Yours faithfully, Tilde. PS: Unloaded dishwasher and tidied away, in case you thought the fairies bin in.'

Julia wasn't quite sure whether it was the fairies or the 'yours faithfully' that brought tears to her eyes, but what did it matter? Tilde was a lovely old soul, and right now her emotions were running so close to the surface that almost anything could make her cry. She looked at the book that was lying flat in front of the kettle. It appeared to be another journal, though it was clearly much newer than those she'd found in the attic. A glance inside at the handwritten dates proved her right: it had been written in the weeks before her father died. Unable to deal with any more now, she simply added it to the other book, and clutching them both to her, she went to lie down on the other bed, and fell almost instantly asleep.

It was the middle of the afternoon when the sound of the phone began penetrating her dreams, until finally it sank deeply enough to wake her. With her eyes barely open, and not having any clear idea where she was, she reached out to answer it, and knocked a small china pot from the night-stand. The noise brought her several more layers to the surface, and sitting up, she realised the phone that was still ringing was out in the kitchen. Throwing back the covers, she stumbled along the short hallway and managed to get to it before the caller rang off.

'Is this too early?' Josh said.

Warming to the intimate tone of his voice, she said, 'No, it's fine. How are you?'

'That's my question. I woke you, didn't I?'

'Yes, but it doesn't matter. I need to get up.'

'I just wanted to make sure you were OK, not sitting there alone, bottling anything up.'

'All I'm bottling up is how much I'm missing you.'

'We need to be together again,' he said. 'I'm going to have a chat with Shannon tonight, because I think it'll help her to know that I don't have a problem with what happened any more.'

Julia's heart turned over. She didn't want to have this conversation now, but knew she had to. 'Do you really mean that?' she whispered.

'Well, I confess, I wouldn't like it to happen again,' he replied, 'and as long as you can tell me you haven't developed a penchant for young . . . Sorry, cut that, it was going to turn into a bad joke, so let's not go there.'

'The only penchant I have is for you,' she told him. 'It always was for you. Nothing's changed that, and nothing ever will.'

There was a moment before he was able to say, 'Same here.'

'Josh, don't cry. Please don't.'

'I'm not,' he said, but she felt sure he was.

Knowing how close to tears she was herself, she said, 'We can get through anything, can't we?'

'I think the last few months have proved that,' he answered. 'I was a fool to have done what I did, worse than a fool, but I'll never let anyone, or anything take you away from me.'

Tears were falling fast as she said, 'I wish you were here. I want to look at you as I tell you how much I love you.'

'Then save it until I'm there. Or you're here.'

'Call me again in an hour. I need to hear your voice.'

'I need to hear yours too. I'll be in a meeting, but I'll only be thinking of you.'

She spluttered with laughter. 'Now you've gone too far,' she accused.

'You're doubting me?'

'Would I?'

He laughed. 'I always knew I was the luckiest man alive to have you as my wife. You don't have to keep reminding me.'

More tears welled in her eyes. 'I'm the lucky one,' she said brokenly. 'I just don't ever want to lose you.'

'Then come home soon. We all love you and miss you, so it's time we were a family again.'

As she put the phone down she leaned over it and began to cry with more heartache than she'd ever felt in her life.

Chapter Twenty

Later that night Fen came over and helped to build a fire, which they settled down in front of with bottles of wine and water to read the newly discovered journal. To Julia it seemed right for Fen to share in her father's last recorded thoughts, because, in her way, she'd been as much a daughter to him as she had. And to do it here, in the cosy sitting room of his house, with a fire flickering in the hearth, and the curtains drawn against the wintry night, felt right too.

'I've already looked through it,' she said, curling into the corner of a sofa, 'so I want to read you the parts that I think really matter.'

Fen sank down on a feathery cushion beside the hearth and leaned back against the stone fireplace, one knee raised to prop up the hand holding her wine glass. She looked every bit the horsewoman she was, Julia was thinking as she regarded her, with her cloud of wild red hair, her lovely ivory skin cast warmly in the glow of the flames, and the obligatory jodhpurs and sweater.

'What?' Fen asked curiously.

Julia smiled and shook her head, then turned to the book. 'I'll start with 24th September this year,' she said, opening it at the page she'd marked. She glanced at Fen again, then to the gentle accompaniment of the wind outside and occasional crackle and shift in the hearth, she began to read her father's words.

'"Julia is mine. How can I even begin to express how happy that makes me? All these years of wondering and agonising, feeling certain one day, and doubtful the next ... Tears fill my eyes as I think of my beautiful girl, who is a woman now, and my heart fills up with so much love, the wonderful love a father feels for his precious only child. I keep thinking of all I've missed, and how truly fulfilled our lives would have been if only I'd made Alice and George prove their claim. I blame myself for not having more faith, but I was so afraid of what it would do to Julia if I'd discovered they were telling the truth.

'"It's tempting to ramble on with all my disjointed thoughts now, as memories come back, and regrets keep surfacing, but I want to write this down as it happened, to tell how I found out this most important and joyful of truths. Perhaps it will help me come to decisions that are eluding me now. It began with a curious visit I had last week from a woman who claimed Rene had sent her. At first I had to struggle to remember who Rene was – had she given the surname I'd have known immediately, of course, but so many years have gone by now that I will forgive myself the rather surprising lapse. She was talking of Rene

Hope, George's wife. A dowdy little creature, as I recall. Never used to say much, but always seemed to know more than she should. That was my perception of her, anyway. I remember writing to her begging for news of Julia after I left, but she never wrote back. Now, all these years later, she sends a stranger to see me, who I believe must be a private detective of sorts, and it's from this stranger that I finally learn that Julia is my daughter, my own flesh and blood. As I write those words I feel so much relief and happiness that my hands are shaking. If only I'd challenged them, but if I'd been wrong, it would have meant abandoning Julia to the horror of knowing that George was much more than her uncle. I couldn't do that to her, so I kept silent to protect her, as they knew I would.

'"I try never to remember the day I caught them together, but the images of that terrible scene are indelibly printed in my mind. It changed my life completely, and I believe I knew, almost from the instant I came upon them, that it would be me who ended up losing everything and I turned out to be right.

'"I'd always known Pam wasn't mine, she was born even before Alice and I met, and though it would be easy to say now that I suspected who her real father was, I don't really believe I did. With Julia, there had never been any doubt – until they planted it. Alice and I had been (I thought) happily married at the time Julia was conceived, and I was there at the birth. It was only later that I felt things starting to go wrong between me and Alice, and even wondered if she was involved with

Pam's father again – the mysterious salesman who'd captivated her as a teenager, and left her broken-hearted and pregnant. It turns out I was right, of course, she was indeed involved with Pam's father again. It would seem that whatever compels her and George to flout everything, from God's word to the law of the land, was clearly too strong for them to resist.'"

Keeping her eyes lowered, Julia reached for her glass and took a sip. Though she'd read these words earlier, they seemed to be having a far greater impact now, and she could only wonder what Fen was thinking, if her mind was recoiling as strongly as hers was.

Putting her drink down again, she turned over the page and continued to read.

'"I'm not sure when I first really started to suspect them, I think it just rose up gradually from the darkest corners of my mind, until finally the terrible reality of it was hard to ignore. But still I said nothing, and still I told myself I was wrong. How could any man think such a thing of his wife, or of a conscientious church-goer like George? I confess, I'd never warmed to the man, but for a long time I detested myself for my own depraved thoughts, rather than detesting him for what I feared to be true. I watched Rene, trying to work out what she might know, or what she was thinking, but I never could.

'"Then one day, the fateful day, I turned up at the house unexpectedly, and there they were. Clearly believing themselves safe, they hadn't even taken themselves off to the bedroom. They were so engrossed in each other that they didn't even hear me come in. For a while I could only stand, frozen in shock, unwilling to accept what my eyes were seeing. Two naked bodies coupling on the floor in front of the hearth. The scene that followed, as I grabbed him away from her and knocked him half senseless, was ugly in the extreme, though nothing could surpass the ugliness of what I had seen. Alice shrieked and wept and begged me to stop, but I wanted to kill him. I wanted to kill her too, but I'd never raised my hand to a woman before, and I didn't then, though perhaps she deserved it.

'"I will relive no more of it, because it distresses me still, all I will say is that the days that followed took me deeper and deeper into a nightmare from which I could find no escape. Alice was unrepentant, even unashamed. She became a woman I hardly knew, nor did I want to. She refused to give him up, and even accused me of being the one who was sick, because I was so obsessed with a child who she then claimed wasn't mine. She threatened to tell the world what I got up to with Julia and I was so appalled I barely knew how to defend myself. I had never laid a finger on Julia in that way, nor would I. Then George started adding his threats to Alice's, and claiming his paternal rights, and I soon realised that if I didn't go, Julia's suffering was likely to be even greater than mine.

'"So they used my love for my daughter to protect themselves. They knew I would never want to put her through the shame of finding out she was a child born of incest, or the stigma of having to live with it after. I didn't even want the word to touch her, never mind the reality, so I never told another living soul what I'd seen that day, apart from my darling Gwen of course. I still wonder how I'd have survived had she not come into my life when she did. God knew I was close to the end of my tether by then, but He must have been smiling on me that day, as He hadn't smiled on me since the day I'd last seen my girl."'

Julia stopped and took a breath.

'Are you OK?' Fen asked softly.

She nodded, then looked around the walls, into the corners and up to the rafters. 'I keep feeling as though he's here in the room, do you?' she said.

Fen smiled. 'Maybe he is,' she responded.

Julia smiled too, and turned her gaze to the photograph of her father and Gwen on the table next to her. Then going back to the journal she started to read on.

"'It has taken me almost a week to come to terms with the terrible feelings I have felt towards Alice and George since learning the truth. At first, I wanted nothing more than to take a bloody and bitter revenge for all the years they have stolen from Julia and me, but as the days have passed I've discovered that Gwen's gentling influence on my life and my heart has been as lasting as it was profound, because I now find myself more rational in my thoughts and able to cope. I no longer have much time in this world, so I have chosen to try and forget their treachery, to let go of all feelings of hatred and vengeance, and think only of my girl. Alas, Rene's messenger didn't bring photographs of her, but she brought some of my grandchildren, and to look at them brings indescribable joy to my heart. A girl and a boy. Shannon and Daniel. So beautiful and so handsome. I feel so very proud of them. To think, I am a grandfather. It is the greatest possible source of happiness a man could know. I only wish I could meet them before I go."'

A tear fell onto Julia's cheek as she turned a page. '"25th September,"' she read. '"After days of much soul-searching and painful indecision, I finally found the courage to pick up the phone and call Julia. I longed to hear her voice, to know how she is, to share with her some of the events of these past twenty or more years, but in the end I decided it would be an act of the greatest selfishness to impose a sick and dying father upon her now, so I rang off before she came to the phone. She has her own life to be going on with, as a busy mother and wife, a successful editor, I'm told, with a husband who's very successful too, and apparently loves her very much. I approve of him just for that. I did get to speak to my granddaughter though, and I thank God for that. I'm only sorry I won't hear my grandson, but I've now decided that this is no time for reunions, when the final goodbye is so close. The gift I will give them will be this house, and all the love it has known through my darling Gwen, and perhaps this book, which maybe, one day soon, Julia will read. But of course she won't, because there is too much in it that I would never want her to know, I just like to pretend to myself that it's possible for me to share all this with her, without causing her pain. I will destroy it soon, but for now it is helping me to remember, and allowing me the pleasure of speaking to her almost as though she were here."'

Having to pause to dab away her tears, Julia

glanced at Fen and saw that her eyes were full too. '"29th September,"' she read, after clearing her throat. '"I have felt too weak to write much for a while, but I am sitting here on the bed now, having made it down the stairs, unassisted, to fetch this book. Fen would be very cross with me if she knew, but I'm feeling rather proud of my little triumph. She came to sit with me last night, as she does most nights. I know her heart is troubled over Bob, but she won't talk to me now, the way she used to. It's because I'm sick, I know, but I do my best to soothe her by holding her hand, and I think she appreciates it. In truth, I think it is me who gets the better end of that deal, because I love it when she's here. She tells me about her day, which is always interesting because of the bizarre and barmy people she meets, and I love to see the way her eyes sparkle when she tells me things I probably ought not to hear. It is my dearest wish that she and Julia should become friends. I hope my passing will bring them together, and that they will know as much joy of each other as I have known of them."'

Julia looked at Fen and they both smiled, knowing his wish had come true.

'"4th October,"' Julia read. '"I haven't been at all well this past day or so. Fen says I should move to the bedroom downstairs, and I think she's right. It would make it easier for everyone, including me. What would I do without dear Fen? And her father, who's been like a brother to me. I'm sure he lets me win at backgammon, because he can't really be that bad."'

Both Fen and Julia laughed, and Fen swallowed the lump in her throat.

'"5th October. I've been wondering today about Rene's motive for sending me the truth about Julia when she did, and I fear that she was hoping to stir up my wrath to avenge her own pain. If I am correct, then I will take only the good that has come from it, and leave the rest to her.

'"Tilde is fussing over me like an old mother hen, and I love to hear her. I asked her if she'd care for a dance just now, and the daft old thing started to cry. (She must have a memory of me treading on her toe.) They're moving me downstairs later and I must remember to take this book with me, though I fear I won't be writing much more. My hand is no longer steady, and my eyes are failing. I feel the end drawing close. I lie quietly for long stretches of time that seem only like minutes, but sometimes years. I fill my mind with the memories I have of Julia growing up, all the laughter we shared, the secrets, and the love. I managed to take some of her things when I left, little mementoes that would remind me of her, but they're in the attic now, so I can't get to them. I imagine her with her lovely children, beautiful and happy, and though I know we won't meet again in this world, I believe there will be a lot of time for us in the next."'

Again Julia had to take a pause before she could read on. '"Julia, my Julia,"' she finally managed. '"How happy it makes me to be able to write that and know it is true. Though I doubt you will ever read this, my darling, because later I shall burn it, I want you to know that I never forgot you, even for a minute, and wherever I might be after I leave this world, I shall be watching over you.

Goodnight, now. God bless. Remember to let the angels know if you're in a mess."'

As she finished Julia's voice was thick with tears. 'He used to say that to me when I was a child,' she said, barely able to utter the words. 'Let the angels know when you're in a mess. He said they'd let him know and he'd come to sort it out.'

Fen gave her a while to collect herself, then drying her own eyes, she got up to refill their glasses. 'Let's drink to him, wherever he is now,' she said.

'And to Gwen,' Julia added. 'Let's hope they're together.'

'To Douglas and Gwen,' Fen said, clinking her glass. 'And to us for making one of his dearest wishes come true.'

After they drank, Fen returned to her cushion by the fire and said, 'He must have slipped the book under his bed, and after his stroke he couldn't let any of us know it was there – which means you were meant to have it.'

Julia smiled and nodded.

'Have you read any of it to Josh yet?'

'No, but I will, when he has time to listen. He's pretty busy right now, with work and the children.' Her eyes were drifting off to nowhere. 'I should go back,' she said quietly. 'I mean I will. They need me and I've been away too long.'

'Have you spoken to Shannon?'

'No, but she finally answered one of my texts today to say she was feeling OK about her exams.'

Fen watched her, waiting for her to say more, but she didn't, so in the end Fen said, 'Something else is bothering you, isn't it?'

Julia's eyes came to hers.

'It's all right, you don't have to tell me,' Fen said softly. 'I think I can guess.'

The next few days seemed to pass in a blur as Julia finished clearing the attic, spoke to the police on the phone, and made a trip into Bodmin with Fen. They ordered a new bed, then wandered down the high street to have lunch at one of the trendy cafés, where they talked long into the afternoon. There was much to discuss, but even the support of such a good friend wasn't helping to ease the new and devastating fear that Julia had building inside. For now though, she kept putting it aside, focusing her mind on the present, and not daring to think beyond it.

She spoke to Josh several times a day, even when neither of them had much to say. It seemed they both felt the need to hear the other, and though he was trying very hard not to press her about coming home, she knew her failure to set a date was concerning and confusing him.

'Would you like me to come and get you?' he offered after five days had gone by.

'No, it's fine. I can do the drive. I'll just hang on here until the new bed is delivered, then I'll be on my way back.'

'When will that be?'

'They said the day after tomorrow.'

He knew very well that Fen or one of her family would oversee the delivery if asked, but he didn't put it to her, and she didn't mention it either. Instead, because it was very early in the morning, and no-one else was up yet, she read him the last entries in her father's journal.

'Of course we'll keep the house now,' he said when she'd finished. 'I'll speak to the probate officer, and get a final bill.'

'Thank you,' she whispered.

After a pause, he said, 'Do you want to live there? Is that what this is about?'

'No, I want to live with you, and you have to be in London. We can have this place for holidays and weekends.'

'Then I don't understand what's happening,' he confessed. 'If you need more space, if you'd rather I stopped calling for a while . . .'

'No, please don't do that. I'm sorry, everything will be fine, I promise. I'll be home by the weekend.'

After ringing off she turned away from the phone and gazed out at the first glimmers of dawn. Rather than think of her promise, she imagined them all spending Christmas here, and how wonderful it would be. She was sure they'd want to, so maybe she'd bring it up the next time they spoke.

Later in the day she returned from the supermarket to find a message on the machine from Rico. It was the first time he'd called for almost three weeks, and hearing his voice turned her so hot inside that she almost felt faint.

'I have all my land in Italy,' he'd told her. 'It is my father's now, but one day it can be ours. You will be so happy here . . .'

She was picturing him in Tuscany, living the kind of life so many English women dreamt of, but it wasn't for her. There was only one life she wanted, and she was going back to it any day now.

She sat down at the table and buried her head in her arms. She must have drifted off for a while, because the sound of the phone ringing seemed to startle her. Realising it was probably Dan, having just come out of school, she forced herself to her feet to go and answer.

'Julia? How are you dear? Now, I've found Shallard's Cross on the map, but you'll have to give me directions to the house. I have a pen handy, but speak slowly and clearly so I can make sure I get it right. I wouldn't want to end up lost now, would I?'

Julia stared at the phone, and felt a terrible sense of foreboding coming over her. 'Rene, you can't come here,' she said. 'You must never come here.'

'Now, don't be silly dear. We've got to plan tactics, and we should do it together. So come along, my pen's at the ready.'

'What do you mean, tactics?'

'You know what I mean, so come along now, there's not a lot of time. They'll be here any minute.'

'Who will? Where are you?'

'At home, in Deakins. Where do you think?'

Julia's mind was spinning.

'This will be my house soon,' Rene ranted on, 'and I intend to will it to you when I go. I thought you'd like that. You deserve it dear, after what you've been through. As do I. After all, I'm the one who's been living with them all these years. Of course, I don't have anything to do with them now. I keep myself to myself, up in my room. You really should have shot them when you had the chance, you know. Now, we'll have to work it out all over again. It shouldn't be difficult, because they'll do anything to safeguard their nasty little secret . . .'

'Rene, I don't want to have this conversation,' Julia cut in. 'You're out of my life now, all of you . . .'

'But I'm the one who gave your father the photos,' she cried. 'I wrote the letter telling him you were his, and how they'd lied. They were lovers even before George and I were married, you know, but I didn't mind, because I didn't want him doing those things to me.'

'Rene, I . . .'

'After Pam was born they swore to give each other up,' she pressed on. 'Of course, they knew what they were doing was wrong. How could they not? So Alice married your father, and for a while I think they were happy. You know, it really is a pity Douglas didn't come and finish them off himself when he found out the truth. I thought he would. Still, things don't always work out the way we want them to, do they? I'd kill them myself, but I don't think I could stand to be in prison. So you should be the one to do it, dear. You cope with things so much better than I ever could, and considering the circumstances, I don't think your sentence would be long . . .'

Having no doubt at all that Rene had completely lost her mind, Julia said, 'I have to ring off now. Please don't call here again.'

After putting the phone down she immediately rang Josh. 'She's clearly lost it,' she said, after relating the call, 'but I can't speak to my mother or George myself . . .'

'Don't worry, I'll do it. Did she say where she is now?'

'At the house, in her room, apparently.'

'All right. I'll call them right away and get back to you.'

When the phone rang a few minutes later she was still standing next to it.

'I spoke to George,' he told her. 'Apparently Rene's locked in her room, and can't get out.'

'They've got her locked up? Well, maybe it's for the best. Did you tell him about the call?'

'Yes. He admitted she's come unhinged, and that she probably needs to go into psychiatric care, but for the moment, they're keeping her there.'

'Because they're afraid of what she'll reveal. Dear God, how many victims are there going to be? Everyone seems to suffer, but them.'

'I'm not going to get into defending them,' he responded, 'but it's clearly not only what she can reveal that they're afraid of, because he told me they've got rid of all the guns now, and she isn't allowed near knives, even to eat.'

'Oh Christ,' Julia murmured. 'Well, they've got no more than they deserve.'

'I won't argue with that, but I'm not sure I like the idea of you being down there alone now. If she does manage to get out, you're pretty remote. Even the Bowers aren't close enough to hear if you get into trouble.'

'I know,' she said, feeling an icy chill run down her spine.

'So will you come home now?' he asked.

'Yes. Yes, I will. I'll ask Tilde to oversee the

delivery of the bed, then I'll call tomorrow when I'm on my way.'

As Josh put the phone down to Julia he turned to find his mother glowering at him across the kitchen.

'So what did she say this time?' she demanded, wrenching open the dishwasher and starting to unload.

'She's coming tomorrow,' he answered.

'Hah, and you believe her? How many times has she . . .'

'Leave it, Mother.'

'I'm just pointing out . . .'

'I know what you're doing, and I don't need it, OK? She's been through a difficult time lately . . .'

'We all go through difficult times, Joshua, but our husbands and children generally come first. So I have to ask myself, just what kind of wife and mother is she, hiding herself away down there in Cornwall, like some injured rabbit? You pamper her, Josh. You let her get away with too much. I'm sorry, but she never was good enough for you, and now all this disgusting business with her family . . .'

'It's hardly her fault,' he shot back.

'She's still one of them though.'

'She's one of this family too, and frankly, I don't appreciate you talking about her like this.'

'Well pardon me for speaking my mind,' she retorted, and pursing her lips she grabbed a tea towel to start polishing the glasses.

Rolling his eyes, he was about to return to his study when she said, 'If you ask me, she's got her fancy man down there, that's why she's not coming back.'

Josh's face was pale as he turned round to glare at her, but though he'd have liked nothing better than to really let rip, they were still far too dependent on her for him to fall out with her now. 'That's got nothing to do with it,' he growled.

'So you say, but she keeps putting you off, and if it isn't him, then what is it, I'd like to know?'

'Why are you being so hard on her?' he demanded. 'You know damned well it was my own affair that pushed her . . .'

'I don't want to go into that,' Emma snapped. 'If she'd been a proper wife to you, you'd never have . . .'

'Don't make excuses for me,' he seethed. 'I've been down that road, and it doesn't change the fact that I'm responsible for what's happened . . .'

'Whatever you did, Joshua, it wasn't done in front of your children, and nor have you left them.'

'She hasn't left them.'

'Then where is she? Tell me that.'

'You know very well . . .'

'I'll tell you where she is. She's hiding, because she's too ashamed to face her own daughter, and she should feel ashamed. But once again she's left you to deal with it all, and look at you, you're exhausted, all this worrying about her, and the children, and all those clients you have. You need her support, not her problems.'

'Mother, everyone has problems sometimes, and we just have to deal with them. Julia's doing it her way, I'm doing it mine, and I'm sorry, but you're really not helping . . .'

'Well, that's rich, isn't it, when I'm working my fingers to the bone, taking care of those children – not that I'm complaining, they're my grandchildren after all . . .'

'I wasn't talking about what you're doing in the house, I was meaning the way you're criticising Julia. She's my wife, and I happen to love her, so please, let's drop the subject, and tell me what I can do to help with the dinner.'

'I've got it all under control, thank you very much, but before you vanish back into your study, I think Dan would probably welcome a little of your time.'

'Where is he?'

'In his room.'

'And Shannon?'

'In hers. I don't know why they have to hide themselves away up there all the time. A big house like this, and they hardly venture out of their bedrooms. It's what comes of letting them have their own TVs and computers. Spoiled they are. And selfish. They must get it from their mother, because you were never like that.'

And I don't remember you ever being like this, he was thinking as he took himself off upstairs. However, he shouldn't be too hard on her, because she wasn't getting any younger, and a teenager with erratic hormones, an eleven-year-old with an unpredictable affliction, a son who was moody, unco-operative and working long hours, and a large house to look after, all added up to far too much for her to handle. He just wished she wouldn't come down so heavily on Julia, though something he'd learned over the years was that women were much tougher on each other than they ever were on their men. He could even see it in Shannon, who'd been much less willing to forgive her mother than he suspected she would be to forgive him. However, she was certainly showing signs of relenting now, even though she wasn't coming right out and admitting it, but she didn't have to. He knew how close she was to her mother, and as much as he knew she loved him, he was under no illusion that he could ever fill Julia's place.

Finding Dan engrossed in *The Simpsons*, he sat and watched it with him for a while, until realising Dan was hardly even aware he was there, he left him to it and went to check on Shannon. For once there was no music or TV blaring from her room, so there was no problem about her hearing when he knocked.

'Who is it?' she called out.

'Me. Can I come in?'

She didn't answer, so taking it as permission, he opened the door to find her lying on her bed, flicking through a magazine.

'No homework?' he asked, going to sit next to her.

'Yeah, I'll finish it in a minute. I just needed a break.'

The nasal sound of her voice was enough to tell him she'd been crying, and a tilt down of the magazine to reveal her face confirmed it.

'Want a cuddle?' he offered.

She nodded, and scooted along the bed for him to lie down next to her.

'So what's upset you?' he asked, as she put her head on his shoulder.

'Nothing.'

He let it ride, knowing she didn't like to be pushed.

When finally she spoke again her voice was mangled by tears. 'I heard what Grandma said about Mum,' she said. 'Is it my fault she won't come home? I mean, because I saw . . .'

'Sssh,' he said, cutting her off. 'No, it is not your fault, so don't think that for another minute, OK? Grandma doesn't know the half of it, and Mum's had some difficult issues to deal with lately.'

'But Grandma said she's down there with Rico, and I thought you said he wasn't there any more. Is she going to leave us, Dad?'

'No, no,' he soothed, wishing he felt as confident as he sounded, but even he was starting to question what was really happening down there now.

'I want her to come home.'

'I know, darling, and she will. She said she'll come tomorrow.'

'But she keeps saying that. So why doesn't she?'

He sighed and hugged her closer. 'This isn't an easy time for her,' he said gently, 'so we need to be patient.'

Dan's voice sounded from outside the door. 'Shannon! Can I come in?'

'Only if you say the magic word,' she called back.

'Shannonisverybeautiful,' he responded.

Josh laughed, which made Shannon splutter with laughter too.

'Can I come in now?' he shouted.

'All right.'

'Oh Dad!' he cried joyously, and diving straight onto the bed, he snuggled in under Josh's other arm.

For a while they heard all about *The Simpsons* and even managed to get caught up in it, until finally Shannon said, 'Maybe we need to go down there and get her, Dad.'

'You mean, get Mum?' Dan said, leaping right in on it. 'Yes, Dad, let's go and get Mum. *Please*. We can go tomorrow.'

Josh smiled. 'You've got school tomorrow, but I'll tell you what, if she's not home by the weekend, we'll definitely go and get her. Is that a deal?'

'Deal,' they echoed, and began a ludicrously clumsy process of high fives to seal it.

The following morning Julia was sitting on the edge of the bath, her head resting on the sink and buried in her arms as though to shield herself from the world outside. The phone rang in the kitchen, but she didn't get up to answer. Tilde came over, and called out, but still she didn't respond. She merely sat where she was, knowing she couldn't get up yet, because nothing in her was able to move. She needed time to adjust to the fact that there was no God, no angels, no father to make everything all right again, there was no anything, because she'd prayed and prayed and prayed, and now she knew for certain that no-one had been listening. The thin blue line had confirmed it. She was carrying Rico's child, and of all the things Josh could live with, or forgive, she knew with absolute certainty that this would never be one of them.

Chapter Twenty-One

Fen's expression was grim as she got out of her car and walked up the steps to the mill house. Having come straight from a morning in court she was wearing a dark suit under a warm sheepskin coat and knee-length leather boots, though from the look of the sky she was likely to need waterproofs later. As usual they were on the back seat of the car, which was where she'd left her briefcase and mobile phone too. She wasn't going to need either for the next half an hour, which, unfortunately, was all she could spare.

Letting herself into the kitchen she found Julia sitting at the table, a look of near defeat on her face. After closing the door Fen took off her coat and boots, and went to sit down. The phone started to ring, but Julia let the call go through to the machine, and whoever it was didn't leave a message.

'You're absolutely certain?' Fen said, having received the one-word text – Positive – as she'd come out of court.

Julia nodded. 'You can see the test if you like. Both of them, because I did it twice. There's no room for doubt.'

Fen didn't query it any further, and since they'd spent the best part of the last few evenings discussing what Julia should do if the test did prove positive, all she could say now was, 'Are you any closer to making a decision?'

Julia shook her head, and stared down at her hands. 'For some reason, it seems harder now I know for certain,' she said.

Fen's eyes filled with sympathy as she looked at her.

'It's not that I'm particularly anti-abortion,' Julia went on, 'it just doesn't feel right in this case. I mean, it's not the baby's fault, is it? And it's not as though I'm unable to give it a life.'

'Are you really so sure that Josh won't accept it? I mean, once he gets used to the idea . . .'

Julia sighed and covered her face with her hands. 'It'll just get worse,' she said. 'No, I wouldn't even want to ask him.'

Fen watched her as she got up and went to stare out of the French doors at the woods.

'It's as though the Fates are conspiring to end my marriage,' she said bleakly. 'We just seem to lurch from one crisis to the next, to the next. Well, I guess victory is theirs now. I can't beat this one.'

'You've come through a lot, and it hasn't changed the way you feel about each other,' Fen pointed out.

'This will,' Julia responded, then sighed again as she hugged her arms in close. 'I just don't know what to do. It'll mean losing Josh if I keep it . . .'

'Shouldn't you at least discuss it with him, give him the chance to speak for himself?'

'I've been married to him for a long time, I know this isn't something he can live with.'

'Well, you obviously don't want to end your marriage.'

'Of course not, but is it fair to end an innocent baby's life because of my mistake?'

'It's not the only child you have to consider,' Fen gently reminded her.

Tears immediately burned in Julia's eyes as she thought of Shannon and what this pregnancy was likely to do to her, for she'd find it no easier to live with than Josh would. Only Dan was likely to be delighted by the prospect of a new brother or sister, until he found out Josh wasn't the father, and his mother wouldn't be coming home because of it. The effect on him could be disastrous, and heaven only knew what would happen about custody if she and Josh split up . . .

'I can't take Shannon and Dan away from Josh,' she said quietly, 'and I don't want to be without them either.' The very idea of it stole through her so painfully that she couldn't continue.

'So would it be fair to sacrifice their happiness, and your own, for one little individual that's barely even human yet?' Fen said.

It was a question Julia had asked herself a thousand times these past few days, but she was still unable to answer it. 'Maybe it's because I'm a mother already that I can't bring myself to go through with it,' she said. 'If I'd been raped, or I knew there was something wrong with it, it might be different, but to do it to make my life easier . . .'

'But it's not just your life, is it? You have to consider Shannon and Dan, and Josh of course. They need you, and they're here. That has to be paramount.'

Having no words to argue that, Julia took a deep, shuddering breath and felt her heart fill with pain and love. 'So you're saying I should have a termination,' she said eventually.

Fen shook her head. 'The decision has to be yours, I'm just pointing out what you know already, and trying to help you get there.'

Julia nodded. Then turning to her, she said, 'What about Rico? He's your cousin, are you feeling he should have some say in this?'

'Maybe he should, I don't know,' Fen responded. 'Again the decision has to be yours. I won't be the one to tell him.' Then after a pause, 'But if you do decide to keep it, I'm sure he'll want to play a part. You know how he feels about you . . .'

Julia looked away, as though to shut out the images of herself in Tuscany with Rico and their child. It wasn't what she wanted, not even for a minute. All she wanted was Josh and her children.

In the end she walked back to the table. 'Tell me honestly,' she said as she sat down, 'if you were in my position, what would you do?'

Fen lowered her eyes as she shook her head. 'I think I would find it as difficult as you do,' she answered truthfully, 'but what you have with Josh is very special. I'd give almost anything to be loved that much, so I guess my answer to your question is, in your position, I'd put my marriage and my children first. But that's easy to say from this side of the table, and I don't want to talk you into something you don't feel is right.'

Wishing she knew what she felt, Julia merely looked down at her hands.

Fen glanced at her watch. 'I'm sorry, but I have to get back to the office,' she said. 'We can talk again tonight, if you like.'

'I've taken up so much of your time already.'

'It's one of the blessings about having your children in school all week and your husband working all hours,' Fen replied, going to put on her coat, 'you have plenty of evenings to yourself.' After tugging on her boots she straightened up and said, 'I'll bring something decadent home, shall I, like fish and chips or pizza?' Then seeing Julia's expression, she smiled. 'No appetite?'

Julia shook her head.

'That'll probably change once the cravings kick in.'

Not even wanting to think that far ahead, Julia got up to see her out.

'Listen,' Fen said, before opening the door, 'why don't you make an appointment to see a doctor? You won't have to commit to anything, it'll just be for a chat, so he can tell you what a termination actually involves. Maybe then, you'll be in a better position to decide.'

'You could be right,' Julia agreed. 'Do you know anyone?'

'Around here I know everyone, and there's an excellent private clinic just outside Truro. I'm on first-name terms with a couple of the doctors there, so I'll make the appointment for you, if you like. I'll even come with you, but I won't be free now until Saturday morning. Can you wait that long?'

'For something like this I could wait for ever,' Julia responded dryly, 'but a day and a half's fine.'

'Will you tell Josh?'

Julia's heart turned over. 'I don't know what I'll tell Josh,' she answered. 'I just know I've never been good at keeping secrets from him.'

'Well, to quote your own father,' Fen said, hugging her, 'sometimes secrets are best left untold.'

After she'd gone Julia went to check the messages on the machine, even though she knew there were none. A quick dial of 1471 told her that the last caller hadn't been Josh, but he'd let her know this morning, before she'd done the test, that he might not have time to speak again until this evening.

She picked up her mobile to check that for messages too, but though there was nothing new, there was still the text that had come from Shannon earlier saying good morning. That had been quite a breakthrough, since it was the first unprompted communication she'd made in weeks.

Since it was still not quite two o'clock, and Josh hadn't mentioned meeting anyone for lunch, she took a chance that he might be working through, and dialled his direct number. She wasn't sure what she intended to say, she simply felt the need to hear his voice.

'Hi darling,' he said, when he heard hers. 'You beat me to it. I was just about to ring you. Vanessa Keyes left a message earlier, wanting to know if we're going to take tickets for the Christmas ball this year.'

Julia's heart started a dull, horrible thud. 'Do you want to?' she asked.

'We usually do,' he replied, 'but if you'd rather not . . .'

'No, it's not that. Did she mention anything about dinner next week?'

'Yes, actually, she did. I said we were still up for it, but . . .'

'I think we should cancel,' she said, and tensed in readiness for his explosion.

But it didn't come. Instead he said, 'Julia, please tell me what's going on. Is he there with you? Is that what this is about?'

'No!' she cried. 'He's not in my life any more.' Then realising that wasn't strictly true, she said, 'I don't want him, I want you.'

'Then why are you still there? You're hiding something from me, that much is clear, so for God's sake tell me what it is.'

'I can't, Josh. I'm sorry, I just can't.'

'Julia, I'm going out of my mind here. You can't keep doing this. I have to know what's happening . . .'

'Nothing's happening. I swear it.'

'Then why won't you come back?'

'Because . . .' Her breath caught on a sob. 'I'm sorry, I don't know how to tell you this . . .'

'Just say it!'

She took a breath and closed her eyes tightly, as though somehow that would hold the devastation back from the words. It was impossible though, and she knew it, so in the end, unable to put him through any more confusion and doubt, whilst aware she was about to push him into a far worse hell, she braced herself and said, 'I'm pregnant, Josh. I'm going to have a baby.'

The silence that followed was more excruciating than anything she'd ever known in her life. She could see him sitting at his desk, taking almost no time to figure out that the baby couldn't be his, then reeling from all the implications that would come crowding in on him. She could hardly bear to think of his pain, or to know what was going through his mind, yet she would almost welcome his anger, anything rather than this awful, terrible, silence. But it stretched on and on, until eventually she realised he'd hung up.

After putting the phone down Josh continued to sit at his desk. The echo of her words was still there, along with the reality of their meaning, but he was holding it all at a distance, afraid to let it in, for fear of what he might do once he did.

He got up and walked to the window, and as he gazed down into the street he found himself imagining scenarios he'd never dreamt himself capable of, for he'd never been a violent man, but the thought of the Italian's child inside his wife . . . He recoiled from the horror of it, then hearing Marina returning from lunch, he picked up his coat and left, with no idea of where he was going. He only knew that he couldn't carry on with this day as though his entire future hadn't just been blown apart.

Once in the car he headed for the Cromwell Road, and for one wild moment he considered following it out to the M4, then the M5 and all the way down to Cornwall. But what would he do when he got there? He could change nothing, and for now it was best that he didn't see her.

As he pulled up in Abbotsbury Road, alongside Holland Park, his mobile started to ring. Seeing it was her, he turned the phone off and stepped out of the car.

The park was almost deserted, just a few hardy dog-walkers, and a couple of mothers trundling pushchairs along the leaf-strewn paths. He walked around the Orangerie, then in through the arcades with their Victorian picnic frescoes, and on to the pond where he sat down on a bench and welcomed the bite of the wind, as though its icy edge might anaesthetise what was going on inside him.

For a long time he merely stared through the glistening cascades of a fountain to the grand windows of the Belvedere restaurant, where they'd celebrated several anniversaries over the years. He hadn't proposed to her there, he'd done that one hot summer's night at The Gate cinema in Notting Hill, during *The Year of Living Dangerously*.

'Would you fancy doing that with only me for the rest of your life?' he'd whispered as Mel Gibson got it on with Sigourney Weaver in the back of a car.

'Yes,' she'd whispered back without missing a beat.

A few minutes later, after the crucial moment was over, they'd annoyed everyone by getting up and creeping along the row, until she began telling people that he'd just proposed and she'd accepted. They'd left a lot of smiling faces behind them that night, but the one he would always remember was hers, as he'd made love to her later, under the stars in this very park.

Now he wondered if he'd ever make love to her again. The idea that he might not folded around his insides as though to close him down altogether. He tried to focus his thoughts elsewhere, but there was nowhere else, only her and their children, everything in the world that mattered to him. He found himself remembering her when she was carrying Shannon and Dan, the womanly swell of her and how he'd never been able to get enough of looking at her. He recalled the many times he'd found her asleep while feeding them, and the love and pride he'd felt while standing watching her, almost unable to believe that this beautiful woman and delicate little child were really his.

Unlike so many men he'd never felt pushed out by his children, probably because she hadn't allowed it to happen, nor had he ever been bored or irritated by family demands. They were the very centre of his life, what gave it meaning and purpose; though of course, he and Julia had had their difficulties and challenges, and the fury with which they sometimes fought could occasionally even outdo the passion with which they made love. Thinking now of how deeply sensual and erotic their intimate life had always been, how demanding, and completely fulfilling, made it hard to understand how they'd come to this. Yet he knew very well that had he not turned to Sylvia, it was very unlikely Julia would be carrying another man's child.

So much pain and jealousy was churning inside him, and fear, and more urges to violence. He'd always considered her body exclusively his, never to be touched by anyone but him, as his was for her. It was hard to accept how badly they'd let each other down, but he was to blame. None of it would have happened had he not yielded to Sylvia's suggestion, convincing himself that it would do no harm. Well, he was paying for it now, with a price so bitter that he could only wonder what his life would be worth after she'd taken the children and gone to her Italian, which was presumably what she'd do once their marriage was over.

Of course, he wouldn't let her take Shannon and Dan, nor would Shannon be willing to go once she knew the truth, though the thought gave him no comfort at all, for the last thing he wanted was to tear her and Julia apart. As mother and daughter they belonged together. As a family they all did, and it was his role, his duty to see that they stayed that way. It was what he wanted more than anything, but he only had to think of her getting bigger and bigger as the months passed, filling out with a child that wasn't his, to know he couldn't do it. Maybe some men could, but he wasn't one of them. Even looking at her would be hard, while living every day with the truth, lying next to her in bed each night, sometimes attempting to make love to her as though everything was normal, would be virtually impossible. And once the child was born, he could no more imagine himself taking care of it as his own than he could accept the idea of its father ever coming to visit. He didn't have it in him to be that kind of man, nor was he going to pretend he did.

So the only answer, if she wanted to save their marriage, was for her to get rid of the child now, but she'd know that already, and though he might desperately want to demand it, he knew he had no rights here. And even if he did try to force her, what then? They'd no doubt end up with the hideous situation of her never being able to forgive him, so what kind of marriage would that leave them with?

In the end, needing to escape this nightmare pattern of thoughts, he got to his feet and started back to the car. His limbs were stiff with cold, his insides tense with suppressed emotion, but as he walked he barely noticed his discomfort. All he knew was the mounting despondency inside him, for whichever way he looked at it, whether she kept the baby or not, he could see virtually no chance of them making it now.

There were several messages on his mobile when he got back to the car, mostly from Marina, but none from Julia, which disappointed him, though he was still far from ready to talk. He wondered what she was doing now, and how she was. Clearly she wouldn't be in a happy frame of mind, for no matter how strong her feelings might be for the Italian, nothing would ever convince him they were stronger than those for Shannon and Dan.

By eight o'clock that evening he still hadn't spoken to her, nor was he any keener to do so. He merely returned home from work, so worn out by the constant fight with his emotions that it was all he could do to pour himself a drink and not snap his mother's head off when she complained that dinner would be spoiled if they didn't all sit down right away. The last thing he wanted was to eat, but he could feel the children's eyes on him, and knew they were sensing his mood. Somehow he forced himself to join in their chat, and even managed to ask a few questions about their day, but it didn't take long for silence to fall. He was hardly even aware of it until the telephone rang, and Dan leapt up, shouting, 'It'll probably be Mum.'

Josh ate some food then, and kept his eyes on the muted TV screen up on the wall. He knew Shannon was watching him, so he winked at her, and tried to eat some more.

'Shannon, it's Gilly,' Dan said. 'She wants to know if you're still going shopping on Saturday, because if you are ...'

'No, I'm not,' Shannon snapped.

Dan said into the phone, 'No, she's not,' and hung up.

'Not going shopping?' Emma clucked, helping herself to more beans. 'Doesn't sound like you, Shannon.'

'We're going to Cornwall,' Shannon stated, looking straight at her father.

Josh glanced at his mother, then at Dan, who was watching him too.

'Dad, you said!' Shannon cried, obviously sensing a change of plan. 'We all agreed, didn't we Dan? You were there.'

'Yes, I was there,' Dan confirmed.

'OK, OK,' Josh said. There was still Friday to get through yet, so time to think up an excuse not to go, and if Julia was intending to come back here, well, maybe she'd like to think again, because now the initial shock was wearing off, a very deep, and very dangerous anger was starting to set in. In fact, just to make sure she was in no doubt of the way he was feeling, the instant he could snatch a few moments alone he sent her a text saying, `unless you do the right thing, consider our marriage dead.`

So much dread was building inside Julia, as Fen pulled off the main road and drove up to the front of the clinic, that she was very close to saying they should turn back. It was only the reminder that nothing was going to happen today, that it was merely a consultation, so there was really no reason to be this uptight, that stopped her. She just needed to get out of the car and make herself walk up to the front of this long white building, surrounded by carefully tended flower beds, which appeared as benign as the gently sloping hills fanning out behind it. It had an air about it that made it seem almost inviting, though there was not a single part of her that walked willingly up to the revolving front doors, or that entered a reception that was so elegantly furnished it could almost have been fronting a five-star hotel.

'Are you OK?' Fen asked, after she'd given her name to the receptionist.

Julia nodded, though she knew that the strain must show in her face, as it did in the tightness of the hand that was clutching her mobile phone. She'd erased the text from Josh just after it had arrived, but it was still upsetting her, even though she understood his anger. She kept hoping he'd call or text again, but there had been no more communication between them since that message, and she wasn't even sure what she wanted him to say.

'You'll like Edmund,' Fen told her as they settled into a pair of wing chairs. 'He's a lovely man and an excellent doctor. I handled his divorce, so I got to know him reasonably well, and I can tell you, anyone who'd put up for more than twenty years with the shrew of a wife he was detaching from is a saint indeed.'

Julia smiled weakly, then tensed even harder as a bolt of nerves came out of nowhere to turn her stomach inside out. She couldn't go through with this, she just couldn't. She took a breath and was about to get up, when she reminded herself again that she wasn't here to make a final decision. The relief that followed was so profound that had she been thinking straight she'd probably have conceded, right then, that she was going to keep the baby.

'Fen, how lovely to see you. How are you?'

Julia looked up as Fen rose to her feet to greet a short, stocky man with springy grey hair, half-moon specs and a smile so warm and sincere that there was no mistaking his affection for his feisty lawyer.

'I'm very well, Edmund,' she said, taking his hand between both of hers. 'Thank you for slotting us in at such short notice. I know how in demand you are.'

'But always available for you, you know that,' he twinkled.

Fen blushed and laughed, then turned to introduce Julia.

'How do you do?' Julia said, her mouth so dry and her throat so tight it was hard to get the words out.

His eyes seemed to close in on hers a little, as though guessing how she was feeling, and in a tone that made her relax a little, he said, 'I understand we're just going to have a chat today.'

Julia nodded.

'Excellent.' He smiled. 'Would you like to come along through?'

After glancing at Fen, who gave her hand a reassuring squeeze, she followed him along a plushly carpeted hallway towards a spiral staircase that created an intriguing centrepiece for a large picture window behind it. However, she barely noticed it, she was too busy imagining how she'd feel if it were all actually about to happen, if she were on her way to an anaesthetic right now, but strangely, unlike a few minutes ago, nothing seemed to be registering. She switched her mind to another scene which saw her leaving here, no longer pregnant, but she wasn't clear how she'd feel about that either. She thought of Josh, Shannon, Dan, Rico, then Josh again. She wished he was here, but of course it was madness to think he ever would be.

'Here we are,' Dr Harris said, pushing open a door that bore his name on a shiny chrome plaque. 'Can I ask the nurse to bring you a coffee?'

'No, I'm fine thanks,' she responded.

'Then why don't we make ourselves comfortable over here?' he said, steering her away from his desk towards a pair of two-seater sofas.

She sat down stiffly, then realising she was still

clutching her phone, as though it were some kind of lifeline to Josh, she quickly turned it off and popped it in her bag.

'So,' he said, sitting down too, 'it would seem that we have a surprise pregnancy.'

Appreciating the euphemism, she attempted to sound droll as she said, 'That's certainly one way of putting it.'

His eyes twinkled, but then he was serious again. 'And you're considering a termination?'

'Just considering. I haven't made a decision yet.'

He nodded. 'Well, before we go any further, are you aware of the medical and legal guidelines covering a termination?'

'I think so,' she answered. 'It has to be signed off by two doctors, and it can't be carried out after twenty-four weeks.'

'That's correct, but there are other criteria that have to be taken into consideration, such as the reason for the termination.'

She tried to swallow, but her throat had turned dry again.

'Would I be correct in assuming that the baby isn't your husband's?' he prompted gently.

She nodded, and wished the world would just swallow her up for how bad that made her feel.

'And it will cause problems for your marriage if you keep it?'

'Yes,' she said, in barely more than a whisper.

He fixed her with his kind eyes and said, 'So how far along do you estimate yourself to be?'

'Five to six weeks.'

'Then you've still some time to make a decision. Would it help for me to talk you through the procedure, what actually happens, how long it would take, the type of anaesthetic we recommend?'

She took a breath but no words came out.

He smiled. 'OK. Tell me, have you spoken to your GP yet? Has he examined you at all?'

'No. He's in London. I – uh ... I used one of the tests from a pharmacy. Do you think there's a chance it could be wrong?'

His expression was regretful. 'Unlikely, I'm afraid,' he said. 'Have you had any symptoms?'

'Some nausea. Tiredness, but I've been going through a difficult time lately. My father died, and things haven't been great with my husband ...' Realising she was trying to talk herself out of her condition, she stopped and let her eyes fall away.

He started to get up. 'Maybe we should take a look at you,' he said. 'If you've been a little run-down anyway, and grieving, it could affect your periods. Do you know the date of your last one?'

'Not exactly, but it was about two months ago, I think.' Meaning that she'd have been ovulating at the time she was with Rico, and now she could hardly believe she hadn't given it a moment's thought. What the hell was the matter with her, just how blind and selfish could she be?

'The examination room's through there,' he said, pointing at a door behind his desk. 'If you want to pop in and get undressed, you'll find a very glamorous paper gown on the end of the bed, all fresh and exclusively yours, and I'll ask the nurse to come and join us.'

A few minutes later Julia was lying on a lightly padded examination couch, feeling so tense and anxious again that she dreaded the very thought of anything probing inside her. Not even Edmund Harris's avuncular manner was helping her to relax now, or the nurse who'd given her a big, friendly smile when she'd come into the room. Now the nurse was standing the other side of the couch, watching the doctor as he sat down on a wheeled stool and started to press his fingers gently over Julia's abdomen.

'Mmm,' he said in a doctorly way. He frowned, pressed again and said, 'I see.'

Julia looked at him, waiting for him to tell her what he saw, but he merely turned away, and scooted his stool a few inches towards the scanner. 'I think we'll forgo the pelvic exam,' he said, busying himself with the controls. 'I expect you'll be happy to hear that, not many women enjoy the speculum.'

Julia glanced at the nurse.

'The cold, unforgiving metal thing,' the nurse explained, reaching across to take something from the doctor.

Julia watched as the nurse coated her belly in a thick, cold gel.

'OK,' Edmund Harris said when she'd finished. 'We're going to carry out an ultrasound, which, as you probably know, won't hurt a bit.'

Nevertheless, Julia braced herself and turned away, for she knew, if she were to take just one look at the image of her unborn child, she'd never be able to destroy it.

The roller was smooth on her skin, sliding over the gel and almost skidding off the other side. She was aware of both the doctor and nurse watching the screen, and felt so wretched about refusing to look that she almost started to cry.

Edmund Harris glanced up at the nurse, then back to the screen. 'Mmm,' he said again.

Julia was starting to feel alarmed. 'Is it all right?' she asked, still trying not to look.

'Oh yes, it's all right,' he replied. 'Very healthy I would say, but I have to tell you, Mrs Thayne, you're much further along than five or six weeks. In fact, the baby I'm seeing here is much closer to fifteen.'

Julia turned to look at him, then at the screen. 'But it can't be,' she protested. 'It's just not possible. My husband and I ... We haven't ...' Tears were welling up in her eyes and strangling her voice. There had to be a mistake, something was wrong ...

'The size and weight leave no room for doubt,' Edmund Harris told her. 'It's still within the legal limit of course, but ...'

'No! I can't have a termination,' she cried.

There was no surprise in Harris's tone as he said, 'I rather thought that might change the picture.'

'If I'm fifteen weeks,' she said, still unable to take it in, 'then I ...' A wave of emotion stole her voice. 'I know it's possible to get pregnant without a man reaching climax,' she finally managed, 'but it never ... I just assumed ...' She couldn't go on, because if this baby was Josh's it changed everything, and she was crying too hard now to speak anyway.

The nurse passed her a Kleenex, while Harris pressed a button to print out an image of the foetus.

'I can't tell you,' Julia gasped, wiping her eyes, 'how happy this makes me. Thank you. Thank you so much.'

Harris laughed. 'I think you managed it without me,' he said dryly.

Julia desperately wanted to hug him, but knew it wouldn't be appropriate, so somehow managed not to. The nurse helped her to sit up, and as she swung her legs off the couch she put her hands over her belly and felt so much love and relief welling up in her that she almost started to cry again. Why hadn't she realised sooner? How could she not have known? Fifteen weeks was a long time, but she'd assumed her stomach was filling out because she was eating so much – and then she'd lost weight, but her stomach hadn't gone down, so she should have known. She'd had a period though, she was certain of it, however, it was hard to remember now, so much had happened, so maybe she hadn't. All she knew was that she'd had her coil removed back in May because it was giving her problems, and with the way things were, they hadn't needed the protection. But what did any of it matter now? The fact was, her pregnancy was fifteen weeks along, and even though she and Josh hadn't planned any more, considering the circumstances this little one surely had to be more welcome than the other two put together, and God knew they'd been wanted . . .

Chapter Twenty-Two

'I still don't know how to break it to him,' Julia was saying half an hour later as Fen drove them around the horse chestnut and over the cattle grid. 'Maybe I should go straight back to London. Or should I call him? I'd rather do it face to face, but I can't bear the idea of him going through this for a minute longer.'

Fen was smiling as she speeded up again to proceed down the drive.

'Oh God,' Julia groaned as a shudder of nerves chased through her. 'I hope he's going to be pleased. I mean, he's bound to be, isn't he? This should make everything all right again. Yes, of course it will. What am I so worried about? We might not actually have planned another baby, but it's here now, and once we get used to the idea . . . I think the children will be thrilled. Well, Dan will. I'm not sure about Shannon. Teenagers can be a bit strange about their mothers getting pregnant, can't they? We're not supposed to have sex.'

Fen's eyebrows arched. 'If you'll forgive me for saying, I don't think Shannon . . .'

'Oh God, don't say it!' Julia put her hands over her face. 'I want to forget that ever happened.'

'I imagine she does too, and frankly, Mummy pregnant with Daddy's baby will probably help, because it'll mean Mummy's been playing on her home ground, where she belongs. Much easier to deal with.'

Julia looked down at the black and white printout of the world's most precious little foetus. 'I should have asked what sex it is,' she said. 'Do you think they can tell yet?'

'I'm not sure. Do you want to know?'

Julia thought about that. 'Only if Josh does,' she answered, and waved out to Fen's mother who was clearing leaves from the lawn. For one ridiculous moment she wanted to leap out and hug her, but managed to refrain. 'It's a perfect winter's day, isn't it?' she declared, deciding to take it as a good omen. 'The sun's out, there's hardly a cloud in the sky and everything smells so wonderfully smoky and . . . Christmassy.'

Fen glanced over at her, and, still smiling, accelerated gently down into the woods, where misty bands of sunlight poured down through the trees to fan out over the stream. 'I hope you'll consider spending Christmas here,' she said, as they bumped along the track.

'Oh, I will,' Julia assured her, 'consider it, I mean. I'd absolutely love to, but right now everything's up to Josh.' She looked down at the rippling reflections on the water and felt another surge of relief mixed with unease. 'You know, I'm going to tell him the instant I get in,' she said, 'because I just can't bear to think of what he's going through.'

A couple of minutes later Fen's voice lilted with irony as she said, 'I think that's a wise decision, and by the look of it, you won't need the phone.'

Julia glanced at her in confusion, then following her eyes to the glade outside the mill her heart did an almighty somersault. 'Oh my God,' she murmured, seeing Josh standing next to a large silver Mercedes, talking to Shannon, who was taking things out of the boot. 'Fen, he's here!'

Fen laughed, and Julia's insides plunged into free fall as, hearing a car approach, Josh and Shannon both turned round.

Almost before Fen had a chance to stop Dan came bursting out of the house and thundering down the steps, shouting, 'Mum! Mum! Look, we're here! Is it a surprise?'

'Yes, it's a surprise,' she laughed, catching him as he hurled himself into her arms. 'Oh my darling, let me look at you,' she cried, tilting his face up. 'You're so handsome and gorgeous and I want to eat you all up.'

'Dad hired a Mercedes so we could all fit in,' Dan informed her. 'He let me choose it.'

'It's wonderful,' Julia assured him, feeling Josh's eyes on her, but unable for the moment to look at him.

Dan was still chattering, ' . . . and Dad said that you and Shannon have to talk about girl things and stuff, so he's going to take me to the Eden Project, and then later he said we can go to a pub or do anything we like.' He spun round to Josh. 'Can we go now, Dad? Shall I get in the car?'

Julia looked at Josh, and seeing how drawn and tired he seemed, her heart twisted with the need to go to him now and tell him the good news.

'Go on then,' Josh responded, turning to greet Fen. He hugged her politely, and even managed a smile, but his pain was too close to the surface for him to hide it well. 'I promised to bring them,' he said to Julia, barely glancing at her. 'They needed to see you.'

She tried to connect with his eyes, but he turned away, looking for Shannon. Finding her behind him, he stepped aside to clear the path between her and Julia.

Then, as Julia looked at her daughter, whom she hadn't seen for over five weeks, she felt more emotions than she could ever express. How had she managed to go this long without her? It seemed inconceivable now, beyond enduring, for there had been a whole part of her missing, which she only realised as she gazed into Shannon's anxious blue eyes. 'Come here,' she said softly, and as she held out her arms Shannon ran into them and started to cry.

'Sssh, sssh,' Julia soothed, tears welling in her own eyes too, 'everything's going to be all right.'

'I'm sorry I ran away from you that day, and that I wouldn't let you come home,' Shannon sobbed. 'I want you to come now, please come now . . .'

'I will, and you've got nothing to apologise for,' Julia told her. 'You're not to blame for anything.' Then, tightening her embrace, 'God, I've missed you.'

'I've missed you too. It's not the same without

you. Dad's always miserable, and I don't have anyone to talk to. Please Mum, say you'll come home. Please.'

Julia held her face between her hands and gazed down into her lovely, teary eyes. 'Of course I will,' she said softly.

Shannon clasped her arms around her again. 'Dad's taking Dan to the Eden Project so we can be on our own,' she said. 'I've got such a lot to tell you. So much has happened at school, with my friends and everything . . .'

'I want to hear all about it,' Julia assured her, 'but just give me a moment with Dad before he goes, will you?'

Shannon drew back and wiped away her tears.

Julia looked at Josh, and, half-afraid he might resist her, she walked quickly over to where he was standing. Keeping her voice low so no-one else could hear, she said, 'I've just come from a doctor. I'm fifteen weeks along.'

His frown deepened, then deepened again as he took in what she was saying, but before he had a chance to respond Dan yelled, 'Come on, Dad! We'll miss it.'

Josh looked impossibly torn, and realising he was about to tell Dan the plans had changed, Julia said, 'Take him. We can talk later,' and after brushing a kiss to his cheek she turned back to Shannon.

As Josh got into the car his expression was showing none of the relief or pleasure she might have hoped for, if anything his mood seemed blacker than ever, but she reminded herself that the news had barely had a chance to register yet. Once it had, everything would be fine.

'Is Ottie home?' Shannon asked Fen as Josh and Dan drove away.

'She most certainly is,' Fen replied, 'I'm about to go riding with her, but we won't be long, so come on over whenever you're ready,' and with a quick wink in Julia's direction she got back into the car.

'So it looks like it's just you and me,' Julia said, smiling down into Shannon's upturned face. 'Do you want to go inside, or, it's a nice day, we can go for a walk?'

Shannon tilted her head as she thought. 'Walk,' she decided. 'Unless it gets too cold, but then we can always come back.'

A few minutes later, after wrapping up in puffa coats and Ugg boots, they strolled arm in arm around to the back of the house, and across the field to a stile in the giant hawthorn hedge that marked one of the boundaries between their land and the Bowers'. 'So what's all this you've got to tell me?' Julia asked, as they climbed over and began to wander along a wide muddy path towards the Bowers' orchard. 'I'm all ears.'

'Oh Mum, you will just die,' Shannon told her, as though no time at all had elapsed since they were last together. 'Gilly's managed to get us tickets to a Robbie Williams concert, and her uncle, who's a musician, or a technician or something, says he can get us in backstage to meet him. Just think, Mum, I'm going to meet Robbie Williams. Everyone is going to be like, so freaked out and jealous, but I don't care. They've all been so mean to me anyway, and they were horrible to Gilly when she had to drop out of the drama group, but it wasn't her fault, and anyway, it serves them right that she's not taking them to Robbie's concert. You won't tell Dad though, will you, because if he knows I'm actually going to meet him, you know what he's like, he'll probably say I can't go.'

Julia was laughing. 'I don't think Dad will have too much of a problem with that,' she said, 'and actually, it's about time he came into the real world where you and the male species are concerned.'

'That's what I keep telling him,' Shannon cried, 'but he won't listen. I mean, I really love him and everything, but sometimes he makes me so mad. It's like he's in the Dark Ages. Anyway, I told him the other day that if he shows me up in front of my friends again I'll leave home. I don't mean it, but honestly Mum, you should have heard him. It was *sooo* embarrassing. The thing is, I think he's really stressed about you not being there, and Grandma Emma is driving us all nuts. She's very sweet and everything, but she can be a real pain too . . .'

As she rambled on and on, getting everything off her chest, from complaints about her father and grandmother, to a detailed description of the new clothes she'd bought, to a baffling explanation of her friends' boyfriend problems, Julia smiled and listened and gazed around at the spectacular scenery that was unfolding in front of them. Her thoughts kept moving to Josh and what he might be doing now, how he was feeling and what would happen when he got back. She hadn't felt such a thrill of apprehension since she was Shannon's age, but it really should be all right now, shouldn't it? The fact that Rico had ever been in the picture surely wasn't going to make a difference to how Josh felt about his own child.

'So it sounds as though you're pretty much on top of things,' she said, as they came to a stop at the brink of the hill and waved to Fen and Ottie who were galloping through the valley below.

'Oh yeah, I'm cool,' Shannon assured her. 'But I really, really want you to come home. It's just not the same without you. And I've got this secret that I can only tell you. Well, like, Gilly knows, but I have to tell you too.'

Julia's eyebrows went up. 'Come on then?' she prompted, already suspecting what it was from the way Shannon's eyes were shining.

'Well, there's this boy,' Shannon began, turning pink. 'I met him at Dad's gym. Dad doesn't know, because I was there with Gilly and her mum, but he's really nice, Mum. I mean, like he's really fit, and clever and things, and I think he likes me.'

Julia's eyes were sparkling as she said, 'So what's his name?'

'Hugh – and before you ask, he's sixteen, which is like, not too old for me, is it?'

'Absolutely not,' Julia confirmed. 'Have you been on a date yet?'

Shannon's blush deepened. 'Sort of,' she answered, peering out from under her lashes. 'I mean, we've like met at the gym, you know, when we arranged to be there, and we've texted a few times.'

'Then it all sounds fine to me. I'll look forward to meeting him.'

'Oh, you're the best,' Shannon cried, jumping up and down and throwing her arms around her.

'I knew you'd be cool about it. I just knew it, and I need you to tell me what to say when I text him and things, so I don't seem too keen, because that really puts boys off, doesn't it?'

Smiling, Julia hugged her back, and resting a cheek on her head she said, 'I'm happy to talk about Hugh as long as you like, but we're avoiding what happened before you left, darling. Do you want to discuss it, or not yet?'

As Shannon drew back her embarrassment was evident. 'It's all, like, in the past now,' she said, looking away.

'OK,' Julia responded, aware that it wasn't, but knowing better than to force it. 'Just as long as you understand that it wasn't done to hurt you – or Dad.'

Shannon nodded, and kept her eyes averted.

Julia waited, understanding that she wasn't quite ready to let it go after all.

'Then why did you do it?' Shannon finally asked. 'I mean, I thought you loved Dad . . .'

'I do, very much,' Julia said warmly. 'And I don't ever want you to doubt that. Not ever. OK?'

Shannon nodded, but her eyes were full of uncertainty.

'What happened with Rico had nothing to do with how I feel about Dad,' Julia said firmly. 'When you're older, and you've had a little more experience of the world, you'll have a better understanding of what I'm saying, but sometimes we feel ourselves being driven to do things we wouldn't normally do. It can happen for all sorts of reasons, because you're feeling sad, or happy, or let down, or afraid . . .'

'So you didn't really like Rico?'

Understanding that Shannon needed this to be put simply, but knowing she was old enough to accept some of the complexity in spite of her reluctance, Julia said, 'Yes, I liked him, it wouldn't have happened if I didn't, but feeling an attraction to someone is very different to loving them, the way I love Dad.'

'But what would you do if Dad found someone else attractive? You wouldn't like it, would you?'

'No, of course not, but I know that sometimes he does find other women attractive . . .'

'He doesn't have sex with them though.'

'No, he doesn't,' Julia said, knowing that to tell her about Sylvia wouldn't help at all, 'but that's not to say he hasn't wanted to, because sometimes we experience very overpowering feelings for someone else, that aren't always easy to explain, or even keep under control. They just happen, and . . .'

'Do you mean, like chemistry?'

Julia smiled. 'That's exactly what I mean, and if you're in the kind of vulnerable state I was at the time it happened with Rico – try to remember I was grieving for my father, and things weren't going so well with Dad – then those feelings can take on a much greater sense of immediacy, and become a lot harder to resist.'

Shannon's eyes went down as she considered what she was being told. 'You don't still want to be with him though, do you?' she said. 'Grandma Emma says you do, but . . .'

'Then you mustn't listen to Grandma Emma,' Julia said, making a mental note to take this up with her mother-in-law at a later date, 'because she's not telling you the truth, and that's another lesson you'll learn one day, about people who interfere, but we won't go there now. God, she's such an old bag,' she muttered, unable to stop herself.

Shannon giggled. 'I won't tell Dad you said that,' she promised.

Julia laughed. 'I probably shouldn't criticise her when she's been so good to you all,' she said, 'but I can't believe she said that to you. She is such a stirrer.'

'I know, but I don't think Dad really believed her. He said he didn't, anyway.'

'You talked to him about it?'

'Not very much, but he said if he could forgive you then I should too.'

Julia held her face in her hands and gazed deeply into her eyes. 'And can you?' she asked.

Shannon nodded. 'You won't ever do it again though, will you?'

'No, never,' Julia promised, hugging her. 'Not with anyone except Dad.'

'And definitely not any of my boyfriends,' Shannon teased.

Julia winced, and knew she'd probably never enjoy that particular kind of joke. Then, tilting Shannon's face up to hers, she said, 'Now it's my turn to tell you a secret.'

Shannon's eyes widened with intrigue.

'I went to see a doctor this morning,' Julia whispered, 'and I'm going to have a baby – and before you start jumping to any wrong conclusions, I'm almost four months along so it's definitely Dad's.'

For several seconds Shannon's calculation and amazement were almost palpable, then finally she broke into a smile that was so like her father's that Julia didn't know whether to hug her or cry.

'That is so awesome!' Shannon declared. 'Does Dad know?'

'You remember I had a quick word with him just before he left?'

'You told him then?'

Julia grinned.

'Oh my God,' Shannon cried, 'he must be like so freaked out. Oh, poor Dad, stuck over there with Dan . . . I bet he can't wait to come back. Do you think he's going to be pleased? Yeah, he will. I know he will. He really likes children, well, sometimes he does . . . Oh Mum, this is so wicked. You are going to be so old when you have it . . .'

'Thanks very much,' Julia retorted.

'No, everyone is these days. Women your age are having babies all the time. I read about it, or saw it on TV. I don't know, but it is so cool. I hope it's a girl. What do you think Dad will want? What do you want?'

Linking her arm to start walking back, Julia said, 'Since I've already got one of each, I really don't mind.'

'I knew you'd say something like that. I bet Dad will too.'

'Do you really think he'll be pleased?' Julia said, ready to take reassurance wherever she could get it.

'He's bound to be,' Shannon declared. 'He's a man, and seeing as they like everyone to know how virile they are, how can he not? And he won't need a Porsche to prove it now, will he? He'll have a pram instead.'

Julia threw back her head as she laughed, and wished Josh could have heard his daughter's cracking little insight into the male ego.

By the time they got back to the mill the sun was starting to set, and the temperature had dropped several degrees, making it seem very warm and cosy inside. Keen to make the place even more welcoming for when Josh came back, Julia immediately set about lighting a fire, while Shannon, eager to show her support, placed candles around the sitting room and hearth, then stood back to admire their mellow, romantic glow.

'Don't worry,' she said, carefully lowering the lights to enhance the effect, 'when they come in I'll take Dan into my room so you and Dad can be alone.'

Loving her concern, Julia hugged her close, then needing the distraction she drew her down onto one of the sofas, and encouraged her to talk some more about Hugh. However, it wasn't long before they heard the sound of a car pulling up outside, and as she felt the hollow of her stomach flood with nerves Julia got to her feet, not even realising Shannon was in mid-flow.

'It'll be OK, Mum,' Shannon whispered. 'He'll be fine. Honest.'

Julia looked down at her, too anxious to appreciate their momentary swap of roles, as she reminded herself that it would be hard for Josh to say much with the children around, so if he was still angry it probably wouldn't erupt into anything too terrible tonight. Then she listened for Dan, feeling sure he'd come in shouting, as he usually did, but though she could hear voices, curiously none was his. 'Maybe it's not them,' she said, going to the window, but it was too dark to make out who was there.

'It's definitely Dad,' Shannon said. 'I can tell his voice, but who's he talking to?'

'It sounds like Fen,' Julia replied, and started down the stairs.

As she reached the bottom Fen pushed open the door and began to stomp on the mat.

'Where's Dan?' Julia asked, trying not to be alarmed.

Fen looked up and smiled. 'Over at the house,' she answered, moving aside for Josh to come in. 'Dad's training him up to be his new backgammon partner, and Ottie's hoping Shannon will come and join us for dinner. Bob and I thought we'd take them all over to David's, but it's too dark for her to walk through the woods alone, so I've come to collect her. If that's OK with you?'

Before Julia could respond, Shannon cried, 'Wicked. I'll get my things.'

Julia watched her charge across the kitchen to grab her coat, then her boots, which were next to the door, where Josh was in the process of kicking his off. Since his back was turned she took the opportunity to look quizzically at Fen.

Fen immediately grinned and winked. 'It's bloody freezing out there,' she said, as Josh straightened up. 'Do you need any more logs over here?'

'No thanks,' Julia answered, her heart starting

an unsteady beat as she realised she and Josh really were going to be alone. 'We've got plenty.' His expression was hard to read, though he definitely didn't look happy, and for one absurd moment she almost wanted to go with Shannon and Fen.

'OK, I'm ready,' Shannon announced, jamming on a woolly hat as she looked up at Fen.

'Here's some money,' Josh said, digging into his pocket.

'Not necessary,' Fen assured him.

'Please don't argue,' Shannon told her. 'I'm broke.'

Josh shot her a look and closed up his wallet.

'Dad!' she cried.

Opening it again, he gave her ten pounds and told her it was only a loan.

'OK, let's go,' Shannon said, clutching her cash, and after zooming back to kiss Julia, she went up on tiptoe to kiss Josh, and in a severe, cautionary tone said, 'Be nice to her, Dad, because she's really nervous.'

Julia couldn't help but laugh, nor could Fen, but as the door closed behind them Julia saw that Josh's sense of humour had failed.

For a while they stood in an awkward silence, listening to the sound of Fen's car driving away, then the churn of the mill outside, until finally Julia said, 'Can I get you something? A drink . . .'

He shook his head, and dug his hands into his trouser pockets. 'I asked Fen to take them because we need to talk,' he said in a tone that did nothing to still her nerves.

'Josh, I – I know how bad this must have been for you . . .'

'How certain are you about the fifteen weeks?' he cut in sharply.

'Completely. The doctor wasn't in any doubt.'

'Then how the hell could you *not* have known?'

'I just – it didn't seem, when we haven't exactly . . .'

'I take it it *is* mine,' he shouted. 'Or has there been someone else?'

'Don't be ridiculous, you know there hasn't.'

His eyes were still smouldering with anger. 'I was practically wishing myself dead,' he growled. 'Do you know that? After you told me . . .'

'Oh Josh,' she groaned, starting towards him.

His hand went up. 'Don't even think about it!' he barked, stopping her.

'But what can I say? I'd never have put you through it if I'd known, you must know that. Josh, please, don't be angry. Everything's going to be all right now, isn't it? Please tell me it is.'

His voice was hard as he said, 'Life isn't that simple.'

'But it can be if you'll allow it.'

He said no more, only stared at her in a way that started to turn her blood cold.

'Do we really want to put any more obstacles in the way?' she cried. 'I want us to be together again. Isn't that what you want too?'

As his eyes continued to bore into hers it was impossible to tell what he was thinking. All she knew was that the distance between them was still there, and now she was becoming terrified she wouldn't be able to close it.

'Today,' he said finally, 'was the first time I've cried since we found out about Dan's problem.'

Immediately her heart contracted. 'You cried then?' she said softly. 'I didn't know.'

'Because I didn't want you to.'

'But you do now?'

He didn't answer.

'Why?' she prompted.

Still he didn't answer.

'Josh?'

'I suppose,' he said, 'because it's a way of telling you that I love you so damned much that the relief of finding out I might not lose you after all was too much for me to hold onto.'

As the words reached her she felt such a rush of emotion that she almost sobbed with relief, but though she longed to go to him, there was still something in him that was holding her back.

'Just tell me you're sure about the fifteen weeks,' he said hoarsely.

'I'm sure. I can show you the printout the doctor gave me.'

He swallowed hard, then pressed a finger and thumb into the sockets of his eyes.

This time she didn't hesitate, and as she got to him he looked down into her face with eyes so full of pain that it brought tears to her own. 'I'm sorry,' she whispered brokenly. 'I'm so sorry.'

He continued to look at her, seeming almost afraid to go any further.

'I love you,' she said.

His eyes dropped to her mouth, then he raised a hand to trace her lips with his fingers. 'Even if the baby weren't mine,' he said, watching his movements, 'I couldn't ever have stopped loving you. I just wish I could tell you we'd have made it work.'

'It's not an issue now,' she replied, 'so we don't have to think about it.'

His eyes came back to hers, and as she felt herself sinking slowly into their darkness she placed a hand over his to keep it against her cheek.

'I know we didn't plan this,' she said, 'but are you OK about having another?'

He raised an eyebrow. 'How can I not be when he or she seems to have safeguarded everything I hold most precious?'

She smiled and turned her mouth to his palm. 'That's a lovely way of looking at it,' she whispered.

His only response was to go on gazing at her.

'I've missed you so much,' she murmured softly.

His eyes stayed on hers as he absorbed her words.

'I think you know what I'm saying.'

She could tell that he did, but still he said nothing, only looked at her and traced her jaw with his thumb.

'I feel the way I always did,' she told him. 'There's no strangeness inside me now, nothing like there was before.'

She saw him swallow before he said, 'If it doesn't work . . .'

'It will,' she assured him. Then, realising that the only way to prove it was to show him, she touched her mouth to his and said, 'Why don't we go upstairs?'

With her lips on his he held her there, his hand cupped around her face, his tongue gently finding hers. She tasted so good and the promise of what was to come was so powerful that he could only wonder how he'd lasted so long without it.

As he followed her up the stairs, he was looking at her long slender legs, and noticing how her hips were very slightly starting to flare. Then he was thinking of how beautiful she was when pregnant, how he could never get enough of seeing her naked, carrying his child. Even as he thought it, and realised it was about to become a reality again, he could feel the bitter-sweet pangs of disbelief and euphoria stirring anew.

When they were standing together in the firelight, hands loosely clasped, he let his feelings show through the intensity of his eyes, wanting her to know that everything he did now was going to be about how much he loved her. Not until he could sense the responses building inside her did he draw her into his arms and kiss her with so much tenderness and passion that it was a long time before either of them could bear to let go.

When he did, she moaned softly in protest, as the need for him was gathering like a soft liquid heat inside her. She was thinking of how well he knew her body, each place to touch, every kiss and caress that would arouse her more, and the moves that would finally make her his. The knowledge of what he could do was already inflaming her to a point where she longed to begin, but she understood that he was in charge, that she had no say in this now, so she would let him do with her as he would, and follow wherever he took her.

As his mouth came back to hers, he tilted her face high, moulding her lips with his own and letting her feel the pressure of his tongue, before breaking away from her again to look into the clouded depths of her eyes. He knew she was becoming desperate for him to put his hands on her body, but they remained on her face, and in her hair, then still without touching her, he said, 'Take off all your clothes.'

Desire instantly flared inside her and stepping back she began to do as she was told, keeping her eyes on his as she removed everything down to a front-fastening bra and sheer white panties. He stopped her there and moved her hands aside to finish the task, and as he revealed her soft, heavy breasts he moaned at the pleasure that rose in him. They were so full and luscious and burnished gold in the firelight; her nipples were large and dark and so ready for his touch that she gasped as his fingers found them. Then they both watched him caressing her, loving the rugged maleness of his hands on her pale, feminine flesh, until eventually her eyes came up to his. Seeing how dazed she was becoming, he covered her mouth with his and kissed her hard.

Minutes later they were in the bedroom and as he sat on the edge of the bed he drew her between his legs so that his mouth moved easily to her breasts and his hands could begin to lower her panties. He knew how she loved him to do this slowly, so he took a long, tantalising time to roll them down over her hips and thighs, stopping to smooth her buttocks and touch her very gently between the legs. Then, taking her panties down to her ankles, he watched her step out of them before undressing himself and drawing her back to him again.

As his hands splayed over the soft mound of her belly, she looked past them and saw the strength of his desire. He was so big and ready for her and she longed to move onto him and take him in her now, but she knew he wouldn't allow it yet. He wanted her pleasure to be more intense than she could bear before he gave her that, and already it was beginning as his mouth returned to her breasts, and his fingers teased the moistness at the join of her legs. Sensation after sensation was leaping through her. He could make her come like this and he knew it, but he was a long way from ready for that. Not even when her legs started to weaken did he increase the pressure. He just held her there, toying with her senses and knowing that this was gradually driving her crazy.

'Josh,' she gasped, clutching his shoulders as she sank towards him. 'Please, Josh, now.'

His fingers started to move faster and deeper, while his mouth was more demanding on her nipples, biting and sucking them hard. He felt her shaking, and sensed the waves almost ready to break, but not until the first one forced its way free did he pull her to him, lying back on the bed, and bringing her mouth to his as she began to cry out.

'Please, Josh, please,' she begged. Then feeling the tip of him starting to enter her, she tried to push herself down to take him, but he wouldn't let her.

'Oh God,' she cried, barely able to stand it.

But he held back, making her come all over the tip of him, clenching and squeezing, trembling and releasing until finally, grabbing her hips, he plunged right into the heart of the storm.

'Oh yes,' she seethed, as the fast penetration rocketed her to a new and excruciating high. He held her tight, feeling her muscles tugging him as though to pull everything from him, then still holding her close he rolled her onto her back and rode her straight from one orgasm into the next.

'Josh,' she sobbed only minutes later. 'Josh, I can't.'

'Ssh, you're there,' he told her.

She clung to him with arms and legs, helpless in the onslaught of so much sensation. He was thrusting in hard and fast, pushing in deep and sending her blazing towards the peak.

'Let it go,' he urged. 'Just let it go.'

Then he felt the might of it breaking around him in big, beautiful waves, carrying them both to a place of no return. He was right there with her, pushing her on and on, kissing her and watching her as she soared beyond his control. She was gripping him hard, digging her nails into his flesh and struggling for breath. She begged him to come with her, but he held himself back, letting her fly alone whilst using everything he knew about her to keep her there. Only when he sensed the pleasure turning to pain did he move more gently, gathering her in his arms and holding her close, as, shuddering and panting beneath him, she finally started to come down.

'Josh,' she murmured. 'Josh.'

'Ssh,' he whispered, kissing her.

Her eyes opened and gazed cloudily into his.

'OK?' he said softly.

'Mm,' she answered. Then, bringing her lips back to his, 'Did I remember to tell you I love you?'

He kissed her deeply, pushing his tongue into her mouth and feeling the final throes of her climax still claiming him, before raising himself up on his arms. They both watched as he moved in and out of her with long, tender strokes, then he lay over her again and held her close.

Loving the feel of him still hard inside her, she said, 'I have to wonder how I could ever have felt so afraid.'

His voice was muffled by her neck as he said, 'Well, I guess I am pretty awesome.'

She spluttered with laughter, then moaned as he pushed in more deeply.

'Do you ever intend to come?' she asked.

'Just let me know when you're ready.'

'That could be now,' she said as he pushed in again.

He looked at her warily.

'Please,' she whispered.

For a long time he moved gently, his eyes never leaving hers as he began taking them back to the heights. He knew she'd be tender now, but he wanted her there with him when he finally let go. After a while he altered his rhythm, and as he found the most sensitive spot inside her, he heard her breath catch in her throat. The twists and turns of her body told him he had her now, and as he rode her he could feel the pressure inside him mounting. He knew, almost before she did, when she started to approach another release, and already he could feel himself going with her. This time he didn't hold back, and when at last it came it was so forceful and fast that it was as though everything in him was becoming a part of her. The pleasure was so intense it was almost too much to bear. He held her tight, threw all his weight against her, then suddenly he spun onto his back, taking her with him, and said, 'Finish it.'

She rode him hard, her hands clamped over his on her breasts. He was still coming, she could feel it in the shuddering of his body, and the rapid spurts inside her. She knew how long he could make it last and wanted to draw it out to a point where neither of them could take any more. She did things to him that only she knew he needed, and as they gazed into each other's eyes they could feel their love circling like an invisible force around them, binding them together and prolonging this ecstasy of release. No-one else had ever come close to making either of them feel this way, and never had they given to anyone else like this. This was what they shared, what they understood of each other, and in the end nothing could come between them, because no-one would ever matter more, and no-one ever could.

Finally she lay over him, stretching her body along his and burying her face in his neck. His arms were around her, holding her tight, his lips were pressed against her, and as she listened to the pounding of their hearts and thought of the child inside her she knew she had never before felt such happiness and contentment.

It was a long, long time later when he lifted a hand to her hair and started to stroke it. 'Are you OK?' he asked.

'Mm. Are you?'

He was about to take a breath, but laughed.

'What's funny?' she asked.

'Shannon, telling me to be nice to you.'

She smiled and snuggled more closely to him. 'I promise not to tell how you excelled yourself,' she said sleepily.

He laughed again and kissed the top of her head. 'Are you about to flake out on me?' he asked.

'I think so.'

It was the last thing she remembered either of them saying until they were woken around eleven by Shannon and Dan coming home. He wouldn't let her get up, nor would he allow the children to enter the room.

'I hope you haven't killed her,' she heard Shannon saying hotly, as he made up a bed for Dan in the sitting room next door.

'I'm trying, but she doesn't go down easily,' he responded dryly.

Julia laughed and listened contentedly as he tucked Dan in, then went to rescue Shannon's guilty secret (beloved teddy) from the car, before coming back again. As he slipped in next to her, she wrapped her arms around him and they made love quietly and languorously before falling asleep again, only to be woken around eight the next morning by the sound of the TV in the next room.

Not ready to get up yet, they moved drowsily back into each other's arms, snuggling in close, until she turned so that her back was to his chest, and his knees came up under hers. It was meant to be a long, luxurious prelude to making love, but his fingers had only just begun toying lazily with her nipples when Shannon knocked on the door, and asked if they wanted some tea.

'Are they awake?' Dan shouted in a whisper,

and before anyone could answer he came bounding into the room. 'Shannon wouldn't let me come in,' he told them, 'and I've been awake for ages. But it's OK, because she gave me ten pounds to stay quiet.'

'If only I'd known it would go to such good use,' Josh muttered, making Julia laugh.

'It's cold out here,' Dan said, jumping onto the bed. 'Can I get in with you, Mum?'

'No, darling,' she cried, grabbing the duvet.

'Please. I'll stay still.'

'I don't have any clothes on,' she told him.

He grinned and looked at Shannon. 'They've been kissing,' he said.

Shannon rolled her eyes and blushed. 'You are such a *child*,' she informed him.

'I know, but I'm good at backgammon. Do you want to play, Dad? I can show you how.'

'Not right now, son,' Josh answered, rolling onto his back.

Julia rolled with him and rested her head on his shoulder.

'Are you going to get up?' Dan asked. 'We can go surfing.'

'Not bloody likely,' Josh responded.

Julia lost her yawn to a laugh, then slipped a hand between his legs.

Immediately he raised one knee to disguise what was happening.

'Anyway, I'm not a child,' Dan said to Shannon, 'because really they were making babies.'

Shannon flushed again as she looked at her mother.

Julia's eyes were shining, then turning to kiss

Josh on the cheek, she said, 'I think now's as good a time as any to tell him, don't you?'

Josh eyed his son meaningfully.

'Tell me what?' Dan pressed.

Julia's hand stayed where it was as she said to Dan, 'How would you like to have another sister or brother?'

Dan frowned. 'What, like now?' he replied.

'Duh,' Shannon chipped in.

'Well, in about five months,' Julia said.

Dan's eyes started to round. 'Oh wow!' he cried, getting it. 'That is so cool.' Then, grinning at Josh, 'Dad, you're the man!'

Julia and Josh burst out laughing, and Josh grunted as Dan landed on him.

'OK, now you know, you can leave us in peace,' Josh declared, somehow manhandling his son back to his feet.

'I'm getting into bed with you,' Dan grinned mischievously.

'Out! Now!' Josh roared. 'She's all mine until you've made us some breakfast.'

'Mum!' Dan protested.

'You know I never argue with Daddy,' she responded.

'Yes you do! All the time.'

'Does anyone ever listen to me around here?' Josh wanted to know.

'Can we spend Christmas here?' Shannon asked. 'Fen knows a great place to get trees.'

'I give up,' he declared, and turning Julia's mouth to his, he carried on as if they were alone.

'We're gone,' Shannon told him, grabbing Dan.

Still ignoring them, Josh rolled Julia back to the

position they'd been in before being so rudely interrupted, and was preparing to do something about the condition she'd created under the duvet when Shannon peeped back in the door.

'I suppose the Porsche is up for sale,' she said, and as Julia let out a laugh, she disappeared quickly, leaving her mother to explain the joke, which Julia promised she would, but not until Josh had finished doing what he unquestionably did best.

The Hornbeam Tree

Susan Lewis

Just as celebrated columnist Katie Kiernan thinks life is over, it suddenly arrives on her doorstep in the shape of her sister Michelle, and all the intrigue she brings with her. Friction, resentment and old jealousies make life in their house doubly challenging, as Katie struggles to cope with a rebellious teenager and Michelle longs for the man she left behind.

After a devastating betrayal Laurie Forbes is trying to rebuild her relationship with Elliot Russell, when she is plunged into a whirl-wind of passion that threatens to tear them apart completely.

Top journalist, Tom Chambers, the man Michelle left behind, faces the greatest challenge of his career when highly classified documents fall into his hands. Realizing how explosive the material is, Tom calls upon Elliot Russell to help with the investigation, and very quickly they are caught up in the deadly efforts to stop them going to print . . .

'A multi-faceted tear jerker'
Heat

arrow books

Just One More Day:
A Memoir

Susan Lewis

In 1960s Bristol a family is overshadowed by tragedy . . .

While Susan, a feisty seven-year-old, is busy being brave, her mother, Eddress, is struggling for courage. Though bound by an indestructible love, their journey through a world that is darkening with tragedy is fraught with misunderstandings.

As a mother's greatest fear becomes reality, Eddress tries to deny the truth. And, faced with a wall of adult secrets, Susan creates a world that will never allow her mother to leave.

Set in a world where a fridge is a luxury, cars have starting handles, and where bingo and coupons bring in the little extras, *Just One More Day* is a deeply moving true-life account of how the spectre of death moved into Susan's family, and how hard they all tried to pretend it wasn't there.

'Susan Lewis fans know she can write compelling fiction, but not, until now, that she can write even more engrossing fact. We use the phrase honest truth too lightly: it should be reserved for books — deeply moving books – like this'
Alan Coren

arrow books

Intimate Strangers

Susan Lewis

Investigative journalist, Laurie Forbes, is planning her wedding to Elliot Russell, when she receives a tip-off that a group of illegally smuggled women is being held somewhere in the East End of London. During her search unexpected and devastating events begin throwing her own life into chaos, so fellow journalist, Sherry MacElvoy steps in to help. Taking on undercover roles to get to the heart of the ruthless gang of human-traffickers, neither reporter can ever begin to imagine what dangers they are about to face.

Neela is one of the helpless Indian girls being held in captivity. Her fear is not only for herself, but her six-year-old niece, Shaila. A disfiguring birthmark has so far saved Neela from abuse, but she knows it is only a matter of time before she is sent for – and worse, before Shaila is taken. Her desperate bids to seek outside help are constantly thwarted, until finally she, and the women with her, agree there is only one way out . . . *Intimate Strangers* is a rich and engrossing story of intense love, heart-break, terror and survival.

'Spellbinding — you just keep turning the pages, with the atmosphere growing more and more intense as the story leads to its dramatic climax'
Daily Mail

'Mystery and romance *par excellence*'
Sun

'Susan Lewis strikes gold again . . . gripping'
Options

arrow books

Order further Susan Lewis titles
from your local bookshop, or have them delivered
dirct to your door by Bookpost

	Title	ISBN	Price
☐	Intimate Strangers	0 09 945329 0	£6.99
☐	The Hornbeam Tree	0 09 945327 4	£5.99
☐	Just One More Day: A Memoir	0 09 948683 0	£6.99
☐	Silent Truths	0 09 941458 9	£6.99
☐	Wicked Beauty	0 09 941459 7	£6.99
☐	Taking Chances	0 09 949104 4	£6.99
☐	Obsession	0 09 941715 4	£6.99
☐	Vengeance	0 09 943509 8	£6.99
☐	Strange Allure	0 09 941457 0	£6.99
☐	Cruel Venus	0 09 944143 8	£6.99
☐	A Class Apart	0 09 943615 9	£6.99
☐	Chasing Dreams	0 09 942635 8	£6.99
☐	Summer Madness	0 09 932055 9	£6.99
☐	Stolen Beginnings	0 09 944318 X	£6.99
☐	Dance While You Can	0 09 942174 7	£6.99

Free post and packing
Overseas customers allow £2 per paperback

Phone: 01624 677237

Post: Random House Books
c/o Bookpost, PO Box 29, Douglas, Isle of Man IM99 1BQ

Fax: 01624 670923

email: bookshop@enterprise.net

Cheques (payable to Bookpost) and credit cards accepted

Prices and availability subject to change without notice.
Allow 28 days for delivery.
When placing your order, please state if you do not wish to receive any
additional information.

www.randomhouse.co.uk/arrowbooks

arrow books